The Protectors

Book 1

By

L. Ann Marie

Contemplating ending the constant barrage of death and destruction that he's seen his whole life brings Christian closer to his family. With Dakota's help, he learns and uses his ancestors to control and manage his visions and abilities. Gaining peace for the first time in his life still leaves him lonely. With all he's been gifted, the ability to be touched is not among them.

Dean thought using her ability to help the police find a killer was a good thing, until she realized she was now the hunted. Losing her parents, in an explosion meant for her, she finds her way to the Princes and a man that not only protects and understands her, but can hold her too.

Christian has his work cut out for him. Showing Dean, the Princes and the MC what all in means isn't easy when it's wrapped around the 'freaky kid' abilities and a crazy MC.

This is the story of Christian and Dean.

*Content Warning: includes language and sex. Intended for mature audiences 18+

This is a work of fiction. Names, characters, places, and incidents are either the product of the author's imagination or used fictitiously, and any resemblance to actual persons, living or dead, business establishments, events or locales is entirely coincidental.

The Protectors: Christian Book 1

Copyright 2016 © L. Ann Marie

Published by: L. Ann Marie

Editor Steph Nordstrom

Cover by Lori Birkett

Bigstock®

Cast of Characters

Aaron 29

Aiyana 26

Alex & Ally 33

Aquyà & Justice 7

Aubrey 16

Ben Knight (Little Ben/Prez) 33

Billy 23

Blaze & Blake 17

Brandon 11

Brantley 29

Brenna 20

Case - Newborn Taylor

Chance 1 – Brantley

Christian 28

Colt & Harley 15

Dakota 28

Darren 34

Dean 20

Destiny 2 - Jessie/Dakota

Devan 22

Diego 25

Elizabeth 26

Honor 4 – Darren

Jacob & Jeremy 22

Jared & Kaleb Baxter 33

Jason & Judy 22

Jax 40

Jess Baxter 37

Jessie 33

Joey 30

Jose 24

Kaya 28

Kyler & Riley 11 – Geek

Lily 32

Lori Baxter 40

Mase 17

Mucimi 3

Nash 2 - Taylor

Phoenix & Teller 5

Ricky 33

Sandy 21

Sheila 32

Stella 6

Taylor 29

Terry 29

Tucker 3 - Digs

Victor 32

Zeke 14

Original Families	Kids	Abilities
Ben James (Pres)-Tracey – *Jessie Danny LaPonte-Dena – Rich Danny-Kate – Devan *Darren & Victor & Aaron *Ally & Alex *Patches Karr Danny-Ben-Kate – Brenna	*Rich-Tess-Patches LaPonte-Karr –* Blaze & Blake & Zeke *Jessie-Jess LaPonte-James-Lightfoot-Dakota –* Justice & Aquyà & Destiny *Darren LaPonte-James-Eliza –* Honor	Danny Rich Blaze, Blake, Zeke Devan, Brenna Dakota Justice, Aquyà, Destiny Honor
VP: Steve Knight, Jess Little Ben & Elizabeth	*(Little) Ben Knight-Lily –* Phoenix & Teller	Steve (Little) Ben (Prez) Phoenix, Teller Elizabeth
SGT at Arms: Tiny Callahan, Nancy – Sandy *Sheila, Ricky, José, Billy, Diego, *Jason & Judy	*Jax-Sheila Jackson* – *Stella, Brandon	Sandy Ricky Judy
Geek Moniz-Marty – Aubrey Riley & Kyler		Aubrey Riley Kyler
Jamie Baxter-Mitch-Kevin – Jess & Jared & Kaleb *Lori	*Jess LaPonte-James-Lightfoot* (above)	Kaleb

Cloud Blackhawk-CJ – Mase *Jeremy & Jacob, Joey & Christian, *Taylor, Brantley, Terry	*Brantley Blackhawk-Holly –* Mucimi *Chance *Taylor Blackhawk-Beth –* Nash & Case	Christian, Jeremy, Jacob Mase Mucimi, Chance Nash, Case
Bob Tailley-Amanda – Harley & Colt		Harley, Colt
Digs Brighton-Penny – Tucker		Tucker
RI Reservation:		Co, Aiyana, Kayak, Chevy
Conn. Reservation:		Nunánuk,

*Adopted

& = biological

Princes of Prophecy Officers:
Prez – Little Ben Knight
VP – Darren LaPonte-James
Sergeant at Arms – Jessie LaPonte-James
Trainer – Taylor Blackhawk
HS IT – Brantley Blackhawk
Treasurer – Joey Blackhawk
Secretary – Air Ops – Dakota 'Eagle Eye' Lightfoot
Covering Everything – Sheila Callahan
New Technology – Jared Baxter
PD – Driscoll
Security IT – Bull
Nomads – Jax
Medical – Nick
Prospects – Lee
Clubhouse – Chris
Other Officers – Aaron LaPonte-James, Chevy
Second Tier Officers – Sebastian, Shilah, Josiah (all with abilities)

Princes of Prophecy Brothers:
Hyde
Cade
Tag
Done
Vinny

MC Brothers
Chet
Racks married to Brenda – Lily's sister
Baker

Need to Know Abbreviations:
HS – High Security
FS – Family Security
KC/KClub – Kids' Club
BS – Baxter Security
RS – Reservation Security

Reservations
Nunánuk – Shaman of the Conn. Mohegan Reservation. Cloud and Aleena's Blackhawks grandmother
Bear – runs IT Security for Conn. Reservation
Eagle Feather – pilot for Conn Reservation, ex-military
Brody and Pamela, parents of – Eagle Eye/Dakota
Raven – Conn reservation
Ted – Conn. Chief
Co – Shaman of RI reservation
Peto – stable hand
Chevy – former Prince
Jet

Different Charters
Hammer – Pres in New Hampshire (deceased)

Art: Splicer – IT HS for Hammer
Snake – NY Ops Lead
Al – Conn Ops Lead
Dell – IT Conn
Big K – Pres Conn.

Dogs
Alpha & Omega – Prez
Prince – Alex
Mack – Mucimi
Delta – Taylor
Hawk,   Nekanis –
Christian
Max – Tess
Ituksq – Dean

Table of Contents

Chapter One

I ride through the Rhode Island reservation's gate fast with Cade following. Throwing chin to Peto I wonder why he's at the gate. They have Security here so a stable hand opening the gate is odd. Aiyana sounded frantic, which isn't a normal emotion to hear in her voice—she's always so even keeled. This isn't sitting well with me. I go right to Co's house and shut my bike off. "I'll be a while. Security is tight here if you want to take a ride around I'll call when I'm done."

He gives me a look. "I was told not to let you out of my sight."

I roll my eyes. "I'm dressed and you can't come into the Shaman's teepee."

He nods. "I'll wait outside. Brantley's telling me not to leave your side, but I get the ritual thing. I'll wait out here."

"What's going on with their Security?" Co shields here, but not when he's in the teepee. This is weird.

Cade is usually pretty good at answering me. He flips his mic off. "They pulled people for a protest and Jeremy called Prez telling him shit is happening and they need help. He's sending a team, but I'm staying at your side, or really outside the teepee. I'm not trying to make this hard on you Brother, just following orders. Jessie would kick my ass if something happened to you."

I want to roll my eyes at him again, but end up just throwing him chin and walk away. I don't bother with the house and walk right around to the teepee in the back. "Co, it's Christian, may I enter?" I ask in Mohegan.

Aiyana is here, I feel her, she's upset and everything is going through her head. Co opens the flap and I walk in

10

greeting him with thanks and appreciation for his and the ancestors time. "It is I that give thanks to you. Aiyana will not settle to get guidance from the ancestors."

I look at her. She's got tears running down her face. "What do you need Aiyana?" I ask sitting beside her.

"We need help," she says, sounding defeated.

"Give it to me Aiyana. Hand me your burden and I'll bring it to Prez. Together we can get through everything." I'm frustrated with my words. Mohegan doesn't give me the 'feeling' words that I want to get through to her.

"This is not a Club problem. It's more vast. A blanket threat on anything that is not understood."

That sounds like a Club problem to me. Fuck. I squeeze her hand for a second and see everything she does. Clenching my jaw, I watch with my heart in my throat. Fuck! When her nightmare ends, I watch her eyes. "We will get through this. I'll talk to Prez and Dakota as soon as I get back. Let's jump and get you some peace."

Co sits beside us as we go. "We can't fight the hatred Christian."

I look at her and smile. "Oh, but we can. We've been doing it all our lives. With Dakota and Prez we have the planning and ability to do anything. Do not underestimate that foresight and commitment to keep our mission going."

She looks hopeful. "You've grown so much since you've been back. I need that confidence you have in our tribe."

It's been a little more than two years since I moved from the reservation. In that two years, I've trained with Prez, Dakota and Jeremy to build shields and enhance the abilities I have. With that understanding and training I've gained confidence. My mom used to always say, 'knowledge is power.' She was right. "I am no longer a child Aiyana. At twenty-eight, we need to be closer to who we are meant to be, there is no more time for finding ourselves."

She smiles, but it's a sad smile. "We will need everything in us to fight this."

"Then that's what we'll give. I have learned that in Brotherhood, just as in Warriors, together we can overcome anything. It is when we don't work together that we fail." She nods as we soar above the lake.

"Aiyana give your doubts to the ancestors. Our Warrior Protector speaks the truth. Our past, present and future lie in the hands of more than one. Take the peace and guidance they offer," Co tells her.

We soar back and I watch the smile come back to her eyes. "It is good Aiyana. Your mind is at rest. We have a month to prepare. Come to Princes so you can get the training." She shakes her head no. I sigh, "It is not crucial at this point, but there is a time you will need to shed the security of the reservation and grow into who you are meant to be. I will not put pressure where it is not needed." She looks surprised and scared. I smile and pull her toward me kissing her head. "That is for another time my Warrior Princess. I must get back. Are you more at peace Aiyana?"

"I am my Warrior Protector. Thank you for guiding me to our wise spirits."

I look at Co, he's sitting here smiling at us, "Soon my council will no longer be needed."

I laugh. "Never happening Co. We'll always need our fathers."

I thank him and our ancestors, then walk out. Keeping my head clear I start for my bike. Cade falls in beside me. "There are two away cars that seemed to have followed us here. Prez has the team in place, but we're running red extract unless you want to wait for Dakota to clear Abel for a pickup."

He sounds like that will make his day. "No. I need to get back now. Tell Prez and Dakota I'll need some time when I'm back."

"Fuck." He repeats my words and doesn't look happy. I don't give him a second glance as I start my bike and point it toward the gate. Chevy is here to let us out. I throw him respect and a smile. He's conflicted, but gives me a chin lift. He wants off the reservation, but feels he let his people down. I don't envy him—the elders here are a tough crowd to answer to. On the ride back, I think about Prez and Dakota. They've trained me to defend with my abilities, but I've never had to use them to stay alive. I hope it's like running pop ups and I can call on them when they're needed.

'Yes Christian,' Jeremy says in my head.

I laugh. 'Get the fuck out of my head Je.'

'Be alert. Car tracking movements.' I look at my hand and see the jammer around my wrist. 'On visual,' he explains. Thank fuck. 'Now.' He sounds nervous.

"Stay alert Cade, Jeremy says it's happening now." I pull my gun and hold it against my thigh.

"Roger Guardian." We fly through the streets without one complaint from him. I smile thinking that I like when he's alert and he's not bitching at me about riding crazy. We've all been riding since we were kids. They call all the Blackhawks crazy, but we're all here and still riding. "Next right! Jump and get to Security! Aaron is on the other side of the block. GO!" Cade yells then turns going around the other side of the car.

I need a fuckin' ear piece. They talk in Ops so it comes over the helmets, but partners talk over the ear pieces. I didn't catch where Cade's orders are coming from. I speed up and jump the car waiting to turn flying over it and landing on the side of another turning car.

13

"Jump again Christian!" Prez yells in my helmet. I hear the crash behind me, but keep my focus on forward and jumping over to the side to blow by the standing traffic. Shots are being fired from everywhere. "Jump!"

I twist the throttle and lift the bike over the car in front of me. "Got it Prez."

"Fuckin' Blackhawks! Christian you're on with me and Prez. He'll guide you around and get you here safe." Billy sounds like he's smiling.

This is good, I think, as a gun is pointed at me from an SUV coming my way. I see it in my mind, but also happening right in front of me. I hit the tires then raise the gun and hit the driver before his shot is off. In my head, I see him crash, but I keep moving forward and don't take the time to look back. "Clear Prez."

'Yes,' Jeremy says in my head.

"Good job Brother. Stay alert, Aaron was pulled away. Taylor is close."

Fuck. I hate being the cause of him being pulled away just for a shuttle service. "I'm good Prez. It's clear for me."

"Roger Christian. Let me check something." He's going to ask Jeremy like I don't know what the fuck I'm doing.

"Prez, he already said I'm clear," I give him a monotone voice.

"Roger Guardian. I'm not used to Ops with you in the mix. No disrespect Brother," Prez says and I'm stunned. He's never done that before.

"Roger Prez." I fly through the streets, jumping what is in my way and making Security in fifteen minutes. "I'm out Prez. Thanks for the eyes."

I pull my helmet off and hand it to the Prospect that takes my bike. No one follows me in, but Hawk is waiting when I walk into Security. I bend and pet him, then follow him to Ops. I'm surprised when my thumb lets me in.

Prez is smiling while he's talking to Taylor. "Not even a smile from him Sniper. You'll need to step it up Brother. We've gotten fuckin' bored with your action hogging feeds. We need laughs Brother. Recruit if you have to Ghost."

"Never thought I would see the day when we would miss Ramsey my great Warrior Leader." Dakota slaps him on the back as he's walking toward me. "We need more than a minute Brother?"

I nod losing the smile. "We do. We need information and to be prepared. Jessie and Taylor are needed and Jeremy and Jacob later, but for now Jessie and Taylor are important."

Prez looks over and watches us. He's shielded from me. We all seem to do that, but Dakota is more open than Prez is. I don't think I need all the shit that goes through his head so I'm good with that. It's so much easier than it was before I got here and started training, but Prez gets shit from everywhere. I don't need more than I have and I'm happy to let him do his job while keeping my focus on mine.

We've found that both Aiyana and Jeremy respond well to me, and Prez asked me to keep him updated with any changes in them. This is the first time I felt a shift in either so it is a new experience that I will be reporting on.

The last two years have been easy on the Club and we've grown more focused and stronger than ever before. The kids clued me into the fact that there was a shift ahead a couple of weeks ago, so I'm not surprised in the least that we're at the crossroad they saw coming.

"My meeting room Brothers. Jessie and Taylor are meeting us there," Prez says handing Billy his headset.

15

"Billy keep an eye on the yard and let Bull and Jax know I'm away from Ops." Billy rogers him and Prez looks at me. "Do we need Brantley and Jason?"

"Not yet Prez. I need to give you what I have first so you can consider it before planning. I'm just checking Hawk's water and grabbing a drink. I'll meet you in the room."

He nods looking at Dakota. "I'll be right in. Brantley let Jax and Bull know you're on the side if needed, but get me information on social media trends around our area." I'm surprised he got so much from me already, but I shouldn't be. There is a lot going on with Prez that people don't normally see.

"I can call Mitch and Carolina, that's what Carolina does. It's like keeping the pulse of the people she said." I hear Brantley just as the door closes. I see Carolina like a shadowy film happening around what is now. She's smiling handing Brantley papers. The vision is telling me it's the right thing to do.

I push through Carolina's shadowy form and grab a water from the fridge. When I close the door and bend for the water bowl, my head is smacked with the edge of the door.

"Fuck!"

The woman yelps jumping back and grabs napkins off the counter then pushes them at me. "I'm so sorry I thought you were done and just moving your dog."

I look at her. Seriously? There is nothing around us, but the wall and the dog bowls. "I'm Loretta. I work in Security. Our break room is out of water and Bull said I could grab some here." She grabs my arm and I see the lie right away.

I hold my head and nod taking everything I can get from her while I stare at her willing her to step back. When she does I smile. "Take your hand off my arm and follow me to Prez's meeting room," I tell her walking out. Hawk follows watching her. I keep her under control while I thumb in, but don't step over the threshold. "Dakota, my new friend Loretta is looking for information. She says she's from Security, but that's not quite right is it Loretta?"

She shakes her head no. Dakota walks out and takes Loretta's elbow. "I have her Brother."

I let her go, but don't see the change in our roles happen on her face. Dakota is fuckin' good sliding right into her mind without her registering the change in control.

Prez laughs walking toward me. "He is, isn't he?"

I nod. I love seeing him relaxed and smiling. It's been a good two years since we've been through any major shit. Even the shit we have caught isn't ours. The 'rents are crazy and we ended up with some blowback from that craziness. I know that smile won't last, but I walk in and sit with a smile of my own. I got here and he didn't send Taylor to babysit me. I thank him in my head.

He throws me chin and sits. "I got the unhappiness in your voice Brother. I don't want to take you for granted, but I see where I'm missing all of your abilities on the lineup in my head. I'll ask Dakota to fill in for me."

I can't help it and roll my eyes. "Why don't you just ask me?"

He clenches his jaw looking at me. Fuck, I need to show him respect or he's going to hit me. Luckily Jessie and Taylor come in laughing. I watch Taylor looking for any residual from this last week. He's had a rough week, but you can't tell from the smile on his face.

'He's good Brother,' Prez says in my head. I throw him chin. Jessie and Taylor talk about training while we wait for Dakota.

17

Aaron walks in with Darren and Dakota following. When everyone sits Prez stands. "What's happening with Aiyana? I can't read her clearly."

"She may be easier now. She was calm when I left her. She has a vision of a wave of hate hitting us. There is no real detail other than brutal death at the hands of faceless people. It's unnerved her."

Aaron sits up. "Hatred by faceless people. So not one person?"

I look at him. "No. It's groups with an underlying anger, but that anger is driving them to extreme violence and that violence will be turned on us from many groups for different reasons. The reasoning is off. I didn't get all of it, but the biggest threat is intolerance."

"We're fighting a whole concept not a person?" Taylor asks and I nod.

Jessie slaps the table. "Jesusfuckin'Christ what the hell year are these people living in?"

I look back at Prez. "The next group that does major damage is religious. They don't like that the schools are teaching Sex Ed as a medical issue and want only abstinence taught. They have a problem with contraception being free in schools and at the clinics. Doc's clinic gets bombed."

Aaron stands up disgusted. "The communities voted on the change! Teenage pregnancy dropped, unwanted pregnancy dropped, STDs dropped! What the fuck did abstinence teach anyone? If we want kids to make adult decisions, they need adult information. Fuckin' people don't see that they trample all over everyone else's rights with violence toward us so they can force their belief on us? Didn't America get populated for that fuckin' reason?"

Prez takes a minute then nods for me to go on. "Different religious zealots come after us for being readers. They hurt us through the kids. The feel I got was like a witch hunt. They actually take some of our people. It isn't pretty. I'll throw you what I got, but you might want to sit."

He watches me and lets his breath out slow. "Do I need Brantley and Jason in here?"

I look at him weighing my words. "I think you need to see first then we can get them to plan."

He nods and leans his weight on the table with one hand waiting for me. I throw to him and Dakota making sure he sees all Aiyana did. The feel is suffocating, that's her description, a blanket of hate. His other hand hits the table and looks like it's holding him up. I look at Dakota and get a small nod. I let the rest go. "Holy fuck," he says with no emotion in his voice. When I finish, he sits hard putting his head in his hands. "I need a minute. Get what the woman has before we call Brantley in." He still doesn't have any emotion in his voice—his mind is trying to process everything.

I look at Dakota. He is looking at his hands breathing deep. Not quite sure what to do, I look at Taylor. "Go ahead and let them have a minute." He and Jessie look worried.

Aaron touches my shoulder. "Anything you need us to do for this?"

I shake my head no and look at the board that shows holding. The woman stands. I move her toward the window that's set high on the wall and have her look at the sky. While she does, I slide in her head and pull what I can. I put questions to her and get some names of organizers. Looking at Taylor, "I need to make a list of names."

He shakes his head no. "Prez will get it when you give him that. Brantley and Jason know what to do."

I nod and ask more of my statuesque prisoner. She doesn't know much more than what I pulled so I let her go

19

and watch her fall to her knees. I send confusion and pain then look back at Prez.

"You're a lot further than I realized. Thank you, Brother. Tell me she's not as bad as the last visions."

I keep my mouth shut. His eyes close and a look of resignation shows on his face. When he opens his eyes, I see determination in his hard look. "Go."

I throw and watch pain slide across his face then get replaced with anger. He's pissed and it throws relief on me. Dakota stands, pulling my attention toward him. He's got his eyes on the board and I watch the woman curl into a ball. He takes her breath.

When I'm done throwing to Prez he looks at Darren. "Brantley and Jason. I need a meet with MC for planning. Dakota get Co and Grandmother at that meeting. Jessie, Taylor and Aaron stay. I need you to get what's at stake here."

I don't really know what to do so I sit and wait. He looks at me. "I need you to throw slower so I can get a list. Brantley and Jason will get it straight for planning. Dakota is too angry and I don't want one fuckin' thing to be missed. Can you throw it again when they get in here?"

I nod and clear my throat. "Yeah Prez." Darren and Dakota walk out. I look at Taylor. "You look good Taylor." I need something to clear my head.

He nods. "I am. It was a hell of a week, but I'm good." He smiles. "The boys and Precious keep me smiling."

"Mucimi go home yet?" I smile thinking of him. The kid is three going on twenty. Since Beth came home with the new baby, Case, he's been staying at their house.

"He said he's got to teach the babies. Since they're babies I don't know what the fuck he's teaching them, but he's not done I guess. Beth thinks it's funny."

20

Jessie laughs. "Mucimi is giving Brantley a run for his money. I bet he's going to be worse than Jeremy to keep track of."

Brantley bursts through the door with Jason right behind him. He puts his laptop on the table and looks at the boards. The woman is gone from the floor in holding. He looks at Prez. "I'm not making a list?"

"You are, but it's a little different this time. I need two lists. One for long term planning and one for the fuckin' psycho that is tied to the group from this morning."

Brantley sits and Prez takes a drink of water. I wonder if he still needs a minute here. He looks right at me. "I got this, but yeah, I'm waiting for Darren and Dakota."

I nod. "Dakota isn't coming back. He's checking on a few things."

He looks surprised, but nods.

"When are you making Mucimi go home?" Taylor asks Brantley making us all smile.

Brantley shakes his head. "He said he's teaching them. I don't know what the fuck to do. Is Beth okay with the new baby and Nash?"

"Yeah. I'm just busting your balls. She says Mucimi is a big help. He ordered lunch for him and Nash today." We all laugh.

"Fuckin' kids. Tell me he called them this time." Brantley wipes his hand down his face.

I crack up. "No, he threw to Phoenix and Aquyà at the school, and they called."

Prez laughs and the sound relaxes me. "I think Jessie's right, he's going to be harder than Jeremy to keep track of. He's fuckin' three."

Brantley nods smiling. "He was throwing the order to Matt at the restaurant last week. I told him he wasn't allowed to do that anymore. At least he listened. Last week he didn't want the Portuguese soup Holly made. When we sat to eat, a Prospect knocked with his order." We all laugh. "Fuckin' kid is too much sometimes."

Jessie looks at him. "I hope to Christ the others don't pick that one up."

"Is Destiny throwing?" Prez asks him.

"Not yet, but she's still getting shit we put up. Justice says she's moving things herself. Dakota thinks it's funny, but what the fuck does it mean when she gets older? Do we have to come up with new shit to teach them?" He's looking at me.

I nod. "She does move things herself. I think we'll need to address it, but she's too young now. It's like Mucimi throwing the orders to the restaurant—we need to wait for shit to happen before we can react. They are very good at policing themselves. They should work out a lot more as they get older and that worry you have won't look so big. With Stella and the boys, the kids have a good sense of compassion and right and wrong. That will be a big help for all the parents."

Jessie nods then looks at Prez. "We were pretty good kids. They should be better, right?"

Prez laughs again and I feel that same sense of relief. "They'll be better than we were, but a challenge because they all have different abilities. We haven't seen any of this before."

"Will they be able to hurt someone like Dakota does?" Brantley asks.

Taylor and Jessie look at me then Prez. Shit. Prez nods. "Some will. Some will be like Jeremy and be healers, so hurting someone will be harder for them." He looks at me.

22

'Do you want this out?' he asks in my head. I nod. He might as well. "Others have the ability to hurt too. Christian has all Dakota's abilities except healing and quite a few that we haven't seen yet. Colt, Devan and Mase all have it and are being trained to control that focus. They all have Protector abilities. Some of the girls have it too, but they are not showing the same interest as the Protectors. Right now, Aiyana, Elizabeth and Blaze are the only ones with the focus. I think Honor, Case and Destiny will also have it." He's right in most of that so I don't correct him.

"Jesusfuckin'Christ. I'm not having any more kids," Jessie says pacing.

We're all smiling when Darren walks in. "There is a good outcome?" he asks looking at Prez.

His whole demeanor changes to hard and fierce in an instant. "No, we were talking about the kids. Dakota isn't coming back?"

"He's following a couple of leads. Co, Nunánuk and the MC can meet tomorrow. José cleared you for the meet." He sits and Jessie stops pacing and sits beside him.

Prez looks at me. "I need them slower so I can get Brantley a list."

I nod and wait for him to sit. When he nods, I start throwing from Aiyana's brutal vision.

Chapter Two

One week

     I walk into Security and go right to the locker room. Taylor is coming through the door with Delta and Hawk. "Found Hawk while we were running the tunnels. He wouldn't stop so I figure he knew what he was doing."

     I laugh and pet him. "He does." Handing him a bone, I pull another for Delta.

     "I won't ride like Alex either. I just open the door and tell Delta to meet me at Ops."

     I smile thinking of Prince sitting behind Alex. "Is that why you're always at the school?"

     He smiles. "Yeah. I drop Nash and Delta every day."

     We walk up to the meeting room and the dogs sit by the door. "They remind me of Hyde and Cade."

     He laughs as Jessie and Dakota walk in. "I thought Delta was like Hyde when I first got him. He's still the same."

     "They do resemble their human counterparts," Dakota says making Jessie laugh.

     "We aren't taking any more dogs Dakota. Two is enough."

     I watch Dakota turn toward him with a smile. "I was not suggesting it, but I am happy to note it is a thought you carry always. Jessica would be happy to know that."

     I cover my mouth and hold my laugh. Fuckin' Dakota.

     "No more dogs," Jessie growls.

     I throw to Jessie, 'He's fuckin' with you.'

He gives me a nod and relaxes. "That could have been fun Christian. I do not get to hold anything over him if you tell him what I am doing."

I nod. "Sorry Brother, but he was planning how to get you back for the dog thing."

"In that case I am happy that you stepped in." He throws me chin.

Taylor cracks up. "All you have to do is pin him to a wall Brother. You've got nothing to worry about."

Jessie laughs. "I'd kill him."

"I believe he would. I cannot use those abilities against Jessie. To use them is an act of offense against a greater tragedy." We all think about that. He's right. I could use it, but I have no healer in me. I think healers have a different mindset to their abilities. He looks at me. "That is correct Christian. Protectors have a different outlook. It is meant to be that way. While Prophets, Protectors and Healers have the ability to harm, their purposes are different."

I nod and look at Taylor. "Mucimi came home telling me he's done with the boys. He'll teach them at school now."

He laughs. "Yeah. I had Teller help me with that. Brantley was ready to lose his shit." I slide in his head. He's had a good week. I'm relieved. He had a couple of bad nights last week. It's been good for a while and I know it doesn't seem to shake him anymore, but I still worry.

Prez walks in with Brantley and Darren. Brantley goes right to the computer and pulls the boards up from Ops then sets the hologram board up on the table. Prez walks closer and we all read everything on it while Brantley is handing papers out.

"They made a try at the MC. The City PD stopped it, but Uncle Danny is pissed."

25

Darren nods. "His second almost fucked it up. My dad jumped on his bike and beat the shit out of the two waving guns. They were going to blow the Planned Parenthood in the City."

"Sonofabitch," Jessie says.

Darren looks around at us. "Yeah." He turns to Prez.

"What we have to go on is fuckin' crazy. Using the information Carolina is pulling is the only heads up we'll get as far as anyone can see. The readers will have regular meetings to help keep us prepared, but we can't count on that for our plan. We'll take what they give us and adjust the Ops plans to fit the visions. Our biggest challenge will be keeping up with a constant defense until we can get information to actually make a plan of action."

"We've done it before and we can do it again. That's how we got through all the wars," Jessie says.

Prez nods. "We can and we did. The last two years we've had no wars other than the MC's blowback. The new HS and Security—even PD—are not familiar or were trained during that time. We'll need the readers geared up to help with this in a way that we can use their visions. This isn't something we've done lately. We all know what this is like. The new people and readers were not directly involved with Ops on this level. Moving fast and hitting hard isn't going to be easy for them. Taylor, I want all maintenance training to run with the old Op guidelines. Aaron, you're a good one to get people moving fast. Push them—for everything—all the time so when we need it that will be the normal reaction." Aaron nods and Prez looks at me. "Christian, I need readers to meet regularly and I want you training them. Your travel will be arranged whenever you need it. We have to have the Protectors ready and comfortable with their abilities. I need to know who's there, who's still learning and what their focus is."

I nod, but I'm confused. "Wouldn't Dakota be better for that?"

He looks at Dakota, so I do. "It is time for you to step in to who you are meant to be. I am a Prophet not a Protector Christian, I do not see as a Protector does. You surpass my protective abilities and are better suited to align your Protectors from here on out. I can help chart abilities, but there are other things I must do as a Prophet to ensure the vision stays on course."

I think about that. He's spread thin, but where does that leave me as a Protector? When did I become a Protector that leads people? I look at Prez. "I am a lead for them?"

"No Christian. You are *the* lead for Protectors. We saw your abilities growing and were told that is your rightful place. You are trained HS and have the abilities Dakota does without his temper." He smiles. "A Protector reacts, but not usually out of anger. We need you to take that place now. You will still have days at the school, but Holly is preparing the kids for you to be there two days out of five. They need your guidance, but we need you in Ops and training the other Protectors. You will move to training the kids and leading Protectors in Ops, but I need to plan for what I have. We'll worry about the logistics when they become an issue." His wording that they 'were told' makes me uncomfortable, but I can't look at it now.

This is what they've been training me for. It all flies through my head. All the time Prez and Dakota spent with me when I first got here, then Prez set up training for me. Dakota had me with all the people they charted as Protectors. Prez kept me close to the strongest—reporting to him on their progress, issues and any visions they had that concerned us as a group. I look at Prez and see he's waiting for something. "On it Prez. Do I have non-readers that support us?"

He smiles at me. "You're my next meeting, but yes, we have non-ability support staff for you." I nod, understanding why I needed the whole day off from the school. I thought it was odd.

Prez looks at Jessie. "Pull apps and get us more Security, Prospects and viable candidates for PD or HS. Extra Security on the old ladies and at the school."

He looks at Darren. "Get us more Nomads. Three or four should work. I want them in training right away. Meet with Bull and Driscoll to pull what you can for Jessie's new schedule. They are not Family and I don't want them that close, but I want more Security with anyone riding off the Compound."

"Got it Prez." He types in his phone.

Prez paces. "We'll need to start using the tunnels to move people around. Brantley, find a way to make that happen. Taylor, you'll need to stop the trainees from shooting down there while we have them open."

"Roger Prez," both Taylor and Brantley say.

"Am I missing anything?"

I look at him. "Yeah Prez. We'll be hit this week with some from the lunatic group that want to stone the readers. You are identified as a witch."

"What the fuck? A witch?" Darren says.

Prez looks at me. "The fuckin' video of me throwing from years ago?"

I nod. "Yeah Prez."

He stops and considers everything. Thoughts are flying through his head fast. Flipping through pictures of Aiyana's vision and ideas he stops on Justice and looks at me, I nod. "Get High Security on the Compound today Jessie. The kids are locked down. Do I need the old ladies on lockdown?"

"Not yet. It will happen later."

He nods and looks at everyone. "Justice throws at them and ends up taken. They do something in the woods, a ritual or some shit and actually stone him to death." There is no emotion in his voice as he delivers this.

"Oh my fuckin' God. They kill a kid under this religious guise?" Aaron says like it's the craziest thing he's ever heard.

I look at Prez and he nods at me. "They do much worse. The list Prez gave didn't paint the pictures, just the need. They are identifying readers and have Jeremy, Aubrey, Darren and almost all the kids."

"Me?" Darren asks.

"The glasses," I tell him and go on. "Later they will go after the old ladies. They rape and beat them. Three don't make it."

Jessie stands up fast and his chair hits the floor. "Jesusfuckin'Christ! This is a religious attack? What the fuck do the racists do?"

"Worse," I say.

Prez looks at all of us. "Not one of you are asking if it's your old ladies. I wouldn't tell you, but it throws relief just knowing that you're all in for everyone."

"Seriously? We've grown up with 'we take care of our own' right alongside you." Taylor's offended by that comment.

Prez is smiling though. "You did, but it is old ladies and the thought to protect what is yours didn't jump out and negate the need to protect everyone."

"Negate? No. It's a hell of a word and I'm glad to see my old friend when we need him, but they're all ours. There is no one worth more because a threat is looming in front of us. We still live in our own world where Badass isn't negotiable. Dakota would say we learned the lessons of our fathers. A threat to one will always be a threat to all," Jessie says with a passion that we all feel at his words. Everyone's thoughts are agreeing with him.

Prez nods. "I need to meet with Christian if there isn't anything else." No one has anything. "Thank you, Brothers." He throws chin and walks out telling me to meet him in his office in five.

Dakota walks in and sits.

"Holy fuck," Darren says. We all nod. "Jessie, get HS on the Compound now. Aaron, keep everyone moving fast. I think Prez is right with the reaction thing. Taylor, get me trainees in the tunnels. *Not* shooting." We all laugh. "Have them on patrol. It will get them acquainted with the layout and give us an extra set of eyes. I want a check of all the exit sensors, feeds and guns. Dakota, if you've got anything here—find a way to get it to us." He stands. "Christian, after you meet with Prez, see me about your Security needs. I have a team of three on every shift for you. MC has your people covered, but you'll need to go over that too. Based on what you're pulling lately, that all may need to change. When you need more people, you come to me and I'll get your schedule beefed up."

"Got it VP." I'm not thrilled with keeping Security with me, but the Protectors will need it while they're training. Some aren't HS trained through the MC.

He walks out and I look at Dakota. He's closed up tight. "I'll need some direction. Am I coming to you for that?"

He doesn't answer right away so I wait. Taylor, Jessie and Aaron stay and watch. "You will seek and find your direction today, but that will not be through me my Warrior Protector. Prez will benefit also." He stands, but keeps my eyes. "I will come to you when I am able Christian."

I nod and we all watch him leave. "I wish he talked in his sleep at these times," Jessie says making us laugh. "Life would be a fuck of a lot easier."

I nod and stand. From what Dakota gave me, I need to get to Prez and jump so he gets whatever he's supposed to from the ancestors.

I walk in the door to my new office and sit, relieved to be alone. Hawk sits by my feet calming me. It's been three hours and my head is spinning. I shuffle through the pages of shit I need to decide on and settle on the schedule and people I need to cover. Prez gave me an overview of what my new job is and it was all pretty clear. Now that I'm looking at it, I keep going back to what Co and Nunánuk said about following the lessons of our fathers. The Indians closed themselves off and defended their walls when they were threatened. I don't think those are the fathers we're supposed to follow. Weighing those words and the way they were said, I decide on calling my dad. I think it's our Club fathers we're supposed to follow and he's a father.

I hang up smiling. They were the first to start charting the kids and did it with rolls of paper and dry erase boards. I call for a Prospect and tell him what I need. While he goes for my hologram bases and new boards, I get the computer on and start making spreadsheets for the boards. I need to keep it all straight. It's not paper and markers, but I'll get the same results.

I spend an hour getting the hologram boards set on my desk and the table in the meeting room that connects to my office. The Prospects get the boards up for me in both places. I'm glad the rooms were already set up for the boards so we don't need anything, but to put them up. While they're working, I go to Darren's office. We get the schedules set and he sends my personnel over to my spreadsheet. I'm ready to go, but he has things to say, so I wait. "You need to talk to Ricky, he'll be your contact for anything you need from them. He has a partner for you, non-ability, to get what you need done up there and keep you updated on the admin shit. You choose your ability Brother, or second, to keep everyone straight. Yeah?"

I smile. "How does Ricky know who to put with me from up there?"

"Elizabeth."

I nod glad they're taking it seriously. "Pres is good with this new department?" Since Pres is one of his dads he should know. I see Pres laughing in his head. It's good. "He understands better than he did and Prez keeps him up to date with the freaky kid shit now. Well most of it. He's cool Brother. There is no resistance if that's worrying you."

This surprises me, but I nod. "Thanks VP. Anything else I need?"

I see it all but wait. "Yeah. This is new and you just clued into what your job here is. It's new for us too. None of us, aside from Dakota, see like you do. Prez doesn't get visions so much as pieces of what everyone else gets. If you need something you have to tell us. Whether it's Brothers to fill your schedule, a hand getting through to Jeremy or someone to listen to you vent—you need to tell us. Because it's new, we'll be looking out for anything you may need, but we won't catch it all."

I nod. It's like with Taylor—I see the net and people that are around it. "I'll tell you VP. Right now, I'm just setting it up so I can look at it all together. Co and Nunánuk were helpful with some direction for me. Once I get it straight and align our objective with the readers and Security I'll probably have questions, but I'm not there yet."

He nods. "I'm glad you're ready when we need you Brother. Seeing you make it back was good for us, but watching you learn—and seeing your Badass shine through—has been awesome. We're all proud of you Brother." He means it—with no doubt about my ability.

That feels good. I throw him chin and see he doesn't have anything else so I stand. "Thanks Brother. I didn't know this is where I was headed, but it feels right. It feels good to be working at protecting and preserving our cause. The ancestors were pleased with our plan."

He smiles. "You'd think with Dakota that wouldn't strike me as funny, but hearing it from you too does."

I'm surprised. "Doesn't Prez tell you freaky shit?"

"He doesn't talk about ancestors. I know he believes in their strength, but he keeps that to himself."

I nod and think back. Prez jumps all the time, but not in front of non-ability. Uncle Danny pops in my head and I push him out. He doesn't show anything and I know it will happen, but it's not yet so I don't bother looking at it. I stand and throw chin again. "Thanks, VP. I need to get this settled in my head. Prez said I have someone coming in at four to keep me straight here."

He laughs. "Yeah. Remember to ask for what you need Brother."

"I will VP." I'm already walking out the door thinking about the schedule and calling Ricky.

At my computer, I add all my people and separate them by where they fall.

Once I have everyone listed, I look at them on the boards. They got me up with enough Brothers to cover all the Security needs right now. I look at my schedule and see I'm at the reservation and MC tomorrow. Pulling tracking I see the reservation and here. It's time to call Ricky. I need tracking from up there and I have questions.

"Brother, it's Christian."

33

"I was just finishing up with part of your team Brother. I have Colby, Ally and Uncle Danny right here."

Uncle Danny? "Who is running with ability?"

"They didn't give me that. I figured you'd move your people where you want them. Right now, I have Ally getting tracking from Jeremy's new cuffs up for you. It will run here in Geek's program, but on the new Protectors program for your department. Like how you run PD and Security separate, but it's still overseen in HS Ops."

"Got it. I have a meet up there tomorrow. I need everyone in the department for that. Do you have that yet?"

"Fuck no. I have you up here, but not the meet. Anything else you need?" He doesn't sound thrilled with me.

"Yeah. Do we have an office up there?"

"Yeah, it was in the KC, but VP moved you to MC-Baxters with the same setup you have there. Can I call you right back? Uncle Danny needs to get to PD and Ally wants to get to HS Ops so she can set up her new tracking."

"Yeah Brother." I hang up wondering if he's not happy with the new department or him being my contact.

Jacob walks in with Terry and sits smiling at me. "I was told to report to you when my IT got here."

I laugh. "I like this. You're my Ops lead?"

"Yeah Brother and Terry is our new control. He moved into my old room at Brantley's."

Fuckin' nice. "Why didn't you tell me?" I ask Terry. I just talked to him two days ago.

"You're the fuckin' reader. You should have got it."

Jacob cracks up. "Jeremy's been blocking it for us. Prez didn't want it hitting you before it was set up and everyone was settled with their new jobs."

I nod, but I'm not happy. He doesn't need to keep shielding me. I'm not the fuck-up I was when I got here. "Let's go to the meeting room so you can see where I am."

As we're walking in Terry asks, "You're pissed?"

I wave him away. "Not pissed, but I don't need Prez shielding me. It shows a lack of confidence in my ability to lead this. Who the fuck would put someone they don't fully trust in this position?" I wonder if that's what's up with Ricky. Maybe he doesn't think I can handle it either. I know Prez isn't completely sold on me and I'm not even thinking about Pres.

"Dude stop and think. Prez wouldn't even think about putting everyone in jeopardy so you can play catch up and find your place here. He just wanted to be the one to tell you."

He's right and I throw him chin. "Thanks. I'm waiting for a call back from Ricky. Read what I have up so far while I take it." They sit and go through the board.

When I answer my phone, Terry pops out the reservation info. "Yeah Brother." I walk through to my office and sit on the couch.

"Sorry about that. I have all your people covered for the meet tomorrow. Tell me you don't need more than three hours."

I laugh. "No, I figured two."

"Good. VP scheduled lunch in for you. I have to tell you Brother, I'm so fuckin' glad they're finally catching on to how bad we need this. Elizabeth has been pushing it for a while, but LB wouldn't budge until he thought you were ready. Thank fuck you're ready. Diego is the only one able to get through all the shit Carolina is giving us and we don't have all the freaky shit organized to understand half of what we need."

35

I smile. I thought I'd have to fight to prove myself, but he just wiped it away. "Didn't Brantley send the board up with the readers' predictions?"

"Yeah and I'm sure it's filling in for HS Ops, but fuckin' VP is our only reader there and getting information from him isn't fuckin' easy. KC has the readers, but they aren't in HS Ops Brother. The readers that are on HS now aren't in fuckin' planning. It's like a vicious cycle. I need to get everything connected so I'm covering everyone the way they need to be."

I can see that. Mase, Colt, Aubrey, Blaze, Harley, and Blake are the only Little Brothers that are readers. Not all are focused with their ability. Mase, Blake and Colt are HS so they're not in KC so much, but are still part of Little Brothers for another year at least. Ricky's job has got to be stressful with the kids running KC and HS Ops. I know a couple are working Security when they're needed too. I think Prez had an easier time because he was based out of Ops not KC. Ricky ran just KC for so long then had to adjust to the kids being retrained and pulled to Ops. His office is still in KC.

"We'll get that straight this week. The new tracking is just Protectors?"

"Yeah. You'll be tracked at Security with the regular tracking chip, but Jeremy has new cuffs with the added chip for the Protectors. That second chip goes to the Protectors Program, HS Ops down there and Geek up here. If you want it available somewhere else, you need to give that to Geek and he'll set it up. He's excited to get this up and running too."

"Good to know. Thanks Brother. I was calling to ask about the tracking up there, but I'll hold any more questions until I get there. Is there anything else I need to know before I get there?"

"Yeah something is up in the twins, each twin that's a Protector is antsy. I noticed it last week and they haven't calmed down this week. The younger ones are more noticeable."

I walk back to the meeting room looking at Jacob. "I saw some of that with the kids at the school. They feel what's coming up. Jacob is here right now, he's not antsy, but does have some unsettling thoughts."

Jacob pegs me a finger. I smile and sit.

"I am so fuckin' glad they're doing this now. You already having that throws relief Brother. I'll talk to you tomorrow when you get here. Let me know if you need anything. I mean anything at all Christian."

I'm so fuckin' relieved. "I will, thanks Ricky."

I swipe him off and Terry nods at the phone. "He's worried?"

"The Protectors are antsy and he picked up on it. He's concerned. We have new tracking coming from Jeremy. Do you know about it?"

Jacob slaps the table. "No. What the fuck? He's not telling me shit lately."

"He's been working at the lab and can't do the little shit when he's up there. You're like a mother hen Jay. It's not like you don't know what he's like." Terry looks at him thinking he needs to calm his shit down and I smile. He looks at me. "Get out of my head Christian."

I laugh. "You're in the wrong place for that Terry. That's what we do."

"Fuck. This is gonna nurse."

Jacob laughs. Only the MC says nurse anymore. I'm hit with a flood of memories and laugh. Jacob gets it, but Terry is just looking at us. "Nurses with fuck doesn't work, and it's not something we hear at Princes. It threw a bunch

37

of memories at Jacob that happened before you got to the house. We used to throw in together when someone lost dessert for swearing. Mom was cool about it, but would swear like a Brother when it happened."

He laughs. "Mase still does it. Jeremy helps when he's around too. No one here says nurses?"

Jacob shakes his head no.

I get us back on track. While I'm gone tomorrow they'll get everyone's bio up on the board and Jacob will pull the information from Ops on what we have so far from the crazy fuckers coming after us. I tell him how I want it set up on different pages and he's got it. Before they leave I ask, "You're good with how I want the pages set?"

He didn't ask a single question about it. "Yeah Brother. It's how Brantley sets up for Prez. It's the quickest and easiest way to get the info on the boards for planning. I never did the boards for anything else so this works for me."

"Good. If you see I'm doing something that you have experience in just say so. All of it is new to me so any advice is welcome."

He's surprised, but nods. "While you're being so democratic am I ever going on Ops?"

What? "You want to be out on Ops?" He's an Ops lead for control now.

"I wouldn't mind a break from the Ops room. I'm not saying crazy shit, but there are going to be Ops that are routine. I wouldn't mind those."

I nod. "Get me the bios up so I can see if I have another lead. I don't know all the people we have listed."

He fist pumps making Terry laugh. "We have three here and VP, Prez, Brantley and Taylor will step in for you if we need it."

Nice. The show of the support hits me and I nod.

I look at Terry. He puts his hands up. "I'm good on IT. I don't like Ops where my glasses never shut down."

I nod again. "I'll work it out Jay. You're good on the control Terry?"

Jacob smiles. "He's awesome on control. VP didn't want to lose him, but this was too important to stop him from moving here."

I look at Terry smiling.

"I'm good. It's easier to see through to a board or monitor than traffic."

I get it. Darren doesn't have that issue, but not everyone is Darren. I swear he's got some type of ability going on. "You let me know if that changes or you need anything."

He smiles and his thoughts are of being relieved. "I will, thanks Christian. This is going to be awesome. I'm going to start tonight. I'll meet you tomorrow when you're back." He walks out and Jacob is smiling.

I wait. His head is saying it's about time this is happening and he thinks it will be good too. When he looks at me his thoughts change. "This is going to be bad isn't it Brother?"

This is the unsettling thoughts Ricky is worried about. "It was going to be brutal. That's changing." I don't say any more. I can't say any more.

He watches and nods. "I get it. I'll see you tomorrow Brother."

"Dinner at Brantley's tonight." I remember and remind him. "Tell Terry."

He waves his hand as he's walking down the hall. "Yeah. Tonight." He keeps going.

I'm going to need to do something to get him some peace and confidence. *Jump*, pops into my head. I sit at my desk and think maybe that will help, but he's always been in Jeremy's shadow. Now he's struggling to live without Jeremy and the silence where he always had Jeremy talking to him is deafening. Jeremy will be moving soon. Well, once Aubrey turns eighteen they'll be moving into their house with Jacob. I think Geek will kill Jeremy if he tries to move her before that. I smile shaking my head, and focus on the work ahead of me.

When I'm stuck, I look in on Darren for answers. You don't see him much, but he knows everything that goes on and how it all works. His head is like a maze, but I keep at it until I find what I'm looking for. Getting my answers, I type it all up and print my part to go over tomorrow, the new training schedule, and the information the readers and Protectors need. "Let's go home Hawk." He follows me out.

Before I leave I check in with Terry and tell him about dinner. He waves, keeping his eyes on the monitor. It reminds me of Brantley. I take Hawk to the locker room and shut the sensor off letting him go through the door. "Home Brother."

I flip the sensor on and hit my watch then jog out to the lot. Cade and a Security Brother are waiting. I fly home hoping I beat Hawk and run into the school. I hate to think of him waiting for me to open the door while he's sitting in the dark stairwell. This is the new section Prez had put in and for some reason the lights switch off after a couple of minutes. Hawk doesn't register on the sensor at the stairwell so it stays dark. When I open the door Hawk and Delta come through and the light is on. I pet them and hand them each a bone. "Good job Brothers."

Taylor comes through in shorts and all sweaty, but he's smiling. "Brothers?"

"They are to me." I start walking up to the stairs. The dogs are waiting at the top of the landing.

"I do the same thing. Jessie thinks it's funny. I'm glad I'm not the only one."

"You need help getting the boys home?" When we walk through the kitchen door Justice and Stella run to me.

"No. I just have Nash. Beth has the baby."

"Uncle Christian we did it! Stella got it working for us." I lift him up.

"Let's go check it out Little Brother." I bend and lift Stella up. "You did good Stella. Let's go see."

She signs, 'Yes.'

I take them to the classroom and the kids surround us. They look at Aquyà. He points to the steam coming out of the pipe on the model at the table. "She got the filter to work and the steam is clean. There are no toxins in the water. Phoenix thinks we can make clean water with it too."

Brandon nods. "I think so too, we need to find a way to do the water too. It's not till next month, but if we do it now we can move on to the engine. Right?"

I love how he picked up Alex's word. "Yeah Little Brother. Let's see what you have happening. If we can catch the steam easily and show it's clean, maybe Jess can get something going with one of the businesses to try it out. Did Holly test the steam?"

Stella starts signing. 'She did, she doesn't know about the water, but she said it might work. I asked Mitch, but she didn't answer yet. The filter works. No toxins. We did it.' She starts wiggling in my arms so I do a happy dance with her.

When we're done, I put her down. "Let me call Jess and I'll ask if she has a minute to talk to you."

Phoenix moves closer. "That would be good. This will keep Stella and Mucimi up forever if they don't get an answer."

41

He throws me oil bubbling out of water. Shit. Another oil leak will throw them. That's what started all this in the first place. I hit Jess. "Do you have a few minutes to talk to the kids about an experiment they're running?"

She laughs. "Definitely. Stella asked me about material, but never said what it's for. She's had me wondering all day."

"Are you at home? We can come down."

"I'm here," she says from behind me.

The kids start jumping around yelling. When Taylor sticks his head in, Nash lets his hand go and runs to the kids with Mucimi following. I missed the hell out of them and it's only been a day. "Let's show Jess what you did and ask the questions you have."

She laughs. "You can answer them you know."

I shrug. "They need to learn to ask the right people for the information they need. I could answer from a book point of view, but you have practical answers and experience that they need. They read you as you're talking and pull what they didn't ask from your experience."

She just looks at me. "They learn like Jeremy?"

"Not all of them, but the rest get different things from people. Stella takes everything you say and files it for when she may need it. Aquyà will pull what you learned. Teller and Justice your experience. Brandon your sense of ecological preservation and Mucimi everything. He's the most like Jeremy."

"Jesus. Will we ever get a break from freaky?" Taylor asks making me laugh.

"All of us have freaky shit Uncle Taylor," Teller says making me and Jess laugh more.

Taylor is shocked. "Don't you lose dessert for swearing?"

Teller looks at me a little nervous. "Not from me Little Brother."

He relaxes and answers Taylor. "Unless you tell my mom, I'm good."

Jess cracks up. "I'm not saying shit."

I shake my head and pull her over to the model. They let Stella explain and Jess is impressed. She calls Jared to ask some questions, then answers the kids. "I can build a prototype. We need permission from Prez to try it out. It has to be a building that's open and has good ventilation just in case of a problem. Did you do the reproduction on the CO sensor?"

Brandon raises his hand. "We tried it out here and in the tank. It only went off when we opened the tank. I think if we open it now the CO sensor will go off 'cause the bags stink when you boil them down."

'They give off toxins. It's not good to breathe it. We can't open the tank until it cools and the steam in the tank settles,' she signs.

"That's right Stella. You need to make sure everyone is safe during the experiments. When you explain it, they understand. Good job sweetie," Jess tells her and gets a smile from all of them. "Tell me about the clean water."

Justice and Aquyà explain, then look at Holly. She tells Jess about collecting and testing the steam. Then they start talking about how the water can replace the gray water system until it's proven over time. Taylor sits and watches them with a smile. I sit with him and wait until they're finished. Mucimi climbs on me and listens to everything being said. I know he's collecting from Jess and keep quiet until he climbs down. When he stands in front of Jess, Mack sits beside him. "Mucimi has questions Jess."

She looks down. "I'm ready little man."

I laugh when he throws her pictures. He's going too fast. "Mucimi slow. She's not going to understand if you throw too fast."

He looks at me for a few seconds and I throw him pictures giving time in between each one. He nods and throws pictures at Jess a little slower. I cover my smile and watch.

"Oil spills are a problem. Yes. With using the plastic you're helping the environment. We can get the plastic from the recycling center. They've helped me out before with the belts and sending clean plastic for the 3D printers. They'll be happy we can take all plastic for the heating. If this works, we may have to get plastic from other places to keep the buildings heated." She smiles at him. "We do need a way to clean the oil out of water. The wildlife does suffer, but right now we're working on a way to help that, right?" Mucimi nods, but has tears in his eyes. "We'll keep working and maybe find a way to keep the oil contained. They say that's what they're doing, but we all know that just isn't true. It's up to us to find a way to make that a reality. In the meantime, we have heating and clean water to perfect. While I'm working on a prototype maybe you can work on the oil issues." She looks from Mucimi to Stella.

Brandon steps forward. "Is this more important than the engine? That's our next project."

Every head turns toward Aquyà. "It is. A clean engine has been built. It needs to be made so everyone can get it, but the water is a problem. If the wells and tankers keep spilling oil, there are places that won't have clean drinking water. The wildlife dies or is changed and can't be eaten. Food and water is more important than the engine."

Stella nods. 'Thanks Brother. It is,' she signs, and Prez laughs behind us. I didn't hear him come in and swing around throwing him chin.

Justice tells him what they've done. Aquyà asks to put it in the sundries manufacturing building. That's a good building to try it in. It's open and a bitch to heat because of the high ceilings and very little insulation. It was a sewing shop before and had heat from the dye tanks that must have been stifling.

"Didn't the dye make people sick?"

I look at Teller smiling. "They did Teller, but it wasn't proven until much later." He shakes his head.

"That's why we need time to prove the water is safe," Aquyà says looking at him.

Jess laughs. "That's right." She bends to Mucimi. "It's not all bad little man. We're making a difference in the important things right now. Feeding people, getting them in homes instead of on the street and getting the military people help to make it in jobs and their own places are very important to Princes."

Mucimi isn't giving up and starts throwing pictures at her faster. Prez picks him up and walks to the other side of the room. I watch how the kids react to him being so upset. Stella watches Prez and Mucimi and Jess gets the attention of the other kids. "As soon as Prez says it's okay I'll start on this."

They all happy dance and I stand up. Prez is saying yes to her and they know he will, but she doesn't. He brings Mucimi to me. "He sees too fuckin' much."

I nod holding his head to my shoulder. "He does. He'll be okay. Stella is already making a list to talk to Mitch."

He nods and waits until Jess is done talking to Stella. "You're going to find a way to stop the oil?"

Stella's forehead wrinkles. 'They need to drilling for it. We have alternatives if they'd stop being greedy long enough to look!' She signs so fast I turn so she

45

doesn't see my smile. She's pissed about greed and drilling and she's six. I wish every adult could see this. Mucimi and Stella are the two that are the most sensitive, but they're so fuckin' smart it takes most people a minute to get that these are real issues that are bothering them.

Prez squats down. "You all need to hear this." He gives them a couple of seconds to focus on him. "We do what we can to make the world better. That started long before you were born. We will keep working, but it has to be like triage. People come first. We need clothes, food and shelter. Then we need help with jobs, energy that's affordable and medical care. We keep working on energy and cleaning up the pollution. You're testing that out, so while that's being worked through, you look for a way to stop water from being polluted. Aquyà and Mucimi are right, we need to stop water from being contaminated and killing marine and wildlife—not to mention the drinking water issues that brings with it. We are a small group that needs time to get from one solution to the next. I have no doubt that you will change the world and the way people think, but you have to keep it in perspective. That means you look at the important things in life and put the world problems in their place. We have a roof over our heads, food, water, heat, clothes, our Brothers keeping us safe, and each other. Those are all the most important things we can help our community with. We branch out and do the extra to help our world. If you don't have food, water, security and shelter you can't help the world. Always find a way to do that first then work on other problems."

The kids all nod at him looking so serious and I wish I had recorded it. Mucimi hugs him. "Thanks, Prez." We all laugh. Mucimi rarely talks.

Prez stands. "Fuckin' kids." He puts his hands out and Phoenix and Teller each take one. "You will change our world Little Brothers, but you need to be patient. We'll get there." He throws chin and walks out with Alpha and Omega following.

Mucimi comes to me and puts his head on my shoulder. He's throwing pictures of dead shit in the water. I throw him a barge that cleans the garbage out of the water and he looks at me. "We do what we can and keep pushing for more. If you're always thinking of the worst, you won't ever be happy. Do what Prez said. Keep it in perspective and work one problem at a time. We won't get anything done if we aren't organized and working together."

"That's what Grampa VP says. We take care of our own, then our community, then the world," Aquyà says touching Mucimi's back. "That's Brotherhood. We got this Mucimi."

Taylor laughs. "I need to get home. They're unfuckinbelievable." He lifts Nash up and walks out with Delta following.

Holly sits by us. "You must have a ton of work with your new job. I have happy boy if you need to go."

"Yeah. What time is dinner?"

"Seven. I think Mucimi needs a pick me up. How about if I let you order happy boy?"

He starts bouncing and the kids laugh. I hold my laugh in, getting the pictures of a Chuck E Cheese pizza party.

I leave them to get my shit done before the big party. I'm shaking my head riding home with Hawk running beside me. Terry is going to love this. We do dinner at Brantley's once a week. I love when we're all together and having Terry here is going to make tonight special. With hats, cake and games. I crack up. I can't wait.

Chapter Three

Two days

We're in KC training and it's going well, except for Elizabeth. I take Blaze's place and work with her, but she's off. "Focus Elizabeth. You'll end up hurt if you don't clear it out and focus."

She gives me a look. "You haven't hit me yet."

I spin and slap her ass with the stick. "Because I've been waiting for you to react. If you can't do this now, just go. We'll work again next week."

She sits down looking completely defeated just like Aiyana was. I see what's going through her head and sit beside her. "We'll get through this like everything else."

She shakes her head. "This is big. We don't even know these people Christian. They want us all dead without seeing any good here."

"You've seen this before. This is no different than any other war we've had. A wise Brother once told me, 'we get through it all together.' Every one of us has a purpose that we defend however we can. We know ours now and we can do this. With focus and solidarity, we *will* do this."

She's watching me, but doesn't lose the thoughts of being overwhelmed going through her head. I put my knee against hers and look around the mat. "Brothers come jump with us." Hawk sits against my back.

They all sit in a circle and we jump. Blake, Devan and Mase see right away something is wrong and give Elizabeth encouragement. When we jump back Elizabeth is more settled. "Let's do this like we're defending all the people we love against these evil fuckers. They are no match for us when we pool our strong," I tell her.

She smiles and stands up. "I haven't heard that in so long. We got this. Let's go Brother I got shit to do today."

I laugh and we begin again. They're all focused and Blaze isn't going easy on Elizabeth. She whips the stick out of Blaze's hand and it flies against the wall. We all clap. "Just like that! Good fuckin' job Brother."

Elizabeth is shocked. "I didn't touch it."

I laugh. "That's your strong showing through. Focus and practice. This new line of defense is counting on each of us to bring what we have. Use your abilities whenever you can, where it isn't seen, so when you need it you're comfortable."

"We won't get a pep talk before we need them so make sure you can control the fuckin' shit you're throwing," Colt says making me smile.

Elizabeth gives him a look. "You kiss your mother with that mouth?"

Colt stops with a stick suspended in the air and looks at her. I'm smiling while everyone watches him and the stick. "Like you don't know my fuckin' parents?"

I laugh. They do swear a lot, but Elizabeth is watching the stick. "Show me how to do that. I can defend without the stick in my hand?"

They get into a conversation then he shows her how to control an object. I sit and watch for a while. When our time is almost up, I pull everything they're controlling and hold it up high. Mase cracks up knowing what I've done. "Gather around Brothers." I wave my arm motioning them closer. When they realize I'm controlling their sticks and the chair Blaze was moving they look from me to the ceiling, but move closer. "You practice on your own or in groups. Every one of you has the ability to suspend objects. Use it in your rooms, at your houses, wherever you're alone. Practice shielding at your next training, but do it by suspending

49

objects to deflect. Yeah?" They nod and look up again. I smile and throw fire setting the sticks to burn. With the sticks burning high I lower the chair and stop the sprinklers from going off.

"Yeah?" I ask again.

"Fuck yeah. Teach us how to do that," Colt says making Mase laugh. He can throw fire already, but he doesn't say anything so I leave it alone.

"I'll see you next week. If you get anything bring it to Mase or Uncle Danny. If I need it right away call to me and I'll take it from you." They're still watching the ashes above us. I send them to the trash barrel lifting it up to collect the ash. When I put it down they look at me again. "Did everyone hear what I said?"

"Yeah, but that was cool Brother," Devan says. "Why aren't they bringing me the visions?" Since he's my second here it's a reasonable question.

"I need you on something else this week. Mase will take everything to Ally, but we have a threat coming our way and I need you and Colt on it." He nods. "Everyone else keeps to the training schedule and I'll see you next week." Mase waits with Devan and Colt. "This is an Op that's easy, but will require you to use your abilities. We need information on the group that's planning the hit to Princes." I hand them the information. "You get close, get the information and take whatever they're using with you. If it's guns I want them. You don't have to bring me shit like rocks." They smile. "They are planning to stone Justice to death."

"Fuckin' hell!" Mase yells.

"Take whatever they plan on using to get him. There's no way they can get him unless they plan an attack at the school or Compound. We need to stop that however we can. Your schedules are clear for the next two days. I need you on this now."

"Got it Christian," Devan says pulling Colt by the arm.

I look at Mase knowing the question before he says it. "Why not me?"

"Three reasons. This is the first Op for us. Sending two that are just realizing their ability says something about us as a group. They do the job and it works for everyone. Two, you already have your focus and fight effectively with your abilities. You have nothing to prove to anyone. Three, VP said you have Ops scheduled and he needs you." He smiles relieved so I go on. "Your Op this week is with these pussies. You use whatever you have to take them down. I mean all the abilities we've been training you on. Your control on reading needs to be more focused, but for this week you run HS Ops and stop these lunatics by any means necessary. I'm going to ask Jeremy to get with you about the reading. He may be helpful with that focus."

He nods still happy. "We have dinner with him and Aubrey tonight, I'll ask him. So, we're not hiding abilities anymore?"

"We're hiding specifics. You use what you have in a fight, but don't start getting your own coffee and donut at the Bakery. The flying shit will cause more of a problem than it's worth."

He slaps my back. "Got it. Thanks Christian. I'll work on the reading. With Jeremy and you it isn't something I really practiced. I will now."

"Good Brother, because we're going to need it." I look around and don't see him. "Hawk, let's go Brother." He runs from where he was sitting by the elevator.

"How the hell does he run like that? He's fuckin' old."

I laugh walking up the stairs to the house. "Mucimi does shit with him. I don't have a clue. The healing thing

51

doesn't touch me. I'll catch you later Mase, I need to get to training with Jeremy and Aubrey."

He nods hitting my fist. "I'll ask them tonight about reading."

On the ride to the Baxter's Compound I stop at the lake on the reservation. My Security gives me space staying ahead and behind me, but far enough away that I'm not crowded by their thoughts. Something has me on edge. I sit and jump. Going through my readers up here I don't find anything, but I'm happy to see the hope shining through where there was doubt. I jump to Princes and see Mucimi is upset again, but that's not my main concern. He's pulling from Aiyana and Kaya. Fuck they're talking to an elder that's pissed about the pipeline fight and a pipeline that broke in one of their river's tributaries. I call Aiyana, but she doesn't answer so I hit Co.

"I have been waiting for your call Christian," he answers in Mohegan.

"I'm glad I caught it. I need Aiyana and Kaya at the pipeline with their Security to stop the oil flow from touching the river and calm the unsettled construction and police force that's showing up there. I'll make sure they have HS with them." I wish I had better words to get my feelings across. I can't let them go without protection.

Co laughs. "I understand my Protector Prince. I will get them travel today."

I blow out a breath. "Thanks Co. I need to calm Mucimi. The boy is going to be depressed at four if this keeps up."

"He will calm soon. Find a way to show the good being done. He sees only what he is allowed. Taking away that block so he sees all clearly will give him peace."

I nod. He's right. "Is he too young to jump my wise Shaman?"

52

"Eagle Eye jumped a harvest moon ahead of Mucimi. He is ready Guardian of the unrest."

I smile shaking my head. "I'll get him on a straight path Co, thank you. Is there anything else I am not seeing?"

"You are a wise Protector. You will learn as the day goes on my warrior. Let it be as it would."

"Roger Co. I need to get to training. Let me know if I'm required."

He laughs. "You will always be needed Christian," he says in English. He really does get my meanings. He hangs up before I respond. I shrug. I didn't know what to say to that anyway. I ride the rest of the way forming a plan for Mucimi. I remember what it was like seeing so much death and destruction that I felt paralyzed by it. We keep the shit away from the kids because they already see so much. Maybe it's time to show them so that the perspective they have to go by isn't skewed to their small part of this world. I look up at the camera outside the Lab and the door opens. Jeremy added me so I can come right in. I walk in his office and step back out knocking on the door jam. "Je it's time for training."

Aubrey laughs. "He already saw. Let's go." She comes out pulling Jeremy behind her.

"Glad you still have clothes on." I smile at him.

"Door's open." He gives me a look as if *him* being caught making out is my fault.

I just laugh following them to the first level testing room. There's nothing, but rock and block wall in here. "Flip the cameras on Je."

He nods and stands holding Aubrey's hand. "Done."

"You both know what's at stake. I need you to be able to get away from a threat using everything in you. Your throw and shield are good. Suspending objects is one way to defend, but we need to take that to the next level. If a threat is so close it can harm you, you need to suspend yourselves and get to where you're not in danger."

Jeremy's brows draw down. "Show me."

I pull the shield so he can read it then take a quick step to the side and flip, but hold my body so it moves slow. "Suspend your body until you are clear of danger. You get Aubrey to where she can do this comfortably Brother. This is one of the abilities that keeps her alive. I'm glad you are both fighting Aiyana's vision. We need everyone to make this work and keep everyone safe." When my feet hit the floor Aubrey's smiling. She's in my head taking everything I left open to her.

Jeremy gives me a sad look and I see what he sees in his head. "It hasn't happened and I'm not giving up. It took me fuckin' forever to get here. I'm not going out that easy. You practice and perfect suspension. Yeah?" In my head, I tell him not to speak of the vision of me. He gives me a look, but nods.

Aubrey laughs. "Got it Christian. I'll be flying by tonight."

I smile and pull her to me kissing her head. "Not flying Little Bit—suspension."

She waves me away. "Flying, suspension it's all the same, I get it." She throws me a picture of her moving across the room.

Jeremy cracks up. I leave them to practice and get to MC-Baxter. I'm happy to see they already have Hawk here and he's waiting for me at the door. In Ops, I talk with Ally and get a hug before I go. She's still so cute, I love this kid. She knows her shit and updates my boards before I'm even gone. Neil flies me to Princes Security and I think about Mucimi. I walk right into Ops and look for Brantley. Jacob is smiling. He shows me Jeremy hanging in the air on his phone. I laugh. "I told them to practice. Aubrey said she'd have it by tonight."

He smiles proud. "She's got it, it's on the video before this one." He has a picture in his head of Aubrey and Jeremy kissing in the air. I don't need that shit in my head so I slap his back and head to Brantley's office.

"Brother." I open the door and close it just as fast. What the fuck is happening today? "Come see me when you're free Brother." I go into my office smiling. My brothers with their women today, even Mase had plans for tonight. I think about that and figure a trip to the Club isn't a bad idea. It's been a hell of a week. Since Brantley doesn't show by the time I'm ready to go, I text that I'll see him on his deck tonight. Texting Taylor, I get Hawk squared so he's not waiting here alone. "Go work with Delta Brother. I'll be home later." I give him a bone and watch him run down the hall.

Terry's at the bar when I walk in, I slap his back and he introduces me to his girl for the night. "It's got to be a Blackhawk thing today," I say throwing chin and walking toward the parlor. Kit isn't here so I keep going to the whores' rooms. The music is loud making knocking pointless so I just walk in. Brothers are everywhere. I see Jacob fuckin' a whore against the wall and keep going.

Kit is just walking out of the hallway and spots me smiling. "Just in time handsome. I was shopping and got back late."

I nod seeing it's true. She turns and I follow her back to her room. "Glad my timing hit right."

She doesn't say anymore. In her room, she doesn't talk. This is just how I want it. I don't need her extra memories or other men flowing through my head when I'm fuckin' her. She bends knowing how this works and I take her from behind and focus on getting relief and making sure she feels my hands on her even though I don't move them

55

from her hips. The pictures in my head get me there and she's running on exhaustion. When I finish, her mind and body are done. I go into the bathroom and clean up dropping the condom in the recycle bin shaking my head. It's like a medical waste container, but it keeps the condoms from clogging the plumbing. The medical waste analogy is fitting, I feel like this is clinical. Walking through I stand at the end of the bed and move Kit to the center of it. The only good thing about her being so tired and dazed is she has no clue that my hands never touch her. I clean her and pull the covers over her never moving from my spot. Dropping money in her jar I close the door as I walk out.

Finding relief is the hardest thing I've ever had to learn. It was Dakota that helped when he saw me completely stripped and shaking as I left the whores room one night. He didn't actually talk to me, but had Prez explain how to get relief with little contact. He was right about the getting relief, but no contact is a hard way to live when you crave a woman's hands on you. With release, my body expects and looks for that intimacy and connection that you get from holding your partner before, during and after. I don't know if it's better to be able to walk away without being in such a vulnerable state or walking away feeling that loss. Either way, it's a release that is never fully satisfied and it fuckin' sucks.

I walk through the parlor and don't see Jacob or Terry. Checking the time, I see why and move people so I can walk through easily. No one ever says anything and I smile going by Driscoll and Bull. These are big guys and I move them like I choreograph my exits. I'm surprised no one ever calls me on it. I throw them chin and keep going to my bike.

There's a problem at the gate. I feel it before I turn in so my gun is ready when I see guards surrounding a car. The woman is scared and the baby is screaming. Pulling right alongside the driver's door everyone stops, but the

56

guards on the other side have their guns aimed at the woman.

"Stand down. She is no threat to me." I get off my bike and throw to my Security hoping to calm everyone down.

My Security takes over for the two guards from that side throwing relief on me. They're nervous about anyone being so close to the gate. I look at the woman and get what she's thinking easily. She's clouded by nervousness and pain, but happy I showed. "What brings you to our gate?"

She gives me an incredulous look. "Do you hear the damn kid screaming? I have a headache the size of Cleveland. You think you can get the rest of the guns out of my face so I can get out?"

I nod to the last gate guard and he lowers his gun. "Done." I don't know if she's a bitch or just cranky, but her thoughts are making me want to smile. I open her door and wait for her to step out. I can't give her my hand so it may seem an invasive move, but I'm not putting my guard down and her hand in mine will throw me.

She stands and moves to the back door. Security moves closer to the back. "Really! The kid doesn't even look a year old. You think he's dangerous?"

I've had enough of the bitchy. "Look we have people trying to get at our kids. We're all on edge here. If you'd tell us what the fuck is going on we can react better."

She leans against the door. "Yes, I can see that would be reasonable, but I have this headache that won't quit and this kid that won't shut the hell up." Her shoulders slump with a dejected look crossing her face.

"Move away and I'll calm the boy." She rolls her eyes at me, but moves. I slide in her head and keep her right where she is then move to get the boy out. He's a cute little thing with chubby cheeks that are red and wet from his tears.

I talk in his head calming him and release the belt on his seat. I can smell the urine on him and know he's crying in pain. "He's in pain. Where's a diaper so I can change him?"

She doesn't say anything so I look back. She's frozen in place. Fuck. I loosen my hold on her and she moves her hand. "There was just the seat. He had a toy in his hand, but that's all."

I see she picked him up just off the exit ramp. Who the fuck leaves a kid on a road like that? I don't have time to look for more. The boy hurts and I need to get that straight. "How did you know to bring him here?" I notice he's having pain breathing and loosen my hold on him.

I see she lives close. "The note on the seat said Princes. I see the bikes pulling in here so I brought him here. If there's somewhere else I need to bring him, you'll have to tell me. I'm new and don't really know where everything is."

Hyde goes into alert mode. I tell him in his head she's not a threat and he relaxes. "You brought him to the right place. I'll take him from here." I lift the boy and put him against my chest gently so I'm not the cause of more pain for him. He calms right away. "Get my bike to my house. I'll need a ride." Hyde looks at the guard throwing him chin and the guard moves toward the gate. Looking at the woman I see she's nervous again. "Do you have any other information for me?"

She shakes her head no. "I'm not sure if leaving him with a biker is right, but the note told me to bring him to Princes. You'll get him somewhere he'll be safe?"

I nod. "He'll be safest right here. I need you to give your information to Hyde. If we need answers you're our only lead."

She relaxes. "Are you the police?"

I smile. That thought relieves her. "Something like that." She turns and asks who Hyde is, but I don't wait. My

58

little guy is calm, but still in pain and dripping piss on my arm. I walk toward the guard and hand him the boy. "He's hurt, something hurts him to breathe. Be gentle." Pulling my cut, I get my shirt off and around him then take him back. He puts his head on my shoulder and I start walking to the gate.

"Hey Blackhawk hottie!" the woman yells. Hyde laughs and I turn around. She's worried. "Can I come see him so I know he's alright?"

I nod and point to the school. "You can go to the school gate and they'll bring him out. As I said, we have people trying to get at the kids. That's as close as anyone will let you get." She watches me for a few seconds thinking about crazy bikers then nods. I start walking again, but stop short. My head whips around and I catch her eyes. She's thinking about telling Dean all about this and asking what to do. Who the fuck is Dean and why is she asking? "Stop!" She freezes. "Who is Dean?"

She laughs like I told a joke. "This is why she brought me here? You'd think she would have told me."

Dean is a reader and dragged them from Ohio to here. She's searching? I pull everything she has about Dean and start walking. "You know this paranormal shit doesn't happen in the rest of the world. She should have told me!" Her cranky is back with a vengeance.

I throw her a wave never looking back and get in the SUV with this poor kid. Before we're off I slide in Hyde's head and tell him I need her information and I'll be going out later to pull what I can. He thinks taking orders never spoken is getting easier. I throw him a picture of a smiley face and hear him laugh as the SUV pulls away.

Mucimi is throwing me pictures and I let him in. He knows exactly what's going on and wants the boy so he can fix him. He shows me Jacob is there and I laugh. I tell Jacob to get water in the tub for the boy and I'm a minute out. Hawk is waiting at the garage when we pull up. I pull a bone before I get out and hand it to him as I'm going by. "You did good Brother. Let's go see Mucimi."

He follows me into the house and Mucimi comes running. He wants to hold the boy. "No little dude. He needs to be cleaned up and get some clean clothes." He starts shaking his head no. "He's in pain Little Brother. He needs a bath and some clean clothes. You can help with the bath. I need him calm so I can find out where he came from."

"Hurt away now!" He's never yelled that I know of and I'm surprised to see this now.

Brantley picks up Mucimi. "Let's take his hurt away in the tub. If you keep putting up a fight he'll hurt for longer."

Mucimi sucks in a breath and his tears fall. "No." He throws the bathtub at me and I start walking. Holly is standing back watching, but doesn't say anything.

"I need Nick and Prez here." She nods and walks into the kitchen. "Brantley, Mucimi is off the chart here. Can you get someone to keep him calm?"

He looks back at me worried. "Won't Jacob do that?"

"No Brother. He's support for healing. We need one of the kids."

"I am here Brother. Prez will work on his placement, but I can calm Mucimi and the adults with you later," Dakota says from behind me.

I smile. He's blocking me completely, but showed when I need him. "Thanks Brother."

"Brantley take Mucimi to his room until the boy is in the tub." He tells me in my head to shield. I nod and throw it to Jacob. I hold the boy up while Dakota undresses him.

"Sonofabitch!" Jacob yells scaring the boy and we hear Mucimi scream.

I close my eyes. We don't need Mucimi seeing this. "Dakota, can you take away some of this before Mucimi gets in here?" The boy has two cuts on him and bruises every-fuckin'-where.

"I am Brother. Jacob I need you to go help Brantley calm Mucimi. Block what you see here."

Jacob pulls the door open. "They better fuckin' pay! I'll do it myself!" He slams the door scaring the boy again.

Dakota takes him from me and holds him against his chest. "Our new friend, we will make it all better for you. Mucimi will make sure of it Little Brother." His words relieve me until I pull his diaper off.

"Jesus, Dakota." I throw him what I am seeing.

"It is not sexual, but a bad infection. The blood is the reason I wanted Mucimi and Jacob away, Christian."

"Thank fuck. He's ready."

He nods. "The water will be painful. I need a minute to help that."

Mucimi is still screaming in his room. He doesn't scream, so it unnerves me. "I need to go calm him down Brother. Let me know when you're ready for him."

He tells me in my head to go. I walk through the bedroom door and see Jacob move across the floor without moving his feet. Fuckin' kids. "Stop!" Jacob stops moving, but he's pissed. This is the distraction I need. "*Never* is it okay for you to move people to get what you want when they tell you to wait." I speak slow and make sure he understands I'm not happy. "We have years of experience and know you need to give Dakota a minute with the boy. You are three. You don't know what we do. Give us the respect we deserve. We earned that respect and what you're doing right now shows us that doesn't mean anything to you. Is that the message you're trying to send?"

His whole body starts shaking. Brantley is pissed at me, but doesn't say a word. Mucimi looks at Jacob. "Sorry."

Jacob nods and puts his fist out. "We're good Little Brother, but Christian is right. That was a disrespectful shit move to pull on your favorite uncle."

Mucimi nods and looks down. "Why is he shaking, Christian?" Brantley's words are clipped.

"He's sorry and doesn't know how to get it out. Mucimi, look at your dad. He is not upset with you. Because you were screaming, he's a little nervous, that's scary to hear from your child."

Mucimi looks up at Brantley. "No more. I bring boy for you."

What? His head is swirling like Jeremy's, I throw this to Dakota and hope to fuck he can get something. Brantley is watching me. I throw to him asking him to give us a minute to calm him and get what he's talking about.

Mucimi puts his arms out to me and I take him. "Prez is here and needs to talk to you Brant." He looks from me to Mucimi. "I'd give my life to keep him safe from anything that could hurt him. Over the next two days I'm going to ask you to trust me and my ability to protect him from everything including the emotion that's causing such extreme reactions."

His whole body relaxes. "I do Brother. I didn't realize it was a lesson. Seeing it, now I do." He kisses Mucimi's head. "Listen to Uncle Christian. It's important little dude."

Mucimi nods and watches Brantley walk out. He asks me his questions in my head. "He is not disappointed just as Uncle Jacob isn't. You learn the lessons of your fathers and make us proud Mucimi. We will learn more about that tomorrow. Right now, Dakota is calling us. He needs your help. Are you calm enough to give that to him now?"

He freezes. "Yes." He doesn't normally talk and I've never registered that he slows his head down to do it. I'm always just surprised to hear his words.

I take him to the bathroom with Jacob following. 'Get this to Prez and we need Nick in here,' Dakota throws then starts throwing everything at me. Mucimi starts crying so I set him down. He's ripping his clothes off and Jacob kneels down and helps him. He climbs in with his boxers on and sits holding the boy's hand. "No!" he cries looking at Dakota with tears falling again.

"Jacob help them." He nods at me and touches the boy with the healing chant spilling from his lips. Dakota stopped throwing shit at me so I go find Prez.

Nick is waiting with Holly at the table. "They need you Nick. Dakota said it's not sexual, but a bad infection. There was blood in his diaper."

His blood pressure rises and it's like watching a cartoon with red rising until it reaches his head then blows out. "Fuckin' bastards better be dead."

He grabs his bag and walks down the hall fast. I'm glad he's pissed; this boy will need all the help he can get and that anger will fuel the determination in the adults that help him through this. I look back at Holly. "The boy needs a home. Dakota thinks we need to keep him close to Mucimi." She nods. "Not even a hesitation. Thank you, Holly. You need to hear what I'm going to tell Prez and Brantley."

She stands and I follow her out to the deck. Prez watches me. I'm closed to him, but I need to shield from Mucimi and throw it to him. He relaxes and nods. "The boy has some developmental issues. He does have ability, but Dakota says it will have to wait right now because he's clouded by pain and the disability. Mucimi connected with him and got him to leave the house he was in. The boy crawled across a road and was picked up by someone with a seat for him heading our way. Mucimi had him dropped at our exit and picked up by the woman that brought him to us." I stop and wait for Prez to get his anger under control. I've been throwing the pictures that Dakota gave me so it's pretty vivid how the boy came to be here.

"Where is he from?"

I throw the house at him then show him inside. "It's south east Connecticut close to the New York line."

"What!" Brantley is pissed again. "Mucimi reached out to some baby and got him here from more than two hundred miles away? Alone!"

"Jesus. Calm down Brother, he's three and doesn't know the danger that would put the kid in," Taylor says walking up the stairs. We all look at him. "Dakota said I need to be with Christian later for Ops. I was just coming to see what's up."

I look at Prez. "I'll tell you about that after the boy." He nods. "The boy has a broken rib, bad bruises on his back, arms and a cut on his side and hand. The cuts were made by a grown man that the boy is familiar with. He has a bad rash that Dakota says is infected and blood was in his diaper, but nothing sexual touched him. His skin looks like it was burned wherever the diaper touched, but it's worse between his legs and at any creases. That's what's bleeding, the creases. He hasn't eaten today and by the looks of him that's a normal thing. His cheeks are the only thing with meat on them." I look around and Holly is crying, Taylor and Brantley are pissed and Prez is waiting for more. "Mucimi said he brought him here for Brantley. He threw them as older laughing with Teller and Justice. I know you're pissed at him for putting the boy in danger, but Taylor's right, he doesn't understand the danger. I planned on taking him to work tomorrow and showing him so he understands what we have always seen. Co said he's not too young to jump so we'll do that too. He's getting too emotional over things we can't control right now. We need to give him—and all the kids—the information we've been blocking from them so they can make better decisions and help keep each other safe. I don't want Mucimi to end up fuckin' up like I did. We can help that by showing him what we see and giving him the ancestors as an outlet to calm and guide him."

We all wait for him to consider what I said. After a minute, he looks at Holly then Brantley. "Are you willing to take the boy?"

"Yes," Holly says right away and Brantley smiles nodding.

"A disability isn't temporary," he says looking at Holly. We all get that, but it doesn't play into our thinking like it would outsiders.

She smiles. "Neither is my love."

He smiles. "Of all the things to settle my fuckin' head you hit it Holly. Thank you. I'll get his information and adoption set when you're ready."

"Now." She's determined. I smile and Prez watches her. "Mucimi won't let him go. He sees him as older and they're happy. I've learned to trust those pictures. I don't have to understand them to have faith that they're right and the Princes, namely you, will not let go or let us fall," she explains.

I laugh. "Never," Prez says.

He looks at me with questions going through his head. "I can't go further with Holly and Brantley here." I look at them not sure how much information is too much for them to hear.

Holly stands. "I'm going to check out my new boy. What is his name?"

"We don't have one. His speech will be a problem. I got pictures, but no words from him."

She nods and pulls me down kissing my cheek. "Thank you."

I watch her walk in and see the vision of her crying alone in the hall. I push it away and look at Brantley. "She'll need you." He looks at Prez and gets a nod then follows Holly.

"I think you're right taking the kids to Security so they see all we do. They're reading from more people now and I didn't get that their perspective is so narrow. I'm telling them to use what they don't know. You should have said it at the school. I'm not giving them what they need, but expect them to react as we would." He's disgusted with himself thinking he's failing them.

"I didn't know myself until I saw Mucimi's reaction to Aiyana's melt down today. I talked to Co and started making the plan. I had no idea he was staging all this with the boy. I was at the MC today and didn't see the kids."

He nods and I'm relieved. "I don't expect you to see everything with them, but the boys didn't throw anything to me. Is he blocking them?"

"Fuckin' Christ," Taylor says sitting.

"Two things that happened today lead me to believe he is. He got the boy here by controlling other people and he was moving Jacob out of the doorway so he could get to the boy. He was angry and feeling the boy's pain."

Prez freezes. "Moved Jacob?" I throw him the picture. "Fuck. How is he learning this?"

The slider opens. "He is learning from Christian." Dakota steps out looking at Prez.

Prez looks at me. "You've learned how to move people?"

66

I look at Taylor and lift his chair up about three feet. He's shocked, but doesn't say anything. When I put him down I look at Prez. "This is what I'm training Jeremy and Aubrey on right now. The Protectors are learning with smaller objects, but Blaze moved a chair today."

He looks at Dakota. "Why am I learning this now?"

Dakota turns toward me. "Christian has all the information on his boards. He has gone beyond what I had listed, but is not shielding that from you." He looks back at Prez. "I am no longer overseeing the Protectors and have been warned of my place when Christian aligned himself with the ancestors and readers. I can only guide his way my Warrior Leader. I believe Christian will be bound to his Protectors soon."

Prez looks down and we wait. "This will take some getting used to. I see where I put you in a position, but didn't arrange for your information to flow to me. I'll fix that tomorrow. For tonight, what is happening that you need Taylor?"

I look at Dakota. "He has a job that will require HS. I have not had a chance to talk with him to give him that information."

Prez turns to me with questions running through his head. I answer before he asks. "The woman that brought the boy is from Ohio. She was brought here by a reader. Hyde has the information for me and I made arrangements to go by there tonight just to get a better idea of why they're here."

We wait. When he looks up I see what he's thinking. "I didn't think Mucimi could do what he's already done. I want to say he couldn't, but I don't know. I plan to get that tonight." Again, I answer what he hasn't asked.

"You're getting in where I'm shielding. Is this new? I'm not able to read you while you're shielding for Mucimi."

I look at Dakota because I have no clue. "He is getting stronger Prez."

"I didn't know. It feels the same to me so I assumed you let it show."

He nods. "Nunánuk and Co made a reference to this happening. At least in the cryptic Indian speak." He's smiling so it's good. "Tomorrow we'll meet and go over all I need to know and how you'll keep me up to date. Take Taylor with the Security you have arranged tonight. Use your Protectors when you arrange for Ops."

I look at him wondering if he just missed it or he wants me to move people around. "He does not have that and will need it to understand the picture you see so clear," Dakota says.

"There are no readers in HS here Prez. I have you and Dakota here, but no HS Ops readers to pull. Jacob is the closest, but he doesn't read like you are thinking."

"Fuck. How the fuck did I miss that?" His hands go into his hair putting a tie in it. "We'll look at that tomorrow too. I'm missing too much lately. I'll get it together and have a better plan when we meet. Dakota I need some time tomorrow to get this straight and jump for some guidance."

Dakota nods. "I will be available when you need me Prez." He stops and I see concern, but he's not going to tell Prez so I let it go.

"Taylor, I'll get your first class covered. If you need longer, text me, and I'll arrange more."

"Roger Prez. What time Christian?"

"Twelve," I tell him.

He walks toward the stairs. "I'll meet you in the garage." I throw him a thanks.

"I will see you tomorrow Brothers," Dakota says following Taylor.

Prez is watching me. "This is moving faster than I thought. I need you to point out what I've missed." He's wondering if I'm getting that it's too important to leave anything in question. He also has a question of whether this is going to work.

I nod. "I didn't realize having a reader on Ops here was an issue. With me and HS backup I thought it was your intention for me to be in that position. I arranged with Hyde for Security tonight. I know that will be with HS support."

He nods. "With me and Dakota here, I never thought about HS. Is there someone we can pull from Mass?"

I think about the ability HS from there. "Mase, Blake and Colt are too young. I don't think the 'rents will let that fly and I need Devan running Ops up there."

He's surprised. "You didn't put Jeremy in there."

I think about how to answer that before I open my mouth. "I know in an actual Op he'd focus to get the job done. I've seen it, but right now isn't the time. He's got shit hitting him that needs his focus. Aubrey is an issue that needs his protection more than anything else right now. We've seen what they do to her." I throw the vision that Aiyana didn't get.

His hands hit the table. "Jesus. Who is the most ready out of the kids?"

"Mase, but he's needed on HS. Jeremy has been working with him on his abilities as he sees them growing, but he's not a good reader. Colt is right behind him in ability, but a better reader. He hits right below Mase on the leaderboard and runs HS, but he's fifteen and not a regular for them."

He waves that away and looks up at me. The vision hit him hard. "I'll talk to Bob while I'm at the MC." He's talking to Uncle Danny and Pres about this department.

I want to ask about Uncle Danny, but hold it for now. "I am able to run HS if Jacob is a lead here."

"I have no doubts where you're concerned. You've done more than I expected right from the beginning. My concern is you getting burned out and not having another reader here that can lighten your load."

I see his concerns clearly, but don't comment on them. I think about the rest he said. "Jacob can handle HS Ops too. If you can put Taylor with me, I have that common bond and an ability to let shit go with him. Taking someone so young from the MC concerns me. We have more Blackhawks here than they do in Mass. Colt would be alone here. That will be a problem for a twin that's his age. Freaky shit aside, he's still a teenage boy that needs his parents comfort and guidance."

His hands are in his hair again. "Fuck. I need some time. I'll work a way to get Taylor on with you or maybe a team of Taylor, Sheila and Aaron? If you have the support of your family will that work for you?"

I nod. "It will Prez. I've been comfortable with the ancestors and my family since I got back here. I just didn't know how to get rid of all the shit before. Now I have that outlet and my Brothers and family supporting me. I'm okay with how it's set up here and would rather the readers be together at the MC. They will need that family support and guidance while they're learning."

He gets it. "I'm going to relax now." He smiles. "This is a new position for me. I was nervous throwing you into it so fast, but you're more than ready and I need to remind myself to trust your counsel and abilities. I had similar issues when Dakota came on board. I will apply what I learned from that and get you where you belong in my circle. We'll start that tomorrow. Do I need anything else tonight?"

"Devan and Colt are on an Op pulling weapons and supplies from our threat that was due to hit in two days. I'm taking the kids to Security tomorrow to show them our world, but also to get them familiar with the tunnels. They will need that and it will keep Justice safe."

He's relieved. "Thanks Brother. I need to see our new Little Brother. I think Holly renamed him."

I laugh and follow him in. Brantley is talking to Nick while Holly has the boy and Mucimi on her lap. I sit watching them. Prez talks to Nick getting all that's wrong with the boy and I look in on Mucimi seeing he's in healing mode. The boy is happy to just be held.

"He likes that you're holding him Holly. I think it's new for him."

She nods with tears in her eyes. "I got that too. He's a very easy boy. I gave him oatmeal; does he need more tonight? He stopped before the bowl was empty."

"You may want to try some applesauce later. It's a picture I got earlier. Keeping him in cloth diapers is good too. He may have an allergy to the plastic."

She nods. "I cut up a t-shirt to make one for now. A Prospect went for some and some clothes for a couple of days."

"I'm taking the kids for the next two days. You're clear to get what you need for him, but he has to stay on the Compound. I'd take him with me, but we're traveling through the tunnels and I'm not sure that's the best place for him to be. It hurts him to breathe and the damp air could make him sick."

She waves it away. "I don't want to leave him and risk him being hurt by someone that forgets about his rib. The poor thing doesn't need any more pain right now and I can get what he needs without leaving the Compound."

"What's his name?"

She laughs. "Chance, because this is his second chance to get a good family that loves him and Mucimi likes it."

I smile. "Perfect."

Chapter Four

I meet Taylor at his safe in the garage. I had to move the time to one because HS was busy somewhere else. Taylor doesn't seem phased by it. "You ready?"

"Yeah. We're just getting close so I can pick up this Dean's thoughts. Since Dakota thinks you need to be here there's something else happening that I don't have right now. I have an HS and regular Security waiting for us at the gate."

"Roger."

We ride out of the gate and a couple of blocks south then east. I feel anger and pull over.

"Aaron, take your second around two blocks and come up to," I'm searching for the house in my head, "Green house in the middle of the block, it's a tenement, 432, a single family on one side of it. Someone's watching it from a van. Dark, at the corner, but they have audio from inside the apartment. Two in the van."

"Roger Guardian." He rides away.

I sit and think. "Jacob, are you on with me?"

"Roger Guardian. I didn't know this was a regular Op."

"It started out just a fact finding, but we hit a problem. If we take the men from the van can we pull their audio?" Now I wish I had worked the KC and knew more about Surveillance.

"Roger Guardian. I'll have it for you by the time you're in. The van is tagged on your board Sniper."

"I've seen Ops, but you'll have to guide me in protocol here. I'm on foot moving closer to the house." I get a roger. "Taylor, cover me, but not too close. Someone else is out here. Aaron, take the van. You're bringing the pussies to holding." I start walking toward the house, but I feel someone watching.

"Roger Guardian," Aaron then Taylor reply.

"Taylor, I'm being watched, but you're not seen." I get a click. I guess that means roger.

"Guardian, Shooter is being pulled to regular Ops for the take down."

I feel my watcher close and click instead of answering. At the start of the block I shut the street lights down and move along the fence line.

"Lights are down Guardian," Jacob says sounding frustrated. I click twice and move faster. "I'm taking that as you did it Guardian." I click again wishing he'd stop talking. I throw to Taylor and jump as a shot is fired.

"Jesus Guardian." I see him closing in on a small man and drop behind a fence moving toward a house for cover. When I see Taylor's gun at his head I move closer to the road.

"I need a pickup."

"Roger Sniper. C14 is on his way."

Dean is aware of something going on and I see the light on the first floor go on. Sitting against the house where it's darkest, I pull everything I can from her. She's afraid for her and her sister. They've moved twice trying to get away from the pussies in the van. She knows who they are and I run through her memories trying for everything on these fuckin' lunatics. They blew up a house trying to get her, but pain stops me from following that memory. I need more time, but she's picking up from Aaron.

"Aaron, block," I say softly.

"I'll tell him Guardian. Do you want him back on with you?" Jacob asks.

"No, get him to shield and move two blocks down. Someone's coming for the van." I get up and start moving away. I need more fuckin' time, but it isn't happening tonight. Now I see why two readers are important.

"Roger Guardian."

I start running and throw to Taylor to move closer to the van. He's at the bikes and pulls away as soon as my leg is over.

"Ops move Shooter one block east. A loaded pickup will be coming up from behind him. Get Clean-up ready and stay alert," Taylor says and I throw him the dead driver.

"Roger Sniper, he's moving now."

"Get him back on with us." Taylor doesn't seem to like the way this is running.

I hear a series of clicks, but I'm watching the vision of the truck. "Hit him Aaron!" I yell seeing the pussy raise his gun.

We clear the block and turn in time to see Aaron shoot. Shots are fired behind us. I throw the shooter to Taylor and he spins his bike around going right toward him. Fuck. I follow seeing the pussy look to the right. "On the right!" I shoot at the same time Taylor does and their hate just stops. "Wow, that's a fuckin' weird feeling." Taylor looks at me. "The hate just stopped."

Aaron is talking to Jacob as we slow and stop by the pussies. Taylor goes to the pussy on the right. "Thanks, Christian."

I nod to him, he has no clue how close that was. "Jacob find out how that truck wasn't tagged."

"Terry's got it Guardian. You're clear to come in to Security. Do you want anyone at holding?"

I find the pussies and see they aren't readers and they're scared shit. "No Jacob. Leave them until morning.

75

They aren't tracked and they're scared. Can you record from holding?"

"I'll have voice to text printed for you when you get in," he says like it's funny. They must do it a lot.

"Roger Jacob. I'm headed close to holding then home. I'll be in with the kids around nine." I look at Taylor. "I'm just going to get some information then I'm out. I'll have Aaron. We're done for tonight with Ops."

He looks at me. "Ops, is tracking clear?"

"Yeah Sniper. We have away vehicles, but they're not moving or anywhere close to holding."

"Roger." He pauses for a few seconds. "Jacob's on with you until you're home. If you see anything, throw it to Aaron and he'll talk to Jacob about what you need."

"Got it. Thanks Taylor." He hits my fist and starts his bike. When Aaron and Security ride up he turns toward the Compound throwing chin.

"Jacob, we need Security on this Dean. That's the green house first floor. She's small, dark hair, cut shoulder length, maybe nineteen or twenty. She doesn't drive and I don't have a clear last name."

"Roger Guardian. I'll get someone on her and look for a name."

We go to holding and I sit outside the building pulling what they have. They think of themselves as soldiers, but never expected to get caught. I'm amazed at the righteous indignation they feel. How do you think killing innocent people is justified in any religion? They honestly believe they're carrying out God's will by ridding the world of evil. I wonder if this is how the Nazis and KKK feel. I've never met anyone so sure in their hate. I need to get away from here. As we're riding back to the Compound I think about their hate. Do we justify killing with a warped sense of righteousness? At the gate, I throw Aaron chin. He's on

76

tonight so I guess he goes back to Security. I need to learn how all this works from the Ops lead side. With this first time down, I have some questions to ask. Hawk is waiting with Dakota on the porch.

"You did a good job Brother. There are ways that the Ops run so it is consistent from one shift to the next. Since you will be working with different team leads it will benefit you to learn their procedures. They in turn will learn your way of throwing pictures instead of commands. It will work for everyone."

I'm glad he's here. That was one of my questions. I can't see me in visions, but I can take them from other people. That's how I saw me die in Jeremy's visions. It just hits me. "I read Jeremy now more than ever before because that's stronger for me?"

"Yes, my wise Protector. There are other changes in your abilities that you will notice, but the Brothers will notice more. Keep in mind that all you can do is new and a surprise to them."

He's not saying something, but I know he won't go there so I nod. "Two things that happened tonight struck me. One was the hate that the pussies carried just stopped when they died." He nods, but doesn't say anything. "The other is that they feel justified in killing. Do we hate like that Dakota? Are we just like them in a blind ignorance to true right and wrong?"

He motions for me to sit and pulls a beer from behind him handing it to me with a smile. "No Christian, we are a peaceful, loving people." I think about some of the wars and smile. That's not so peaceful. "You are right, but let me ask you, have we ever brought our beliefs to anyone and forced them to live our way?"

I look at him like he's crazy. "We moved into a town and killed drug dealers, Outlaws and anyone that put up a fight. Then moved to more towns doing the same thing. We completely control this corner of our world."

He smiles like I'm a kid and he's the teacher. I relax realizing that is exactly the way it is. I'm still learning. "That is so and as a Protector you will grow and continue to learn every day. We have never taken over a town without being asked. We remove corruption from hurting the people of the towns and take the drugs and death out of communities replacing it with good to help all. People are happy to live in drug-free zones because it touched them even if they did not use. It is not just the users and dealers that were removed. It was a daily worry for parents, kids and the PD. Our towns live in peace— happy and with a drive to spread that good to more people in the community. What we do is defend our communities and family. We do not look for people to have a problem with, they come here. The woman, Dean, did nothing to warrant grown men planning her murder. She is a known reader and helped the police with an investigation. She did not look for people to bring harm to. She stopped innocents from dying. What we do is justified, but for actual good. She came here for that reason."

I think about that and drink my beer. We stop kids from being sold. Stop the senseless killing that the drugs bring with them, stop families from being devastated by the drugs and corruption like he said. Greed is not what motivates us. Keeping people safe and happy is all I see in Prez's head. He's always looking for ways to keep ahead of threats and promote good in the community. That looks a hell of a lot better than the complete hate I felt from the pussies. I nod having settled it in my head. "If we worked through hate like they do I guess that's all we'd feel too."

He slaps my back and stands. "It is Brother. We cannot allow hate to motivate us. We always work from the light." He laughs. "The ancestors would not allow us to use our abilities with hate in our hearts."

"Thanks Dakota." Using the ancestors is fairly new to me, but I think he's right. He's made comments about the wrath of the ancestors and I can only imagine what that would look like. It's not a pretty picture. They're based in light and push for happiness and peace within the tribe. That can't be bad.

✳ ✳ ✳

"Thanks for showing Brother, but I've got them."

He nods. "I need to get to Security anyway. I'll run back later with Delta." He lifts Mucimi up and carries him through the kitchen.

I look at Done. "We're going to Security through the tunnels. I need you to see how to disable the sensors. You may need to use them at some point."

He nods. "Brandon, come with me Little Brother. We need to follow Uncle Taylor." He's thinking Brandon should see this in case they need the tunnels without an adult present. It's a smart idea so I let it go.

Brandon follows Done and the rest of the kids stand in a line waiting for me. Alpha, Omega, Dexter and Hawk are standing ready. I tell them to follow and lead the kids to the basement door carrying Nash. It's slow going down the stairs, but we get there and make it to the tunnels with no problem. Taylor is talking to Ops and I'm reminded that I need to get an ear piece today. The kids get a kick out of the lights turning on as we walk. Taylor sends Delta ahead on a straight run so they can see how they work. Aquyà and Teller notice the cameras. Taylor explains how they run, then why they were put in.

The kids look at me wondering if it's true. It's the first time they realize the threats we're constantly under. This sparks a conversation about the closed-up doorways and the guns trained on them. While it's scary, I don't think it's a bad thing for them to know. I let them ask all the questions they have and answer everything or ask Taylor to explain what I don't know.

Mucimi is throwing pictures at him and the kids stop talking. He must be throwing so everyone sees.

I need to ask Dakota if they're strong enough to pick up what each one is thinking. Justice and Phoenix stop and look back at me. "Yes," Justice says. Okay then, maybe I'll ask how I can block them more effectively. Phoenix rolls his eyes and they start walking again. I laugh.

In Ops, Done, Cade and Darren help us get the kids up the stairs. They all watch as Cade turns the sensors back on. Honor wants to know why we keep the sensors on and doors locked if the doors in the tunnels are blocked. Darren answers and they all watch him, but don't ask any more questions. I see he's got a memory of people using the tunnels to hurt the Club and figure they see it too. We take them right up to the meeting room and I put the Ops boards up so they can see what Ops does.

They sit and watch while Done gets them drinks. All the dogs are sitting by the door as if they're guarding the kids. I hold my laugh when Prez comes in and does a double take. "Good job Brothers," he says to them before he turns and stands at the head of the table. The kids are watching the boards and don't look at him.

"They're looking at everything from tracking to the tagging," I tell him.

He nods and waits for them to take it all in. "I think we can take them through a mini training session so they see and understand what is happening here."

I think it's a great idea. I had planned on two days here; that will save me some time.

"We want to learn this. Now we can see what you do to keep us safe. This is big." Brandon looks at Prez signing as he talks then back at the boards.

Prez goes to the computer. "Billy come to the meeting room. I need you for an hour."

The kids look at him. "Billy will explain about the boards. When you're done, Taylor will take you through his class rooms, pop ups and the range so you can see how we train people. Aaron will explain about the PD and Bull will take you through Security so you can see the jobs they do and how that side works. Do you have any questions for me right now?" he signs as he's talking and I'm glad he remembered.

"What do you do?" Aquyà asks.

"A little bit of everything. My job is making sure everyone is safe, that doesn't mean just the Princes. We have towns full of people that we keep safe too. I run Ops when I'm needed and make decisions for the Club, our towns and the jobs in Security."

"Like the President," Brandon says.

He laughs. "That's why they call me Prez. I'm the President of the Princes of Prophecy. I have a whole Club of Brothers to help me keep people safe."

Mucimi is throwing Prez pictures fast and I turn around so he doesn't see me smiling. "Your dad runs IT for HS—that's the whole Club and all the businesses. Sheila is an HS Ops lead and works Security for the Women's Center. Taylor is an HS Ops lead and our main trainer. Dakota does Aerial Ops, training, and he's our Prophet. Jessie is a trainer, an HS Ops lead, fills our positions with membership and takes care of any problems at the PD. Jax is the second at the PD and runs Nomads. Eliza is an HS Ops lead and works Security at the Women's Center. Darren is the VP, he takes care of Transport, HS Ops, and a bunch of other things that I or anyone else needs help with," He answers as fast as Mucimi is throwing pictures.

"What does Uncle Christian do?" Teller asks.

"He's an HS Ops lead and runs the new department of readers called the Protectors. He'll still train you and teach at the school, but it won't be every day. We are already looking for someone to work at the school to help Holly."

Billy comes in and looks at the kids then smiles. "Bring the kids to work day?"

"Yeah. Can you get the Ops up on the hologram board then show them how it works?"

Billy looks shocked. "You want everything open?"

Prez nods and turns to the kids. "You have an hour here then Taylor will come get you." He looks at Billy. "Done will be outside. If you have bathroom or any other issues, you shut the boards down and get Done in here."

"Roger Prez."

He looks back at the kids. "You tell Billy if you need anything. The bathroom is right there." He points to the door. "Done will be right in the hall if you need him."

"How come he can't see what we do?" Brandon asks.

"He's HS Family and knows most of what you're going to see today, but only HS Ops leads or controls see everything in HS Ops. When we have a need for IT or other support in HS Ops we shut down what isn't meant to be seen by everyone. We don't talk about what we do in HS Ops. It's another way that we keep people safe. If everyone knew what we do and have here, we'd never be safe."

'Us too?' Stella asks.

Prez smiles at her. 'I want to tell you that you are the most important people we keep safe, but you'll see that everyone matters here. We spend most of our time keeping the towns safe. When we have wars, we are keeping our families safe. The family is the first thing the bad guys focus on so Family Security and HS will always be there to make sure you stay safe.'

Billy pops the hologram board up and moves to the table with a tablet.

"Me and Christian are in my meeting room if there's a problem," Prez says walking toward the door. "You have one hour Brother."

"Roger Prez." Billy starts dropping the boards so he can show them one at a time. Stella moves closer to him. I walk out smiling. This is going to be good. Her little brain will absorb everything she sees and spark her to perfect the things she can.

"Cover Taylor for his next class, thanks Brother." He stops at his meeting room, swipes his phone off and thumbs in. I hit the pad and follow. Taylor and Jessie are here watching the kids in the meeting room. "Sheila is covering your next class."

Taylor throws him chin. "I have the kids for an hour?"

"No half, they can go with Aaron for the other half. Done is ordering lunch for them then Bull can talk to them."

Taylor types on his phone then looks at me. "We need to talk about last night. I asked Prez to be here because we need a few things from him and he needs to know how this will work."

I'm feeling a little under the gun here, but nod.

He looks at Prez. "Christian hasn't trained at Ops lead. He needs that or he's going to start throwing with someone like Sheila and she'll lose her shit. I'm used to Christian and Jeremy throwing shit regularly, but people that didn't live with it aren't going to react well that first time."

I nod. "I talked to Dakota about that last night. He agrees it would be helpful for me to learn the procedures and to work with my people so they learn how I react."

Prez nods. "How has it been with Hyde?"

I smile thinking of him at the woman's car. "He said it's getting easier to take unspoken commands."

Taylor laughs. "Has he seen you fly through the air? I have to tell you Brother it shocked the shit out of me."

"It's not flying. We all flip through the air and learn about body and space through martial arts. I just slow it down and suspend in the air. I'm not flying."

Jessie looks at me. "The word offends you?"

I think about it before I answer. "Flying implies different laws of physics. I'm not navigating through different air streams using the wind or air density to stay up."

"What-the-fuck-ever Brother. If you're in the air without wings or strings you're fuckin' flying in my book too. That will take some getting used to." He looks at Prez and I roll my eyes.

"He jumped to avoid a bullet and stayed up until I was behind the pussy. It was fuckin' crazy to see." Taylor is shaking his head.

I watch Prez. "You avoided a bullet." He smiles. I nod and he looks back at Taylor. "What else?"

"Doesn't have an HS bike, an earpiece or the gear for what he'll be doing. He shut off street lights and they turned on while he was riding away. He threw commands and talked about what he sees over the helmet. I had a concern that he wouldn't be able to handle the earpiece, but he did fine with the helmet. If you know to expect him to throw commands he's easy, alert, can ride and is a fuckin' dead eye."

Prez takes a minute to answer. "Most of what you said he'll get from some training in procedures and he'll get it to his team. The lights concern you because it shows what he has?" Taylor nods. "We're not hiding it. Abilities will show as he needs them to. He didn't have Kevlar on so avoiding a bullet is a good fuckin' reason for you to see his ability to suspend. I think even with the gear he'd avoid getting shot. So, that leaves a bike, earpiece and gear?"

"Yeah." Taylor isn't happy.

"I think Prez is right. He was seen throwing a lightning bolt through a crowd. Hiding what they have at this point is stupid. We need them now more than ever. Showing ability may keep other people from coming at us."

I shake my head no. "For right now that statement isn't true. The woman that I went to get information from is running from people that are trying to kill her. She helped in a murder investigation so she was put out there. Because she's a reader she got the attention of a group that is trying to wipe readers from the planet. They have an organized network that reaches throughout the country. This isn't just hate. They think they are right to rid the evil they see. I was struck with the hate when we shot the two in the road. The hate just shut off. It was strange to feel so much, then like a light switch turning off, it was gone."

Prez stops pacing and looks at me. "The feeling touches you?"

"Not in the way you're thinking. The complete hatred was all encompassing. There was nothing good in what I could see before the hate was just gone. I've never met anyone with that kind of hatred. It was uncomfortable to see and feel, but I think I was looking for anything that made them human to me."

Jessie looks at me. "That's how Ops leads work. We process and assess very quickly and react based on that split-second assessment. I think the feelings you're getting will

85

govern the way you react. As a Protector, I would think this is exactly what we want." He looks at Taylor. "The abilities are what we're protecting here. Whether they're seen or not I still don't think is relevant. With what he's telling us, we have a bunch of yahoos out there hunting down readers. If one already showed here, I'm guessing we'll see more."

"Two showed. The baby Mucimi brought in and this woman," I tell him.

He's shocked. "Mucimi brought a baby here?"

Dakota didn't tell him? I look at Prez. "Jessie had a job last night." He looks at Jessie. "Brantley has him. That's the job you were on. The man used a knife on the boy. He has a broken rib and fuckin' bruises everywhere. Anywhere a diaper touched him is burned, the creases in that area are infected and actually bleeding."

"Jesus, a kid lived there? There wasn't any sign of a kid. Not even a bottle." He's searching his memory and I see the house again. "That's why you had me bring the box of papers?"

"Yeah, there was nothing in it, but we were looking for paper on the boy." He looks at Taylor. "Your worry over Christian is on a personal level. He did everything right last night and caught six from this group that we didn't know existed. He got information on the organization and we still have three in holding. Seeing him use the abilities should throw relief on you. You said yourself he's not only ready, but fuckin' good. With procedure training and gear he'll be better."

Taylor runs his hand through his hair. "Yeah. He's my little brother, knowing he's HS and seeing it, are two different things. It took me by surprise. The fuckin' flying was nothing like lifting me in the chair. That's going to take some getting used to."

I laugh and Prez smiles. "From what I'm getting you need to get through that quick. We have Protector Ops going on that we haven't heard about yet."

Uh Oh. "I was going to talk to you about that today."

He nods. "We will. Right now, I need to get you gear. While the kids are busy you're in with Jacob and Terry. They'll walk you through procedure and give you a book to study from. Ask questions before they become an issue whenever you can. The other side of that is with readers— you'll handle things different than regular Ops leads. You don't have a reader running that, so your non-ability people need to know how you're going to react to situations so they can be ready to cover you." He looks at Taylor then Jessie. "Christian needs to be at the Security meetings from now on. I want everyone going into Princes Security and all of HS to be trained with whatever you come up with on new procedures for Ops with readers. Jacob and Terry can help, but I think you already have some ideas. We need to incorporate everything they do and add so it's second nature. Dakota isn't saying much, but being prepared is a key phrase he's repeated. Co, Nunánuk and the ancestors feel the same."

"We need the Ops going on if we're getting reactions to base training off of," Jessie says looking from me to Prez.

I get a nod so I tell him, "Colt and Devan are taking weapons and supplies meant for these lunatics' planned attack on us tomorrow. They've already confiscated quite a bit and haven't been seen yet."

Prez's eyes snap to mine. "Yet?"

I smile. "Colt decides to make an exit driving a box truck they steal with all they collected from the pussies."

"Jesusfuckin'Christ. He's not legal." Jessie waves his hands in the air like that's a fuckin' point.

87

"We're fuckin' bikers killing anyone that walks into our little part of the world and decides to sell drugs, but a fifteen-year-old kid stealing and driving part of what was going to be used to take our fuckin' family is bad? He's fuckin' HS and you're pissed that he doesn't have a license?" I ask calmly hoping the calm I show isn't betraying what I feel. My body is tense and rigid with anger.

"If he gets picked up? With fuckin' guns?"

I smile at him. "They're both able to throw commands. They're both able to project and they're both trained to use whatever they have to accomplish what they're doing. They won't be stopped, detained or jailed because they'll make that happen with the abilities they have."

"You know this?" Jesus, he isn't letting this go.

"I'm a fuckin' reader. I'm the one training them. Yeah, I fuckin' know it!"

"Watch how you talk to me or my only problem isn't sending fuckin' kids on Ops with no fuckin' Security to assist."

I lift his chair and stand up. "Two things are happening here. One you have no fuckin' clue about abilities and what we can and are trained to do and two I'm not a fuckin' kid anymore so stop seeing me like that. Your inability to see me as the person calling the shots for THOSE THAT I TRAIN is your fuckin' problem not mine! Colt runs fuckin' Ops with VP. He's trained for more than you realize."

"Put my fuckin' chair down or I'm killing you in your fuckin' sleep!" he growls out.

I lower his chair excruciatingly slow. "I'm a reader with more ability than you know. I see it will never happen, but you need to see I won't ever allow it to. I'm not the fuck-up I used to be. Open your fuckin' eyes and see that."

As soon as the chair is down he flies across the table at me. I jump and move to the other side slow. He pulls his gun and I throw it. He jumps and I put a chair in front of him. "I see your next moves Jessie. If you want, I'll get you help." I throw to Taylor to try and catch me. He stands, but is saying no. "Help him catch me Taylor."

He's still shaking his head no, but I'm moving him toward me. "Cut the shit Christian! I'm not helping him." I move his arms up to grab me and I pull him holding him in the air then I look at Jessie and hold him the same way. I throw to Darren and pull him to us. "You need me to find someone else?"

Darren walks through the door and laughs. "You didn't drag me here for this, did you?" He looks at me.

"Yeah I did. If you can see me as an adult that has his shit together I think they should too." I'm still fuckin' pissed and spitting out my words.

"Put them down," Prez says and it's not a question. I lower them and expect them to come after me, but they sit. Taylor is even smiling. Prez paces. "You were allowed to show them because they needed to see it. If you ever pull shit on your Officers again you deal with me. I have no problem dropping your cut and I don't give a fuck whose family you're in. Are we clear on that?" I nod. "We need an amendment about using abilities against our own. Fuckin' hell." His hands are in his hair.

Fuck, this probably wasn't smart—he's threatening to take my cut. "No disrespect meant Jessie and Taylor. I was pissed. It won't happen again." I pick up Jessie's gun and send it over to him laying it on the table in front of him. When I put all the chairs back Taylor cracks up.

I look at him wondering what's funny. "No wonder your house is always clean."

I smile because that's how I got good at directing objects. "You see in our heads like Prez?" Jessie asks, but isn't looking at me.

I hesitate and look at Prez and get a nod. "Better. More like Dakota or Jeremy, but with control to pull what I want. I don't look unless I need it or I'd go crazy with what everyone is thinking. I've learned to control what comes in and what I listen to."

He looks at me. "You're right. I see you as that depressed unconnected boy you once were. That is my problem and I'll deal. You've done nothing to earn my doubt and I didn't realize I was throwing it at you. No disrespect Christian and I won't doubt you again. How do you use your abilities here? Dakota can't."

I look at Prez. "He isn't a Prophet, but a Protector. His abilities are meant for different purposes. According to Dakota, healers only use abilities in extreme situations where the outcome leads to lives saved. Protectors are a whole different ball game, they will use the abilities as needed. Apparently showing you those abilities was needed today."

Jessie nods and Taylor is still smiling. Darren opens the door. "Since I'm released and free to move wherever the fuck I want now, I got shit to do. Later."

Laughter bubbles in my chest and I cough covering my mouth. Taylor laughs. "I'm sold Prez. Colt isn't getting stopped and I can see how they'll make sure of it."

Jessie nods and I'm relieved. I move my hand and show my smile. Prez throws me chin. "Get with Jacob and Terry. I'll get your gear here today and let you know when I'm ready to meet. I have the kids covered until lunch. You'll need to take that over after they eat."

I nod knowing they go to Aaron and Bull. Throwing him chin I stand. "On it Prez." I'm out the door and walking by Done before I start laughing. I don't stop until I'm at the new console Ops put in for Jacob and Terry. I can't believe I just did all that to Jessie and I'm still breathing.

Jacob looks up at me. "You good Brother?"

I start laughing all over again. "I'm breathing and that's good." He nods giving me a strange look. "Inside joke sorry."

"We need to get on the Ops issues. Tell us the joke later," Terry says handing me a pad.

I look at it. He thinks I'm taking notes? I move the pad to the desk and pull up a new doc. The keys are moving and Jacob pushes his chair back as if I need the room. I smile and look at Terry. "Go."

Jacob laughs, but Terry starts talking as if nothing new is happening here. I get an hour and a half of procedure and think I got this. At least road names and shit. I need to remember Terry is Mimer. I got Jacob's Lightfoot. Dad has used it for years. The rest is crazy and we don't need all of it. Jacob said I can write in my book where the procedures would be different. It's a whole fuckin' book. I take it thinking Patches has more influence than he'll ever know. This is crazy, but I guess it got us this far.

Dropping the book on my desk I open tracking and check on the kids then the reader and Security. The sister left, but the reader hasn't even looked out the window. She probably knows he's out there.

I check on Aiyana and Kaya. They're watching the water with a group of tribesmen. Aiyana is pissed about something, but she's focused on the water right now so I pull away and get back to here. Devan and Mase are still hidden and collecting shit in the truck. I smile knowing they do a good job. I hope it's enough, but don't pull what they have for information. I'll be getting it soon enough.

Phoenix throws me lunch. I close everything down and head to the meeting room. Prez is here talking to them about tracking. He throws me chin and I sit and eat.

"Aiyana and Kaya are stopping the oil," Teller says.

I nod smiling. "Did you get that or is Mucimi throwing it?"

He smiles proud. "I got it. I can watch her now."

Since she's the most focused reader we have that's not surprising, but I'm reminded we need to jump. I'll do that before Mase and Devan get here. They need a way to get rid of the stress they'll have by getting what everyone is doing.

Prez is watching us. "Aiyana isn't at the reservation?" Fuck he's got that fierce look in his eyes and he's trying to block me.

"No Prez. Every time I try to get through what everyone is doing I'm sent out or you have something else pulling you away."

"Outside." He gets up and walks out, but I know that calm isn't really calm. He's pissed. I follow him out and he sends Done in. "They ordered you lunch." Done looks at me then throws Prez chin going into the room. Fuck, he feels bad for me. It's not like I had a fuckin' chance to say anything.

He walks a couple of steps away then turns back. "Aiyana is off of the reservation, but I'm not told. What the fuck are you thinking? She's one of the most powerful readers we have."

"We haven't met yet for me to give you all I've done. Every time you ask I get through half of it. If I told you no, when you sent me away, you'd be pissed. I'm trying to catch up with MC protocol, but you being pissed at me isn't reasonable. I've done everything you asked when you've asked. When we meet, I can tell you everything."

"Now! Tell me now because I've got two of ours in fuckin' God knows where and they're being hunted. Tell me what the fuck made you think it was okay to send them any-fuckin'-where."

Jesus. He's ready to hit me. "You telling me I head up Protectors made me think you meant it. I'm doing the job you gave me, but I'm fighting everyone's assumption that I'm still a fuck-up. If you'd take a fuckin' minute and listen I can explain."

Fuck! He's got his hand wrapped around my neck and I'm slammed against the wall before I can even register he moved. "I don't give a fuck whose family you are. I deserve more respect than I've seen out of you. If you can't get it together then drop the fuckin' cut now."

What? I've given him respect. I'm trying to think of when I've been disrespectful to him then just give up. "You know what, take it. You're not listening, but threatening me. Take the fuckin' cut and I'll go back to the school with the kids. Pick someone you trust to lead the Protectors because I'm not it and I'm fuckin' tired of having to prove myself. I'm done." He steps back shocked. As soon as his hand loosens I move breathing heavy. He knows what putting his hands on me does. Walking down the hall I shrug the cut off and send it back to him. "I'll be waiting in the locker room for the kids when they're done. Hawk will stay with them."

"Christian!" Shit is flying through his head.

I spin around pissed. "No Prez. It's not so easy walking away! It hasn't been a fuckin' week in the job I didn't ask for! I've done everything for both the MC and Princes since I was eleven fuckin' years old! I've given up everything I get for both Clubs and I *just* started getting that level of commitment back from you. No one gave me shit before I got here. Now I'm told to move to a job that no one wants me in. I jumped when you told me too. I even asked how fuckin' high, but it's not enough. Fuck that. I was happy where I was. I don't need the Brothers or Officers bringing me down again. Take your doubt, your threats and the fuckin' cut that I worked so hard to earn. I'm fuckin' out." When I turn Jessie and Taylor are standing here. I walk by and head to the locker room. Walking the tunnels will calm me. I throw to Brantley that I'm heading down and disable the sensors.

Jeremy is in my head, but I stop him. 'I need a fuckin' minute. Nothing you say will change this right now. Give me that. I promise I'll always help to keep Aubrey safe Brother. Just give me a fuckin' minute.' He quiets and I walk.

Since I was a kid I've gotten this shit and have always given them everything. It was to the point that I was so disconnected I only saw my family after they escaped the shit that I saw. People would get pissed when I didn't tell them shit so I stopped showing for most of that too. Jacob was the only one that saw what was happening and tried to help. He didn't get the process of the ancestors so what I gave him hurt him, but didn't change anything for me. I stopped that too. He was younger than me and didn't need my shit in his head. It would have been helpful if anyone took a fuckin' minute to explain the ancestors to me, maybe how to use meditation, or some training on the reading. I got help right at first, but nothing after. When I came to the Compound, I finally learned all that shit and have been training to grow my abilities. It hits me how fuckin' long that took and I'm pissed all over again. *I was a fuckin' kid.* I'll make sure the kids get it and never walk with that depression or feelings of not being good enough to get the extra training. I'll give it to them myself and fuck what the Brothers think. They haven't done a fuckin' thing, but train me for two years. While I'm grateful and appreciate the ability to see and use the ancestors, I worked for a fuck of a lot longer for them than they ever did for me.

A peace settles over me as I walk back from the waterfront. The kids will be ready to go soon. I push everything from my head and shield so nothing comes in or goes out. I need some space from the Club and all the shit they throw. I wait at the door and see Done disable the sensors. I brace myself because Prez, Darren, Jessie and Dakota are waiting with the kids.

When the door opens, Hawk moves to my side. I don't know whether to say Brothers or not so I throw chin and reach for Nash. "Thanks, we're good if you can help them down the stairs."

"We need some time with you Brother," Dakota says.

I smile. "I wasn't sure if I say, 'Brothers' so I just threw chin. I need to get them back. My job is them. I'll do that to the best of my ability. No one had a problem with me when I did that job."

Dakota is throwing and I shut him down. "I'm not doing this with them right here. They get more than you know. I'll explain their new abilities when you come for that at the school. I'll train them with the new they have so that keeps growing. Tomorrow I'll teach them to jump so they have that to fall back on when it all gets to be too much. I won't let them down and I'm good where I'm at with all this."

Dakota nods and puts his hand up like he's stopping them from saying anything. I don't even look at Prez, but take Honor's hand and start walking. On the way, we talk about how Security works. I'm relieved when Done answers them. I keep my head clear, but it's not easy.

In the school, I get them settled and we get through the rest of the afternoon. They have more to think about now and are ready to jump in, but I keep them on the clean water for the sundries building. Jess comes for the boys and Destiny, then Lily shows. I leave with Mucimi and Honor when Jax pulls in.

"Done, move Honor with me and Mucimi. We're headed to Brantley's."

He looks at me and nods. "Are you good Brother?"

I look at Mucimi then back at him. "Not sure if the Brother still works, but I'm good."

His hand wipes down his face. "I've been here a while Brother. If you need an ear I'm around."

I smile. He's a good Brother to have. "Thanks, Done. I don't see me, but I think this needs to be this way. If I need it, I'll call. I'm good though." His head nods, but he's seeing my cut in Prez's hand.

I walk out and put Honor on my shoulders. I'm relaxed and enjoy the quiet walk home thinking tomorrow I'll teach them about the ancestors. Holly is reading to Chance when we walk in. Mucimi runs to him and kisses his cheek. I put Honor down and she does the same thing making Holly laugh. She stops and looks at me. "You gave your cut back to Ben?"

Fuck. I pull a shield and see Mucimi throwing her pictures. "Stop Mucimi." He looks at me, but stops with the pictures. "This isn't something I'm talking about with him right here."

She looks disappointed. "Since he doesn't understand maybe you should. He worries over so much lately. He shouldn't have more to worry about especially from you. You're connected in a way I don't see. He needs something here Christian."

"Sonofabitch." I sit. "I did hand Prez my cut. My whole life in the MC I gave them all the visions I could. I didn't know about help from the ancestors for me. I thought they took Jeremy because he had the healer abilities. No one talked to me about the shit I saw. When people got pissed because of what I didn't tell them, I pulled away. It wasn't until I moved here that I got the help and training to release all that. Now with control and more abilities they put me in a new job, but don't trust me to do it. I can't make them see that I'm not the fuck-up I was and they can't get past it." I don't tell her Prez can't get past it.

"You're not, and from what I've been told have *never* been a fuck-up Christian. If they didn't give you the tools you needed maybe they didn't know that you needed them."

I shrug. This view of me not getting from them just hit me today, but it isn't wrong. "They worked with Tess and Jeremy then Aubrey. I wasn't ever anyone that was worth what they are. It was me talking to Brantley that drew Dakota to me. The Clubs didn't do anything, but take what I had seen. I'm not saying this pissed for what was. It just hit me today. I'm sick of jumping when they need me to. I'm good at the school. It makes me happy and I'm all for living with happy instead of the death and destruction I didn't know how to get rid of."

She nods, but she doesn't look happy about it. "If this makes you happy I'm all for it, but what happens to the new department?"

I pull my hair back. "I can't keep worrying about what I can't control. That's how I got so far away from my family and Brothers. I see their disappointment and how pissed they are and I just barely started. I'm not willing to go back Holly. They'll figure it out. They always do."

"I don't want you seeing that every day. I'm proud of you Christian. I don't understand why they'd be disappointed in you, but seeing that every day will affect you. I don't want to see the unhappy man I first met again. I like you happy. Since you're so good at your job, I'd be happy to see you happy every day teaching the kids." She smiles and I open to see she means it.

Looking at Mucimi I see he's watching, but not throwing anything at me. "Did you understand little man?"

"Yes."

97

"No questions? You can throw now."

He shakes his head no. He's trying to block me, but I see what he does. "I can only control me Mucimi. It's not cool to try controlling how people see me and I'm not wasting my time trying. I have this group of kids that needs me to teach them about right and wrong and how to control all the freaky shit."

He signs, 'Yes.'

Since I don't know what else to say to him I look at Holly. "Can Honor stay?"

She smiles. "Of course."

I kiss her cheek and walk out the back. Shit, Mucimi is trying to block me now. "Let's walk Brother." Hawk follows me down to the water and we walk a couple of miles down the coast. I pull all the shields and check on my people. Colt and Devan are here and laughing with Dakota and Jessie. Aiyana and Kaya are on their way back with Co, but they aren't happy. I keep their thoughts away and move to the reader. Thank fuck they still have Security on her. Her sister is back and they're talking about the woman's work. The reader is worried about money. I decide I can fix that and start planning. Without the Club, I can still get shit done, but it's going to be harder. I'll work around it. Uncle Danny says you can work around anything if you just think about it. I got this shit. "Let's go home Brother. I got shit to do."

I'm smiling until I see Jacob. He's pissed sitting on my porch. "Jeremy is pissed you're blocking him."

I shrug. "I'm not anymore. I told him I'd keep Aubrey safe, I meant it."

"This isn't about Aubrey's safety. We know you'd never let anything happen to her."

"Then why are you so upset?" I walk by him and open the door.

"What the fuck Christian? You quit the Club and it doesn't even matter to you?"

I control my temper and breathe. "For years, I've given everything in me to the Clubs. It wasn't until I was ready to end it that I talked to Brantley, and Dakota showed for me. Prez put me against a wall today and threatened to take my cut because I was too busy jumping through his hoops for him to listen to me. I'm done Jay. I'll do what I can, but I'm not fighting my own fuckin' Brothers for that same respect they refuse to show me."

He looks away. "You were going to kill yourself? Suicide is what you're saying?"

Fuck. "You have no clue what it's like not being able to touch anyone. People being pissed at me because I didn't tell them what I saw. How disappointed even Dad was in me. The visions don't fuckin' stop Jay. It's not like Jeremy. He gets hit with something and it's gone. I'm hit all the fuckin' time. It's never ending and I had no relief from it. No one stepped in. I wasn't important enough to step in for. Everyone saw me as a poor thing that was lost, but no one did a fuckin' thing to help until Dakota showed. I see what you all think of me all the time." I look away. "Even Prez thinks I'm still a fuck-up."

"You're wrong. I've never thought of you as a fuck-up. I tried to help Christian. You pushed me away too."

I look at him. "You did, you're the only one that did. I gave you what I saw and saw it hurting you. It gave me nothing, but more hurt Jay. I saw what that did to you down the road so I stopped."

He watches me and I see him getting it. He nods. "What can I do Christian? How do I help?"

I smile. "For me there isn't anything I can do to change what everyone thinks so I need to go around them and do what I can for the reader. She's worried about money. It's something I can fix. Help me do this and I'll let you

99

know what else I come up with when I get it straight in my head."

He nods, but he's worried about Prez. I put my hand up. "I got this. I don't want you doing anything that gets you thrown out too."

He gives me a look. "You didn't get thrown out you walked away."

"Be careful here Jacob. I see your disappointment. With training and control I'm more confident and I'm not stepping back into that fuck-up role I was in. The Brothers say one thing, but think another. I see all of it. Thank fuck for my family. You are the only ones that see who I really am. Prez doesn't believe in me. I've been giving them visions for fuckin' ever and he doesn't believe in me or my abilities. There's nothing for me to fight for if no one has faith in me as a person. Their thinking comes in loud and clear Jay. Me walking away is just semantics."

He rolls that over and looks at me. "Jeremy is saying it's true."

I nod. "I caught that. I got some shit to take care of. I'll talk to you tomorrow." I walk by him and up the stairs to the loft. I need a shower and some time to think my plan through.

"Christian." I turn and look down at him. "I believe in you, so do Jeremy and Aubrey."

I smile at him. "I know you do Jay. The whole family does now."

He nods and walks out thinking they let me down too. I can't fix it now so it will have to wait.

Once I'm showered I sit at the computer and get an SUV ordered then have it set to be delivered to Jax at the garage tomorrow. It will need tracking. I call to Jeremy. 'I need tracking for the new reader on an SUV. It's at the garage. Can you do that for me?'

'Yeah. We need to talk.'

'I know Je. I'll get there and talk to you soon. Tomorrow I teach the kids about the ancestors. Maybe this weekend I can come up.'

'Take Security.'

This would require me asking for it. I'm not asking anyone in the Club for anything. I get some cash and throw a coat on to cover my gun. "I'll be back Brother," I tell Hawk as I walk out.

At the gate, I have to wait for the guard to open it. "We don't have Security here for you Brother."

"I'm not a Brother anymore so I don't need it." I move him to the gate control and have him open it. Once I ride through I wonder if I need to move. I put it aside and ride to the reader's house. Keeping Security looking the other way, I shut the street lights and open the sister's car door. I stuff the cash above the visor and lock then close it. When I'm riding away I release the Security Brother and let the lights go. Instead of going home I ride to the fish place we like off the highway. I keep people away from me and sit. A waiter comes and takes my order and I open to the people. I feel anger and look to my right. A woman is pissed at her husband. I block them and keep moving. No one is thinking about me, but a woman at the bar. I ignore her and watch my waiter walk toward me smiling. "I told them it was for you so they took it from a pain in the ass at the bar. They're making him another order."

I see the guy, in his head, giving the bartender shit and smile. "Karma. Thanks buddy." He laughs walking away. They do know me here. He even brought the malt vinegar.

I eat until I feel anger directed at me. I look toward the door where Taylor is walking toward me. "What the fuck are you thinking Christian?"

101

I look at him wondering where this is coming from. "I was thinking I was hungry."

He sits. "Don't give me that shit. Why are you without Security? The guard says he opened the gate, but didn't want to. You did that, didn't you?"

I nod. "I did. I'm not a Brother and don't need Security. Do you have Security with you?"

He leans back in his chair and looks at me. "You take Security with you whenever you leave the Compound. As for you not being a Brother that's a whole different conversation."

"No."

He looks like I slapped him. "What do you mean no?"

"I'm not taking Security with me. You don't have Security with you, Jessie doesn't take Security neither does Aaron. Because I don't know your words doesn't mean I'm not qualified to keep myself safe. If I need help I'll ask you or Jacob or even Brantley for it."

"Jesus you're a fuckin' pain in the ass today. Security is always with you Christian, you've always had it."

I throw money and stand. "I hit higher than all of you on the leaderboard. While everyone was living a real life all I did was train. I did that alone because that's how it was for me. Now I'm here and you see my ability, but you're still treating me like I can't get from one place to another without Security—who don't come close to me as soldiers. Tell me Taylor, if someone told you you're not allowed to move around without Security what would you do?"

His first reaction is he'd laugh at them. I don't give him time to answer. "You laughing at them is my point. I'm ahead of you too Taylor. Why the fuck do I need someone not trained as well as me on my right? You don't." I throw my leg over and wait for him to get on his bike then ride away.

He's thinking about me without Security when he turns toward the Compound. I keep going and ride along the water until I hit our last town. I don't want to push my luck too far so I turn around and head back. I see bikes with the lowlights and like the look of it. I need to talk to Jax about getting some on my bike. I always thought about them for HS, but they're cool and I want them. I laugh. Losing my cut has been an uplifting and an enlightening experience. A car moves over the line and I push it back and fly by. At the gate the guard has it opening as I'm turning reminding me that I'm still tracked. I throw him respect and ride home.

Chapter Five

I run down the stairs and open the door. I swear if he wasn't my brother I'd hit him. "Activity Center breakfast." He walks away.

"Jay! What's going on?" It's like six in the fuckin' morning.

I'm not getting anything. I look for Taylor and Terry, but get nothing. What the fuck? He doesn't stop. I run up the stairs and get dressed. I hear the chopper, but I'm getting nothing from anyone. You'd think the quiet would be welcome, but I see my brothers and Officers gathered. This doesn't bode well for me. I call to the ancestors for strength.

Co answers making me laugh. 'We are with you Guardian of the unrest. Go with peace in your heart and a smile on your face son. The ancestors like when you smile.'

I'm still smiling when I walk into the Activity Center. I stop short at the door and Hawk stops with me. All the Officers are here right in front of me. I look around and see the kids and my family to the side. The MC Officers are here standing with my dad. All the Protectors are here from the MC and reservation. Co and Nunánuk stand with them.

I'm pulling from all of them, but the Shaman are closed to me. I look at Jeremy. "You can stop I'm through." He nods smiling. I look at Prez. "I know Dakota and Aiyana are shielding for you, but I can read you if I'm looking at you." He nods and Co laughs.

I want to walk back out, but Jeremy yells, 'Stay!' in my head. I look at him, but he doesn't give me anymore.

Pres steps forward. I watch him then look at Prez. He wants me to listen. I turn back to Pres. "You can come in Christian. This is us fixing a wrong."

I roll my eyes and step forward five paces. Since there's nothing, but open space this seems a little ridiculous. I'm struck again with them all there and me on the other side with no one behind me. This feels like shit. I turn, but Jeremy moves behind me holding Aubrey's hand. Mase, Jacob and Terry move. Then the Protectors do with Co and Nunánuk. When the kids and Done move with Holly behind me, my throat closes up. I swallow throwing them chin and thanking them in my head.

"Something we should have seen and done as well. Our intention is fixing what we fucked up. We've spent all night getting everyone's take on how you've been let down by us and are a little tired. You should know we all have your back. Thank you, Jeremy, for showing him."

I look back and Jeremy throws me chin. They've been here all night?

"I transported the old ladies this morning," Dakota says. I nod and look at Prez.

My dad steps forward. "I find I'm in this position a lot. I should have shown you the peace you get with the ancestors. I didn't know how to get through, but never thought to show that to you. It was such a simple solution. Nunánuk told me I should, but Jeremy was trying to get to Mitch and I forgot all about it. It's not an excuse—but an apology. Dakota and Prez were pissed at me again, but I didn't understand how close we came to losing you. It was when Taylor was going through his shit and I didn't think about the meditation until Danny told me. I tried to fix it, but I see now how that was too little too late. Christian, you are worth and loved as much as your brothers and sister. There is so much more that I should have done for you and didn't. I'm so sorry I wasn't there for you Son."

I hug him and hold on. When his hands touch my back I feel all he does. "I don't know how you're still sane Dad. We weren't easy that's for sure." He laughs and kisses my head. "You are a great Dad." My mom comes over with tears on her face asking if she can hug me. I pull her to us. When I can't take anymore I let go and step back. Jeremy puts his hand on my back pulling the energy away. "Thanks, Je."

Pres comes closer. "We got help for Tess, Jeremy and Aubrey. Now the kids help each other. We had no idea how to help you and dropped that. That's on us Christian. Little Ben was always watching and asking for ways to get help for you, but not understanding how your visions worked—we didn't know what to do. As you know, doing nothing is what actually happened. As adults, we should have been there for you. We always thank Jeremy and Tess for saving so many of us, but it's you that brings the majority of visions to us or sends them to Jeremy to give us. You alone have the ability to see so much more than we'll ever understand. It wasn't until Jacob and Taylor talked that we got a piece of what you go through daily. You see as we're speaking, you get all that's unsaid, you can't just shut it off like Tess and Jeremy." I nod feeling relieved that he gets it. "Even walking in, with everyone shielding, you still get it. I tried to give you peace here and still couldn't." He shakes his head, but he's smiling.

"I saw everyone gathered, but didn't get anything until I walked in. That's why I told Prez so he knew I could still read him."

He nods. "If all these people can't shield from you, I don't know how the hell you get through a day."

I smile. "Dakota and Prez taught me how to control and shield. It's good now Pres. It was a nightmare some days, but that's over for me. I don't think Rich and Tess understood how much I was getting. The blocks they taught me only worked for a short time. Janelle's door was the same. I've trained and now take in what I want. I still get the visions the same, but I manage them instead of them taking me over."

He nods. I see he wants to hug me, but keeps himself back. I step forward and hug him. "I'm sorry for letting you go Christian. We've learned so much. It won't happen again."

I step back shaken. "Thanks Pres." Jeremy's hand is on me and I feel the energy move out fast.

Prez steps forward. "It's been an eye-opening night for us. Especially me. Aiyana was going no matter what I said." I nod. "You made sure Co knew and she had Security?" I nod again. "I was wrong. I told you to go with Jacob and Terry, I went to meet Chance, both times telling you that I'd listen better, but I didn't. The biggest thing that hit me, Christian, is you leaving without Security. Taylor came back and I got what you told him. You know I looked up where you're at?" I shake my head no feeling like shit again. He had to check? "That's when it hit me. I was looking at your scores and realized you knew exactly what I was thinking because I was doing just what you said I was. I doubted you. I swear I've never let you go Christian, but I didn't show you respect either. You saying it should have been enough for me. I am sorry Brother. You had every right to give me back what I was throwing at you." He looks to the side, but I'm looking at what he's thinking. "Mucimi threw everything you told Holly to the kids. My boys made sure I heard it all. I told everyone word for word. Jacob told us about how we had no faith in you when your whole life with us has been living in hell with visions on our behalf. Taylor told us how you not needing Security is another way that we don't show you the respect you earned. Elizabeth, Aiyana and Jeremy told me I am an ass for not showing you my faith in your ability." Everyone mumbles. "Nunánuk and Co told me the ancestors are not happy with me and I'm fuckin' afraid to jump." I smile. He's telling me the truth. "Christian we have asked you to give us everything without giving anything in return. Starting now I want to fix that. Will you give us a second chance here Brother?"

I take a breath and look at everyone. They all believe I should. They believe in me and I'm feeling it from them. I swallow hard. "Yeah Prez," I say looking at him. I'm shocked at the look of relief on his face.

"You had every fuckin' reason to say no there, Brother. I'm so fuckin' glad it was a yes." He whispers and I throw him chin. "We have your cut, but we're asking for a little more from you Christian. Will you serve with your Officers as the new Protector Officer?"

No fuckin' way? "Seriously?" He nods. "I'm not asking for that Prez. I just didn't think anyone saw me. The real me."

He nods. "For years, you've protected us. You know the history. I gave you a job and you stepped into it without complaint. You ran Ops saving Taylor and Aaron. Even showed what real Brotherhood is, getting money and an easier path to a woman that you've never met." Oh shit. I look, but he's not pissed. "You earned this and we'd be honored if you'd wear the Officers cut and take back the job I pushed you away from yesterday."

I look for my dad. He's smiling and gives me a nod. "I'd be honored Prez."

Again, he looks relieved. I look at Dakota. "We will not take you for granted again Christian, but Prez feels relief knowing he was mistaken in his doubt of your ability."

I nod looking at Prez and feel Jeremy's hand on my back. Pres and Jessie are standing behind me. Jessie steps closer. "I was a dick. I got it right away, but wanted you to know I meant what I said. I won't doubt you again Christian." I throw him chin.

"Can I touch you to get your cut on?" Pres asks. I can't believe Pres is putting an Officers cut on me. I shield against his thoughts.

Jeremy answers, "Yeah I got him."

Prez smiles. "I was surprised when they asked to do this too. You understand Brotherhood, so telling you to extend it is pointless, it's second nature to you. What this cut means, for all of us, is that we owe you respect for all you have done, do now and will do, to honor that Brotherhood and our Club. This cut is our way of showing the 'all in' that we dropped when you needed us. Your commitment and worth to us will never be questioned Christian. Your cut is an HS Officer's, but also has the new Protectors colors. It is us that are honored Brother."

I'm fuckin' stunned and it's not just because Pres and Jessie are touching me. Jeremy is taking it away.

"Brothers, I don't think he can handle any more hands on him so give a cheer to welcome our newest Officer Christian Blackhawk head of the Protectors for the Princes of Prophecy."

The room explodes. Between the war cries and the whistling I don't pick up on the Officers moving closer. I'm watching my dad, smiling at his war cry. "Brother, we have your new gear and a house on the Compound that Uncle Danny will make yours." My eyes snap to Prez.

"Thank you for this. It is more than I ever thought I'd be here."

His smile falters. "We'll fix that Brother."

"Can we eat now?" Uncle Danny says and we all laugh.

"Prospects!"

People start moving away and I move my foot so Hawk will get up. "I'm good Brother." He stands by my side, but keeps his body against my leg.

Mucimi is throwing me pictures and I look for him. "Here," Jeremy says and I look his way.

I pick him up and give him a hug. "Thank you, little man. I know what you've done here."

"Love you."

I laugh. "I love you too Mucimi."

"How come you can hug the kid, but we can't touch you?" Tiny yells from behind me and I jump a fuckin' foot.

"You fuckin' touch him and I'm shooting you that's why! Get away from him!" Jessie yells and the Officers are laughing again. I don't get it, so I take Mucimi to the table of Blackhawks.

We jump back with the kids and Dakota is smiling. "You are a good teacher my wise Protector. The ancestors are happy with the children visiting."

I throw him chin, then look at the kids. We have Mucimi, Teller, Phoenix, Justice and Aquyà. "We will jump after every training class. That's two days and we jump again. When you're ready you can jump yourselves, but it's dangerous to do that alone until you can control your spirit guide. You can jump with me, Dakota or Jeremy. Even Prez and my dad jump. If you need to jump, you find one of us and we'll help you. Me and Dakota don't need to be with you to jump with you. We can do that from anywhere. Do you have any questions?"

"What happens if we jump alone?" Aquyà asks.

I look at Dakota, he shows a girl on a bed with elders around her and a woman crying. "The place you can get hurt is not of this world Little Brothers. It is difficult to get back here if you are hurt there. What Christian says is right. You do not jump alone until he tells you that you are ready. It will not be long for that to happen. You already show control with your spirit guides. Christian believes you are responsible enough to learn this now. It is important that you show him you are worthy of that responsibility by respecting his knowledge of your abilities. He has much more to teach you and will need that respect and show of responsibility to move with you to the next level of training. If you show him that you are not responsible, he will not be confident to move you any further than where you are right now. Do you need me to explain that?"

They all shake their heads no. "We'll show him and our fathers we're learning right Daddy," Justice tells him.

I smile because they're all thinking the same thing. Mucimi climbs on my lap.

"He asks if we have to talk Mohegan always," Teller says.

I look at Dakota. "It is good to speak the language of the ancestors when we are in their world. I was taught by Co and our old Shaman and have never spoken any other way there. It makes the ancestors happy to hear their language spoken. You saw the beautiful colors they showed for you." They all nod smiling. They're so fuckin' cute. "That was because they were happy to see children and hear their language."

Aquyà moves to Dakota's lap. "Are there other kids that visit the ancestors?"

"Sadly, there are not many. Today, people do not believe in the ancestors as they once did. Children are not taught to visit until they are much older and the ancestors do not hold the same meaning for them as they do for us. Some parents do not have the time to teach the children safely, so they do not learn at all."

Justice sits up. "That's why we waited for Christian? 'Cause he can teach us to be safe?"

I wait for him to answer. If Co said Mucimi is ready to learn why didn't he teach his boys?

111

"Part of the reason was Christian, the other is you are so close to the younger boys that we did not want an accident, like with the girl I showed you, happening before everyone was ready. Mucimi can read all of you. He could have been hurt without the knowledge Christian is able to get through to him. It was important for us to keep that hidden so he would not come to harm."

I nod. He's right and I'm glad they had the conversation taking him into account. I give them a minute and see they're all good with this. "Two days we jump again. If you need to jump before that, you do what?"

"Find you!" they yell making me laugh. Mucimi giggles and it makes me laugh more.

"That's right Little Brothers. I need to get to work. Is there anything I need to know before I leave?"

Mucimi is throwing me pictures, but it's Phoenix that speaks. "The people at the pipeline get hurt. An elder did a bad thing and the people get hurt."

Teller touches my arm. "The reader lady is going to get hurt today too. The bad men think she hurt their Brothers." Jesus.

I look at Dakota. "We must get to work to stop that from happening. Thank you, boys. You have grown in your abilities in a very short amount of time."

Mucimi stands up and hugs me. "Love you little man. I got the reader." He nods with tears in his eyes. We take the boys back to the classroom and wave to Holly.

Done slaps my back as I'm walking out. I throw him chin. He's happy to see the cut. Outside Dakota stops and calls Prez. While he's telling him what the kids said, I find my reader. She's home and appears safe. I look for her Security. Fuck! I pull my helmet on. "Guardian on. Lightfoot, are you with me?"

"Roger Guardian. Mimer's pulling, but something's happening at the reader's."

"I'm on my way now. Get someone for the Security Brother, he's out." I fly out the school gate with Dakota following. "Get Eagle Eye on with us."

"Roger Guardian." I hear the clicks. "Eagle Eye you've been switched to Protectors control. Guardian, Security is down. We have a truck being tagged now. It's on your boards."

I look, but decide I don't need it right now and make the corner just as two bikes are coming our way from the other side.

"Lightfoot, have them take the truck. It's the fuckin' lunatics again."

"They're regular Security Guardian. HS is leaving now."

Fuck! "Eagle Eye get to the reader, she's in a closet hiding, a pussy is at her door. I got the truck Lightfoot." I pass Security and they turn around following me. Before the pussy gets out of the driver's side I see his vision aiming at me. I shoot and stop at the door pointing my gun at the passenger. "Hands up or I'm shooting you where you sit. Lightfoot get Security on him."

"Roger Guardian, they have him." One guard opens his door while the other has a gun trained on him.

"Get Clean-up here and we still have Security down."

"Roger Guardian."

The reader screams and I run. "Move my bike!" I yell, making the corner.

I'm up the stairs and in the apartment as Dakota is holstering his gun. "Clear Lightfoot. We need Clean-up in the apartment."

"Roger Eagle Eye."

I take my helmet off and flip on my mic walking in further. I find her in a tiny closet off the hall. "I'm opening the door."

"I have a gun!" she yells back.

"No, you don't. Dean, we took care of the lunatic in your house. You know Princes have readers and we protect them. I'm here with Dakota and we're both readers. I'm the man your sister brought the boy to. We aren't a threat to you. I'm opening the door." I turn the knob slow. She's scared out of her mind so I keep moving slow. "It's okay. We're here now. You're safe."

She's crying and watching me. "I can't read you."

I nod. "That should be a comfort. You can read the men that want to hurt you." I want to help her up, but I don't want to touch her. "I can't touch you Dean."

She's not moving. "I couldn't read the guy in the room."

I look back at Dakota. I didn't see one already in here. He walks down the hall and throws me a picture of the guy on the floor with blood around his head. 'An aluminum bat Brother.'

"Guardian, Sniper and Ghost are coming in."

"Roger Lightfoot." I look at the girl. She's still terrified to move. "My Brothers are here. They aren't going to hurt you either. I can have Ops call your sister and let her know you'll be at Security. You'll be safe there."

She relaxes. "Princes Security?"

"Yes." Taylor and Jessie walk in and she tries to burrow her body deeper into the closet. I look at Taylor. 'Help her out. We can't touch her.'

114

He throws me chin and moves closer bending down. "I'm Taylor, Christian's brother. We're going to take you to Security. You'll be safe there and Prez will get you somewhere these pussies can't reach you. Yeah?" He puts his hand out.

She looks at me with tears running and a red nose that I think is adorable. "I can read him."

I'm fuckin' glad she can't read me. Dakota laughs. "Then you see he isn't going to hurt you. We're all about the helping Dean." I smile hoping it puts her at ease.

"Yeah," she sobs out and takes his hand.

He pulls her up and tries to hold her to his chest, but she moves away fast crying with her head down. He looks at me wanting to be anywhere, but here. "Let's go before more pussies show."

I smile. "Lightfoot, is there an SUV close?"

"Roger Guardian. Right outside. I have your bike heading to Security."

Taylor is relieved. The girl laughs. "I'm not usually such a wimp. Sorry mister." She steps further away and grabs a towel from the closet wiping her face. When she's done, she looks at me. "I'm ready Christian."

Jessie cracks up and Dakota is smiling. I shake my head and give a nod toward the door. "Jessie, Dakota and Taylor will follow us to Security."

She follows Jessie and Dakota out. "Can you tell them not to call Serenity? She can't leave work again or she'll get fired."

I nod. "Did you hear that Lightfoot?"

"Roger Guardian. Prez is on his way with the MC Officers. He wants her in the meeting room."

"Roger Lightfoot."

115

She gets to the SUV and Taylor opens the door. "You're married to Beth?"

Oh fuck. 'No! Don't say anymore!' She looks around him to me and nods.

"Yeah," Taylor says looking back at me.

"One of them is Justice's Dad?" She points to Jessie and Dakota.

"Jesus. Yeah. Can you get in so we can get to Security?"

Taylor's hands hit his knees. Fuck. I look back at Dakota. 'Delta isn't here. He connected that Beth is one they go for.'

Dakota moves fast. "Breathe Brother." His hand is on Taylor's head.

"Yeah. I got this." He doesn't stand up, but his head isn't too bad.

Jessie watches wondering what the fuck is going on. I throw it to him and his eyes narrow on the girl.

"Guardian, you need to move out. A car and van are heading your way."

"Roger Lightfoot. Taylor get in the SUV. We need to move now."

He stands and looks at me with hard, determined eyes. "I'm not letting these fuckers out Brother." He's breathing heavy, but not shaking, I nod.

Jessie pulls him to his bike and I run around the truck. "Keep him safe Jessie."

They're gone before I'm in the truck. Jacob is telling them where the car is. "Eagle Eye we're headed to Security."

"Roger Guardian. I am right behind you."

116

I pull out and floor it. "Lightfoot get the school covered and let Prez know the old ladies have a threat. We need the Clinic and Center covered by noon."

"Roger Guardian."

We get to the corner and I stop a car coming our way. Dean braces her legs and holds her mouth, but doesn't make a sound. "We're good Dean. I won't let anything happen to you."

She cries. Shit. "It's been so damn long since I've been safe."

I see that's all that's in her head and relax. We make the next corner and I see a vision of a van coming at us. "Eagle Eye the van will try for us from the front."

"Roger Guardian." He flies around us and I slow down.

"Eagle Eye and Guardian, LP1 is coming up on your left."

"Roger whoever you are."

"VP, Guardian. We switched you to Ops when Prez got in."

"Roger VP." I stand on the brake pedal lifting my ass off the seat. "Jesus he's fuckin' nuts." The SUV's rear end swerves and I let the brake up then hit it again. Uncle Danny jumps a car and hits the driver of the van then Dakota hits the tires slowing it down. I stop the cars coming our way and veer around the van speeding past them.

"You're clear Guardian. LP1 and Eagle Eye, Prez said to get him here and stop fuckin' around. He'll keep the traffic away from them himself."

"Roger VP," I say smiling. What part was fuckin' around?

"Roger VP. I will keep his tires on the ground," Dakota says and I laugh. He can't, but I'm not telling Uncle Danny that.

"No more stunts VP," Uncle Danny says then laughs jumping the front of a car. The car stops short and I move it back so I can pass. "Not my fault there, VP."

"Guardian to Eagle Eye, control the fuckin' lights."

"You can do that?" Uncle Danny asks as we fly through the light and into the Security lot.

"I can LP1, but did not think to do it," Dakota says and I laugh.

"Thanks Brothers I'm clear," I say shaking my head and walking around the SUV fast. Opening her door, I see she's smiling. She puts her hand on my arm and I move away fast. "We need to get you inside." I cover her, but don't let my body touch hers. "Touch affects me."

She nods. "Me too. I was checking."

I laugh and follow her up the stairs. We hear shooting and she moves faster. I put my thumb on the keypad and open the door keeping her in front of me. "Take the hall on the left." Hawk is waiting. I pet his head walking by him. "Good job Brother. Meeting room." He goes down the hall and waits at the door. I hand him a bone and thumb us in. "Hawk stay. I'll have a Prospect get you coffee and something to eat. I need to get to Ops, but I'll be back." I flip the last board on and pull the control that's Velcro'd to the bottom of it. "TV if you want it."

She nods. "Thanks. I should have brought my laptop."

I stop at the door. "I'll send one in and have yours picked up. If it's not tracked, I'll send it in." She pales and I wait until she's settled. "We won't let them get at you Dean. Mucimi would never forgive me." I get a nod and step out then lean back in. "The room is on our surveillance."

She nods looking at the ceiling.

I stop a Prospect and tell him to get her a laptop with limited access and full surveillance. In Ops, I see the whole fuckin' town with cars and shit happening everywhere. Prez is on Air Ops and Pres is running Clean-up while Darren and Uncle Steve are running HS teams. Jacob is still running and I move closer to him.

He looks from his boards to me and holds his mic. "I'm running Security and Team Three."

I nod and step back so I can see everything. They all have Security Teams and the MC is mixed in with Princes. It's different than the MC Ops I've seen. Eliza is at the Daycare and Sheila is running a team. I've never seen either running and like that they're out there. I'm impressed with the professionalism everyone has. I see where Jacob is different with me and wonder if the changes will confuse the other leads. Taylor and Dakota are running together and they're brutal. They don't ask anything, but keep moving— leaving behind bodies for Clean-up. I look in on Taylor and see he's all about keeping them away from his Precious. Since his head is clear, I slide out and look for Jessie getting basically the same thing so I stop looking. Watching the process of control and lead, I see how well Terry does compared to the other controls. I'd put him right with Jason who's running with VP.

Uncle Steve looks at me. "Over here." I step closer to his console and he motions me in. "Watch. Control is key. Runs Jason, Terry, Billy if you don't have Brantley." I nod, I guess that's the order. He throws me chin and says something to his team that I translate to mean they have cars coming at them from the front within three blocks. He said like four words. He smiles, so I must have got it right.

As he's watching his boards I notice he's scanning everyone else's. He throws commands to the other leads, but keeps his Team running the entire time. I look in and see he's red. Everything flies by, but he throws it out just as fast as it hits him. When he likes something, he holds it, talks, then lets it go. It's interesting to see the process.

As the Teams start rolling in, the leads hand headsets in. Prez hands his to Josiah and looks at me. "A little different than the other side."

I nod. "It gives me a better understanding of how it all works together. It's different than I remember."

He cocks his head to the side. I wait for him to consider how to answer. His brain works like no one else I know. Maybe VP, but not quite the same. "I think we've come a long way from where we were, but it's because we have new technology that wasn't available back then. With that, we have people working to perfect where we are lacking. Being open to new ideas helps with what we've learned works and doesn't. Sharing between the two Clubs helps too. We're all on the same page so them jumping in here isn't a problem. The same works for us working with them."

I nod. "I see how that benefits both. Keeping the process the same is important. Will changing how readers run affect the leads from one shift to another? All these words spoken is distracting when you're listening, running through a vision and need to guide or get more information."

Pres hands his headset to Billy and walks closer. Prez shakes his head no. "The training classes will address some of that, but the leads and controls we have understand and adjust for the people. If Taylor is running, Jason knows what he'll look for. He doesn't need the same guidance that Cade does. The same for Dakota, but with Dakota he doesn't need anything, but a direction. All the leads know how all the Team Leads will react and what they need. The same will happen for you and your teams."

I nod; this is good. I don't know if I could change the picture throwing. Pres steps up. "This will be where all Protectors are running Ops from. At the MC, we have more readers, but you're their lead. VP and Devan will run lead until our leads understand how this all will work. We need the book and the training you, Taylor and Jessie come up with, but for now we're covered. Once this is up and running, Ops will switch to here."

I nod, having no clue that this is where they'd run from too. "I had no idea it would be this big."

He smiles throwing relief. "We didn't either. We came up with it around three this morning. Danny pointed out that without one central location, the disconnect and you bouncing back and forth was bound to cause problems. It's a way to keep everything under one control and not drop shit." I can see that and nod. "Can you show me how you fly?"

What? He's serious. I look at Prez. He nods smiling. Shit. I look around wondering if he means right here. "Only HS in here it's okay," Prez says.

I step away and flip. "I don't fly, but suspend the time I'm up." I move slowly to the other side of the room. When I step down everyone is watching. Jesus.

"Are you only able to move from up in the air? Like when you flip?" Pres asks.

I move me toward him about a foot off the ground and stop where I started. "No. Suspending isn't just in the air. It isn't always me I move either." I move him back about five feet.

"Fuck! Don't do that without warning people. Fuckin' Danny would shoot you."

I look at Prez, he shakes his head no so I keep my mouth shut. He looks at Pres. "He hung Taylor and Jessie in the meeting room and moved Darren in from his office while they were hanging."

"Mase said he lit their sticks on fire while they were up in the air in KC," Jacob says watching us.

Pres looks at me. "Is that how Colt and Devan got the truck and the weapons?"

I look around. Prez nods to me. "Yes. They can move objects right now."

I pull the shield and see he has a million fuckin' questions, but thankfully doesn't ask them. I throw to him, 'I'm not comfortable talking about it in here.'

He's surprised then smiles. "I didn't think you were. Can you read me?"

"Yes, when I need to."

"He is able to read everyone. If he has a need for information he can get it from any person without speaking with them," Dakota says walking in. It sounds like a warning. I throw him chin. "Do you want the choppers on Surveillance Prez?"

"Yeah keep them up until we have at least two hours of clear then go back to high alert procedures until tomorrow."

I'm not sure if I should say it. Dakota knows, but he isn't going to give him anything. I watch him then decide I need to tell them. "This was it Prez. The lunatics had nothing to fight with. Now their army here is minimal. They have four that got out. It's enough to warn and get more people here, but they have nothing to come at us with right now."

Both Pres and Prez consider that. "The religious fanatics?" Prez asks.

"The MC will be hit again next week. The readers are safe until the witch hunters are organized again. That's about two to three weeks out."

They look at each other and think similarly. "Elizabeth, Devan and Tess are your best readers. They'll be helpful if you ask them the right questions. Blaze and Blake are focused, but can't hurt anyone so they don't talk much.

122

Readers aren't just going to tell you information. Unless they have the vision to go with it they'll be nervous about causing future problems. For that you need Tess, Jeremy and Aubrey. The readers will take information to Ally and if I'm not available she'll get it to Jeremy and/or Aubrey. Based on what they say, it will filter down to you. If I'm available or they call directly to me, I'll get it to Prez."

They nod, but Pres still has questions. I let him ask. "When won't you be available?"

"If I'm on Ops." He's going to follow it up so I just answer. "Visions happen all the time for me. On Ops, I see the next thing playing out, have a lead in my ear, the team to direct, and read from all of them—the pussies to my team. I can't take calls from away at those times so I block—keeping only what I'm doing in my head."

"Jesus. How the fuck do you run Ops with all that shit?"

I look behind me and shrug at Jessie. "I don't know how to do it any other way. Visions and hearing people doesn't stop. I just learned how to shut out what I can. Now the visions are like a ghost movie. I can see through them to keep moving, but with Ops running I need to shut out the other readers."

A hand on my shoulder has me moving. My head swings around. "Sorry Pres." I don't move back, but he isn't offended.

"No, I forgot. I had no idea it was so much. Do the other readers have to deal like that?"

Prez shakes his head no. "Dakota, Aiyana, Elizabeth, Tess, Jeremy and Aubrey all have controllable visions. Mucimi, Phoenix and Aquyà are getting better at that control. None of them are like Christian. He sees more, but now he sees a bigger picture and uses what everyone else has to manage what he's seeing. Dakota is probably the closest with the vision, but Aiyana isn't far off."

I shake my head no. "All the boys, Destiny and Honor will have that level soon. Aiyana is equal to Dakota in vision, but she's focused on the reservation and the impact to her people. The Protectors hit all ranges, but they are meant for different purposes. Reading and visions are two different things. Some with visions don't read well some that read don't have vision. The kids have both. They already see and work through visions. Mucimi did it with Chance. I would put him above someone like Mase or Colt because he has the ability to control people from long distances whereas Mase and Colt can control objects and read, but don't have vision and the ability to control people unless they're close. Devan would be up on that list too, but he's just recognizing his ability."

They both are surprised, but Jessie more so. "Jesusfuckin'Christ! It's a whole fuckin' army of freaky shit. How the fuck are we supposed to keep up with who can do what?"

"It's on the hologram board. Terry and Jacob put bios up so Prez could keep up. We'll keep them updated so anything new is tracked."

Prez nods. "I haven't seen the board, but this is already different than what Dakota has charted."

"It is, but they're training different now. All the readers at the MC can suspend objects. Jeremy, Aubrey and Mase can suspend themselves. Soon Jeremy and Aubrey will suspend larger objects, I mean bigger like vehicles. Jeremy learns like the kids. If someone has it and opens to him he will learn it."

Pres laughs. "Meaning you."

I smile and nod.

"Let's see the board, then we need to deal with your reader. Do you need time to get information from her?" Prez asks.

"I got it while I was waiting in here. Do you want it now?"

Uncle Steve laughs. "Fuckin' good."

"My meeting room after we see the board." Prez starts walking and I follow the parade out. "Brantley, I need the hologram boards running."

"On it Prez," he says handing his headset to Jason.

I smile and wait for him to run by. He's always thinking he needs to hurry. My shoulder is touched and I move the hand looking back. "I think they're just cluing into what you live with. I'm glad it's easier now."

"Thanks Uncle Danny."

"You didn't mention how touch affects you."

I stop and turn. "Prez and my family know. I don't think the entire Ops room needs that."

"I think they do. We know with Dakota because we saw. If they don't know they can't help."

How can they help? "I move people away just like I moved your hand. I can control that touch. If someone touches me it's because I allowed it."

I feel him and throw a shield. He smiles. "They're waiting for you."

I turn and smile. Yes, they are.

* * *

Finally, we get to the reader. Knowing all the information and answering their questions took a fuckin' hour. They're too much. Ability kids have been here their whole lives and they're just getting what that means. They really didn't know about how the visions and reading work together. Thank God Dakota was able to answer most of their questions. I know he could feel me getting pissed and stepped in.

"Where is the reader with ability?" Pres asks.

I look at Dakota, but he isn't going to answer. "She's equal to someone like Blaze or Sandy. Very singularly focused and it's mostly by touch. She can read if you're close and she can see you, but she doesn't get through shields. If another reader is close and lets her in, she can follow their focus, but can't get there alone."

Prez is watching me and I see his questions, but I wait for him to voice them. "How did she know to come here?"

I smile and look at Brantley. "Mucimi threw her pictures. At first it was small things, warnings. She got out of a house that was set to blow because of his picture. She lost her parents in it though. He sent pictures of a newspaper and she got our location and the Princes' name."

"Tell me you can stop him from bringing more people here," Pres says.

"Why?"

He looks at Prez then Uncle Steve. "With him. Why? Kid's savin' lives like us. Just farther away. Must be people we need."

"He brought a baby here! The kid made it across a road, was picked up and dropped on the road at our exit, then picked up again!" Jessie yells and Dakota smiles.

"Nothing was going to hurt the boy. Mucimi was able to control how it all happened. The boy made it here and he got the help he needed with a family that included Mucimi for the support he will require. He will become who he was meant to be here. That would not have happened where he was. He was destined to die at the hands of the man you killed." Dakota is smiling, but he is not happy.

126

I look at Prez, we need to finish this shit already. "The reader. She helped with an investigation in Cleveland and it was put on the news as a sensational piece. The PD there was open to her help and had another case for her to work on. They would have offered her a job, but she left after the house blew. She was almost caught by one of the lunatics, but fought him and got away. She read enough with his touch to understand who was after her. We have more than she does on the organization, but she can be helpful in what we do here. She understands readers, but not anything else. She doesn't know about the different ranges or how to control. She has no hate in her except for the men trying to kill her. That comes in loud and clear because of her parents. It's still fresh and you can feel her pain. Her sister has been working to keep her hidden. She takes whatever job she can find for basics. They don't have much, but they don't seem to require much to be happy."

Prez nods. "You want to offer her a job?"

I nod. "I do, but first they need a place to live that's safe. The house they were in will never be that. Here she can work with Jacob. He has reader ability, but can be taught to block. He doesn't get what she can. With some training, she'll be able to pull from what she sees, it won't be just touch."

He looks at Dakota. "Do you feel she'll work here?"

He smiles. "I cannot answer what you want to ask, but I can answer that. Dean feels like an addition that will surprise the Princes, but only in good ways. I do not agree that working in Ops is the best place for her, but training and the kids will be important to her."

"Training and the kids will be important to her," Prez repeats—hearing the same thing I did. "You think she should be at the school?" He waves his hand like it wipes the question away. "I think we should see if she'd like working at the school."

Dakota smiles and I laugh. "I think my wise Warrior Leader makes very good decisions."

Pres laughs. "That's a hell of a way to get information." Everyone laughs.

Prez looks at me. "Does that work for you?" I nod. "Keeping her in one of the houses behind the school work for everyone?"

"Works for me. She'd be under surveillance and close in case of shit hitting." Jessie says. Taylor agrees.

I watch Darren. "You're all okay with someone we don't know with our kids?"

"Mucimi brought her here, Christian read her, Dakota approves. I don't know how much more we can get on her, but she isn't in the gate, she'll be on the feeds at the school which is monitored by Security here and in person right there. I could call Jeremy, but what's the point?" Prez says.

Darren looks at me. Before he can ask I answer. "I am bound to the kids as a Protector. That's like the bind that holds Prez, Dakota and Jeremy. I can't put them in danger, it's just the opposite, I would give my life for them."

He looks at Prez. "I'm in."

"Let's go hear her story and offer her a job," Prez says and we stand. The MC Officers stand and Prez looks at them then Brantley. "Get the meeting room up for them."

Uncle Danny laughs and sits down. "We need dinner too."

"I could eat," Jessie says and Prez pulls him out.

"Brantley, order fuckin' dinner before they both start."

I hear them laugh before the door closes. "On it Prez."

Everyone walks in smiling and Jessie laughs. She's asleep on the table with music playing on the TV. She sits up fast and I see she is scared.

"Dean, this is Prez, VP, and you know Jessie, Dakota and Taylor." She moves to the other side of the table and looks at each one. "You can read a little by looking at people, but Prez and Dakota read and we all grew up learning how to shield. They won't be so easy to get anything from."

She looks at me. "Are you in charge of readers?"

I look at Prez. "He is. He is the most powerful reader we have, but he has other abilities that you will learn through training. Please sit. These are the Officers of the Princes of Prophecy. The MC Officers are watching from the next meeting room. We have all worked to get rid of the threat to you. No one here will hurt you. We need information on how you came to be here." I tell them to sit, she's nervous. Everyone, but Prez sits then Dean does.

She tells them the same thing I did, then about the pictures. She has no idea how she got them, but she got her sister to drive them here then explains about her sister keeping her hidden. When she tells about the men chasing her you can feel the hate roll off her.

I send tissues to her and Darren laughs. Fuck. I put my head down and wait. Jesus I'm fuckin' stupid at times. No one is saying anything so I look up at Prez. He's not pissed and I look around, everyone is smiling. I just shrug.

"Can I learn to do that?" she asks and I clench my jaw.

"The ability to suspend is not available to everyone Dean. Christian is not just a reader," Dakota tells her.

"So that's a no?"

Jessie laughs. "Back to the point?" He looks at Prez.

129

"We can put you in a house outside the Compound that has surveillance surrounding it. It's directly behind the school. We also have a job at the school working with kids with reader and other abilities."

She laughs. "There are kids with reader abilities here?"

Prez looks at Dakota then Dean. "All of our kids."

She looks at me. "Is he for real?" I clench my jaw and nod. Swinging her head back to Prez she says, "I want to work. I can work if I'm safe. Will you keep me safe?"

Prez smiles. "It's our specialty Dean. We need you in the new house today. The threat is gone for the moment, but I'm told that's only until they regroup. I will have your belongings moved and someone with you tomorrow to start your new job. Your sister will need to come here and I'll have Security bring you to the new house." I throw him the SUV. "The car will need to be replaced. The new one will have tracking so we can keep your sister safe. We also have jammers and personal tracking cuffs that will help. We have businesses that your sister can work at that are under surveillance. If you are a target and the car is tracked, she will never be safe outside the surveillance area. We've learned that family is the first thing everyone tries for."

Her hand goes to her mouth. "I'll do anything. She's all I have left." She grabs a tissue and I look at Prez.

"We will do everything we can to keep you both safe, but you work with and not against us. Meaning you need to understand that this is what we do. We are not putting you in a prison here. If you follow some basic safety protocol you can move freely through our towns."

She nods looking surprised. "I'll do anything I need to and I know my sister will too. I can go out?"

Prez looks at me, so I answer. "If you can do it safely yes. No one lives in a prison here. Until the threat is

130

gone you will need Security. That doesn't mean you have to stay inside, unless something like today happens. When the threat is gone and Security levels are lowered, you keep tracking on, but won't have the shadow."

She looks from me to Prez. "Thank you."

"Do you have any questions that I need to answer right now?" Prez asks and I know she gets that he has other things to do by his voice.

"I have a bunch, but I'm not sure you personally have to answer them. Can I ask someone else?"

Dakota laughs and stands up. Prez looks at Darren. "VP can answer if Christian doesn't know."

I turn my head, Darren is calling him a bastard and Dean laughs. Prez smiles. "If you need anything let Holly or Done at the school know." He walks out with her nod. Taylor, Jessie and Dakota follow.

She looks at Darren. "Will we make enough to afford a house and new car?"

"Princes own the house and the price is reasonable. We live green and have very few bills. The car was donated specifically for you and your sister. The car she has will be stripped of tracking and taken to Mass to be sold. There are no strings here. You work and pay your bills, and you should be able to live comfortably on what you both make. What does your sister do or did she do before she started shielding you?"

She takes it all in pretty quick. She's smart and processes fast. "She was a DM for a promotional company before I helped the police. Now she does whatever she can that won't check and alert the freakazoids that are chasing me."

I cover my mouth. "So, management. We have two manufacturing companies that are in need of a go between

131

from plant managers to the old lady that oversees them. Is that the type of management she does?"

"I don't really know. She worked with three locations, but I don't know what she did exactly." She's getting excited. She thinks this is exactly the kind of work her sister does.

I throw it to Darren. "We can ask when she gets here or I'll stop by later. What time will she be here?"

"She gets out at six."

He nods and does a time check then pulls his phone. "Call the sister and get Sheila to escort her to Security." He pauses. "Get the SUV from the garage over here and have them wait for the car. They'll need a wand. Once tracking is off send it to Racks. I'll check with Prez, but it may go to my mom."

She sits up straighter. "Your mom needs a car?" I smile at the hopefulness in her voice.

He swipes off and looks at her. "She runs the Women's Shelters at the MC. The women coming out sometimes do that with nothing. It could be donated if we get the okay from the person that donated yours."

She nods very happy with that idea. I throw to him to give it to Kate. He nods without looking my way. "Do you have anything else?"

"No one asked me about the freakazoids."

I smile at the word again. "We have information on them. Christian said it's more than you have."

She looks at me. "I've found the name and different cities they run out of."

"Yeah. We have that and some of their top people. Since you've been here we've taken two teams plus what happened today."

132

She pales. "The van at the corner?"

"Yeah and a truck." I throw her the picture of the men. "They had feeds and audio from your house."

I see her tears and hope she doesn't cry again. "You'll be safe here. Right along, we've had Security with you. Today, they took him down and got close. We still got you out and safe."

She nods. "Why are you helping me?" She looks at Darren.

He shrugs. "You live in our town. We take care of our own. For us to do that you just need to live here."

I see Sheila and smile. "Sheila left the car. When she explained, your sister didn't want to drive it. They'll be here in a couple of minutes."

Darren stands. "Are we good?"

"Yes, thank you and all the people that helped me today." She stands, but doesn't go close to him. "I don't hug people, but I would if I could."

His head jerks back. "Touch affects her," I tell him.

He smiles. "I'm good with the thanks and I'm sure my Brothers will understand. We have others like you."

She smiles like she won the lottery and it changes her whole face making her look younger and happier than I've seen from her.

We watch Darren walk out then I look at her. "If you need anything there will be a number left for you to call. If you see something that I need to know, call to me and I'll get to you or send help. You can reach out to me right?"

'Christian!' she yells in my head.

I smile. "Just like that."

She has more questions so I answer them before she has to ask. "There are many readers here, at the MC and the reservation. They are all tracked and when needed have Security as a shadow. You will be treated the same. I train the kids every couple of days at the school and we'll work on your control when I'm there. The readers have training here to grow their abilities. We do not hide that they read anymore. We do keep other abilities close. Sending you tissues was a mistake that I won't let slip again. It's not something non-readers see. The Officers, MC Officers and the Shaman from Rhode Island and Connecticut all know and will help when we need them. There is nothing expected, but for you to do your job and work with us to keep you safe. No one will ask for anything else. You making it easy for Security is a bigger help than you can imagine. Here there are six towns that you can move through freely. Someone will explain the borders when you're brought home. If you have to go outside our towns, you make arrangements with Security so you're covered. Did I get everything?" She nods smiling. "Good. Sheila and your sister are here."

"You can see that or you read it?" She's smart.

"Both." I hold the door open for her and Hawk. We meet the SUV out front.

"Thanks Sheila."

She throws me chin looking at Dean. "The reader?"

"Dean. Yes. She'll be working at the school and I think VP has a job for her sister."

She nods. "Serenity."

I look at Serenity. "Good to see you again."

"Thanks for keeping her safe. We saw shooting, but I didn't know Dean was in the middle of it." She's watching Dean and I see her throwing the information she has up until now. Serenity is like Jacob for Dean.

When she's done, Dean looks at me. "Thanks for waiting."

I nod and look at Sheila. "Do you know who is taking them to the house?"

"I am. Apparently, my job changed to fuckin' Welcome Wagon today."

I laugh. "They need the borders, number for Security, cuffs, and what they need to stay safe." She rolls her eyes at me. I look at Serenity. "VP will be by later." She nods, but she's nervous about Sheila being pissed. "She's harmless unless you threaten people or her kids. She was brought up MC so you're just seeing Badass."

She smiles. "I can deal with Badass."

Sheila laughs. "That's good because with a reader I have a feeling you'll see a lot of them. Just so you know, they're all fuckin' crazy."

I laugh throwing Dean chin. "I'll see you at the school tomorrow morning unless I'm called away."

"Thank you Christian."

I go back into Prez's meeting room where some are still eating. I look around and Jessie slides a tray over. "Thanks Brother."

"I had to guard the fuckin' thing. Uncle Danny was eyeing it."

I make a sandwich with the chicken salad and slide the rest over to him. "I'm good. I have food at home ready to cook, but I'm starving."

"What are you cooking?" he asks and everyone laughs.

Pres is shaking his head. "I don't know how you're not six hundred pounds."

Uncle Danny looks at him. "I had breakfast and this. Did you eat lunch?"

Pres nods smiling. "I had a sandwich while Ops was running."

"Bastard." Everyone's laughing again. Uncle Danny ignores them and looks at me. "We need to decide what you want on the house."

I nod finishing the roll. "Can it be like the patio?"

He bobs his head swallowing a forkful of potato salad. "I can do that. Let me finish and we'll go look at it."

I stand. "I need to check on the readers. The kids are worried about the pipeline. They said people are going to get hurt tonight."

Prez stands up. "Is Aiyana going back?"

I shake my head no. "Not tonight. Co won't go unless I get them Security from here." I throw chin and look at Uncle Danny. "I'll be about a half hour." He nods and I walk out.

When we hit the hall Prez asks, "Not tonight?"

"She's pushing to get back, but I think we can help from here."

He doesn't want her leaving after the run on us today. "These pussies are going to be pissed."

"Yeah, I've been sending it to her hoping to keep her there."

In my office, I pull up tracking. Prez sits on the other side of my desk and it feels weird. Everyone is in their spots. "I need to get Jeremy and maybe Aubrey to jump."

"From here?"

I nod and look for Aiyana and tell her what I'm doing. She's getting Kaya to help. Jeremy and Aubrey are

136

ready and have Elizabeth with them. "They're ready. Do you want to jump? I think we could use all the help we can get."

He nods, but hasn't done this before. 'Just like they were here.' He closes his eyes and I jump with him. We fly through, then over the lake. Jeremy, Aubrey, Kaya, Elizabeth and Aiyana are waiting on the rock. We land beside them.

"Prez," Aubrey and Jeremy say.

"I did not expect to see you our great Warrior Leader," Aiyana says bowing her head to him. I smile, but I'm thinking that's a bit much.

Elizabeth laughs. "Happy you're here Little Ben."

"We need to calm what's happening at the pipeline. The boys were concerned with people getting hurt tonight. We can stand with them together. Try to touch the PD and Security men so the tribesmen stay safe. Use what they're thinking. If someone isn't sure about being there give them a push to walk away. If you can control, do it. If you can shield do that. Whatever it takes to get them through another day. Any questions?"

"How do we get there?" Prez asks.

"Me and Aiyana can get us there. Stay close. We need to touch to do this. Jeremy and Aubrey, we need you to keep the energy from being too much. The ancestors will help where they can. Anything else?"

No one has anything. "Kaya get between Jeremy and Aubrey. Keep hold of us." They nod and I'm glad to see Prez and Elizabeth open to us and trusting the ancestors. I look at Aiyana. "Close your eyes and jump to the ancestors. The tribe is ready for us and are sending strength and safe passage through their ancestors."

"I am ready my Warrior Protector."

Co flies in. "I will help guide you warriors and princesses. The ancestors are pleased with the peace you are offering."

I nod. "Thank you my Shaman. We are ready."

"Trust in the ancestors and your Protector," Co says then closes his eyes.

We jump and we're flying through blackness. "Feel the pull of the ancestors. They guide us to their people of another tribe. They're chanting for our safe passage." We hear then repeat their chant. As they get louder we're hit with freezing water. "Hold together!" Fuck it's cold. "Prez, Jeremy shield!"

When the water stops, I open my eyes. "Fuck. My eyes are burning."

"Mace is being thrown too," Kaya says.

"Throw a shield over the tribe." I start chanting for wind to push the water back. Jeremy and Aiyana help. Tribesmen move closer to us and chant. "Feel them, the ancestors and tribe are helping, use it and push all together. Now!"

"It's working Christian look!" Aubrey is pointing to the wind blowing the water and Mace back at the fuckin' idiots shooting it.

"Connect with them. Slide in. If they show you a way, push them to leave. If not move on to the next. Work quickly and touch as many as you can. Keep the shield on the tribe and go."

"We have help Christian. They have two that can help if we open to them."

I look at Aiyana. "Take one. Jeremy take the other I need to get to the leaders here. Go! We don't have much time."

138

Prez is focused on the men with the fire hoses. I look for who's calling the shots. These men are not happy. I hit as many as I can, telling them these are American citizens just like them protecting their land, water and ancestors. The water is stopping. "Keep going Prez. It's working."

Men are walking away. I find the leader and see I'm not getting anywhere with him. He thinks the tribes have no rights here. I hold him in place while they work through people.

"Shut the water off!" A man yells and all the water stops. Since it was hitting them I had no problem with it on, but this shows we're getting in.

"Don't stop. We need them to leave for the night," I tell them.

"Christian they're turning in their badges!" Kaya yells.

I smile. "Keep moving from one to the next." I start chanting for strength from all the ancestors and hear Co chanting with me.

When a truck pulls away the tribe lets out a war cry. I chant louder and hear the tribesmen close to us start to chant. The pussies are putting the hoses away and another war cry goes up.

"My Protector it is time to return," Co says stopping me.

I don't get it. "It's working Co."

"You have done what you traveled for. Our people from another tribe are safe tonight because of your belief in our ancestors' power. You must return before your strength will not allow it." He's not asking.

I release the leader leaving him dazed. "As you will my wise Shaman." I look across to Aiyana. She's ready.

"Jeremy and Aubrey throw to us before we leave." I feel a blast of energy and nod to Aiyana. "Now." We jump.

I start chanting and feel the pull. Co is beside us. "I would not have believed it could be done my wise Protector. The ancestors are pleased and grateful for your help."

I move away and open my wings to feel the healing of the ancestors. "It is us that are grateful to the ancestors for allowing and helping us keep the tribesmen safe. Thank you Co for guiding us with your wisdom." He nods and is gone. Jeremy moves to me. "Thanks, Je. It didn't feel like so much until we hit the rock. Aiyana, are you okay?"

She's away from Elizabeth and Aubrey is touching her back. "I will be Christian. Thank you for doing this."

"I was not alone Aiyana. It took all of us and Co to make the journey and back. With some practice, it will be easier, but we did it and tonight the tribesmen can sleep in peace."

She smiles. "We did."

Prez smiles. "It is not often I see you smile Aiyana. I'm glad I got to see it here."

Mucimi is throwing pictures. "We need to get back."

"You need to stay," Jeremy says.

"Dakota is waiting."

He nods and takes Aubrey with him. Elizabeth watches me, but I look at Aiyana. "Co is waiting for you." She nods and flies with Kaya thanking us for our help.

"Thank you for believing in me Christian. If I can help again I am happy to."

I look at her. She's come a long way from the quiet little girl she was. "You have earned your place here Elizabeth. I am sure there will be more you can help with. I am honored to have you beside us."

140

She throws chin and is off with a smile. "Little Ben."

"Bye Brother. Thanks for your help." He looks at me. "Mucimi and Phoenix are happy."

I smile. "Yeah."

"Have you done this before?"

I look over the lake happy to see the colors so bright. "I traveled here, but never farther."

He laughs and I follow him smiling. When I open my eyes, he's smiling at me sitting in front of my desk. "Fuckin' Blackhawks. Thank you for keeping our people from the other tribe and Aiyana safe." I nod. "You're a good leader for your Protectors, Christian. I'm proud of the man you've become. That was by far, the craziest, scariest and most amazing thing I've ever done. Thank you for taking me."

I love hearing that, but he worked right with me. "I couldn't have done it alone Prez. If any one of you didn't show, we wouldn't have made it. I had no idea what we could do, but everyone's belief in the ancestors and their abilities worked in our favor."

He stands shaking his head. "Are you okay?"

I nod. "A little shaken, but okay."

"Tomorrow you'll have to explain what the fight is about. I think I'm missing some information here."

I just nod. I'm trying to collect myself right now. I'll get him information later.

When he opens the door Dakota walks in. "It has been an eventful day for our new Protector Officer."

I laugh. It fuckin' has.

"He's earned the respect of the ancestors across the country. You were right our Prophet. He is the leader you've

141

shown us he could be. I need to change, I didn't think I'd get back and be wet. At least my eyes aren't still burning," Prez says walking through the door.

Dakota closes it. "Can I help get you to where you can walk my Warrior Protector?"

I smile. "Please and thank you for helping. I know they didn't see, but you helped shield when we needed it. Next time I'll be better prepared." He puts his hand on my head and I want to lay across the desk. "I'm fuckin' tired."

"Perhaps you will sleep tonight."

"I fuckin' hope so, or I hope it's a quiet night," I tell him already feeling lighter. "Thanks Dakota. Prez said Phoenix was happy. I didn't get anything from him."

"He was throwing with Mucimi. You were weak from the energy it took for you to jump and supply abilities so far away. Co and Nunánuk are impressed with your strength and knowledge of abilities in your Protectors. It was an impressive Op to watch."

I give him a look. "You were right there. How come Prez and Jeremy didn't see you?"

"Co helped me get there. I was only able to help with the shield and the energy before you jumped back. My abilities are not what yours are Christian. I did not want to be seen as the weak link, Brother."

I crack up. "Next time show yourself. Just knowing you're there will keep them motivated. It won't always work like tonight."

I see he already knows. "I will Christian. How do you feel?"

I shake my head moving his hand. "You know I'm good. Just because you're not answering Prez doesn't mean you don't know."

He laughs. "Very wise Brother."

I stand up trying out how that feels. I'm good so I throw him chin. "Uncle Danny is waiting for me." I'm drained, but I need to get this day done.

* * *

The house is directly behind Brantley's. Jacob is right next door behind Taylor's and I wonder if this will be Terry's new street soon. The only other Brothers on it are Aaron and Alex at the end and Hyde at the corner. Since there are two houses before mine I'm guessing Terry and Mase will fill those.

Uncle Danny walks me through telling me what he can do. Since I like the loft he can make it here on the same side. Hawk checks out the house while Uncle Danny talks. When he's done, he looks at me. "Yeah," I tell him.

He laughs. "You have to be the easiest Brother yet."

"No one ever says no to you. I'm not looking to be the first and I don't need to be convinced."

"Good enough. We'll be done next week."

"Thanks Uncle Danny. What do I need to do to own the house and get this done?"

He looks surprised. "It's yours. The MC and Princes are paying for the renovation to show their support for you Christian. Didn't LB tell you?"

"No. Just that I had a house and you'd do the work."

He smiles. "I guess that's all you need to know. We'll be done next week. You want Hawk's door on the bedroom and the back or just the back?"

"Just the back. Thanks. I need to see Mucimi before he goes to sleep. I don't mean to cut you short here."

143

He starts walking to the door. "We're done. I'll draw it up and start over the weekend."

"Does Kate ever complain about you being down here so much?"

"She never has. It gives her a chance to miss me." He smiles back at me.

I laugh walking up the deck and watch him go around the house to the road. He gives Pres time with her. That's a good thing to do.

I knock and open the slider and Mucimi comes running. He's throwing pictures of a group from the tribe chanting and onlookers smiling. "They're safe little man. So is Aiyana. Thanks for the heads up." I pick him up and carry him back to the living room.

Holly is holding Chance on her lap. When we walk in she's smiling. "He's been a happy boy all afternoon. I've seen more pictures of smiling people today. I'm glad you were one of them. Good day?"

I laugh. Mucimi gets down and pets Hawk. "I got my cut back, became an Officer, ran Ops, jumped with the kids, and just left my new house. It was fuckin' awesome."

She laughs. "I heard I have a new assistant. She's not a teacher?"

I shake my head no. "She's a reader that lost her parents because of the lunatics trying to get rid of readers." She's shocked. "She helped the police on a case and was picked up on the nuts' radar. Lost her parents in an explosion, but got out of the house thanks to someone sending her a warning." I look at Mucimi. He doesn't look at me, but keeps petting Hawk. "She got a picture of a newspaper and made her way here hoping just being close would keep her safe. Her sister has been helping to keep her hidden, but it's been hard for them. They have no other family."

She can't wait to meet her and she's already making plans to keep her and her sister close. I want a woman like Holly. Someone that wants to make life better for other people. I shake my head. This isn't an option when I can't handle someone's hands on me. Who the hell wants a man that can't touch them?

Holly is watching me. "The Princes believe in you Christian. I haven't seen that sad look in a while. Are you going to be happy where you are?" She's wondering if I should stay at the school.

"I am Holly, it wasn't that. Something just hit me. I need to go and change. I wanted to see Mucimi before he went to bed."

"He's been good, thanks for checking on him." Chance moves and Holly sets him down gently. He uses the table to walk closer to Mucimi and Hawk, but looks up at me.

I squat down and smile. "Hey Chance. Are you having fun with your new family?" I see the park. "You went to the park?" He smiles surprising me. He's a cute kid. Mucimi holds his hand and I see Holly holding him then holding his hand while he walks. I look at Mucimi. "You can focus him?"

"Yes."

I chuck him under the chin. "You're going to make a great big brother Mucimi."

"He's my brother." He gives Chance a gentle hug and kisses his cheek.

"He is little man. You're going to be good together. Always and forever."

He smiles. "Mucimi."

I kiss his head. "Love you Mucimi." He throws me a picture of me kissing Chance so I do. "Love you Chance." I get a smile from Chance. "Be good Brothers. I need a shower and change of clothes. I'll see you tomorrow at school."

Mucimi signs, 'Yes,' then Chance does. I laugh messing up their hair. "I'll see you tomorrow Holly. Let's go Hawk."

We walk around to my place and I laugh at Mucimi's pictures. Dean is talking to the kids at lunch tomorrow. The kid is cute.

Chapter Six

One week

  Walking down the beach I open and think about my week. I've been starting my days at the school just connecting, training or jumping with the kids. It keeps me settled. I like the way this has been working, but Prez was wrong about my days. I don't have any full days at the school. The Protectors are a motivated and determined group that are keeping me hopping. I know this settles down, but for the next couple of years they'll be busy. I'm not complaining. Just the thought of doing more for the kids and our Security makes me smile. I loved working at the school, but this job and knowing that I'm worth something to the Clubs feels fuckin' good. Teaching the Protectors their value and how to defend themselves and our families works for me.

  A scream rips through my head, my breath catches and I stop. Aquyà! I run. Phoenix screams and I'm torn. Mucimi screams and I see why. He's throwing pictures of me. Fuck! "I'm here Little Brothers. I'm okay. I'm right here. It's not a new vision, it's from before the Protectors started." I'm coming up to Aquyà's and Dakota says he's got him. I keep going to Prez's talking to them. "Mucimi look and see, it's not a new vision."

  I get a 'yes' in my head and I'm glad he's calm. Phoenix is still screaming and I walk right in. Alpha and Omega are at the stairs, I command them to stand down and they move so we can pass. Prez is pacing with Phoenix in his arms. "Let me try." He gives me a look then hands me Phoenix. 'I'm here. I'm fine Little Brother. The vision is old. Connect to Mucimi and you'll see it's not now Phoenix.' I walk across the room and back. By the time we're close to Prez again Phoenix is calm. I feel the other boys, but they're not screaming. I hand Phoenix back.

"Listen Brothers. We need to jump. I want you all to sit with me. We'll jump together and calm you all with the ancestors' strength and reassurances. Yeah?"

Teller comes running in and pulls Phoenix's leg. Prez puts him down and they sit with Teller holding Phoenix's hand. I look at Prez. They need a minute for Teller to see Phoenix is okay. "I had Lily take him out and was keeping him shielded."

I shake my head no. In my head, I tell him, 'You can't separate them like that. Teller would have calmed Phoenix, he sees more clearly and isn't as sensitive.'

I sit with the boys, but Prez is still standing. He's pissed, but I'm not answering him. I have six boys, Dakota and Jessie waiting to jump. I let Brantley know what we're doing and he sits watching Mucimi and Chance. 'Just be there Brant. I've got them.'

He's good, so I look up at Prez. He sits and I pull the boys closer in my head. "All at once Little Brothers, close your eyes and jump now." I stay with Mucimi while he guides Chance.

Dakota guides us all to his tree and we sit. "Feel Little Brothers. Let the ancestors wash through you. Take the gift of peace they offer."

Prez is shocked that they got here on their own. I don't say anything, but help them receive the strength of the ancestors.

"Our wise Protector is right to bring you here when you are so unsettled. The ancestors can help in ways our mere human minds cannot. Let them replace your worry with peace. Christian is right, the vision you saw was old and has changed," Dakota says and Prez relaxes. The boys smile.

I look at the boys waiting for them all to focus on me. "Visions hit all the time. I get them continuously; Jeremy and Tess get them and they're gone. We decide if it's

148

safe to tell, based on the next vision, if we alter what is to happen. If the outcome is changed in a good way we tell Prez here or at the MC. If altering will cause more harm, we come here and get peace from the ancestors to help us put it in its place. It isn't easy seeing people close to you get hurt and holding that inside when you see them every day. You must do that though. You can't alter a vision just because it hurts you right now. The outcome doesn't always come to you right away. Until you see that outcome you can't change anything. Do you understand?"

Phoenix is shaking his head no. "If we don't tell you, you'll die."

I touch his back. "That may be, but if telling me hurts more people, you can't tell me. You have to look at the bigger picture. If all we thought about is how we feel right now, we would not make very good Protectors. It has to be how that vision impacts life for people beyond what you feel. I think Protectors with visions are the strongest people I know. They have to sacrifice what they want to happen and allow things that hurt in here." I touch his heart. "When you have to make that sacrifice you come here and get help. The ancestors will give you the strength to deal with it and a healing peace so your mind will not keep fighting what hurts your heart."

He nods, but his tears fall. "It is not an easy job Little Brothers. It is not a happy one on some days, but it is the job we were given. If you couldn't do it, you would not have that ability to use. You will learn how to harness the ancestors' strength and use it even when all you want to do is tell so your friends and family will not be hurt. It takes a will of steel, a strong heart and wise guides to become who you are meant to be. Look at who is here with us. You would not be here if you didn't have a will of steel. The ancestors would not have given you the abilities, if you didn't have a strong heart that they trust to do your job." They nod so cute. "You have some of the strongest guides I have ever seen. The ancestors are very powerful. Your dads, your

149

grandparents and the other Protectors are always here for you. Look to us for your lessons, advice or as a comfort for what is not easy. We are here for you always."

Phoenix jumps on me and I roll us through the air laughing. "You will feel it all Phoenix and it is as it will be. You find happiness and live in light Little Brother. It is not all bad. The Clubs and your family will make sure you get what you need for happy." I set us back on the branch and the boys are all smiling. "Mucimi and Aquyà are you at peace with all I've said?"

"No, but it is as it will be and you and my dad will help," Aquyà says looking at the lake. He has tears, but Dakota has him.

I look at Mucimi. "Jeremy showed Aubrey the vision."

I give a quick look to Prez then back to Mucimi. "Yes. It was from a while ago."

"He didn't get a new one." His tears fall and I hold him.

"I know little man, but they don't always get them. I saw me teaching you to jump after that one. I know it was changed. Because they get the vision doesn't mean they always see the outcome. Especially Jeremy, he is a busy Brother and not always open to receive. We help Brothers like that. I've always helped him. It's who I was meant to be. You need to see this now so you know it's not all on you. Protectors work together. You may get a vision that is the change for Aiyana's vision. You bring it to the ancestors and me or your dads. You will learn who should know and bring it to the right people. You'll also learn who can heal you when you need it. For me it's you, Dakota and Jeremy. We are bound and you all are my healers."

He nods and I let him go. "Take your time here and gain all the peace the ancestors give to you. When you are ready, you jump back together. Justice stay in between Mucimi and Chance and help get Chance back."

"I am here my wise Protector. I will guide them back safely," Co says making me smile. I wondered when he would show himself.

"Thank you my wise Shaman." I look at Prez, Jessie and Dakota. "It is time to let them heal each other and learn the power of the ancestors."

Dakota nods. "As you will Christian."

I look at Jessie, but he's just watching. He hasn't said a word this whole time and is okay with what I decide. Prez isn't happy, but won't stop this. "Believe in the ancestors, the boys' abilities and me, my Warrior Leader. We will not put them in danger." He nods at me and we jump.

In the boys' room, he is watching me when I open my eyes. "When?"

I know what he's asking. Fuck. "Last week. The vision was from a month ago. I couldn't say and asked Jeremy to hold it."

"Fuckin' Christ!" He stands and paces. "You've been without Security all this time."

I stand. "I will continue without it. Prez, I can't always tell and I wasn't giving up. I took the warnings and adjusted my movements. I'm here and it worked. Co, Nunánuk, Jeremy and Dakota all knew. They also knew telling you was wrong. It happened the way it was meant to without anyone getting hurt now or in the future."

He nods. "Jeremy isn't a Protector?" He's thinking I'm keeping him apart from the rest for a reason.

"He is, but not with the purpose the rest have. Aubrey either. All the Protectors have different purposes. I put the focus on the boards so you could see that. Their focus is where their purpose is aligned."

He takes a minute to go through the boards and get it straight on the list in his head. "Aiyana and Kaya are meant only for the reservation?"

He's getting it. "Yeah, but they are a strength we can use for other purposes. Like us helping them, they will be here for us."

He nods. "The boys are ready to come back. Do you need to get to Brantley's?"

I shake my head no. "Mucimi can get Chance back, but for the first time I wanted him to have the support from Justice. Telling them he might need it will have them all helping. They need to build that bond between them."

He stops and takes a deep breath. "You are a good leader for them Christian. Thank you."

I sit and wait. Teller and Phoenix open their eyes and I look for Mucimi. He's hugging Chance. Phoenix looks at Prez. "Mucimi did it." He smiles.

Prez nods. "He is young, but very strong. That doesn't mean you let him go. Always watch and be ready to step in if he needs it."

Teller hugs him. "We won't let go Dad. We're going to be like you and make sure we hold all our Brothers."

I laugh. "You're going to make excellent big Brothers." I stop and feel Dean. "I need to go. I'll see you at school tomorrow."

"She needs you now," Teller says looking worried.

I nod and mess his hair. "I'm on it Little Brother." I look at Prez. "I'll see you tomorrow and can answer your questions. I need to go."

He throws me chin and we're out the door running to the gate. "Stay with me Dean." Serenity is looking for my number. "I'm on my way," I tell her and she slumps on the counter. She's crying and I can't get much from her so I focus on Dean. The guard opens the gate and we run through.

Serenity is at the door waiting for us. "She won't wake up. It's never been this bad." She tries to touch my arm and I move her away.

I know she won't hurt me, but I need everything to get through to Dean. "I got her." I walk by and hear her crying, but she doesn't follow.

Dean's thrashing on the bed. "Up Hawk." He lays beside her and I touch her hand. Her body relaxes, but she's stuck in the dream. "We're here Dean. Come to me. Follow my voice and come to me." The shit going through her head is brutal. "We can get past it. Fight Dean you can do this. Come to me."

"They're killing them!" she screams, and Hawk lays across her legs.

"No. It hasn't happened. Come to me and we can work to keep them safe. I need you to help do that. Come to me Dean so we can make sure it doesn't happen." I call to Dakota. 'I need you.'

'I am here Brother.'

'Help me pull her away. She can't get back.'

She screams then her eyes open. Thank fuck! "Thank you, Dakota."

"They die!" She sits up and holds onto me crying. Fuck. After the initial energy, my body calms. Dakota didn't let me go. I thank him and hold her feeling calm and alert. I'm a bastard, but I like the feeling of her body plastered to mine. Dakota laughs in my head. 'Fuck off Brother.'

153

He laughs again. 'I am no longer needed Christian. Your night will be good.'

I'm glad she can't see my smiling face. "Thanks Brother."

He's gone and I'm still holding her with a clear head and energy that I can manage. My smile gets bigger and I hold her tighter while she sobs against my chest. "We use your information to keep everyone safe Dean. Together we can get through this. That's what we do."

She calms and loosens her hold on me, but I keep her tight against my chest not wanting to let go. "I need tissues." She hiccups and I smile.

I'm fuckin' sick. I let her loose and pull my shirt off. "Use this."

Handing it to her she looks up at me embarrassed. "We can keep them alive?"

I nod. "That's how the readers help us. Your information will keep them safe. It's a fuck of a way to live, seeing all the bad shit, but the warnings are always taken seriously and we will do everything we can to keep them safe."

She's skeptical, but nods. "Thank you for being here. How come you can hold me?"

"Yeah. I can't touch her for that long. How come you can?" Serenity says moving into the room and sitting on the edge of the bed. She's a fuckin' mess. Jesus. She's still shaking.

I tell Hawk to move to her and look at Dean. "Dakota was here and helped with the initial energy. I don't know how I can still touch you now that he's gone and I'm a fuckin' lunatic too, but I don't want to let you go."

She leans against my chest again and I don't stop her. "Don't let me go." Her arms go around me and I'm hard as a rock.

Serenity laughs. "Me being right here means nothing to either one of you?"

"No," I say giving her a look that tells her I don't give a shit if she stays.

She moves fast walking out. Maybe I threw what's in my head to her. "I have to get some sleep. I have a job to get to tomorrow." I laugh watching her walk away.

"You'd think she'd be happy I can touch someone." Her breath hitches, but she's still calm.

"People don't know what this feels like. They've always had the ability to touch anyone they want. I saw the boys touching you. They do that a lot knowing what you feel from it. They did the same thing for me. I can hold them anytime and manage the energy alone. My family has a ten second rule. They let me go before that usually. I hold the kids longer."

She nods. "I love them all so much. How do we keep them safe?" She's getting worked up again so I slide in and calm her.

"We will. To me the visions come in clear. We do this and with your information we will do it right. It takes all of us, but we'll keep them safe."

"How?"

Jesus I just want to hold her. "Tomorrow I'll bring it to Prez and we'll plan with the other Security Officers. Tonight, I'm holding you so you can sleep. My boys were up late and everyone needs some sleep." I'm never sleeping with the fuckin' hard on I have, but I don't need sleep like they do.

"It won't be too late?"

155

I lift her and move us to the headboard. "Come Brother." I sit her across my legs and pull her so her head is on my chest. Hawk leans against us and relaxes. "Sleep Dean. You're waking up safe in my arms, but for right now sleep."

"Christian?"

I want to will her to shut the fuck-up so I can just hold her, but push against the frustration. "Yeah."

"Is this why Mucimi brought me here?"

What? He told why he brought Chance, but didn't say anything about Dean. "I don't know. I can't see me."

She yawns, thank fuck! "Okay."

This time I use her sleepiness to keep her quiet and focus on where she's leaning against my body. I kiss her head smiling and sleep.

Chapter Seven

We walk into the school holding hands and both Done and Holly notice. I throw to them to leave it alone. With sly smiles, they watch—but don't say anything. The kids are all around Dean. They saw and were worried, but she smiles and bends so she's at their height. "Christian explained it and I understand now. I'm just a piece of the puzzle."

They nod and Justice hugs her. "We all are Dean. Uncle VP says, *together, we can do anythin'*," he says it like Uncle Steve would.

Holly cracks up and I give her a look. "That's right Little Brothers, we'll get through it like we always do. I need to get to work early. Is everyone good here?"

I look in on them and see concern, but nothing over the top. Even Mucimi is calm.

"We're good, Christian. We'll stay together and do what Done tells us to." Dean stands up wondering if she should kiss me.

I hold her face and kiss her lips. "Good. I'll pick you up later."

I walk out smiling with all the questions hanging in the air. Holly and Done are shocked, but Taylor and Sheila, who just walked in, more so. I fly to Security laughing at their expressions. When I pull in I remember Hawk. Fuck! He's at the school. I throw to him to keep Dean safe and see him sit by her. I'd rather him be with me, but keeping her safe is good and I don't want to go back showing them how much that kiss affected me.

Dakota laughs behind me. "It was a good night?"

I throw him chin. "The best. Nothing happened, but me holding her. I know nobody will get how big that is, but it was fuckin' awesome."

"I am one that understands Brother. You need to know she has no experience. She could not touch either."

I stop and turn. Fuck. "What do I do? I've never been with anyone, but Club chicks and whores."

He looks embarrassed. "Call Patches." He walks by blocking me. Fuck. It was just a question.

We grew up seeing sex as part of life around the Brothers and Club. It isn't a subject Brothers are embarrassed to talk about. "Dakota didn't live like we did Brother. He isn't comfortable talking about it like we are," Prez says coming out of Ops. I need to shield better coming in here. He laughs.

"He told me she doesn't have experience then to call Patches. He's a little old for this one, isn't he?"

"No. He made lists for the Brothers as we were growing up. He'll cover you better than anyone else. You can touch her without the need to release the energy?"

I smile probably looking like a pussy, but I don't care. "Yeah. I woke up with her in my arms. It was fuckin' awesome."

He slaps my back. "Good Brother. Call Patches. Another piece you've been missing is falling into place. Don't move so fast you miss the good in it."

"Not a fuckin' chance I'm missing out on any of it." He laughs. "I need some time. What she saw is another attack. The kids, then her last night. That isn't a coincidence."

He gets serious fast. "In the Security meeting or alone?"

"The meeting room is good." I follow him into his meeting room. Jessie and Aaron are already here. While they talk, I connect with Ally and Devan. The Protectors are nervous. I check on Aiyana and Kaya seeing Aiyana's concern, but Kaya is settled and Co is aware. Nunánuk tells me to trust in the lessons of my fathers. When Taylor and Jessie come in I pull back and settle here.

"You kissed a girl," Taylor says, and I smile, but don't answer. I did and I'm fuckin' ecstatic.

Everyone looks my way, but I'm not talking about this here. "Is Jeremy here?" Aaron asks.

"No, he is managing the energy himself," Prez answers for me.

Jessie sits forward and catches my eyes. "So, we can touch you without Dakota or Jeremy around?"

"No Brother. Touch will still affect him. Dean is the same, but they have a bond that will bridge that for them," Dakota says saving me from saying too much or telling them to shut the fuck-up. Who cares how as long as I can touch her?

Prez steps closer. "They are bound together?"

I roll my eyes, we have shit to talk about that doesn't have to do with me holding Dean. Dakota saves me again. "Not as you and I are. The bond is in shared ability and isolation. The ability for simple touch is not easily explained to people that have never experienced life without it. Thinking you will spend your life without the ability to touch happens early and is a part of your being from a very young age. With Jessica, my life has changed in ways I never expected. It was a dream I never thought would be attainable for me. I was okay with the way my life was before, but I cannot imagine living another day without her touching me. It is a lonely existence when you do not have it."

159

I nod hoping I never lose this feeling. Fuck. I look at him while they talk about Sheila needing touch. 'Is she the one Dakota? Am I going to lose this?' Jesus my throat closes and I swallow hard.

He doesn't answer and I walk out. Fuck. I lean against the wall and slide down with my head in my hands. It was one night. I had that. I woke up holding a woman in my arms. I can be happy with that or find a way around whatever Dakota sees to have another. 'Jeremy, is she the one?'

I feel Prez and hear the door, but I don't look up. 'It is good Christian.' I let my breath out and think. He's not saying she's the one, but I'm good with what he's giving me.

"I can't tell you I know how you feel. I can't imagine a life without my Brothers, family or kids touching me. What I can tell you is Tess is happy for you. We can lay down and accept what you have as enough or fight like the Badasses we were taught to be and get you more." He's sitting beside me and I feel what he's thinking. He thinks I can do this and he's willing to help.

I smile at him. "I was just thinking I need to find a way around whatever Dakota sees. Nunánuk said to trust in the lessons of my fathers. Not one of them would give up. My head was clear when I opened my eyes Prez. I held her and woke up feeling fine. I'm not giving it back."

He laughs. "Let's go find a way around it Brother. I don't want you to give it back either."

Darren comes down the hall. "New meeting?"

Prez laughs. "Christian found his girl and we're going to help him keep her."

"Fuckin' nice. Who am I shooting?"

We laugh walking back in. Dakota is surprised, but doesn't say anything. I should be pissed he's blocking me, but I let it go. I have to get the kids safe, the Protectors

160

calmed, and my girl back in my bed for another day. I let him see it, but don't look at him to see the reaction. No one says anything and Prez starts the meeting.

I tell them what she saw and about the boys seeing the old vision. Connecting with Devan I get what the readers up there saw. I give them that too. Terry has new information and I pull the board up so we can see what they have. The information all connects and I'm hit with the new threat against me. I look at Dakota and see that's what has him concerned. I throw it to Prez and he stops talking and looks at Dakota. After collecting his thoughts, he looks for a way to get an answer. "Christian will have HS with him until this new threat is gone." Dakota doesn't say a word.

"Me, Aaron and Taylor will cover him here and Uncle Danny and Chet in Mass," Jessie says.

Dakota looks like the air is let out of him. "That is a wise plan Jessie. With touch affecting him, having people that understand is very important."

I close my eyes feeling so fuckin' relieved.

"I want everyone in HS knowing that touch affects him. The kids locked on the Compound, old ladies on high and I need a meet with the MC as soon as possible. Christian get the Protectors paired so no one goes anywhere alone and I need anything new coming in."

I nod and Jeremy tells me, 'it's good' again. I smile and look at my hands. It feels good to know they have my back.

* * *

While Prez and Brantley are meeting with MC inner circle I meet with Patches then get to KC for training.

Elizabeth is determined and focused. Harley is a good match for her. I watch Devan and Mase. They're throwing everything at Colt and he's defending, suspending and hitting back just as hard. Blaze and Blake are suspending with direction from Aubrey. Jeremy watches everyone and steps in when he needs to, but never says a word out loud.

I was happy to see them here today when I walked in. Jeremy already had them started and seems to be pushing them by throwing information and how to achieve the next level.

When they're all exhausted, I call them over. "You know the new threat. Pres and Prez will get me the new information once they have a plan. What I do know is no one goes anywhere without a Protector by their side. You stay in pairs and stay close to the backyard unless you're called for. Mase, Colt and Devan you have a Protector or HS with you out of the backyard. This is not to be taken lightly. Keep your partners close and follow high alert Security procedures."

They all nod. "Let's jump and see what the ancestors have to say." We sit and jump together. I'm so glad again for the ability to let the ancestors soothe our worries and encourage our strengths. Jumping back everyone is at peace with where we are at. Jeremy and Aubrey stay while the rest file out.

"Happy campers," Aubrey says making me laugh.

"Thank you for being here. It was good to see how far they've come." Jeremy throws me chin. He's worried. "Let's get to your training. You can suspend easily, but can you defend while you're in the air?"

"Oooh we didn't do that yet." Aubrey is excited for something new.

Jeremy holds her hand and suspends. It strikes me as wrong. "Aubrey, can you suspend without Jeremy's help?"

I pull them back down and Jeremy's pissed. "She's good. My partner."

"She's not good if she can't suspend alone. If she's with the old ladies, then what?"

"My partner. I'm there." He's telling me in my head to let it go.

"No. Why can't she go alone?"

Aubrey stands in front of Jeremy. "He's just helping me so I don't have to work so hard. I can stay up and move suspended alone."

I look at him pissed. "You fuckin' know what the vision is. You'd put her life on the line so she doesn't have to work so hard?" I throw the pictures of her naked body floating at him.

"Stop!" He has tears in his eyes and I'm shoved back.

He never moved and I'm relieved. "Good! Fight and let her learn to fight with you! She's got the ability! Why the fuck would you make anything easy on her when it's her life we're talking about?"

He stops trying to push me breathing heavy.

I turn toward her. "Aubrey this isn't helping you. Making it easy isn't saving your life. The vision hasn't changed." I watch her face pale.

Jeremy moves fast holding onto her. "No! I'll teach her."

"You better. We're running out of time Je. This isn't a fuckin' joke and I'm only one person." He gives me a sad look, but I'm not giving in. He's not a fuckin' kid anymore and needs to realize they aren't all going to end well for us unless we do what we need to do to alter that. He nods.

"Thank fuck. Let's see what you can do in the air. Aubrey, you practice every fuckin' day."

163

She looks around him. "I will Christian. I thought it changed because you're still here."

I shake my head no and Jeremy spins around to face her. "You'll learn. Tonight, we'll train."

"Let's get to training, I don't have much time." I suspend about ten feet up and wait for them. Once Jeremy has her up she's stable in the air. I move closer to the rock wall and lob energy at Jeremy. He rolls his eyes and hits it to Aubrey. She falls a foot when she hits it back to me, but lifts right back up. I give him a look and hit it harder at him. After a couple of minutes I switch to fire and he's taken by surprise. I stop the fire holding it in front of him. "Ready for anything Je. You got this." He nods and I release the fire. He hits it to Aubrey, but moves closer in case she needs him. "I got her Je." He moves back watching her deflect it easily. "Aubrey we're going to hit hard and fast. If it's too much, say so and we'll work together. You can work with Jeremy later."

She nods, but she's not happy. It just hit her how going easy isn't preparing her.

I whip fire at Jeremy and he hits it away. Aubrey moves toward it deflecting it to me. "Good!" I yell switching to a big ball of energy.

"Hey!" Jeremy says deflecting it.

"Use it Jeremy. Use everything in you. Deflecting will only work for so long. You need to push and direct it."

I throw a chair at him, he lifts another and stops it. He pushes me back and I laugh throwing fire again. He hits it to Aubrey and I throw energy. He takes his eyes off Aubrey throwing it back at me pissed. I smile moving in front of it and use it as a shield for the fire Aubrey throws my way. I push them both at Jeremy and he laughs using it just like I did. I throw a table at him and it burns up before it hits him. "That's it Je! Use it however you can." He throws a chair laughing. I roll it in energy and throw it at Aubrey.

164

She's not ready and I stop it. Jeremy yells and I look at him—he's falling, but catches himself about five feet from the floor. "I told you I had her. Trust me Brother. I won't ever hurt her. This is why she needs to practice. Yeah?"

"Yeah," they both say.

I lower myself to the floor and get the chairs back where they belong and the ash cleaned up and into the trash. I turn fast hearing clapping. Fuck! Jeremy and Aubrey are standing on the floor when I look back. Ricky, VP, Uncle Danny, Pres and Prez are here. "I didn't know you were here." I don't know if they're supposed to see this. "I don't know who to ask about you seeing shit." I guess asking them would work. Jeremy laughs and I peg him a finger behind my back.

Prez steps forward. "I wouldn't show everyone, but I think we're all okay to see."

I throw him chin. "Jeremy will work with Aubrey."

He nods. "Are the other Protectors able to do that?"

"Not like Christian. He's hard," Aubrey says and I clench my jaw to stop from laughing.

Jeremy steps in front of her. "No. Was me. We'll practice."

Pres looks at him. "Going easy on her will only hurt her Jeremy. You of all people should have learned that lesson."

Jeremy looks down and nods. "We'll practice. Now." He starts walking toward the stairs.

"Where are you going?" I ask.

"Lab," Uncle Steve says.

I nod. "Call to me later. Anything hitting her hurts you. Make sure she can keep you safe too Je."

165

He gives me a look, but throws chin pulling Aubrey out with him.

Uncle Danny laughs. "I think you're the only one that talks to him like that. It's good for him."

"My brothers stopped shielding him." I pull what they see. "He's still the only one here that reads everyone, has visions and works daily at the lab to keep us all safe. He sleeps like three hours a night and still trains every single day. What he's doing with Aubrey is wrong, but he'll fix that now."

Uncle Steve throws me chin. "Yeah. Shouldn't be taken for granted either."

I shake my head no and look at Ricky. "Sorry about the table. I didn't expect him to torch it."

They laugh. "That was fuckin' incredible Brother. I'll get another table."

I throw him chin. I have no idea why they're all looking at me. "Do you have questions?"

"Do the other Protectors have this ability?" Prez asks again.

"Some. Jeremy and Aubrey were teaching them more today. He's pushing them where he was easy on her. Mase, Colt and Devan are getting very good with defending while suspended. Harley and Elizabeth are right behind them, but able to see the next move and plan a defense. Blake and Blaze are learning to suspend, but they are the more focused readers." It hits me. "We shut the feeds down while we're in here. Do you want them on?"

"No. I don't think anyone else needs to see this," Pres says and I nod throwing a shield over his thoughts.

"We came to tell you the plan and see if you had anything to add." Uncle Danny walks by me and sits at the kitchen table.

I follow because they're all looking at me weird. I don't want to look at what they're thinking so I block them all. He's smiling when I sit. I smile because I know he knows.

✷ ✷ ✷

I update my spreadsheets on the chopper and hand Terry the flash when I walk into Ops. Jacob is pissed. "Let's take a walk Jay." He follows me out. 'Walk Hawk.' We take him out to the back lot. "What's up?"

His arms go out and his frustration is right there for me to see. "He's not training her Christian. He gets pissed, but he's not doing his part." He's scared for Aubrey.

"He's training her now. They're at the Lab. I checked in on them and he isn't playing anymore."

"Because you threw her fuckin' dead body at him! I get nothing from him then get slammed with that! He should have known going easy on her *hurts* her!"

I touch his shoulder. "I'm sorry Jay. I had no idea he'd throw it to you. I needed to get through to him. It wasn't a new picture for him, it's the vision. It hasn't changed."

"Fuck." He's got his hands on his knees and he's breathing heavy.

I think this is learned from Badasses. Everyone does the same thing. I push it out of my head and touch his shoulder again. "We're doing everything we can to keep her safe. She's learning now and we'll be ready. Neither MC nor Princes are letting it go."

He gives me a look. "He showed me you too Christian."

Fuckin' Jeremy! "He shouldn't have. They aren't letting it go Jay. Everyone is working to keep that from

167

happening." If he showed the kids I'm going back up there to punch him in the fuckin' face.

'No! I was mad, you're right.' Jeremy throws at me.

'Stop acting like a kid! This isn't a fuckin' game and that was a shit move. Our whole family has enough to deal with without you throwing a fuckin' tantrum.'

He yells, 'I said you're right! Sorry.'

Jacob stands up and starts walking. "Prez has HS with you."

"Yeah, Taylor, Aaron or Jessie."

He stops and looks at me. "You're okay with them shadowing you?"

I smile. "I'm not fuckin' stupid Jay. There's a vision of me dead out there. I'll do everything I can to change that without hurting anyone else."

His arms go up again. "You think you can stop throwing dead out like it's nothing!"

"Sorry Jay. I just mean I'll do everything I can to stay alive."

He smiles. "That's a long fuckin' way from suicide so I'll take it." He's worried I wouldn't fight for myself. Fuck.

"It was a pussy solution. That's why I talked to Brantley, Jay. I was looking for a way out instead of around. I got around it and never thought about it again."

He watches me and Jeremy tells him it's true. He nods and starts walking again. "Stop watching here and go teach her the fuckin' right way!" he yells.

I'm smiling as we follow him in. At Ops, I check in with Terry. Jacob hasn't told him what Jeremy sent so he's not all over him or pissed. It's refreshing. He's got everything on the flash transferred to our boards and looks around. "Does 'suspend and defend' mean fighting while flying?" he asks softly.

"Not flying, but yeah."

"Like what you showed Pres, but fighting?" He's picturing a *Star Wars* like scene and I stop myself from laughing, but smile.

"Without light sabers, yeah."

"Jesus fuck. That's cool and fuckin' scary Christian."

I laugh. "We're hoping for effective." He nods seriously. The visions have him worried too. "If you don't have questions I'm out."

He shakes his head no. "Taylor is working with the procedure book. He's happy with all you have for it and started the new training today."

I slap his back and move to Brantley at the center console. "I'm out Brant. I'll check on Mucimi and Chance while I'm at the school."

He looks at me concerned. "You doing okay?"

"Yeah. We're working through some kinks, but we'll be ready when we're needed."

He rolls his eyes. "I mean you Christian, not the whole fuckin' department."

I put my hands up. "I'm good Brantley."

He's got Holly in his head telling him I looked upset yesterday. Before he asks I throw to him, 'It had nothing to do with anything you're thinking. Things hit me and I'm not always going to wear a smile.'

"If this starts getting to you, find me. No matter when or where. Yeah?"

"I will Brant. I'm happy where I am right now. The visions don't stop, but I'm still a long way from when I first got here. I'm never going back to that. I'll talk to you first."

He goes through what I said again and nods. I see his worry isn't me, but how people treat me. It's something he'll have to see himself and it's so new that I don't have anything to give him for that. He'll see soon enough. "I checked you out, go see your girl."

I smile. "On my way. I need to get Hawk in the tunnels."

He starts typing. "Taylor has trainees on patrol, but Hawk's clear to go down."

"Thanks Brantley." We walk toward the door and I'm thinking about Dean. I've looked in on her all day long and she has been happy, but I want to feel her hand in mine. I hope it's the same as last night and this morning. I don't want Dakota to have to show every fuckin' day. I'd be lying if I said I didn't want more, but I can do slow if I get what my Brothers have in the end.

I get Hawk in the tunnel and reset the sensors then hit my watch so Security knows I'm on my way out. Aaron is sitting behind my bike when I hit the lot. "Protector service. If you go out tonight I'm your shadow." He thinks I'm going to argue.

"You want fish or the deli?"

He laughs. "Fish."

I nod thinking Dean will like going out. I see Serenity laughing with Aaron, but it isn't yet. I push it away and get to the school so I can let Hawk out of the tunnel.

"Tell him to sit here," she says looking toward the bar.

170

"He won't. His job is Security for me."

She doesn't understand. I keep the smile off my face and let her go on. "There is a guy outside watching us."

"He's your Security and Aaron's eyes outside. If Security wasn't high, he would sit with us, but he needs to be where he is to see the whole place. He's not watching us. Just relax." I've been shielding her since we walked in. Crowds are a problem for her and I hope what I'm doing works.

She's going to keep going. "All my life I've been with Security. I get that it's new for you, but we've been doing this for a long time. You saw why he's here. We have to take the precautions so what you saw doesn't happen. It's always worked for us. Relax. This is our first date and I don't want to spend it talking about Security or the Club."

She's fuckin' funny, but I don't smile or react to what's going through her head. "Since you know everything about me and I know about you; what exactly is there to talk about?"

"How do you like your new job?" That surprises her and I smile.

Her face lights up and I see her happy. "I love it. The kids are a trip I'll tell ya. I love them all already and they like me too. Holly is so easy to work for. I've only ever worked with the police and they weren't like bosses because I volunteered." I nod. That's how she ended up losing her parents and running for her life. She pushes that away and focuses on the school. "I want to take the rest of the online classes and finish school. Now that we're here, can I do that?"

I look for why she's asking me. "You aren't in jail here. If you want classes take classes. Online will make Security happy, it'd be a pain in the ass for them to follow you around campus." I'm thinking she'd never make a campus if she can't block.

171

That makes her happy. "I'm going to. Holly said I don't need to, but the kids are so damn smart."

I laugh. "They are. Stella is something else, but the boys aren't too far behind. She lets them figure things out for themselves. Soon she'll widen that gap, but she's happy right now working at their pace."

"Why won't she wear the glasses? I don't get that?"

"The glasses will be important later, but the boys sign and throw to her. She doesn't need them right now. They're good about including her in everything they do. Sometimes I see the glasses on her when she goes out with Sheila and Jax." I throw her the picture.

"Sheila is funny. I like her. I haven't met anyone yet that I don't like." She's thinking it's like Disney World.

I laugh. "We're just people like everyone else. The difference here is there are a lot of us and we've found a way to promote good while keeping us safe from the lunatics outside our borders." She's going to argue it and I hate to do it, but she isn't seeing the bigger picture. "Take your parents. They sheltered you keeping bad away your whole life. They found a way to work around you reading that left you happy and content with your life. We're no different. There are just more of us. The MC is over five hundred members and we're close to them. That's a lot of strong concentrated on good and keeping us safe."

I see the pain hit her, but she pushes forward. "That is a lot of good. Has it always been like this here?"

I wait until our order is in and the waitress walks away. "We grew up in the MC. They weren't as big as they are now, but they've always been about keeping women and kids safe. They got bigger and worked for the community then the towns they took over. They weren't set up like we were when we started, but they control the PD in three towns and the City. Even the towns with real PD are trained by the MC."

172

She's fighting through pain and I want it away from her. "Why didn't my parents move us here?"

"No one knew about the readers until Prez threw energy while cameras were running. He pretty much outed us then and decided he wouldn't hide the readers, but that wasn't that long ago. They may not have heard of us or were afraid of the biker thing. Not everyone accepts bikers like our towns do."

She nods and I see her put it away. "I love the job and kids and keep wondering how you can leave a job like that. You're really smart like the kids. You must miss them. Do you like your new job?"

While I read her easily she can't read me unless she's touching me, even then it's very little. "I love the new job and miss the kids, but I see them every day. I miss watching them figure things out, but I can see them through the visions all day if I want to."

She doesn't understand the visions, but she isn't going to ask. "I'm out."

I laugh. "Don't you want to know about my family or tell me about Serenity?"

Her sister's face passes through her head. "Holly tells me all about your family. They're amazing. I can't wait to meet Joey and your mom. She says they're just as intent on doing good as the guys."

I nod letting her see what I do thinking about them. She smiles. "They are. I'm so proud of my family and what they do for the community and the kids. My parents are fuckin' saints. They raised every one of us to be who we are today." I don't tell her what a fuck-up I was.

She's nodding with that smile. "I heard. They must be incredible. I feel like that about Serenity. She sacrificed everything in her life to keep me safe and hidden. She even

173

moved here without asking a single question. She loves her new job, but she gave up everything for me."

She did too. She had a good job and walked away. She took as much money as she could out of her account via ATM, but hasn't touched the account or her credit cards since they've been on the run. Brantley helped me get the cards paid, but she still hasn't used them and Darren is talking to Serenity about the life insurance from her parents. Her sister is like us. "She's a good sister. Maybe she'll find her happy here and life will be easier."

She laughs, I memorize that sound and the smile on her face. She's beautiful. "She already loves it here. Now that she's not worried about money and I'm working to help pay the bills, life is easier. She loves the house too." We move so the server can drop our plates. "This looks good. You have the best seafood here."

I smile. "We're kind of known for it."

She smiles and I see her question, but wait to see if she'll ask. After a couple of bites, she looks at me. "Do you date a lot?"

"Never been on a date." She thinks I'm lying. "There are things I can't tell you, things I'd rather not talk about and things that could get people killed if I talked about them. One thing I won't do is lie to you. I've never been on a date because I couldn't touch anyone without seeing the men before me. It's not something I want to see on a first date."

She nods. "So, you only date virgins?"

I laugh. "I've never been on a date Dean. I grew up in the Club, whores and Club chicks are everywhere. I've never been with a virgin. No."

Her face falls. Fuck, she thinks I'm laughing at her. I reach for her hand and try to figure out a way to say this. "I shouldn't have laughed. I'm sorry. Being with women requires a level of intimacy that I can only handle a certain

174

way. Without the details, I can't touch or hold anyone the way that should happen naturally. You are the first woman I've ever held like last night and I didn't want to let go. I don't want to fuck this up so you'll need to ask me if you want to know something. I promise I won't laugh."

She nods and goes back to eating. I liked her hand in mine and try to figure a way to get it back while she eats. A waitress comes toward us with boxes and I look at Aaron. He swings his finger around and I pull money out throwing it on the table. "Have them deliver fresh meals to the Compound. Christian Blackhawk." I hold my hand out for Dean. She looks confused. "Sorry babe, but we need to go now." She's up and following me without question.

"Mr. Blackhawk?" The waitress calls, I stop and turn. "Is this going with Mucimi's order?"

I laugh and nod. "Sure."

Aaron meets us at the door and I see we have vehicles tagged and being tracked coming toward us. Since we're just off the highway that's not unusual, but with Security high, Dean needs to be away from the threat. I shouldn't have been blocking them. As soon as we're out the door I feel it—then see it. Aaron steps closer to me. "Truck green, two men paid like mercs." I throw to get the old ladies covered. He nods. "Babe, I've only run Ops on this bike once. I need you to hold on and move with me. No matter what's happening around us, keep your arms around me and don't let go. Yeah?" I say as I'm pulling my gun.

She nods and I see she's scared to death. Fuckin' great. Aaron nods, he's tag and will keep my six. I smile at him thinking it instead of saying it and wait for Dean to move up. When her front hits my back I nod to Security and follow him out. The truck is coming up on us fast. I throw the picture to Dean. "Hold on baby." I speed up and pass Security throwing to Aaron. 'I'll drop her and get to Prez's office.'

"Roger Guardian." He repeats what I said to Jacob.

"Guardian, we have a truck just south of the gate. Ghost is closest at five out."

"I don't have five Lightfoot. I'm two out. The green truck is headed for the Compound."

"Roger Guardian." He has Jessie moving toward the truck.

I fly around the corner stopping everything in our path and Dean holds on tighter. "Lightfoot, they have snapshots of Prez, me and the kids in the truck by the gate."

"Jesus. Roger Guardian. Prez and VP are coming from behind. They're one out."

I see the vision; the pussies get a call. "There's a watcher giving them Prez coming their way."

"Guardian hit them. I'll keep one breathing from the other truck," Jessie says.

"Roger Ghost." Like I'd let them hit Prez.

'Hold on Dean.' I throw and feel another watcher. "Black Chevy, Lightfoot. I just passed it. They know I'm coming."

"Roger Guardian. Coder is coming through the gate."

I see the gun and shoot. Dean screams, but quiets right down. 'We're good.' I hit the passenger and fly by then into the gate. "That truck has paper in it Lightfoot."

"Roger Guardian," he answers in between giving Jessie and Aaron directions. I feel Prez and I'm glad he goes right by us to the watcher in the black car. Darren already has Clean-up picking up the other pussy. At Brantley's, I pull Dean into the house. "Holly I need to leave Dean here for a while. She isn't going to be safe outside the gate tonight."

When I turn Jess and Serenity are here. "Good, girls' night in. I need to go. Oh yeah, Mucimi ordered food from the seafood restaurant."

They all laugh. Holly's shaking her head. "He didn't want pork chops?"

I shrug and turn Dean to me. "Sorry babe. We'll try for a better second date. You did great. I'll be back as soon as I can and we can at least eat."

She nods, but is still scared. "I'll be here."

I kiss her and get it back. Fuck, of all the times for her to open her mouth. I smile putting my forehead against hers. "We'll finish that too." I turn before everyone can see how that worked for me. Jesus, like I'm a fuckin' kid.

At the gate, I ask Jacob where I'm going. "Prez wants you at the Chevy."

"Roger Lightfoot." I ride the two blocks and pull up alongside the car.

Brantley is here with Prez. "Took you long enough."

I look at my watch. "Seven minutes. He wasn't armed."

He smiles. "Just fuckin' with you Christian."

I look at the pussy Prez has against the car. His mouth is taped and hands are cuffed. "He's been here for about four months. That's before Dean moved here. He has detailed information he's been gathering. The truck had a copy, but I didn't get this one. His laptop is in the car with everything on it." I see a vision of the man dying. I can't say I'm sorry. "He's been looking for someone to pay him for the information. He has a tie to the MC." I look for more and the guy starts moving. Prez punches him and he stops. "He's got Elizabeth, Aubrey and Harley's pictures. He's looking to hurt VP." Prez looks at me and I throw him what I have.

177

"Lightfoot get Eagle Eye to the meeting room when this one comes in. Tell him I want this fuckin' asswipe in pain."

"Roger Prez."

Jacob answers Aaron then Jessie. He's got shit going on everywhere. "Where do you need me Lightfoot?"

"Clean-up is clear at the truck. Eagle Eye is in Ops. Unless you see something I can't, I'm clear Guardian."

I look at Prez. "Dakota will handle holding again. You're clear to go finish your date Brother."

I nod. "We have the laptop."

Brantley opens the car door. "I need to get everything off it. It will take some time to get it on a hologram board."

"Go Brother. We got this," Prez says.

I look, but don't see anything to concern me. "Thanks, Prez, Brantley." I throw chin and get back to Brantley's.

Parking at my house I get Hawk and walk over to Brantley's, going in through the slider. The women are laughing in the living room, but Mucimi comes running to me.

He's throwing pictures of the truck. Jesus. "They're dealt with little man. Prez and Dakota will handle it." He nods.

I pick him up and walk through to the front when I hear the knock. "I got it," I tell Holly. She sits until the bags come in. I put Mucimi down and he runs to the hallway. I hold my laugh in, but I'm smiling. Fuckin' kid is too much.

"Mucimi!" Holly yells and starts hunting him down.

Jess, Serenity and Dean help get the bags in the dining room. We're all smiling. "Guess they didn't have enough pork chops." They laugh.

"Christian he's hiding again!" Holly yells and they laugh more.

I pick up Chance, "Let's go get your brother out of trouble." In Mucimi's room Holly is looking in the closet. "I got him. He ordered for everyone and the Brothers."

She throws her hands up. "He can't just order food everywhere. How is he paying for this?"

I look and take a second to make sure I don't laugh. "Brantley's allowance account. He has money in his own account if you want him to use it you have to tell him."

"Mucimi has an account?" She's shocked.

I look the other way so I don't laugh. "All the kids do. When they're born, birthdays and holidays the MC and Princes deposit into the accounts."

"I thought they got gift cards?" She's thinking so I wait. "I've never seen the gift cards."

"Joey takes care of it for them. They all have their own IDs. Just tell him to use his own number."

She walks out disgusted and I laugh. Chance puts his head on my chest. "Let's get your brother." I walk out of Mucimi's room and into the office. When I open the closet door, he looks up at me. "I think you're losing dessert little man."

He nods looking sad and puts his arms up. I lift him and take him into the dining room. When they're both sitting Mucimi looks at Holly. "Sorry."

"You can't keep ordering food happy boy."

179

He looks down. "I pay," he says without looking at her again. I clench my jaw and look away. Holy shit he's fuckin' funny.

"It isn't about you paying. You should ask me and wait for my answer. Maybe I wanted Italian." She smiles.

Mucimi looks at her. "You want fish."

Brantley and Prez walk in to us all laughing. I throw to them what happened and Brantley's smiling. Holly glares at him and Prez laughs. "Worse than keeping up with Jeremy," he says catching my eye. He throws Dakota getting information and Terry will have my boards updated in the morning. I nod. Dean is watching everything around the table. Prez looks at Serenity. "I need you on the Compound tonight. With a threat to Dean you're on high alert. You'll have Security with you off the Compound. Yeah?"

She nods. "Thank you. Where am I staying?"

"Christian's loft is empty. The Prospects moved everything earlier," Holly tells Prez.

He looks at me. "Dakota tells me I may want something more permanent, but that will work for tonight. Are you good with that?"

I see Serenity in a house down my street across from Aaron. "Yeah, thanks Prez."

He looks back at Serenity. "I'll have a Prospect get you enough for a couple of days."

She nods completely intimidated by him. He smiles knowing what's going through her head and Dean laughs looking at Prez. "She's fine, but she needs to learn how to block from you guys or at least you."

I clench my jaw. Mucimi raises his hand. Cracking me up. "You're going to teach her?" Prez asks him smiling.

"Yeah." He's so fuckin' serious and looks Prez in the eyes daring him to say he can't.

180

"Good job Little Brother. Make sure you throw slow enough that she understands."

Mucimi relaxes and I'm clenching my jaw again. "I will do good."

Dean laughs and Mucimi gives her a look. "Important to do good." He starts throwing shit at her.

Jesus. "Stop. I'll explain it to her. We don't show visions to anyone, but Prez, Dakota, Jeremy or me," I tell him.

He nods and Prez throws him chin. "Good job Mucimi. Remember the lessons of your fathers so we all stay safe."

"I will. Sorry Prez." He's talking slower and Prez looks at me. I throw him, 'Like Jeremy.' He nods.

When he leaves, Serenity and Mucimi both relax. He looks at me to see if I'm mad. "You're okay little man. No one expects you to remember everything right away. You'll get it." He nods and looks down. Shit. I look at Brantley. 'He thinks he did wrong. Mistakes are okay, but he needs to learn from them.'

Mucimi looks up at me. "I will." I can't do anything, but laugh.

Jessie comes in and sits by Jess kissing her like no one else is here. She slides a tray over to him. "You miss all the good stuff. Mucimi ordered your food."

"Yeah, I told him to get for everyone. Where are the boys?"

We all look at Mucimi then Jessie. Holly doesn't know what to think. Dean starts laughing again. At least she's happy. I sit by her and take her hand loving the simple contact without the energy throwing me.

"Alex should bring them back soon. They went to see a new dog Steve trained."

181

Brantley sits and everyone starts eating. "I told the Prospects to leave your pictures for you to put up Christian."

I saw them against the walls and nod. "Thanks Brant."

Everyone starts talking, but Dean is watching me with a smile on her face. I lean in knowing just what she's thinking, but let her tell me herself. "I like you holding my hand." She shrugs thinking it's stupid.

"Me too. Not something that happens every day for me either." I get a smile with her eyes flashing happy at me so I kiss her. I look at Brantley. "Doesn't translate like you think Brother."

He laughs. "I'm not sure I like the new and improved Christian. Get the fuck out of my head."

"Get used to it. It took him fuckin' years to get here. I like him just the way he is. You, I can still hang in pop ups," Jessie growls at him and Dean squeezes my hand. I look at her smiling.

When Jessie is done, he stands. "I need to get to the meeting. Mucimi did you get Jacob and Terry's food?"

"Yeah." He points to the bag on the counter.

Jessie kisses Jess and grabs the bag throwing chin. "You're on the Compound tonight. With everything going on HS is spread thin."

I nod. "If I'm needed I'll run the tunnels or use Prez's office."

He walks toward the door. "I'm glad you're going to be fuckin' easy."

I laugh when the door closes. Serenity looks at Jess. "He's a little scary."

She waves it away. "He's a big teddy bear."

Holly says she'll show Serenity around the loft so I clear our trays and pull Dean up. "I like the service here." She has everyone laughing as I guide her to the door. Since my hand is on her back, like my dad does for my mom, I don't give a fuck what they're thinking. Hawk follows us out.

At my new house, I walk her through. "It's beautiful."

"Uncle Danny finished it this morning. He always does a good job."

"Are you behind Brantley so you can be close to Mucimi?"

I think about that. "Maybe. Prez gave me the house, but didn't say why here. There are about twenty empty houses on the Compound. I lived at Brantley's, or the apartment on the side of it, until today. He could have thought I'd like being close. Taylor is the next house over from Brantley and Jacob is next door to me."

She giggles making me smile. "Blackhawk block?"

I laugh walking her to the patio. "The glass in here is solar panels. Jess is testing them out. This is my favorite room." I pull her down as I sit.

"Serenity has a place to sleep, but no one said anything about me." She's hoping I ask her to stay here.

"I told Prez about waking up holding you today. He probably thought I'd want that for more than one night."

All kinds of shit flies through her head. I kiss her and it stops. When I lift my head up she's looking at me surprised. "I needed to stop all that shit in your head. No one will judge you here. You can read enough to see it yourself. I've grown up with almost everyone here and they know since I hit twelve or thirteen I haven't been able to touch people without getting every fuckin' nightmare they've ever had. They're happy for me and they like you."

183

"They do? They don't know me." She thinks she's in Disney World again.

I smile and kiss her again. I like anything that makes her happy, but kissing her makes me happy. Patches gave me a four-page list with everything in the world on it. Kissing and making her comfortable with everything we do is on the list first. Since it's new to me too, I have no problem experiencing every minute of how this feels.

She pulls away from my mouth and puts her head on my shoulder. "I've never done this Christian."

"I know baby. I haven't either. We'll go slow and get it right. Now that I've found you, I'm not willing to let you go."

She looks up at me. "Do we stay together?"

"I saw you older, so I want to say yes, but I don't see myself. I got it from Mucimi. I'm not taking any chances here, we need to do this right."

She laughs. "This is the weirdest place I've ever been, but it's a nice weird."

I kiss her head. She's cute. "Most people just think we're crazy." She thinks they're right, but isn't going to tell me. "There are some clothes for you in my closet and anything you need for the morning. The Prospects brought some stuff over today."

She laughs thinking we're all crazy. Since she's probably right I leave it alone.

We spend the night talking and kissing. When it's time to walk Hawk, she comes with us down to the beach. "Can I ask you something?" She looks at the water and I'm not seeing everything clear in her head.

"Anything." I call to Jeremy. 'Something is wrong Je. I can't read her clear.' He fuckin' laughs in my head.

"Why me?" She thinks she's not good enough?

184

'Jeremy, what the fuck?' I don't like this at all.

"Why not you? You're funny, honest, loyal and beautiful." I'm touching her and looking right at her. Why the fuck can't I see her clearly?

'It is the way Christian. I do not read Jessica unless it's extreme emotions. Prez cannot read Lily either. You will feel more than read her,' Dakota answers me. Thank fuck.

I stop her and turn so I'm looking right at her. "I'm having a conversation with Dakota about why I can't see you so clear. I'm getting some from you, but it isn't so clear anymore. He says it's the way. He doesn't read Jess either."

"Thank God!" She's smiling.

What the fuck? Why is she trying to hide from me? "That makes you happy?"

She looks unsure. "It's a relief. I must be entertaining as hell, but I don't know how to do any of this. It's hard knowing you can read every stupid thing in my head."

"New isn't stupid. I keep telling you it's new for me too. I've kissed two women my whole life babe. Never held anyone's hand unless it was my family, even then it's for short amounts of time. I've never done this either. Relax and give yourself a break. We'll learn together. Yeah?"

She nods with a smile. "Yeah. I like how everyone does that. Yeah?"

I pull her into me and hug her loving the feel of her up against me. "Yeah." I kiss her head and we walk.

Back at the house I get Hawk a bone and some clean water then bring Dean up to my room. "I know they brought enough for a couple of days. I don't know where they put everything. If you start over here I'll look in the other dresser."

185

She starts opening drawers. I open every drawer, but don't find anything in this dresser. When I look she's not at the dresser. I definitely don't like not reading her. I hear her in the closet and go look. "There's panties, but nothing for bed." She's looking at her clothes, but won't look at me.

"What's wrong?"

Her hands go up. "All these people think I'm sleeping with you and I don't need clothes." She's still not looking at me, but I can feel her frustration.

I pull her to me. "First, I don't give a fuck who thinks what. Second, why does this upset you? Do you want to sleep at the loft with Serenity?"

"No. Yes. I don't know!"

What? "You don't want to sleep here?"

She doesn't answer so I step back. She's crying. Fuck. "Tell me what's happening here." I wipe her tears.

"I just met you. This is scary and I don't have anything to wear to bed." More tears fall.

I hug her smiling. "I have clothes you can wear. I don't think we're ready for more than sleeping, but I want you here where I know you're safe and I can hold you while you sleep."

"Are you smiling?"

Shit. "No ma'am, I am not smiling." I wipe the smile off my face and look down at her.

She gives me a look. "I think you were." I don't say a word or smile. "What can I wear to bed? I'm tired." She sighs.

I take her hand and bring her to the dresser. "Shirts are here, shorts in the next and sweats in the bottom."

She takes a shirt and a pair of basketball shorts and goes to the other dresser for panties. When she's in the bathroom I look in the panty drawer. I close it fast. Fuckin' women and the panties. Patches' list pops in my head and I get my laptop to order more.

When she comes out of the bathroom I'm in the drawer getting her size. "Need help?" She smirks. My shirt on her body does something to me. I feel it in my chest and my dick swells. Maybe it's looking at all the panties on the site.

"No. I needed your size." I close the drawer and go back to the laptop. I get a box from the Princesses and one from Victoria's coming. I check her clothes in the closet and send the sizes to Nancy so she can send some clothes. What the fuck is a one? Women's clothes are weird. They should have inches or something that works better than 'one'. My clothes all have my size by inches even with the medium label they tell the size in inches. How the hell do they get clothes with one?

She's on the bed when I come back in. "Done." I sit on the edge of the bed admiring my shirt on her. I like this. "The women are crazy with panties. The Princesses came up with environmentally friendly material, but the Brothers always bought from Victoria's. I don't know what you wanted so I got both. Nancy will send clothes or send you pictures for you to choose."

"You bought me panties?" She's looking at me like I'm crazy.

"Well, they might be for me. Some of that shit is hot. I got Superman, Ironman and Flash. Captain America was sold out. How come the sizes are different than your pants? And the shirts are different too." She's laughing like it's something I should know. I clench my jaw, grab some shorts and go take a shower. I look in on the kids then my Protectors. Everyone is a little antsy tonight, but they're holding it together. When I come in the room she's laying at the very edge of the bed. At least she's not laughing at me anymore. I climb in and move to the middle then pull her

187

over to me. "You being as far away as you can get doesn't work for me." I settle her against me and kiss her head. "I like this much better."

"Is it normal for men to order women's panties when they meet?"

I laugh. "Babe, we're fuckin' crazy bikers. Everyone I know orders their women panties and clothes from Nancy. It's just the way it's done."

She nods so serious and I miss seeing what she's thinking. "Are there other things you do that I should know about?"

I think about my mom and dad then Patches' list. "I'll get you a car tomorrow and have Joey get you an ID and card for house stuff."

She sits up. "You're buying me a car? Isn't that a bit much?"

I shrug. "I think it's the way they do things. You need a car to get around the towns and the card so you can get what you need. I order groceries so, I just pick them up and paper products come in on the first. The gate guards will deliver takeout, but you need the ID to order unless you have the guard order. They have the number for me."

"You just order like a hotel on TV?" She doesn't believe me?

"Yeah babe. Just tell them what you want and they'll order or order and they'll deliver it to you."

"You think this is all normal?"

I don't understand where she's going with this. "You saw Mucimi order tonight. It's normal for us. It's the way it's always been. In Mass, it works the same way. The guards deliver or order. Paper is on the first. The Brothers order clothes and panties and make sure the women can get around safely. Women are our weak link. The last thing we

188

want is one of our women stuck on the side of the road. No one is safe that way." She nods looking a little more relaxed. "I'm not about to lie to you. I want this. I want what we can be and I want to do it right. It's worked for the MC Brothers and the Princes. Since better Brothers than me still have their women, I'll follow their lead. Yeah?"

She smiles. "If you think this is normal who the hell am I to say it isn't. I've never had a boyfriend. Are bikers boyfriends? Is that what I call you?"

She's cute. "Christian works, but I like that you think of me like that." I smile liking the way that feels. Prez and Brantley called her my girl. I think of her that way. She's mine.

She lays back down. "Thank you Christian, but I have to tell you it's a little crazy. I never saw anything like this. I know my dad didn't buy clothes or do shopping. Do you clean and cook?"

"Yeah," I say smiling. "Cleaners come once a week, but I do the in between."

"I like you even more now." She yawns.

I laugh giving her a squeeze. "Since you're not giving me shit for how we live, I like you more too."

She giggles sounding so young. It makes me smile— like Mucimi's little laugh. Her arm goes across my stomach, I don't move so she can sleep, but her hands on me is fuckin' with my head. The wrong one. I push it away and think about eating at the restaurant then walking on the beach. I held her hand the whole way. It was another good day and she's in my bed, in my new house. I jump and fly the reservation thanking the ancestors for sharing their strength and wisdom. When I jump back I'm tired and fall asleep aware of all the places Dean's body is touching mine.

Chapter Eight

Christian

I feel her on me and open my eyes. Jesus I need to get out of bed before she wakes up. My dick standing at attention will embarrass the shit out of her. I suspend her—slide out—then move the pillows over so she's comfortable. Lowering her—she moves her arms tighter around the pillow—but doesn't wake up.

Throwing on shorts I take Hawk for a run. I'm showered and dressed before she opens her eyes. "Morning babe. Coffee is on, but I didn't know what you wanted for breakfast." I lean over and kiss her surprised face.

She smiles. "You don't know what I want?"

I pull my hair back. "No. Nothing is clear with you. I don't like this. I could have had your breakfast made already."

She giggles. "I like it." When she sits up, she hugs me and I like that so I don't say anything. She doesn't hug me fast and move away like everyone else, she holds on and my dick jumps, but I don't let her go. I don't want to miss these little things.

"I'll make some eggs when I'm dressed." She puts her head on my shoulder as if she likes being in my arms. I'm glad she's comfortable right here, but I wish I could see her clear.

"I got it."

Fuck, she sits up. "I better get moving or I'll be late."

I should have kept my mouth shut. I stand up and lift her off the bed. "I'm glad you're here Dean." I bend and kiss her. My shorts almost cover her legs. It's cute.

She pulls away embarrassed. "Bad breath." Her face is red as she goes around me to the bathroom.

I shake my head and go start our breakfast. If she's embarrassed, she's not comfortable. It's a good indicator of where we stand. I hate not seeing her. I run through my people. Seeing some nervousness in the kids has me digging deeper. Phoenix is holding something for me. It has Beth clear, making me smile. When I jump to the reservation and find Aiyana—I'm pissed. I call Co, but keep breakfast going on autopilot.

"I need to keep her on the reservation Co. It isn't safe with paid bad men having her marked."

"She is headstrong, but understands my Warrior Protector. I will not arrange travel for her right now."

"We have threats coming at the MC and Princes today. I'll try to get people together so we can get back there maybe tomorrow." I'm thinking of the other Protectors and who can control. Maybe Mase and Colt. Then we'll need more to get them there. Jesus.

"As you will Christian. It will ease her mind." He's gone.

"I need to teach him goodbye."

"Who?"

I spin around and my breath catches. She's smiling with happy in her eyes. "You're beautiful babe."

She walks right over and lifts her face to me. I turn and shut the sausage off then lift her up against me so I can kiss her the right way. I'm hard in a New York minute. Jesus I need to control this. I put her down and put my hands on her face to kiss her lips. "I don't think I'll ever get enough." She smiles liking that or maybe she feels the same. "Sit baby, I'm almost done here."

She gets a cup and fills it with coffee. Shit, I should have made it for her. I'll remember tomorrow. While I'm getting the plates filled, I get Hawk his food. She laughs and I turn setting her plate down. She's watching the cup pour Hawk's food in his bowl.

I shrug and sit. "I have some other abilities."

She's wearing a cute little smirk. "So I see." She starts eating. "Thanks for breakfast. I'll do supper."

I nod watching her. Really, I'm trying to read her. She doesn't ask and I'm wondering why. "You're not going to ask?"

She shakes her head no. "You said you don't talk about abilities. Or maybe that was the kids." She shakes her head. "Either way you're not supposed to talk about them. I'll just watch for them."

I'm surprised, but nod. Okay. This isn't what I expected. I planned on telling her the obvious ones. I eat. When we're done, she stands to clean up. "Sit." I get everything cleaned up and the dishwasher packed while we sit and talk about the day. She's going to look up classes.

"You're sure it's okay?" She looks nervous.

"You don't need permission from me babe. Do whatever makes you happy."

She giggles. I love that sound. "You make me happy."

I love hearing that too and lean over to kiss her. "I'll take you to work. Once I order the car, Jax needs to get it tracked. I'll bring you another cuff tonight. It will keep you safe."

She nods, but her forehead scrunches making little creases across it. "I don't have a license, so I don't think I need a car."

"How do you not have a license?"

192

She smiles. "I can drive, but I never took the test."

"I'll get the car to Jax and we'll get you a license. You need to be able to come and go as you please. Being chained to the Compound isn't a life babe. What kind of car do you want and what color?"

She gives me a smile. "Smallish and blue."

"You want a smaller SUV?" I like that idea, she's so damn tiny, at least she'd be able to see in front of her.

"I've never had a car so whatever you think."

I smile. "Blue, fun and sporty SUV."

She laughs. "Okay then. I need to get to work."

She does. I take her hand and walk her out. "The gate Hawk." He starts running while we get on my HS bike and follow. At the gate, I tell the guard I'm at the school for an hour then I'll need an HS shuttle to Security.

Walking into the school I call Uncle Danny. "I wanted to thank you for finishing the house yesterday. It's perfect."

"Glad you like it. You were easy. Your girl like it?" How the fuck does he know about Dean? "Jessie called last night."

I laugh. Right. "She loves it."

"You got a date?" He's fuckin' nuts.

"After two days? No. Bye." I swipe the phone off while he yells something about wasting time. Fuckin' crazy bastard. Two fuckin' days.

I let Dean's hand go and pick up Nash. "Hey little buddy. You're here early." Dean walks into the classroom. I watch her go—thinking about getting another kiss before I leave. I'm turning into quite the pussy and smile at the thought.

"Prez has us all in early. He said we have a warning," Taylor says from behind me.

I turn to look at him. "The meeting still at nine?"

He nods. "Inner circle is meeting first." Dakota isn't telling them anything so I don't know what that's all about. "Beth wants you to come to dinner tonight. She's asking Serenity too."

"We aren't making dinner tonight Taylor. Shit is going to hit us hard." Phoenix is waiting by the classroom door. I feel him trying to connect and throw to him that I'll see him next.

Taylor is watching me, trying to figure out how to ask so I answer. "The old ladies need cover. The kids need extra Security today and you need to make sure HS has good tags. They'll try to take out HS so they can get at the kids and old ladies."

He nods. "I'll let Prez know." I can't tell him Beth will be clear, but it would ease his mind. We need that fierce fight today so I leave it alone and let it happen as it should.

"I need to see Phoenix."

He kisses Nash's head. "Love you little dude." He looks at me. Wondering if he should ask for more, but he doesn't. "You want Hawk at Security?"

"Not yet." He watches me for a second then heads toward the kitchen. He'll run the tunnel today. They'll see a lot of action down there. I hope to Christ we're ready.

In the classroom, I put Nash down and take Phoenix's hand leading him out to the empty daycare room. He's throwing me what he picked up and I let him get it all out. I throw it was from another's vision and shows a good end to a bad day. He nods with a smile. He asks in my head if everyone stays safe today. I'm glad he asked because it shows he understands that what they're seeing isn't a whole picture. "We will do what we do and work to keep everyone

194

safe. It will be scary, but you need to trust in your fathers and work to keep the Little Brothers safe. I need all of you to look out for each other. Yeah?" He isn't happy with the answer, but he understands. He hugs me and goes back to the classroom having never said a word.

I shake my head smiling and wait for Mucimi and Aquyà to come in and sit. I don't wait long before Mucimi is throwing pictures at me fast. "I know little man. Slow down and sit." Aquyà waits at the door. "You too Aquyà."

I think of my wording and start. "Today the MC and Princes will be hit. Because of what can happen I can only say so much to prepare them for that. Phoenix gave me some information that tells me one will be saved. I need that to happen as it will and will do everything possible to make sure everyone else is safe and nothing alters the future. You need to trust in our fathers to do their jobs. This is no different than any other war we've had. They're very good at their jobs. Mucimi, I need to talk to Aquyà. You throw to me if you need me little man, but I see everything you do. I need you to trust that I'm doing the right thing—even if you don't understand. Yeah?"

He gives me a nod and gets up. As he's walking out Aquyà throws, 'He's worried. He's too small to worry so much.'

"He is. We'll work on that, but for today I need you to focus on keeping the Little Brothers safe." He nods so I go on. "Brandon knows how to get in the tunnels. You use them if you need them and get everyone to Security. Hit your watch twice so Ops knows you're moving and take the dogs with you. Holly and Dean need to follow. Yeah?" He nods so serious. "We will use everything we have—including the Little Brothers. It's the way we've always worked. I know it will be scary, but you need to lead them today. Use Mucimi to calm everyone. If he's focused on that he'll get less of what's happening."

I get another nod and put my fist out. "Good luck Little Brother."

"I love you Christian." He hits my fist and hugs me.

I see he has the vision running through his head. "Love you too Aquyà."

When he leaves, I call Uncle Steve. "You need Devan and Colt running today. Elizabeth, Harley and Blake are a help with HS beside Blake. I'm pulling Blaze to Ops. She's a focused reader that will also be a help for you."

"You takin' Mase?"

His mind is running so fast I can't grab at anything. "Yeah, we need him here. They'll try to knock out HS first. Cover the kids and old ladies."

"Sendin' Mase with Cloud. Anythin' else."

"Jeremy needs to stay with Aubrey. Together they keep each other safe. Blaze will help with that. That's all I can give you right now."

"This isn't just church pussies." He's not asking so I don't answer. "Good luck Brother," he tells me.

"Thanks VP. We're going to need it."

He's gone, so I connect with Aiyana. She's still pissed about the pipeline. Jesus. This is like walking through the Club. I have to choreograph all the people just to get to the fuckin' door. 'I need help Aiyana. We don't have Protectors here like the MC. I need everything you have focused on us today. Anywhere you can freely step in will be a help.'

'I'll be there Christian. There is much hate today. Will it be enough?'

'I'm counting on it my Warrior Princess. Together we can make it through this. I need everyone.'

'I will have help in Co and Kaya. Be safe my Warrior Protector.' She's already moving to talk to them.

I take a deep breath and hope to fuck this works. We've never fought like this. Coordinating everyone is one thing. Getting them to fight with all they have is another. I jump and let the ancestors settle me—which they do. Whatever I'm doing is helpful.

I go over everything in my head and see a couple of problems with me being in two places at once. I'm going to need Mase's help. 'Je, I need you with Aubrey today. You keep each other safe however you can Brother. Blaze will be at Ops, you need to listen to her today, it's important that you do.'

"I will Christian. She saw.' He sounds upset.

Fuck. 'You can do this. Stay with her, no matter what is happening around you, you stay with Aubrey.'

'Yeah. Good Luck Christian.'

'Love ya, Je. Stay safe.'

'Kuwômôyush.'

I find my girl and kiss her like it will be the last time, hoping it isn't the last time. "I'll be late babe. Follow Aquyà today. He knows what to do." She gives me an odd look, but nods. I wish to fuck I could read her. Leaving Hawk with the kids feels right. They'll need any extra protection I can get them.

When I get to my bike Aaron is waiting. "I'm just shuttle and going for the Security meeting."

I nod and we fly through the streets to Security. Since Aaron is Uncle Danny's he has no problem riding hard and fast. I never get shit from him and today that's a relief. I don't need shit today. I run everything through my head again as we're walking into Security. Running with Mase should give us the help we need. Aiyana is a bonus. I need to talk to Devan, Ally, Terry and Jacob after the meeting.

In my office, I call Uncle Danny. "A tractor trailer will cross your path today. Do. Not. Shoot it. Don't shoot *any* box trucks. Get them up to Baxter's to unload before VP sees what's in them. Blake can help you with that."

"Anything else?"

"Rich may be helpful."

"Thanks Brother. Good Luck." He didn't ask about a date so I look in. They're in a meeting of their own. Perfect.

I do a time check and walk to the meeting room. I see everyone in Prez's and thumb in that one. Taylor and Aaron aren't here. I throw chin and sit. I'm a little nervous now about how this will all play out.

"Good night Brother?" Prez asks.

I smile. "Yeah. I love the house and Dean stayed with me."

He nods happy for me. I like seeing him so clear. "I can't read her though. Last night got harder, but today I don't get anything. It's like a complete block."

"I can't read Lily either. It's just the way it works. I think it evens the playing field and keeps us working for our women," he says and Dakota laughs.

I look at Dakota. "Women will always be a mystery to men. This is no different Christian. If you cannot read her you are too close. That is not a bad thing, but a very good one."

I smile. "Yeah." Being closer to her is a good thing in my book.

"Since Dakota isn't in an answering mood today, do you have anything for us?" Prez is frustrated, but not mad.

Dakota is blocking me so I look Prez in the eye. "It's going to be bad. There are things we can do to make that easier. Mase is getting dropped by my dad. He'll need to run with Aaron or Jessie. Taylor needs his gear, but he'll be helpful in the tunnels later. They'll aim for HS first. Dakota needs to cover." I look at Dakota. "Don't shoot the trucks. They expect us to run like we have in the past. We need to change that." Dakota nods and looks at Prez so I do. "If the kids need to move, Aquyà will alert Ops he's on the move. They can disable the guns and make it to the tunnels. The MC is aware of the trucks and what I could tell them. I'll call Devan and Ally when we're done here. Aiyana, Co and Kaya will help where they can."

He has everything running in his head then he runs through what I said again. Jessie leans forward. "What can Aiyana do? Are they hit too?"

I shake my head no. "They'll help here. We don't have the Protectors here like Mass does. Aiyana and Kaya can help here with Co guiding them."

He doesn't understand and I don't know what he needs to know versus what he can know so I look at Prez for help. 'I don't know what to tell him.'

He smiles. "Freaky kid shit Jessie. They'll be on the reservation, but can help with their abilities here. It's fuckin' crazy." He looks at me. "Jeremy?"

"Focused on keeping people and Aubrey safe." He gets it. I wait for the questions he's got going through his head.

"You see what I'm thinking. If you can't answer don't. Is there anything else that I need here?"

"Me to stress *don't* shoot the trucks and *don't* run the same plays you've used before."

His head cocks to the side. "This isn't the religious fanatics?"

199

I think about what I can say. "The group has been watched and now have others mixed in their groups collecting information and watching their next moves. At first, it's the lunatics. After is the plans of a bigger group with an MC axe to grind." Dakota sits up and I stop. Prez takes note of how that worked and throws me chin. He gets it without me explaining anymore. It's not ours to tell.

They start talking about the run on Saturday. Since I'm going, I listen while I get some coffee from the side table. Taylor and Aaron come in.

"Everything is set, if we need them, they're secure," Taylor says walking toward me. I hand him the cup and make another.

"Thanks Brother." He sits and I see he's talking about securing the tunnels.

I didn't think of that and I had Aquyà using them before I even knew if they were safe. I sit thinking I need to pay better attention to the details.

"You talked to Aiyana, Jeremy, the MC and the kids all before you got here. You don't need to think of everything. That's on me. You get your Protectors ready and tell me where I can help or the plans you've made. I'll do the rest. It takes every one of us to do this Christian." I nod and realize he's right. "Jason get the boards up and Brantley explain what we've got so far."

The lunatics don't have a good plan, but they know a lot of HS patterns, all the family and readers with Darren, Jessie, Sheila, Aaron and Brantley mixed in. From what the board shows they think all family are readers.

Prez gives us a plan and warns about shooting the trucks and not being predictable. He has to explain to Taylor and Aaron and stresses watching for the Teams. I'm surprised when he tells us Driscoll will run the PD while Jax is running some high-ranking officers as Security for us. This is more than I saw and I'm glad for the help. It's another layer to get through. When he tells Dakota he's flying, Dakota throws him chin making me smile.

When he's done, he looks around the table taking everyone's thoughts in. "Are there any questions?"

"Who is Christian partnered with?" Brantley asks.

I didn't think of that either. "Jessie," Prez says like it was already decided.

I look in and see that it was. Dakota did tell them something. I look at him and throw him chin getting it back with a smile. I may live yet. He laughs.

Prez watches not catching what passed between us. "Jessie and Aaron are running with the Protectors. I'm on Air Ops, but we'll be working with you to make sure nothing gets dropped. Jessie will get information through to me if I need it."

I nod thanking the ancestors he thought of that too. He looks around again. "Anything else?"

I wait until everyone is filing out and stop Aaron. "Mase is HS. He works with VP when he's on. I don't know if he'll just start throwing to you, but he'll need to focus on what he's doing. He's good or VP wouldn't let him run."

He's good with Mase. "You don't have to convince me, Christian. I was one that helped train him."

"I didn't know that. Sorry Brother."

He nods thinking I was going through shit myself. "Is he going to fly?"

I laugh. "Suspend. He may."

Mase is waiting in the hall. "Dad said you wanted me here. I can't believe VP okayed it."

"I'm the only one here. We'll need the help. I need to talk to Devan and Jacob. Grab some coffee and something to eat and meet me in my office."

He's glad to be here and wonders if we'll need more help. I let it go and call to Jacob to bring Terry up. On the way, I call Devan and tell him the plan and what to watch out for. He's ready and Pres brought him into their Security meeting. He didn't know what he could tell them so he didn't say anything. He's a smart Brother. VP is running Protector Ops and he's relieved. The questions he has never get spoken. I tell him what I can and hang up as Jacob and Terry come in.

"Leave it open for Mase," I tell Terry walking toward the meeting room.

"Jeremy is worried," Jacob says sitting down.

I nod and wave Mase in. "He needs to focus on Aubrey today. It won't be easy with everything that's going on."

He talks to Jeremy about getting his shit together and keeping their girl safe. I wait for him, looking at Mase and Terry. Since they know what he's doing they don't have a problem waiting. When he checks back in, I tell them the plan and what I can of what we'll be dealing with. I let Mase know we'll have help in Aiyana. He's relieved. Jacob doesn't have a problem running with Prez and Terry's head is clear and relaxed.

"Any questions?"

Mase raises his hand and Jacob laughs. "Do Aaron and Jessie know what's coming?"

"No and we can't tell them. I can't give them that without changing what's meant to be." I see his concern, but he understands. None of them want to chance another Aubrey nightmare.

"If no one has any questions, Jacob and Terry you can get to Ops and watch for vehicles coming in. They've been smart about tracking, you'll want to keep a close eye on any vehicles just roaming, even if they're not tagged." They throw chin and come around to my side of the table. I stand knowing why.

Jacob hugs me. "Good luck Christian. Keep Jessie close. I'd like to see you tomorrow." He lets go quick and steps back.

"I just got the girl. I'm not going out that easy Jay."

He watches me then nods. "Kuwômôyush." He walks away and I can see how hard this is for him. The threat of losing Aubrey and me is a lot to handle, but he's determined to do everything he can to stop that from happening.

"Love you too Jay." I smile hearing him give Jeremy a pep talk as he's leaving.

When I turn, Terry is standing in front of me. "I know I don't get everything the others do, but I know enough to be worried. Stay safe Brother. Kuwômôyush." He man hugs me and walks away.

I look at Mase and see tears in his eyes. I turn away. "It will all work out Mase."

"Has anyone gotten a change for the vision?"

"No, but the ancestors were encouraging."

He stands up pissed. "Not on my watch Brother. Stay away from the fuckin' trucks. Jessie should know so he can be prepared."

I shake my head no. "There's more at stake here Mase. We need to keep clear heads and just do the job. Your job is clearing the threat any way you can. Don't hold back and show no mercy Brother. If we all work together we can get rid of this threat and have a beer with Prez at the Club."

"Does he know about the visions?" He's only got bits and pieces, but they're running through his head.

"Not all, no. We just need to do the job Mase. I'm not chancing the kids or old ladies to save a Brother. They wouldn't want that and we can't guarantee the outcome."

He watches me and I see him weighing my words. "I'll do everything I can Christian. No matter what happens I won't quit Brother. I'll work until it's done."

I hug him. "Kuwômôyush."

"I'm headed to the locker room. Call to me when it's time." He walks toward the door.

"Mase." He stops, but doesn't turn. "I'm proud of you little brother. Out of everyone I could have chosen I knew you'd understand the dangers of saying too much and you're fuckin' fierce when you need it. Don't hold back. Throw everything you can at these pussies. Aaron will have your back and he can't wait to see you suspend."

He laughs and continues walking. I blow out a breath and plop down on the seat. When I open my mind, I see the visions playing through. The only one that's changed is Beth. If that's all we get today, it's still worth it.

I call to Nunánuk asking for the strength and peace of the ancestors for all of the Blackhawks today. She eases my mind saying, 'Mucimi Christian.'

I head to Ops with a smile.

Jessie throws his leg over watching me to make sure I got all he's said. I throw him chin to go on. "Reload is with a relay team of HS. They'll take our place and we drop back to reload. There's one per town." He's got nothing else for directions, but knows I'm not the only one destined to die today. I wait for him to ask knowing that I can't answer. "Aquyà asked who becomes President if the Officers die. Are we all fighting for our lives today?"

It's not the question that was in the front of his mind and it throws me. "I would say that's every day. We fight for good every day Jessie. This is just another day."

"Fuckin' cryptic messages." He starts his bike.

I smile thinking life is rarely simple, but every day there are those moments that cause a simple smile. "Fuckin' A, Jessie. Fuckin' A."

He laughs and looks behind him. Our Team is ready to roll.

Jessie: "Ghost to Protector Ops, Team One readied."

Jacob: "Ghost you're on with Lightfoot on lead and Mimer on control. Roll on my one. Three, two, one."

We roll out heading toward the highway. While there are no tagged vehicles congregating, there are too many cars and trucks that seem to have no destination. Darren has Jax move PD closer to them.

I see a vision of Jeremy throwing shit at a car, just trying to keep ahead of it. 'Speed up and come at him. Run offense Je. Aubrey can throw with you.'

Our boards light up and Jacob is moving Mase and Aaron. I throw to Jessie we need to move.

Jacob: "Team One move toward the Compound. Coder has a utility truck moving fast."

Jessie: "Roger Lightfoot."

A box truck turns right in front of us and Jessie raises his gun.

"No! Stand down!" I move the truck and hold the driver. "Lightfoot get someone on the truck. I won't be able to hold him much longer."

Jacob: "Roger Guardian. The utility truck is thirty seconds out."

Fuck. This is earlier than I thought. Fuckin' lunatics can't even keep a schedule.

Jacob: "Prez said to tell you the kids are moving everyone to the kitchen."

Me: "Roger Lightfoot. Ghost we're running out of time. I can't hold the driver Jay." I start moving cars out of our way and speed up.

Jacob: "Security has him Guardian." I move to the middle of the road and stop everything from coming close to me.

Jessie: "Roger Lightfoot. He's off the fuckin' chart Brother."

Jacob: "The utility truck is in the gate and a couple of feet through the front door Ghost." Fuck!

'Aquyà get out of the building. Get in the tunnel now!' I see Sheila shooting as a van pulls in, fuckin' pussies are running out of the back. Done is right behind her, but falls. Jesus someone is in the building. I throw it to Sheila and she spins around ducking behind the truck. That was too fuckin' close.

We take the corner and Jessie's shooting at everyone. I pull right to the door and run in. Aquyà isn't going down. He throws Mucimi and Holly. She's got the baby, but won't move from the pantry. Mucimi is trying to pull her out. 'Push. I'm here Mucimi, make her go.'

A shot just misses my head and I duck throwing a shield around me. I turn, but no one is there. At the kitchen, I see Holly walking toward the basement door shaking her head no. "Go!" She runs holding the baby against her. Shit, I wish we could have prepared them.

Mucimi veers toward me and a pussy steps out, pointing a gun at him. "The most dangerous one of all." His finger moves and I throw fire then roll pain through him starting at his head so he can't think.

206

I raise and move Mucimi away from the pussy then set him down at the door with Aquyà. I don't want to leave the lunatic to go closer to them. "Go! Get to Security. I'll reset the sensor here. Keep moving Little Brothers. You did good." I look at the pussy then back at them as the door closes.

Jessie moves to the sensor control and looks at me. "Get the fire out before the building goes up."

I shoot the pussy then throw water at him. "Done was shot," I tell him.

"Where the fuck did you get water?"

What? "I don't know. Is Done okay?" I see the kids close the tunnel door and breathe easier. "They're in the tunnel."

"He was taken to Nick, a shot high on his leg, he'll be okay." He throws the switch on the sensor.

I nod. "They're clear. Cade is down there with them." 'Good job Aquyà.' I throw to my little guy and turn. "We need to get to the town center."

Jessie: "Team One clear. We're moving to the town center."

Jacob: "Roger Ghost. VP has Enforcer on the clinic."

I push it away and find Mase. 'A truck is coming your way. They're going to try to block the Security building. I'm four out.'

Mase: "Roger Guardian."

At the bikes, Jessie puts his hand on my arm. "What did you say to him?"

"I'm four out. We need to go now." I start my bike and roll to the gate.

"We go together Brother."

"Always." I look back and watch them roll up to me.

He throws chin and I'm off. "Jesusfuckin'Christ." I don't hear what he says to Jacob as I'm clearing our path. The MC just had a truck blow, BS was hit and we have a truck that's going to blow if we don't make it. I throw a pussy raising his gun from a doorway to Jessie and hear the shot, but keep moving.

Jessie: "Ghost clear. Send Clean-up Lightfoot."

Jacob: "Roger Ghost."

'Dakota they're trying to block the Security building. Watch for anything getting close. Do not shoot the trucks.'

'Roger Guardian.'

A minivan flies out of a side street and I veer away pushing it back. I throw the driver to Jessie and hear him tell Tag to shoot him. 'Mase, we're coming up to the Café.'

Mase: "West two blocks, north one, Guardian."

Jacob: "Two trucks Guardian! One is stolen from the Brewery."

Me: "Get someone stopping traffic around Security. Eagle Eye stand ready. Do NOT hit the trucks HS."

Dakota: "I will thank you in advance Brothers. The trucks are expensive."

I hear people laughing, but push it away and call to Aiyana. 'I need help Aiyana. The trucks are loaded with explosives. They're going to try to level the Security building. I only see after. Help me clear the trucks then keep Security clear. If you have to, focus on shielding the building just do that.'

'We have time my Warrior Protector.'

Thank fuck. "Mase focus on the truck. I got the driver. We need it away from the buildings."

Mase: "Roger Guardian. I can stop it, but can't move it alone."

Me: "We have help. Stop it now!" I hear Prez talking, but have the driver held and push the truck from the corner. "Help me Aiyana!" The truck lifts and slides to the center of the road. "Lightfoot get the driver and someone to drive the truck to the service road behind the Club."

Jacob: "Roger Guardian. Second truck four blocks south."

Me: "I need the driver cleared Jay I can't do both."

Jessie: "43 take the pussy until he's picked up. Go Christian."

As soon as 43 has the door open I hit the throttle. There are fewer cars and that makes thinking easier. The visions aren't fuckin' quitting and we're running out of time. 'Aiyana shield the building. Just like with the water protectors. Make a wall.'

'We are Christian.'

"Mase we clear the truck then shield the building. Prez we need your help. I need the kids to help shield the building."

Prez: "Roger Guardian." I see him walking out of Ops. Thank fuck he didn't ask questions.

As we come up to the truck it swerves and tips with two wheels off the ground. "NO! Mase stop the car!" I slow and push with everything in me. The driver turns the wheel and the truck leans heavy on me. "Mase!"

'We cannot leave the building Christian.'

"Mase has it Aiyana. Stay with Prez."

When the truck is back on four wheels I look at the driver and roll energy through him. He falls forward. Jessie opens the door and shoots him.

Jessie: "Truck to the service road Lightfoot."

Jacob: "Roger Ghost."

Jessie looks at me. "Where to?"

"There are two more, but I need to get to Security." I see Sheila shooting in front of the clinic. "Beth is clear."

Jessie: "Get VP to move Enforcer to clearing the two trucks Lightfoot. We're at Security."

Jacob: "We don't have the trucks Ghost." I throw a yellow flash on Terry's board marking the trucks. "Got it Guardian."

Jessie flies by me heading for Security. "Stay away from the building."

Jessie: "Roger Guardian."

I pull up to him and roll into the lot. He stops when I do and stands with me. "Tell us what to do."

I look at him and sit down. "Throw me everything in you, we need energy to cover the building."

He looks at Tag and 43. "You heard him. Jump into Never Never Land and help shield the building."

I almost smile, but see the kids. "Throw Little Brothers all together. Push together." I feel it as soon as they do. "Keep going. See the shield cover the building and push Little Brothers."

Jacob: "Christian!"

"No, we shield the building Jay. Keep pushing Little Brothers."

Jacob: "Ghost a car is coming toward you. Everyone is every fuckin' where."

Since they aren't adding much energy I focus on the building and let them go. 'Dakota I never made it here Brother. Tell me what I need to do.'

'Shield the building. I am sorry Christian.'

I push his sorry away seeing the truck at the north side of the building. "Push NOW!"

My arm is pulled. "NO! Don't touch me I need the energy!" Hands are all over me. I push the energy to the shield and feel the ground shake. "Don't let go Prez!"

Jessie yells and I'm dragged a few feet. They're shooting and yelling, but I'm pushing everything to the shield. My body is screaming in pain and I throw it. Another explosion rocks the ground and Jessie's hands are on me again.

'Christian!' Justice screams.

Jessie's pulling me again. My world is out of focus and I'm fighting to get it back.

"Christian! Stay with me Brother. You did it. They're clear. Prez said Aiyana sees them clear."

I open my eyes and focus on his words. "They're clear. MC got hit again. One from Security is dead and one BS shot."

"Jesusfuckin'Christ. What do you need Brother?"

I can't see what the fuck is happening here. "Mucimi and the Little Brothers. I can't move Jessie."

"I got you Christian. Jessie get the door. Darren get Dakota here," Prez says. I didn't feel him close.

I'm lifted and moan. Jesus I hurt. I wake up in Prez's meeting room. On the table to be exact. Fuck. Dakota has the boys around me. "I'm good Dakota."

He gives me a sad look. "You are good Christian, but you are not fine. Nick will be here soon. You have a

211

broken leg and many bruises. The boys and Kaya are helping with what we can."

I nod. "Are we clear Dakota?"

I get the sad smile again. "We are. Devan has Aiyana working with Blaze and the Protectors. They will be clear soon. I could not shoot the trucks without losing Brothers Christian."

He's worried? "We did it Dakota. The building is still here. Everyone is safe. I didn't see this far."

"We wouldn't let you go Christian," Justice says and I laugh then moan.

"Thanks, Little Brothers." Mucimi climbs up and lays his head on me. I close my eyes glad for the heat rolling through me.

I feel Dean before my eyes open. "Babe."

"Right here Christian. A doctor is here. The boys went to get him."

I open my eyes and see the worry on her face. "I got this babe. I'll be fine."

Dakota laughs. "He will be." He leans over me. My neck is sore so I'm glad he does. "There is a concern of Nick touching you. Prez is worried about the energy. Brantley had to be removed. I do not think he would have let Nick do what must be done for you." I smile trying to see it. "Pain clouds your vision."

I nod and hurt so I stop that shit. Jesus. "The boys can help."

"Prez thought the same thing. They will travel with us. Co said the ancestors are happy today Christian. You have done well in their eyes."

I smile. It's always good to keep them happy. He smiles, but something is sad in that smile. I can't focus to see what's going on. "Is everyone okay?"

Nick comes in and I hear the boys moving around the table. "Fuck you look like you got hit by a car Brother."

I look at him then back to Dakota. "Who did we lose?"

Prez leans over me. "Hawk, Christian. He broke through the door and was running to you when the second truck hit."

Hawk? No. My heart stops and breath catches. Hawk. I jump hearing Dakota tell them I'm with the ancestors. I go to Nunánuk. She's waiting on the rock at her lake. "It is good to see my warriors together."

What? I look behind me and see the boys and Prez. "We aren't letting go," he says.

I turn away and wipe my eyes taking a steadying breath. "Thanks, Prez." They sit with me and I feel the strength in them. It's flowing to me freely with the ancestors' calming presence. "He died trying to save me."

"He did Christian. He died with you in the first vision, but Dakota couldn't shield him while flying. We didn't know until it was too late. I'm sorry Christian," Prez says gently.

I nod and look away. He was my only companion for years. RIP Brother. I feel a peace flowing through me. "Nunánuk is Hawk here with the ancestors?"

Mucimi puts his hand on my face and turns me so I'm looking across the lake. "Hawk!" My tears fall and I fly to him landing on his back. "I'm so fuckin' glad to see you Brother." He barks making me laugh. "Thank you Nunánuk and my fathers for giving me this peace." I feel everything run through me warm like the love from my family. They are my family. "Take me home Hawk." He runs and I hold on for dear life. At the rock, he jumps and I almost go flying.

The boys laugh. "Now he's mucimi Christian," Mucimi says and I smile. He is.

"Hawk will keep me company my grandsons, go see your Shaman so he can heal your bones my Warrior Protector. We will see you when you return." Nunánuk stands and I watch as Hawk moves beside her.

"As you will Nunánuk. Thank you my all-seeing Shaman." I throw her my appreciation getting a smile before they walk down to the pathway. I look at Prez. "I'm ready. I got this Prez. Thank you, Protectors."

The boys nod and we jump. Nick has a stretcher waiting and Prez and Dakota move me. The boys climb in the ambulance with Dean and Dakota and I close my eyes seeing Hawk with Nunánuk.

Dean

I stand back with tears in my eyes, but not where he can see. The guy got run over and lost his dog. Now he's here and has to fight the mind-numbing feeling of being touched by the doctor and Beth. This day can't possibly get any worse. I broke my wrist when I was fourteen and passed out from doctors touching me. He's so much stronger than I am, but damn!

"Dean?"

I wipe my eyes and move forward so he can see me. "Here."

He puts his hand out and I look at where the boys are touching him. I can't handle all that. "It will be okay."

214

I look at his eyes. I can actually see his pain and my heart breaks all over again. Moving closer I take his hand. "I am so sorry Christian." I see Hawk with an old woman.

Dakota laughs. "Nunánuk, his grandmother, Shaman of the Connecticut reservation. Hawk is with the ancestors of Christian's tribe. He will be a source of comfort and peace for Christian, always and forever."

"Mucimi," I say amazed by these people. Holly told me that's what Mucimi's name actually means. I like the thought of Christian having Hawk forever. When I look back at Christian he's smiling with that pain still in his eyes. "I'm so glad you have that. What can I do for you Christian?" With these incredible people around him, I doubt I have anything he needs. I could have lost him today. I throw up doors and decide I'm not wasting a minute with him. Every minute we have should count. My dad always said that, *make the small things count as much as the big things*. I'm doing that.

"Keep his hand Nadine. The relief of seeing Hawk with Nunánuk does not shield him from the loss of him in our world." Dakota squeezes our connected hands and steps away.

I see it on his face and decide they'll need more than the Security they have here to move me. Jessie's face floats through my head. Okay so he would be enough, but he's not here. The kids laugh. "Stop reading me."

"My dad would help you hold on Dean. He wouldn't take you out," Aquyà says so serious.

I can't believe such sweet boys came from the scary looking guy, but I nod hoping he's right. Dakota walks out laughing.

Christian passes out when Nick and Beth's hands are on him and I feel their touch. I have to let go, but don't move away. Beth puts a heavy shield on me while they X-ray his chest, but doesn't ask me to leave. It takes hours to get

215

everything X-rayed and his leg in a cast. Dakota stands right with the kids helping with the energy, but Christian still passes out a couple of times worrying me.

When we are getting ready to leave, Prez walks in with Jessie. I almost stick my tongue out at him for being too late to move me, but catch it and smile. He has no idea what I'm thinking. I blame it on nerves. Prez smiles at me. "We need to get him to the Club for status. You're welcome to join us."

The Club? He got run over today. He nods. "You can always read me?"

"Yes."

"Then you know I'm not leaving him. If Jessie couldn't move me, you have no chance."

They all laugh. "Glad you're with him," Jessie says surprising me. "Someone needs to keep his fuckin' stubborn ass in line. He doesn't listen to me."

I smile. Maybe he is a big teddy bear. While they're laughing Prez and Dakota get him in an SUV. He isn't saying a word and I wonder if it's the loss of Hawk or if he's in pain. With his leg stretched out on the seat and bruises everywhere, it could be pain. Since they do things so different than anyone I have ever met, I don't know what to do, or say. Demanding they bring us home doesn't feel right and the scary guy is right here this time. I hold his hand and sit quiet. Christian isn't afraid to say what's on his mind. I'll wait until he says different. Then I'll pitch a fit.

Christian laughs drawing my eyes to his. "Prez threw what you're thinking. Shield Dean." Damn! I nod. "I need to have a beer and the shot in honor of Hawk." The pain is there. I don't just see it in his eyes, but feel it too.

I just nod. This is important and I thank Prez for making sure he gets what he needs. They know more than I do. I need to keep my thoughts to myself so they don't see how stupid they are. I move lifting off the seat and kiss him.

His hand lets mine go and he's holding my cheeks kissing me back. Holy Cow! "Thank you." He doesn't say anymore and I have no idea why he's thanking me so I nod again.

The Club is loud, the guys are huge and the women are so sweet. Except for Sheila—she isn't scary, just funny. I think she's sweet too, but I can't say it. Apparently, the reasons are a mystery, but the word can't be used with the Brothers or Sheila and Eliza. I learned that too. All men are Brothers and Sheila and Eliza think they are Brothers too. Jess said they aren't, but I don't want to ask and cause trouble. They have a lot of rules for bikers. I thought bikers didn't have any rules and that's what made them dangerous.

"We live by a different code than other people. So, all the Brothers are governed by those rules, but not the rules of society. Thank fuckin' Christ because society is going fuckin' crazy." I look at the guy. I've seen his picture. "Mase, Christian's favorite Brother."

Everyone around us laughs. "I'm Dean. It's nice to meet you, but I thought Brantley was his favorite." His smile falters and I smile. "Just messing with you. Stop reading me." There's more laughing, but I don't care. If I don't tell them it's not cool, how would they know?

"Touch affects her," Christian says to Mase then hugs him and leans back against the bar. "Thanks for saving our asses Brother." I feel the emotion flowing from them. They're a close family like me and Serenity.

Mase shakes his head. "It was all you Christian. I'm just glad I got called to help." He looks at me then back at Christian. "Are we clear now?"

"For a while. Is Dad picking you up?"

"They had some losses so he needs to be there. He'll be here tomorrow morning. I'll stay at Jacob's."

I can't read him. He must be one of the Protectors like Christian. He laughs and looks at me. "I'm not even close to him, but I'm working on it. I am a Protector, but we're all different with different abilities and focus."

I nod and think he needs to stop reading me if I can't read him. He laughs again. "Christian needs to teach you how to block better."

"With all the readers here, I'm not learning fast enough."

Everyone cheers and I look at what they're cheering for, but I only see a wall of men looking at the door. I rise up in the air for a few seconds and see Prez walking toward the middle of the room then I'm lowered again. This is so cool! I step on the rung of a stool and kiss my biker boyfriend for being so nice. "Thank you."

He laughs. "Anytime baby. I'm shielding for you right now. If it gets to be too much tell me." I nod, but look around. A war cry goes out and I'm stunned. Christian squeezes my hand and points to Dakota. "Just getting everyone to quiet down."

"Brothers, we have had a day! It seems this month has been riddled with one fight after another. Thankfully the Protectors are standing with us from the MC and the reservation. For those that haven't seen them in action I'm sure Brantley will have some video floating around." Everyone laughs, but I look at Christian. He's really going to show the abilities. I want to see.

Mase laughs and kisses my head giving me a zap. "Don't fuck it up. I like her."

Prospects are handing everyone a shot glass. Christian takes two and gives me one so seriously I don't even try to tell him I've never had a shot. When everything quiets down Prez goes on. "The vision had Security hit with the Officers, kids and two old ladies inside. We were supposed to lose all of us, another old lady, Aubrey, Jeremy and Christian. With the Protectors knowing the trucks held explosives we lost one. Most of you have seen Hawk with Christian. He's been a constant companion and Security for Christian since he was eleven. The loss cuts deep Brothers. To our Security Brother Hawk."

Everyone says, "To Hawk." I take a sip and think this is not making it down my throat. I hand it to Christian and he swallows it in one gulp. I guess that's how you do it. His arm goes around me and I think about my parents. All I wanted was someone to hold me. I hold onto his arm across my stomach hoping it's a comfort for him.

After a minute or so Prez goes on. "We have Done on the injured list. He took a shot to the leg and Nick just told me he's doing fine. Christian got hit by a car shielding the Officers, kids, old ladies and Brothers in the Security building. As you can see he's here and will be fine after some down time. Outside of Security is a mess. It took two hits, but did not get close enough to damage the building. Thanks again to the help of our Protectors." A cheer goes up. Prez holds his hand up.

"Brothers." Everyone quiets, but the Prospects are handing out shots again. I never finished the first. "The MC did not fare so well. MC-Baxter's sustained some damage to the corner of their building, but I'm told it's not too bad. They had loss as well and quite a few injuries. BS26, name is Johnny, was lost today. Also, a Security Brother, Hank Mello. After the run Saturday, Hawk will be buried in Mass and we have some Brothers showing for Johnny and Hank's family. You can get the details from the website tomorrow. To our Brothers Hank and Johnny."

"To Hank and Johnny!" everyone says again. They must do this a lot.

219

"Today we kept our towns safe. Nothing touched the town's people. Your training and skill made sure of it. Pres sends his thanks to us for sharing Christian's knowledge and training. He said today would not have ended quite so well without either. Please remember the Brothers that have passed and our injured. Have a drink, go home to your families, hang with your Brothers. Whatever you do be happy knowing your skill and training got us through another one. I'm proud to call you mine and will be happy to see you all tomorrow."

Everyone grumbles, but it isn't heartfelt by the smiles they're wearing and Prez laughs. "Whatever you decide to do, have a good time Brothers." A cheer goes up and everyone is loud again.

I turn toward Christian. "What an awesome thing to do. I'm so proud of you Christian!" He hugs me and I hold on.

"Brother." I step back and turn, but Christian keeps me against his side with an arm around my back. "There is no way for me to thank you for what you did today. You made sure everyone in my family made it out alive. I am so fuckin' proud of you Christian. You had no time to get what you pulled off today done, but you did it. Brace yourself Brother. It deserves more than the hug I'm giving you, but that's all I thought of so far."

Christian laughs and lets me go leaning forward. "It's enough. Thanks Prez and thanks for handling Hawk."

"Love you Brother." Prez lets him go and steps back.

Jessie steps close to us. "I'm on watch. Dakota said you're not a hundred percent. If they get too close, I've got it."

I smile. He is a big teddy bear. Mase laughs and bends to my ear. "He's a deadly Brother, but for his family and Brothers he's always got their backs. No one will get

220

close to Christian and he can relax, drink or just leave. Jessie will make sure he gets what he wants."

"Teddy bear," I whisper.

He nods. "Whatever the fuck you want to call him Shorty."

Christian laughs and Jessie turns. I stop talking and smile at him. He does the chin thing and smiles. He's not so scary when he smiles. People come by and talk to Christian about Hawk and thank him for keeping the Officers safe. This is the strangest group of scary men I have ever seen. Considering I was home schooled and never went out much, I haven't seen many scary guys so what do I know? Some buy him a shot, some beer. I wonder how he's still standing. The people and their thoughts are smashing through my doors, but I stay by his side. Some of these guys are scary.

Mase moves back toward us and something passes between them. Christian touches Jessie's arm. "I'm out Brother. There are too many people and I can't focus." I'm so relieved I squeeze his hand.

Jessie nods and presses something on his neck then talks to someone. They're like Secret Service. He's got a radio in his ear. I bet it's got the squiggly cord to it.

Mase leans toward Christian. "Don't fuckin' lose her. It's like Holly all over again. Mom and Joey will love her."

Aww. What a nice thing to say. I look at him. "Stop reading me. I've never seen any of this and I don't need you reading my stupid."

He stands straight. "Yes ma'am." He's smiling so he probably doesn't mean it. He laughs and I know he doesn't. Damn readers.

Christian holds my hand and hobbles to the door. People are moving and look back, but no one says anything. "Are you moving them?"

"Yeah." He doesn't stop or even turn around.

At the stairs, Jessie and Dakota put an arm under his shoulders and carry him down. Dakota holds on, but Jessie walks to the SUV and opens the door. "You are still full of energy Brother."

Christian nods. "I'll jump when I get home." That's what he does with the kids. I hope he's okay.

Dakota looks at me and smiles. "He will be fine Nadine." Damn readers.

At the house, they help get Christian up the stairs and into the bedroom. "Call if you need anything Brother," Jessie tells him.

When they leave, I help him undress. His pockets are full of bullets, tie things that they use for cuffs, wire, tape, a small dream catcher and he has two guns with a knife in one of the holster. He is ready for anything and that was only one leg. I dump everything into his nightstand drawer and help him undress trying not to look at his package. Not an easy thing to do.

"Babe." I look up at his eyes. "I can't take a shower with a cast and that look requires a shower." I turn fast and get him shorts. He laughs. I am so embarrassed. I tell him to sit and get the shorts up to his knees. He smiles, but stands and pulls them up.

Before he lays down he gets his laptop. "I need to order your SUV."

I kiss him. He's a really good boyfriend. "It can wait. Do you need anything?" He shakes his head no and pulls his leg up on the bed. I watch him move pillows and wonder again why he picked me. Everyone here could be models, but Christian has a soulful look to him. You know as soon as you see him that there's more than what you're seeing. He has secrets that will never be told, and a body that's like a picture of the perfect male specimen. Even

222

banged up he's gorgeous. I want my cheek on his chest every day. Then I get to see those abs. I shake my head trying to erase where those thoughts are going. As if that's happening. Damn I have it bad. He settles and looks at me with a question in his eyes. "I'm taking a shower."

He smiles and I want to sigh. Thank God I don't. I think I've embarrassed myself enough for one day. "Looks like you're still standing here looking at me. Do you want me to help you shower?"

Oh. My. God. I actually feel my eyebrows move to my hairline. "I don't know and now I can't think." I'm going to hell for lying. My brain is thinking of his hands everywhere. Like everywhere. And his lips. A shiver runs down my whole body at that thought.

He smiles and I want to climb on the bed with him. "Go shower babe. I'm going to jump and order your car. We can think together when you're done."

Oh, dear Lord. I want to think together now. He needs to jump. I throw up doors in my head and turn toward the bathroom then remember the clothes. I need a lobotomy to get rid of the package and lip pictures going through my head. At twenty I'm an expert on packages and I've memorized his and all the ways it moves when he does. In the shower, I regain some control over my thoughts. I never thought I could have someone's hands or mouth on me. My parents never had to worry about me and I hated that. While it must have been a relief to them—it's not normal for a teenage girl. Now Christian is right here and he's got no problem touching me. And oh, how I want him to touch me. I slam doors again. I need to act my age. I chuckle. I've always been older than my age, but teenage raging hormones is exactly what I'm feeling here. Giddy with excitement and scared to death is a horrible feeling when they're mixed together. How teenagers get through this is a mystery to me. I wash my hair and get me out, trying to think like an adult. I know what I want. I need to be brave enough to take it.

* * *

Christian

I jump back feeling settled. Just seeing Hawk waiting for me settled me. I shake my head. The ancestors may not like that competition, but just the sight of him had my mind and heart working together again.

I hear the water shut off and wonder about the little spitfire in there. While she was watching me, I got a glimpse of her head thrown back and ecstasy etched on her face. I'll never lose that picture. I pushed it away and fixed fuckin' pillows. If she wasn't right there, I would have gotten the relief I need. Jesus she's fuckin' beautiful when she comes. I shake my head. I need to go slow here.

Pushing thoughts of her out, I connect to Jeremy. 'Je, you did fuckin' awesome today. How is Aubrey doing?'

His laugh hits me and I smile. 'Perfect. She can fight.'

I can see him shaking his head and laugh. 'She can. You did it Je. I'm proud of you.'

'Thanks for making me teach her. I couldn't do it alone.' He sounds embarrassed.

'We need all of us Brother. The old ladies have always worked with the Brothers, this is no different, her job is different, but the purpose is the same.'

'Yeah. I got it today. I'm glad you're okay. I watched Nick and Prez. You did it too Christian. You kept both Clubs safe.'

I smile. It feels incredible knowing I didn't fuck it up. 'Yeah.'

'Watch Mucimi. He's bringing more in. VP has a surprise for you. It's good. I gotta go.'

Fuckin' kid is gone. Mucimi's bringing more. Jesus I hope they aren't fuckin' babies. Dean walks out of the bathroom and my dick is hard. Fuck. I put Mucimi away and watch her.

She's nervous so I put my arm out. "Got you a blue Patriot. It's an SUV, but small and cute like you."

She's on her hands and knees crawling toward me and stops. What a fuckin' sight she makes just like that. "I like the name."

I smile, she has no clue about cars. "That's why I picked it. The Compass is too small. This one you can fit a kid in the back." Her expression changes to confused. It hits me. "I don't have kids. I hope you want them."

I get that smile. She sits facing me. "I never thought about a husband and kids. It's different when you can't touch people."

I got that from her when I could read everything she thought. "I was the same way, Dakota too, so I think it's normal for people like us. For me it's like a whole new world opened up for me and I get all those dreams I missed out on as a kid."

She smiles nodding her head. "That's exactly how I feel. I was thinking it in the shower. I'm slammed with teenage raging hormones. It's about time."

I crack up. She's cute. She hits my chest and I hold her hand there. "Let's explore your raging hormones." I give her hand a tug and she lands on my chest. I push the pain away and kiss her. My hand slides under her shirt and right up her back. She pushes her tits into my chest and I moan loving that feeling. I move her so she's straddling my dick and not pushing on my chest. Fuck this may not have been a good idea, but it feels fuckin' good right now. Sitting up I break the kiss and look in her eyes. She wants more, but she's scared. "You stop me when you need to. Yeah?"

225

She looks like she doesn't believe me. I wait needing to hear her agree. "You're not a teenager Christian." She doesn't say anymore and I wish for the millionth time I could read her.

"That means I know better than to take more than you're willing to give. This isn't about me babe. If it doesn't feel right, you tell me and we stop. Yeah?"

All her worry leaves her face. "Yeah."

I pull her shirt off watching her eyes. "We start here. I get to put my mouth anywhere and I want it on your tits. My whole fuckin' life I dreamed of doing this." My hands slide up and I take her hard nipples rolling them while she watches my eyes. She lets out a soft moan and my dick jerks under her. Jesus. Her hips rock against it and I moan.

She stops. "Is it okay to do that?"

"Anything you want is what you do baby. There is no wrong here. Your pussy grinding into me feels fuckin' good." I can't wait and get her tit in my mouth—moaning again. She purrs and I'm lost in the feel of my tongue on her nipple. I've pictured it a million times. Giving the whores what they need to get off is one thing, but actually feeling it is indescribable. I don't want to get her off with my mind, I want to feel every bit of it. She runs her hands down my shoulders to my arms and grinds down harder. "You're fuckin' beautiful Dean. I love your hands on me. Show me where you want my mouth baby." She grabs my head and moves me from her neck back to her tit. I lick and nip getting the most erotic sounds I've ever heard. Her hips are moving faster. "Slow baby. It will feel better." She slows and moans.

"I don't know what to do to." She's breathing hard and sounds frustrated.

I smile against her tit. I know what she's looking for and I want the first taste. I look in her eyes. "Trust me." She nods and I flip her to her back on the side of me. I suspend

226

me over her and her eyes are bugging out. "The cast babe." She nods looking relieved. I kiss her and move me down—making my way to her shorts. She's pushing up into me, but not stopping me so I slide them down smelling her sweet scent as I do. Just the thought of my mouth on her has me ready to come. When her shorts are off, I look at her panties covering where I want to be. Women and the fuckin' panties. I rip them and she moans. "Baby put your hands on your tits. It will help you get to where you want to be." She gives me an embarrassed look. "Me too, nothing like seeing a woman please herself." Her hands move and I moan. "Fuck baby just like that. Jesus that's beautiful." She watches me lifting her hips up. I give her what she's looking for and put my mouth on her.

"Oh, my God." She moans loud and I lose myself hitting everything she needs and loving the taste of her. I want her scent all over me. Jesus I'm like a fuckin' Neanderthal, but I want everything from Dean marking me as hers. I have no doubt of her being mine. When she's ready to come, I raise her up at an angle so I can watch and stroke her inside on that little bump that will send her into that ecstasy I saw on her face. She screams and I roll her clit one last time. I watch her come and think using my mind to get her off isn't so bad if I can touch and taste her like this. Her body is bucking and shaking and that look is fuckin' with my control. I put my mouth back on her taking everything she's giving to me and lose it grinding my dick into the bed. Holy fuck do I lose it, exploding into my clothes, for-fuckin'-ever.

Laying my head on her thigh I catch my breath then smile. She's all over my face and I fuckin' love it. Raising up, I suspend over her—kissing her delicious body as I go. When I get to her mouth I kiss it smiling. She's zoned out. She kisses me back, but has nothing left. "Thank you my beautiful Little Pixie. You taste as good as you smell." She moans and I laugh. "You're spent babe. Let me clean us up and you can sleep."

She pulls my hair and kisses my lips. "Amazing."

I smile and she yawns. Not what I was hoping for, but I get what the release does to women so I'm not offended. "Let me clean you up babe."

A towel comes to me and I take it and wash her up. I dry her with the next and send the wet towel back so I can clean the fuckin' mess I made of myself. She's smiling with her eyes taking longer to open. I like that smile or maybe I just like knowing that I put it there and I did it touching her. Her eyes don't open again. I kiss each one then her lips and position myself so I'll be laying beside her again. Before I lower, I lose my clothes then clean myself up. I send everything to the washer while I lower back down and pull her over to me. Her naked body has me hard and I think of teenage raging hormones, laughing quietly.

I jump so I can tell Hawk I did it all with my hands and mouth actually on her body. I'm not telling him about stroking her g-spot. He wouldn't understand.

Chapter Nine

Dean

Oh. My. God. My hips and eyes roll at the same time. "That feels so good," I mumble out.

"Mmm. You grinding against my leg just wasn't enough my Little Pixie. I moved us so I can get you what you need."

I open my eyes and my breath catches. We're in the damn air. Like *above the bed* in the air! "Christian!"

"Shhh baby I won't ever hurt you. Just feel. You're so fuckin' wet. Feel my fingers sliding against your pussy."

With one hand on my ass and the other rolling my clit I can see the benefit of being in the air and roll my hips with his fingers. He pushes his package into me and I look down wanting to touch him. He's watching his hand so I do. Not sure if he's going to get mad I watch his face as my hand wraps around him.

His body moves out a little and he moans looking at my face. "I love your hand on me baby."

"Show me what to do." He's hard and silky soft, it's an oxymoron I think and smile when my hand tightens and moves down then slides back up. "Let me." He smiles and I move my hand myself.

"Fuck, yeah." He slides a finger in me and my breath catches. "Trust me baby. Just relax."

I grip him tighter and try to relax. His thumb moves and I forget everything, but how amazing his hands feel on me. His mouth goes to my nipple and I'm ready to float away. I hold his head right there loving when he bites down. His hand moves and I feel pressure at my ass, but can't stop moving with his hand. "It feels so good Christian," I moan out, pushing against his hands.

"It does. I'm going to come with you babe just let it happen." He's breathing fast and it's turning me on. I hold him tighter and he moans. "Fuckin' perfect. Come for me Dean."

My whole body shivers then ignites. "Christian!"

Christian

I think about her coming on my hand the whole time I'm drying her. Jesus. I shake my head and look at her face. She's smiling. "Go get dressed baby."

She bends to kiss me and laughs. "You need to put me down."

Fuck. I lower her and she walks away laughing.

I wash and throw shorts and a Security shirt on. Considering I look like I was hit by a Mack truck, I feel pretty good. I get coffee going and a bagel in the toaster then suspend my way down the stairs. I could have gotten up to the room last night, but Dakota and Jessie needed to bring me. When I get to the kitchen, Dean is standing in the doorway. I stop and take her in. I'm a lucky bastard. She's a tiny pixie built like a wet dream and she's mine. "Dean?"

She turns looking like she's ready to laugh. "I wanted to see you make breakfast."

I smile and hug her. "It's a habit." I keep my hand on her back and guide her to the table. Keeping my hands on her is never going to get old.

"I like it almost as much as you babying me." She sits and I get us coffee sending the bagel to her. "Do you have cream cheese?"

I get it and a knife for her while sending another bagel to the toaster. "Babying you?" I sit looking at her.

"Giving me a bath like a baby."

I think about that. "I like my hands on you and it's how it's done."

She spreads enough cream cheese on her bagel to choke a horse and stands up walking to the fridge. "I like your hands on me too. I didn't know it could be like this. I'm so glad we moved here." She comes back with jelly and sits. I don't need to read her to see what she's planning and get a clean knife so I'm not eating cheese with my jelly. She smiles plucking the knife out of the air. "Serenity hates it too."

We talk about the day and she's surprised that I'm going to work. "I'll be okay and I can come home if I'm not. You need the address here so you can get into classes. Do you need money for them?"

She's staring at me. "No, and I can use my address."

What the fuck? "Prez is moving Serenity onto the Compound so she'll be safe. You're staying here."

I feel her getting pissed and I don't like it. "Would it be too much for you to ask me questions before you just decide how I should live?"

"I'm not deciding how you should live, just where. Do you want to leave?" She'd have to walk over my dead body. Now she's going to cry? I'm never understanding women.

"No, but ask me first. You order things like I'm one of the men in your Protector army. I'm a grown woman that wants to be treated like one."

"There's almost as many women as men in that army. I'm not trying to order you to do anything. You'll

231

need an address for the school. I was just going to get your phone and put it in."

Her whole body relaxes. "Sorry. This is new for me. I don't know how to live with someone, and your words come out like orders. I'm living here, driving a new car, getting my license, my sister is being moved, I get a card and ID, have to shop when you do and I was given a job all because you said so. At some point, you need to learn to ask. I have money to pay for school. I need a bank, but I'm sure I can find one here. I've never made decisions just for me. Leave me something so I can do that."

I think about what I said. Maybe saying, *you're staying here* was a bit much. "Can I put the address in your phone?"

She rolls her eyes at me and I want to laugh. "I don't have one, the phone we used is Serenity's."

"I'll..." Fuck. "Can I order you one? It will be here by the time you're done with work."

She smiles. Jesus this is almost too much work. "If the bill comes to me."

"Princes own the satellite. It's not much of a bill."

Her hands move and I watch the cream cheese and jelly shift on the bagel. "The bill still comes to me." I nod and a glob falls on the table. With the towel right behind her she grabs the knife and scoops the mess back onto the pile on her bagel. "Thanks for not rushing to clean it up for me." She smiles like it matters that I didn't.

I send the towel back to the sink thinking I can clean the table before we leave. I'm not saying another fuckin' word or doing anything that she might not like. I thought she was going to be easy. Eating my bagel seems safe so I do that.

She laughs and I look at her. "That's driving you crazy, isn't it?"

I look at the table then back at her. "Yeah."

Her whole face gets soft. "You can clean it. Are you OCD?"

I put the towel back before she thinks I *am* OCD. "No, but we've never lived with anyone. Even at Nunánuk's we lived above her garage."

I feel her pain and watch her eyes fill with tears. She doesn't say anything and finishes the mess she's calling breakfast. I'm too much of a pussy to ask, so I get up and actually rinse then put the dishes in the dishwasher. I turn taking a breath to call Hawk and freeze closing my eyes. 'Sorry Brother.' She's watching me when I open them.

"That's going to take some getting used to." It comes out soft. She hugs me. I said we. That's why she had tears in her eyes. I kiss her head; my sweet Little Pixie doesn't understand about the ancestors. We have a lot to talk about but not time to do that now. "Ready?"

She nods against me. "I just have to get my purse." She moves fast and I wash the table. I'm waiting at the door for her and see her look at the table as she walks by. I shrug seeing her smirk. "I think I hit the lottery." She puts her hand up. "Gorgeous, has great hands, cooks, worries over my safety and is a neat freak." She ticks each finger.

"I'm offended." She stops moving. "My mouth didn't make it in there and gorgeous doesn't work for me."

She giggles as I guide her out. She steps toward the HS bike. I'm surprised to see it here, but move her to the Harley. "I need to sit back and this one has a peg for my leg." I flip the peg and suspend to get my leg over. When I'm on she climbs behind me and moves close. Uncle Danny used to tell us there's nothing better than your woman's arms around you. He wasn't wrong.

At the school, she kisses me and goes to the classroom. I wait for Mucimi in the daycare room. He sits in front of me with Teller. "Yesterday you saw what people are like. Outside of our towns isn't safe for readers. If you bring people here, that's with the adults helping to keep them safe. Yeah?"

He nods throwing me pictures. I put my hand up. "Stop." Teller squeezes his hand. "We will have a meeting and you can throw your pictures to the Security team so we can do this the right way. No more bringing people here without being able to do that safely. Chance could have gotten hurt in a million different ways. We work together and make sure the readers are covered and make it here."

Teller nods. "I told him that too. There's a man that needs help right now. He's in the woods near Grampa VP. He doesn't have food, Christian, and he's sick."

I look at Mucimi. "Give me this man and I'll get him to the MC. Today I'll talk to Prez and set up a meeting for the rest." He throws me the guy and a million fuckin' pictures of trees. I look for him and see a shop. "I got it. Thanks, little man. I'll let you know about the meeting when I get a time."

"Today?"

I smile and mess his hair. "Yeah, I'll try for today. There's a lot going on, but I think this is important."

He nods and Teller hugs me. "Thanks, Christian."

At Security I go to my office and connect with my readers. The MC is shaken, but they're pushing through it. Aiyana is pissed about the pipeline again and I look for time to get people with her. I call down to Jacob to get a phone to Dean and make sure the bill goes to her at my address. He fuckin' laughs. Shaking my head I go to Prez's office.

José is yelling at someone and I smile waiting at the door. "Well you could have been dead! Did you see the trucks that blew up at Security? They were on the road with you. The Brother moved you to keep you alive. You could just say thanks and stop calling me to point out the fuckin' obvious." He swipes his phone off and I laugh. Prez gives me a look, but fuck he's funny.

"José, I think you can be a little more tactful and less confrontational. People were scared."

His arms go up. "I don't do stupid. They're fuckin' stupid. Some moron wants us to send someone over to move his neighbor's garage. Like we'll pick it up and move it five feet back so he can see down the fuckin' road, and he's a repeat. I don't have time for stupid Prez. I have holes as big as craters to get filled in and Uncle Danny coming down to check on the tunnel and building on top of my regular shit. Move his fuckin' garage." He shakes his head and walks by me disgusted. "Next time don't be so fuckin' flashy with moving shit."

I put my hands up in surrender. "I'll try Brother." He doesn't believe me, thinking I should take the stupid calls. I clench my jaw and sit. "Sorry."

Prez waves it away. "He didn't ask why I called for him, but seeing that maybe I'll get Dakota on it." He types on his phone and looks up. "You should be home."

"Nothing to do there." I throw him the guy in the woods. "Mucimi is bringing other readers here. That guy is up toward Boston. He's being hunted and is living in those woods. Right now, he's sick and hasn't eaten. He has others, but I told him we need a meet with the Security team before he tries to get anyone else here without Security. After what happened yesterday, he's waiting for the meet."

His hands go through his hair. "The MC was just hit. Pres is off. He was willing to let the Protectors work, but ordered Elizabeth and Harley away from the truck that hit the building. Elizabeth said they were too far away. My dad's pissed and Uncle Danny isn't talking to him. I don't know what kind of help I can get for the guy."

He's really worried about this. "Pres will apologize and I have the people. I just need the okay and a place for him to stay. I'll have the Protectors work with him."

He smiles pulling the tie out of his hair. "That I can do. Have someone pick him up and I'll get a place and food for him. I'll call Kate, she'll do it and have Doc waiting for him." I nod seeing he has more. "Mucimi. How many are we talking?"

I shrug. "I didn't take it from him. He needs to learn this has to go through the right people. It isn't for him to just decide and do alone."

He nods thinking that's smart. "Have him brought over at three."

Fuck. I need to work Aiyana in later. Unless, "If I don't get Aiyana back to the pipeline she's going alone. If I can work the people will you help us again? At like four?"

"Fuckin' pipeline. I read everything I could find. They were fucked right from the beginning. If they didn't agree with selling their land, the government took it under eminent domain and they got nothing. They don't have casinos or other businesses supporting them. No money meant no chance at fighting the government or the fuckin' company that stole their only source of income. There's a barbed wire fence stopping them from getting to the water. They can't even get food. Who the fuck does shit like that?"

I put my hands up. I know the story, but he's on a roll.

He takes a breath. "We need more people hearing the truth from up there. A group that everyone believes in to stop this insanity."

I see it and smile interrupting him. "Vets." I actually see them standing in front of the tribe and throw it to him.

He stops and looks at me. "That would work. I can get ads up all over the country. Mitch would love to help with this." His mind is spinning.

"Prez?"

He shakes his head and looks at me. "Anything else?"

"Can you help with Aiyana later?"

He stands up waving his hand. "Yeah. I need to get José to call Mitch for this. Dakota can see if the Vets from the houses are willing to go up. I'll fly them there. They'll need places to sleep and shit. I'll see you at the meeting." He walks out and I laugh.

Darren comes in and looks around. "He went to José's office. I was just leaving."

He nods. "You did a great job yesterday. Pres is kicking himself today, but he was impressed when he saw the feeds this morning."

I shrug. "He saw me training with Jeremy and Aubrey. He knew what we were capable of."

He's thinking it was the women, but he doesn't get it either. "I don't think he doubts you Christian."

"Elizabeth and Harley are two of the strongest Protectors we have up there. Just because they won't let them on HS doesn't mean they aren't capable. I'd take them here if I thought VP wouldn't try killing me and Harley was older, but they need to be partnered together. Separating them would be a mistake."

"You and Mase did better here than all of them up there." He thinks they aren't as strong.

I shake my head no. "Their threat started as the lunatics, but ended with a bigger fish they've been fighting too. They had hits everywhere. Ours were concentrated on the kids and Security. That's why I only took Mase. They needed all the Protectors they had. If they would have used them right they wouldn't have lost anyone. They shot the first fuckin' truck Darren. Uncle Danny is pissed about the truck because they were warned. That's where they lost BS. Sidelining Elizabeth and Harley got them damage to the building. Jeremy and Aubrey kept each other safe and helped stop the truck that almost went into the building. A minute later and the Officers would be dead today. That truck was loaded to take out the entire building. They were fuckin' lucky."

"Sonofabitch. Why are you telling me now?" He thinks I'm holding back.

I shake my head again. "Because you can talk to Pres in a way that I can't. He didn't get the warning for a reason. Giving it to Uncle Danny got it in the meeting and everyone, including VP was aware. I gave them all I could. If they aren't listening, using the information and the people they have, they'll all end up dead. Their trouble didn't end with yesterday's run on them. Someone needs to get through." They won't make the next one, I think, but don't say.

When I turn Prez is standing there. Fuck. With the visions hitting me I've been shielding too much. I didn't feel him close. He looks pissed. "Were you going to tell me?"

"No."

Yep he's pissed. "Why the fuck not?" He walks around his desk and I'm relieved. Last time he put me against a wall.

"Pres isn't listening to you. Ricky is still in KC, they won't put Elizabeth on HS and she's been HS for fuckin' years, Harley should be on HS—Colt is, I gave them warnings and they didn't listen. Jeremy got shit for going to MC-Baxter when he was told to go to the Compound and they fuckin' saved every one of them. Do I need more?"

He puts his hand out waving me to a seat.

"Jeremy helped with the truck?"

We all turn and look at my dad. Jesus. I nod my head. "How much did you hear?"

Fuck he's pissed. "Not e-fuckin'-nough." He growls and my head falls forward. I throw to Prez he heard all I said.

"Good. Maybe something *someone else* says will get them using the people and abilities they have," Prez says throwing a file across his desk. At least he's not mad at me.

"What did I miss?" my dad asks.

I look at Prez. "Before you get into all this I need to set up the meets for later. Ricky will need to pull people for me."

"Are you holding back more shit?"

My head goes back. "Yeah Prez, but I tell you everything I can. With Pres, nothing you've said has made a difference with the women. I was telling Darren hoping for a better outcome." I look at Darren and my dad. "Jeremy needs to be off the leash. Him and Aubrey together are able to do more than anyone gives them credit for. Off his leash, he's free to help where he's needed. Of all the people in HS, he shouldn't be the one taken for granted."

My dad nods and Darren throws me chin. I get up and make the door. "Christian."

I rise up and turn back. Darren laughs. I'm watching Prez. "Work your Protectors from the MC however you need to. Ricky, VP and Uncle Danny are behind you. I'll run interference with Pres." I nod and get out before he sees I was planning on it.

I suspend down the stairs and hear laughing behind me. "I guess you didn't need us to carry you up the stairs last night," Jessie says.

"No Brother. I was going for coffee, but didn't think making and sending the cup up would be good here."

He cracks up. "You may be right, but seeing you fly down the stairs ranks right up there with floating cups."

"I don't fly Jessie."

"What-the-fuck-ever." He walks toward Ops.

Back in my office I call Ricky and get Harley and Elizabeth on the reader in the woods. Ally is set and VP will run it for them. He'll pull what we need for the meet at four. I call to Aiyana and Co letting them know we'll meet at four. Aiyana is surprised I'm working, but happy to get to the pipeline by jumping. I call to Ops and get the kids a transport shuttle so they'll be here on time for the meet with HS Security. Connecting with Mucimi, I let him know the man will be picked up today and the meet is set. He knows, making me smile. These kids are going to be a trip when they get older. They're a fuckin' trip now and they haven't grown into all their abilities.

My last call is to Jax. He got the call on the Jeep and will have it later today. Trapper will get it to me as soon as he can.

With everything done, it's Hawk's walk time so I jump. He's waiting for me and we walk. I run through everything in my head with the ancestors and feel settled when I jump back. VP and Uncle Danny are sitting in front of my desk. I really need to stop shielding in the building.

VP smiles. "Hawk's there? Where you go."

"Yeah. He stays with Nunánuk."

He nods thinking it's good. I look at Uncle Danny. "I don't think the tunnels are safe. I have transport bringing the kids in."

"No. They need some reinforcements. I have a meet with LB for it. You put the kids here knowing they would help?"

I look at the door, thank fuck it's closed. "Yeah. I needed them to shield or we would have lost everyone." I expect them to be pissed, but they're not.

"Use what you have," VP says.

I nod. I plan to use every bit of ability we have to keep people from dying.

Uncle Danny sits forward. "The vision was all of them?"

Fuck. Since it's past and he's not asking about the next, I guess it won't hurt to say. "Both buildings went with everyone inside. I got it from Jeremy. I was taken out by a truck before the buildings were hit."

"Fuckin' Christ. That's why you called?"

"Yeah. You needed it so more weren't lost. What the fuck would have happened to the Clubs without the Officers? No one would have recovered from that loss. Losing the kids wasn't an option either. With Prez and the kids inside and Aiyana and Kaya helping from the reservation they had a chance of shielding here without me. Mase would have done it if I didn't make it, but it worked out."

He nods then looks at VP. "Pres needs this."

"Yeah. Jeremy?"

"A minute later, you wouldn't be here to ask."

He sits back. Uncle Danny stands up. "Why didn't he say?"

"He sees shit you have no clue about. His brain is running so fast all the time he can't always slow it enough to talk. For you a vision is all you hear. For us it plays then the

241

result plays. If he's trying to run different scenarios he can't say until he knows. Maybe him getting shit wasn't worth slowing his brain down to explain. He knew I told you. He knew the vision didn't change and he was trying to keep his Officers safe. I wouldn't give a fuck if you were pissed at me either."

"Got hit savin' *your* Officers." Uncle Steve points out.

I smile. "No one gave me shit over it either."

Uncle Danny laughs. "Jessie wasn't happy."

I shrug. "His family is alive. Thank fuck he moved me, but I'd do it again if I had to."

"Good Brother." VP is throwing thanks at me. I throw him chin. "Got you somethin'."

I see and close my eyes. Fuck. Uncle Danny opens the door and a dog walks to VP and sits. "Know it's soon. You need him. Still got Hawk where you go. Need protection here. Already trained for you. Kids and Alex kept him."

I look from the dog to him. "You knew?"

Uncle Danny sits. "A few months ago, Teller said Mucimi was healing Hawk. He was old Christian." I look away and swallow. "VP started looking for the right dog, he found him, then trained him for you. He helps with the energy like Hawk did. Jeremy tested him for us."

I throw chin and a thanks to Uncle Steve. "What's his name?"

"My brother."

I smile and call him over. He sits on my foot and I pet his head. Nekanis is a hell of a name, but it's better than dog. Hawk will like him. "He calms me."

Uncle Steve nods. "Works good. Changed out Hawk's stuff with his. Thought you'd like that better." I nod not able to talk.

They stand. "Is there anything we can do for you Christian? Seems like you saved everyone that means something to us."

They'd do the same for me. They have done the same for me. My truck jumps in my head. "There is. My truck is at the reservation and I could use it here. The Harley works with the cast, but I can't use the tunnels and I need to get Nekanis home."

"You rode in? How the fuck did you make that work?"

I laugh at his expression and shrug. The Brother has one eye and never had a problem.

"Done," Uncle Steve says and walks out. Uncle Danny throws me chin and follows him.

I look at my new dog. "How they kept you a secret is beyond me. Let's find water," I tell him in Mohegan. He stands and waits for me.

* * *

In Prez's meeting room the dogs stand at the door. Prez walks in and looks at Nekanis. "Who got a dog now?" He looks at Aaron.

"Me. VP said I need him."

"Jesusfuckin'Christ. It's been a fuckin' day," Jessie says making me smile.

"Mucimi was healing Hawk. When they found out, he found Nekanis and trained him for me."

Aaron leans forward. "Good name."

243

I nod. I didn't name him. Prez looks at me. "Are you okay with this?"

I shrug. "He didn't give me any options. They replaced all Hawk's stuff with his and brought him here. He calms me, so I guess it works. Jeremy said he takes the energy too."

He nods. "Why don't I know this shit?" I shrug again and it's starting to feel like a bad habit, I'll have to watch that.

The kids come in and Uncle Steve and Danny are right behind them. Prez looks at the ceiling and we all smile. He looks at Uncle Steve. "Tell me you're just dropping them."

"No."

The whole table laughs. Prez looks at me. "I thought this was Mucimi?"

I almost shrug, but catch myself. "They're Brothers. He needs them like you needed Darren and Jessie, and Jeremy needs Jacob."

He nods. "These are the Brothers that help make decisions for the Princes." He gives a look to Uncle Steve and Uncle Danny. "And the MC. When there is something happening, we all work to find a solution. We have the man from the woods in the yard with the MC. Christian will talk to him tomorrow and see if he can be a help to us. What I know is that he's being hunted. He's happy to be protected by the MC and Amanda is checking in on him. He's going to be fine."

Mucimi nods. "Monia."

"Pneumonia, but yes he's sick and Doc saw him...you already know. He'll get better."

Teller stands on his chair. "He helps Jeremy."

I hold my laugh. Prez looks at me and I nod. His hands are in his hair and I look away before I start laughing out loud. "Why didn't you tell me this morning?"

Phoenix stands and Teller sits down. "We tell Christian about visions. He tells if we can talk about it. He said we have to meet to help with this one. We can tell you now."

Uncle Danny cracks up then Jessie then Aaron. I clench my jaw and watch everything go through Prez's head. He looks around the table with his eyes flashing a warning. "I'm standing here being given visions by kids seven and under. If you can't get it together then get the fuck out." Everyone stops and looks at the kids.

Prez nods at Phoenix and he sits. "That's as it should be and good that you learned so quickly. You're right, that should pass through Christian in case it would alter something else in the future." The kids nod so serious. They get it. "What do you have today Mucimi?"

He stands on his chair and looks at the boards. "On TV?"

Prez looks at me. "You can put them on the board Mucimi, everyone here is cleared for it," I tell him. Teller takes one of his hands and Aquyà takes the other. The boards flash on and we see faces flash on all three. A woman is running and tackled to the ground. A man is running dripping blood from his head. I turn back to Mucimi and see his tears. Phoenix and Justice are holding Aquyà and Teller's hands. I call Nekanis to Mucimi. He jumps on the chair and leans into Mucimi.

"Fuckin' hell. These pussies are fuckin' nuts," Taylor says.

I throw to Prez, 'We need to get a list and slow him down. He's never going to make this twice.' His eyes find mine and he nods. I stand behind him and touch his shoulder. "Mucimi we need you to go slower and give me a little

245

more. Can you do that?" His little face looks at me with tears running down it. He nods. "I need locations so I'll need you to show more with each person." He lets the boys' hands go and turns to me. I lift him up and look at Prez.

"Brantley, we need a list."

Brantley opens his laptop. "Ready Prez." He looks at Mucimi and thinks, 'You got this my big boy.'

Little man nods. "Yeah."

I sit and call Nekanis. "Dakota, can you help?" He stands behind us and touches Mucimi's shoulder. "One at a time until we get locations on all. Little Brothers if you get it, tell Prez." They nod and look at the boards. Mucimi throws the woman that was tackled first.

"Seminole County, Florida," Jessie says. We see a building. "Winter Park Medical."

"Next Mucimi," I tell him softly. He's shaking trying to move slower for us. I throw it to Prez. He nods watching.

We spend close to forty minutes watching people beaten or hiding. Mucimi is spent and the boys are all shaken. I turn Mucimi and he puts his head on my shoulder. Uncle Steve takes him from me. "Dakota fix him." He throws his chin toward me. I feel Dakota's hand on my shoulder and call Nekanis to me. I have twenty minutes to get my shit together. While they talk, I jump. Hawk comes running and I sit petting him. Feeling the ancestors always settles me. I jump back and see the boys watching me. 'Jump?' They nod so we jump. 'Now Little Brothers.'

Dakota is here. "It is good to ask for the peace you need. The ancestors are always happy to help."

He gets nods, but no words. When they're ready they tell me they're jumping. I feel good opening my eyes. They're smiling and I see Prez is relieved. Brantley has Mucimi and is talking to him away from the table.

246

When Uncle Danny and Uncle Steve take them out, Prez sits with his head in his hands. "He's fuckin' three. I don't even know what to say to you Brantley. If you think this is too much for him tell me and we'll figure something out."

Brantley looks at me wondering what could stop visions. "I want him away from anything that has the potential to hurt him. After seeing what happened to Christian, I know that keeping it in and having no relief is not what I want for him. I also don't want him so shielded he's a danger to himself. I'm going with whatever Christian thinks at this point. He's lived without the release and seeing what happened with Jeremy affected him. He's the closest to Mucimi and he wouldn't let him get hurt. If Dakota was giving advice I wouldn't turn it down." Prez looks at Dakota.

"Very wise decision Brother. There is no way to stop what is coming in to Mucimi. Isolation is not a good solution and will do more harm than good for him. Christian cannot put the boys in the way of harm. It goes against the abilities he was given. While Mucimi was throwing, he had the support of his Brothers. They all took from him even when it hurt. They will not allow him to go through anything alone. He will always have that from them."

Brantley nods and throws me chin thinking he trusts whatever I decide.

Prez stands. "We have a meeting with the reservation." He looks at his watch. "In five minutes. Christian, do you need anything?"

"Nekanis needs to go out."

Aaron stands. "I have him Brother." Darren, Brantley, Jessie, Taylor and Delta leave with him.

"Will you be able to do this?" Prez asks.

I nod.

He walks out and Dakota moves beside me. "You have exceeded the hopes of the ancestors Christian. They are collecting to assist us for their people from another tribe."

"Good. I have more to help, but we'll need the strength to get them there and back."

"Jeremy is waiting with Cloud as well."

I'm surprised and fuckin' happy about that. I've been shielding again and drop them enough to see my Protectors. I'm so fuckin' proud and happy to see them all together with my dad in the KC. 'Thank you Brothers and Dad. This is more than I expected. When we are set here we will jump. For the Brothers that don't know how, just relax and let those that *can* guide you.' They tell me they will.

Prez comes in with bottles of water and hands me one. When he sits we jump. Aiyana is here with more help. They are not Protectors, but they are elders with ability. I show respect and appreciation. The MC Protectors show and Aiyana is smiling. Nunánuk shows with elders and some RS and I smile when I see Hawk.

I explain what we're doing and what to expect. I move people so we form a long line with strong on each side of weaker links. "You don't let go. No matter what happens you don't let go. Spinning and pitch black will throw you. Hold onto your anchors and they'll guide you through. Co and Nunánuk can you take the ends?" They move and I put Jeremy and Aiyana in place then I take the middle. "Hold on and jump now!"

I feel the push and know Dakota is guiding us with the ancestors. We give a chant for strength then safe passage. When I open my eyes, I see we're in the middle of another fight. "Hold on and move in front of the tribesmen." Elders from the tribe start chanting and some of the water protestors move toward us chanting with them. "Connect with the pussies and sway them to leave. If they don't budge move to the next. Aiyana, Mase, Colt, Devan hit the people with the hoses. Shut the water down. Jeremy, Dad, Kaya, Elizabeth, Harley, Blaze and Blake shield the tribesmen."

Shots are fired. "Rubber bullets!" someone yells behind us.

"Elders keep up our request for strength!"

I hit a gun away and move to the next. People are yelling everywhere. A truck crosses the tape. "Mase!"

I stop it and feel Dakota and Aiyana throwing to me. "Colt, Devan help us move it!"

The truck raises up in the air and everyone stops yelling. "Push Brothers. Now!" The truck flips and lands twenty feet away. The protesters let out war cries. Shots are coming faster. Jesus don't these people ever quit? "Hold the shield. Colt, Devan, Mase hit the guns away."

If I wasn't jumping from place to place, I'd probably be laughing. Guns are flying backward, the protestors are still yelling, the pussies are pissed, but don't know what to do and the water isn't flowing.

"Christian maximum damage to their equipment!"

"Colt, Devan, Mase, you heard Prez, maximum damage. Disable vehicles, cut hoses, let them freeze, take their food, whatever you can."

The pussies are running to the vehicles in the back and Prez tells us what to hit. I take out their generators and send a truck rolling down the hill. Prez yells to get cameras on the PD. Mase has food floating to the protestors. The elders are chanting louder and I realize more protesters are helping. Devan starts laughing and I see clothes moving to the water. The water goes on at the tanker truck and the pussies are running to get away from it. Fuckin' Colt is controlling the only hose left and he's hitting everything they have. The water goes off and the only thing I hear is the chanting. It changes to a chant for peace. The pussies are moving together.

249

Prez moves, but Jeremy doesn't let him go. "They can't jam your signals. Get feeds up now. Ask for help from Vets. Ask for media help. Keep sending out what you can while they're down. You are American citizens in need of protection. People aren't getting your message. Put it out while you can." Jeremy pulls him back.

"Christian we must go," Co tells me.

"Remember your fathers and sleep in peace tonight." I look at our group. "Hold on. It will be harder, but together we can do this. Draw from each other and jump. Now!"

It seems like it takes forever to get back. As soon as we hit I sit down. Holy fuck that was crazy. Everyone is talking, but I gather what I can from the ancestors. Jeremy moves to my side and touches my knee. 'Brother.'

"Yeah, fuckin' crazy." I lay back closing my eyes. Hawk sits against me. "Thanks Brother." When I can, I sit up giving thanks to the ancestors and everyone that showed. The elders thank us and are gone.

My dad kneels in front of me. "So proud of my boys tonight. All of our people matter. It's good to see my sons fighting with them. When you need me, call, I'm honored to stand with my sons." He hugs me and stands. Mase and Jeremy fist bump me then the MC is gone.

Co and Dakota sit beside me. Prez comes over and stands behind Dakota. Co touches me and I feel almost human again. "I have made calls for help from the men of war. We have many tribesmen that have fought for this land. They will show to help. The ancestors are pleased with your efforts my Warrior Protector. Your abilities are increasing and new are showing. With your Prophet and Leader, you are aligned and will be bound to all your Protectors allowing the sharing of abilities and skill. This is not given lightly, you have proven yourself with the children, the Protectors, and your people. Showing respect for all you have been given pleases the ancestors and shows them your understanding of the power of those gifts. Seek your Prophet and Leader for guidance and remember your fathers."

I look at Dakota, "It was a test?" He nods and Prez laughs shaking his head. "Take me home. I need a drink." Co laughs and I look at him and my grandmother. "Thank you Co and Nunánuk for your guidance and wisdom."

I open my eyes and fall forward putting my head on the table. "Holy fuck." I hear Uncle Danny laugh, but I can't move to see him. Nekanis leans against my leg. "I feel like I've been hit by a truck."

"Why is he so drained Dakota?" Prez asks and I want to laugh, but can't.

"Do you remember carrying Taylor? Christian carries the weight of those that cannot jump. The readers are helpful, but a heavy burden on him. He is not recovered from being hit by a car either. Luckily Jeremy showed to help."

"Sonofabitch. You think you can give him a fuckin' day off Prez?" Darren says and I laugh then moan with my head still on the table.

"He will need to guide the readers Mucimi gave here. Some will need assistance to get away from the hunters."

"Mase, Colt and Devan can do the shit he does," Prez says and it sounds like a question.

Dakota puts his hand on my back and I feel heat flow through me. "They are not able to transcend space as Christian does. Without him, only Mase is able to get to the ancestors, but he can go no further."

"He brings all of us?" I want to sit up so I push on my arms. Dakota pulls me up the rest of the way and I lean back in the chair. I want the answer to that too.

"With ancestor help and the Shaman."

251

"And you Dakota," I say and sound drunk. I could use a drink.

He laughs. "Our Warrior Protector could use a drink. I am able to help by throwing energy at him to make it through. I do not have that ability and am told it is not necessary for me to have it."

"Shit," I say thinking that would make this easier. They all laugh, but a glass is put in front of me so I drink and tune them out. When I put it down it's refilled. I drink more and sit back. "I need a ride home." They stop talking and look at me. "What? I got a new dog and I'm done for today."

Uncle Danny laughs. "Let's get you home Brother."

Dean

Two men bring Christian in and I'm scared to death. What the hell happened to him today? He's supposed to be taking it easy because he got hit by a car *yesterday*! This is nuts. Jessie and Taylor come in and sit at the table. "There are two men and a dog upstairs putting Christian to bed."

Taylor laughs. "That's Uncle Steve and Uncle Danny. They would give their lives for him and you. Right now, he's exhausted and maybe a little drunk."

"Dakota is on his way," Jessie says like that's going to help.

I sit down not knowing what else to do. "Why is he exhausted? He got run over yesterday!"

Taylor waves his hand. "Something about carrying all the readers to the pipeline and stopping them from hurting the protesters."

"And the kids. Getting the places and names of people that are being hunted had him jumping too."

Are they kidding? "Do you people know what it's like to be hit by a car? He was supposed to have an easy day. To... oh, I don't know, *recuperate from that!*"

Taylor laughs. "It was easier than yesterday. That was fuckin' sick."

Sick good or sick bad? They're all nuts. Dakota comes in with Mucimi and Jacob. They all nod to me and walk right by. Taylor and Jessie don't seem to have a problem with this. "Do I have to stay here? That big scary guy said, 'Stay.'"

"You should stay then," Taylor says.

Eliza and Beth come in and I wonder why everyone is looking at each other. Beth makes coffee and Jessie and Taylor walk out. Nuts I tell ya. Nuts!

Eliza sits down and smiles. She's nuts too. "We thought you might need female support. All the testosterone has got to be making you crazy by now."

"It is. He was hit by a damn car yesterday and by the sound of it, he was fighting again today. What is wrong with these men? What the hell are they all doing up there?"

Beth puts coffee in front of me and sits down. "Dakota and Mucimi are healers. They can help where doctors can't. They helped Holly after she was attacked. Dakota also helped Taylor through his worst PTSD episodes. If Jeremy were here he'd be up there with them." I nod because I've heard they heal. "The Brothers will always work to help anyone in need, but especially their families. That's what they're doing. Christian needs them and they're here for him and you."

"That's nice and all, but he was already hurt."

253

Eliza turns and looks me in the eye. "When you needed help, Christian took out teams of men trying to get at you. When they sent more he went to your house and brought you to Security. He didn't ask if you wanted him there. You *needed* him there and he showed up. That's what they do. When Taylor was going through the bad times he showed up for work and did his job. When I was held by the Outlaws the Princes showed up and freed me. They didn't ask for anything, but let me walk away a free woman after being a slave." She was a slave? She pauses then goes on. "There is a threat to readers. They're being hunted and killed because they can read. Just like you. What the Brothers do is fight for good. We fight for right and we fight hard. This isn't normal, but it's happening right now. It has to stop and you of all people know why. The PD isn't helping the innocent readers. They didn't ask to be born reading, but they're marked for death because of it. Christian is the guy that can help them. He reads, has visions and a bunch of other abilities that he'll have to explain to you. He's not the guy that will let a broken leg stop him from saving a life. Yesterday he saved the Officers, kids and you. Today he saved water protestors and got the leads to save readers all over the country."

I think about all she's said, but can't get past him being carried in by those guys. "What if he dies?" I can't do this again.

Beth gets tissues and hands me the box. "With the Brothers, he always has someone at his back. He isn't going to die. Are you happy with Christian?"

I wipe my eyes. "Yes, I know it sounds crazy, but I love him."

Eliza nods. "You make everything count. They do what ordinary men won't. You stand beside him proud that he's willing to fight for right today and feed the homeless tomorrow."

"He feeds the homeless?"

254

They look at each other. "Feeds the homeless, builds houses for them, helps keep Vets off the street, works with the teen runaways, is a support person for PTSD servicemen, helps the reservations with anything they need and works with the kids training and shit," Eliza says. I can see him working and smiling as she's saying it.

I sit back shocked. Holly didn't tell me all this, but I can't read her like I can read them. "When does he sleep?"

Beth laughs. "Christian doesn't sleep or he doesn't sleep much."

I'm looking right at her and I know she's telling me the truth, but I've slept with him. Maybe only I slept. How damn weird is that?

Eliza lifts my chin and I get a zap of energy from her. "The thing with Brothers is everything they do is hard. They fight hard, play hard and fall hard. When they find the one, they don't look back and do everything they can to make her theirs. They do that fast. Warp speed fast. Every old lady, but Lily spent a matter of days with their men and were moved in. Every old lady loved their men in that time. It's just the way it works. The men follow a code with the old ladies. They don't cheat, leave or give up. They treat us like princesses and all they expect back is our love. That's it. They do everything with some weird sense of showing us how they feel and expect only love in return. Don't ever try to cut the grass. I'm just sayin'."

I laugh. I see Darren taking the mower away from her and beating it with a hammer. "Okay. That explains a lot. They do a whole panty thing and washing you like babies too right?"

They're both nodding. "If I can shower alone once a week I'm lucky. Taylor's crazy. He wanted to shave me so I'd get in the tub." Beth's hands are flying with a disgusted look on her face and I laugh.

Eliza is nodding. "I just let him. It's easier."

255

They're funny and I can't help laughing. "I thought he'd lost his mind."

Shaking their heads no, they get serious. "It really is something passed down to them. The Brothers that go 'all in' don't do divorce. They stay together for life. I've been with Darren for years and he hasn't stopped treating me like a princess yet. His mom and dads are the same. Kate is treated like a princess too. It's like it's all they know." Eliza is very easy to read and sets my mind at ease.

I nod. "So I let him do all his nutty stuff and just love him? What do I do today? The guy is hurt and weird things are happening up there."

Beth waves her hand like it's nothing. "He'll be fine tomorrow. It's an energy thing with him from what I'm told. Jeremy and Dakota are like that too. If they get too much energy or expend too much they need time to regroup or something."

I get that. "So, he isn't hurt today, but has an energy issue?"

They nod. We hear footsteps coming down the stairs and turn toward the doorway. The scary guys walk in. The one with the patch smiles and kisses Eliza on the head. "Glad you made coffee." She smiles. She loves him. He looks at me. "I'm Danny and I'm going to help myself."

I laugh and nod. "Nice to meet you. I'm Dean."

I look at the other guy. He's way scarier, but smiles. "Steve. Dog's with Christian. Learned Mohegan, but knows some English. Two cups of food tonight. Stuff's out and new toys for him."

I nod, but have no idea what he's talking about. Hawk died yesterday. Do I tell him that?

Danny smiles, I bet seeing the confusion on my face. "Christian has a new dog. He helps with the energy and protects him. He learned commands in Mohegan, but knows some English. He works best with thinking the commands. His food pail is in the pantry, he gets two cups tonight and in the morning. He'll need to be walked. There's a chest on the back deck with his toys and one in the living room. The living room just leave open and he'll put his toys away when he's done."

I nod. Steve smiles. "What he said." I laugh.

A woman with a crutch comes in with an Indian. "Hi everyone!" She's beautiful and smiling like she hasn't seen us in a year. "We came to check on Christian too. I'm Joey, Christian's sister. He sent me an email about you Dean. This is Sebastian."

I nod telling her it's nice to meet them. Danny stands giving Sebastian a look. "You got a date yet?"

Joey rolls her eyes. Beth and Eliza laugh and stand up. "If the family is showing we'll get out of your way," Beth says with a big smile.

I nod wondering who else is showing. Serenity comes in and I think I should lock the door. Steve laughs. My head swings toward him. "You're a reader too?" They all nod. "Damn you all need warning labels on your foreheads so I can keep up."

They think I'm cute. Like every single one of them think it. Sebastian tells me he reads too. I just roll my eyes. Serenity thinks this is funny and I give her a look. Steve and Danny leave behind Beth and Eliza. I look at Joey. "They brought him home and told me to stay. Dakota is up there with Jacob and Mucimi. I don't know anything else." Sebastian walks toward the stairs. "Is he a healer too?"

She smiles and I love how happy she is. "Not at Dakota and Jeremy's level, but yes."

Okay then. "Would you like some coffee?"

She sits waving her hand. "My office is attached to Dunkin'. I am full of caffeine today. I'm fine and if I get thirsty I can get a drink."

I nod and look at Serenity. "I like her."

"Did the old ladies set you straight with the crazy shit the Brothers do?"

I giggle. "Yes. They're quite the boyfriends and husbands."

"They are." She giggles.

Serenity laughs. "I expected you to be a basket case."

"Oh, I was. Eliza and Beth explained and I get it now. Well not the healer thing, but the rest. He had an energy problem, he didn't get hurt again."

She's surprised. "Energy like you? Someone touched him?"

Joey is watching us with a smile. I look at Serenity. "Similar, but different." She doesn't ask and thinks she doesn't need to know. I agree so I stay quiet.

Joey tells us about her family. I've heard most of it, but she's funny and so damn happy. When Sebastian comes down she stands and asks if she can hug me. "We have a ten second rule and Christian is my biological brother. I get the touch thing."

I stand and hug her moving away fast, but she's smiling. "I'm so glad he found you! It took him long enough." Sebastian pulls her to the door. She didn't get to see Christian. Maybe Sebastian tells her.

Serenity looks at me. "They are the craziest happy people I've ever seen."

"You don't know the half of it." I tell her all that's happened and she's shocked. When I get to the panties and baths, I tell her what Beth and Eliza said, and she's laughing.

"I wish a man would treat me like that. This is priceless. You deserve every minute of it Dean. Don't let the little things slip by." She's smiling, but I know she's thinking of Dad. I just nod.

Dakota, Jacob and Mucimi come down. "He will be fine. Nekanis is with him and will help. Do not be alarmed if he does not respond. He jumped to the ancestors for strength."

"Thank you, Dakota. You too Mucimi and Jacob." Mucimi giggles and we laugh. He's so damn cute. I look at Dakota. "Nekanis?"

He smiles. "His dog."

Okay then. They leave with Jacob doing the chin thing and I look at Serenity.

"Is it me or do they all look like models?"

I laugh. "Every one of them. How do you like the job?"

She's happy. "It's the best job I've ever had. Everyone is respectful. Weird, but in a good way. I love Jess too, she's a trip. The woman has her shit together and is so smart."

"I heard that too. I'm glad you're happy."

She stands. "I'm getting out of your hair. I wanted to check on you and make sure you're doing okay. Do you need anything?"

"No. Christian is determined to take care of everything. Oh, I didn't tell you my news. I have a phone! The bill is mine before you go spastic about it and I enrolled in school. I have the money for that too." I take my phone out and call hers.

She presses, buttons and smiles. "I'm so proud of you!" She hugs me quick. "Letting him take care of you doesn't mean you lose your values. I'm glad to see them show." I nod smiling.

When she leaves, I run up the stairs. Christian looks like he's sleeping and Nekanis is laying against him. When I climb on the bed I'm nervous the dog will bite me, but he watches and lays his head back down. I move closer and lay my head on Christian's chest. His arm goes around me pulling me closer. I smile and fall asleep.

Chapter Ten

Christian

I open my eyes and smile. Dean and Nekanis are on each side of me. I look for the time and see it's just after midnight. Checking my people, I see all are settled so I get some work done. Mucimi's list is all over the fuckin' place. I get the laptop hovering above my legs and put the readers in an order by need then run through it. Pulling up a map I pin each location and get it all on spreadsheets. We need a place for processing. I make a list for Prez and send it by OC.

Nekanis jumps down and wants out. Suspending us I move the pillows around and get Dean comfortable. It's almost four, but I think she'll stay sleeping. I kiss her head and take Nekanis down to the beach. He runs ahead and I laugh telling him to go. When he comes back I throw a stick for him. He's happy and full of energy. I sit and jump with him. Sitting on the rock I'm happy to watch Hawk running around the lake with Nekanis following.

I feel Dean. She's terrified of something. I call to Nekanis and jump. Nekanis runs while I move a foot above the sand, then grass and road. It looks like every light in the house is on. "Dean!" I yell coming through the door.

I move up the stairs hearing her crying. "Dean!" What the fuck happened? I feel her hurt and scared.

She's on the bed crying. "Oh, my God! I'm so glad you're okay."

Fuck. "I'm sorry baby. I thought you'd sleep until I got back." I lift her to me and hold her against my chest while I spin and sit. I should have left a note.

"I thought something else happened."

I kiss her head. "No baby. I just took Nekanis for a walk and lost track of time."

261

She sits up and looks at me. "You're fine after yesterday?" I nod feeling like a shit for making her worry. "You were just walking the dog?"

"Yeah. I don't sleep much so I walk the dog, work or work out at night."

She nods. "They said you didn't sleep much."

"Who?"

"Beth and Eliza. They were here before. I didn't know. I checked everywhere."

The old ladies came to talk to her? They must have seen something wrong. "Are you okay?"

She waves it away. "Now that you're here I am. I was so scared. Something has me nervous, I thought it was you being hurt again. Once it was in my head nothing else got through. Nothing else mattered."

I clench my jaw to stop from smiling. I'm a dick, but nothing mattered if I was hurt. I shut the lights off in all, but this room and stand up. "I'm fine my worried Little Pixie. I should have left a note or told you where I go. I'd never leave the Compound without telling you. Uncle Danny put a gym in the basement for me and I work from here or walk on the beach."

She nods. I strip her clothes off and she's smiling. "I'll remember it next time and look for you there first." When my clothes start coming off she laughs. "You didn't actually walk on the beach did you?"

"No, more like over it. I didn't want to get sand in the cast."

She doesn't ask any more questions. I kiss her moving us over the bed. "I missed you last night." I kiss down her neck.

"You held onto me and I fell asleep. That feels good. I only woke up to feed the dog and let him out. When I came

262

back you did the same thing." She moves my head to her tit and I get to making her forget about talking.

Since it's working, I move lower and breathe in that scent I've been craving. Then I taste her. Jesus I'm never going to get enough of this. Her hands are in my hair traveling down my shoulders and back up until she screams. I love her touching me and move up her body. "I love to hear my name when you come baby. So fuckin' beautiful." She kisses me like she can't get enough and I'm grinding into her.

"Love me Christian."

Jesus. I move me up and look at her. "We've got time baby."

"I don't want to wait another minute Christian. I love you. It's just wasted time if I don't show you."

My mouth crashes down and I hold her tight while showing her what that means to me. Patches' list runs through my head and I raise up. "I love you too Dean. I never thought I'd get the chance to say it and here you are. Let me show you baby." She's got tears in her eyes, but she's smiling. "Are you sure?"

"Positive." She's serious and I see the truth of that in her eyes.

I picture my hands all over her and she moans. I get a condom over to me and she snatches it out of the air smiling. "I love your hands touching me everywhere even though I see them right here."

My finger slides into her and I get a moan. She's breathing heavy when I slide a second in. "You're so fuckin' wet." The package in her hand tears and I pull the condom out moving it to me. She watches with a purring sound deep in her chest. When I'm covered, I kiss her, moving her legs out and bending her knees high. "I love you my beautiful

263

Little Pixie." The tip of my dick touches her entrance and she tenses up. "Relax baby. I'll make it good for you."

She watches me and nods. Taking a deep breath, she lets it out, "I'm ready."

As soon as she relaxes I slide in. Holy fuck I'm not going to make it. She grips my arms. "I'd never hurt you babe. Relax for me." I picture the little bump inside her and stroke it lightly. Her whole body relaxes and I see my hands all over her. She moans and I slide in until I'm stopped. With my mind touching every part of her I watch her eyes and pull back. Stroking her g-spot harder, I push through. Her breath catches and a tear falls. I lick it away and kiss her eyes waiting for her to be ready for more. "Tell me when baby." Her eyes close. I'm going to die here. When she opens them she nods. I picture my hands moving faster and hold her tight. "So fuckin' beautiful baby. You feel incredible." I pull out moving slow. She rolls her hips into me and I move. Never have I felt this close or so fuckin' good. My head is spinning and she holds me tighter. Fuck. "We're going Dean just hold on."

"Christian!" She grabs onto my back and rolls her hips.

Jesus. We're at the reservation and everything is flying through me. "Feel them Dean, the ancestors are happy today. You can feel them." I'm awed by the touch of the wind and colors swirling around us. She's already tight, but when she's ready I lose my breath. "Dean."

"I love you Christian." She squeezes my dick again and I hold my breath hearing her scream.

Holy fuck. I open my eyes and laugh. Fuckin' freaky just jumped to a new high. Dean is against my chest and still holding me tight. She's out. Shaking my head I raise us off the bed. I'm glad she's out and doesn't see the blood or me smiling the whole time I'm cleaning her. She gave that to me. Swear to God, I feel like beating my chest. I calm myself and bring us back to the bed so I can hold her.

I go through my people and don't see anything concerning. I open and see the woman from the top of the reader list talking to Dean. Interesting, but I push it away. Prez is talking in front of the Baxter's plane. I push it away. Mucimi running stops me. I watch it through and try to get time. He's scared, but I can't see when it's happening. Aquyà is calling to him to keep going. Mack runs past him. I look around and see Brandon run toward him and fall. Fuck! I close my eyes trying for time again, but it's gone.

I jump holding my girl and sit on the rock with Hawk. The ancestors come, throwing relief over me. Co tells me to relax and spend time considering all around me. I thank him and the ancestors and jump back much calmer.

It's not five minutes and Dean moves. "How do you feel baby?"

"Like silly putty." I laugh. Silly putty is good I guess. "What happened? Don't get me wrong, it was the most incredible feeling, but I don't think that happens to everyone. No one would ever be seen again."

I can't help laughing again. "I don't know babe. We were here, then it's like I was sucked into the spirit world with the ancestors. They were happy we were there. All the colors and them flowing through me was like a show of them accepting us. It's not anything I've ever felt before."

'It is so Christian. The ancestors are pleased with your union and were showing you that pleasure,' Dakota says.

'Seriously dude? This isn't the time for you to be throwing shit in my head. I can talk to you later.'

Dean looks at me. "Fuckin' Dakota telling me the ancestors are pleased with our union."

265

She cracks up then I do. When we're both quiet I ask again. "Do you want me to run you a bath? It might help if you're sore."

"I feel good Christian. Thank you. I can take a quick shower. I must be a mess." I see her face turn red before she puts it on my chest.

"You're clean babe. We both are." I kiss her head smiling again. "Nothing between us should embarrass you. Every woman gives herself to someone and every man should be honored to receive that gift. We are no different. Well, the ancestor thing was different, but I am honored and so fuckin' glad you chose me."

She giggles making me smile. "The ancestor thing was cool."

"It was. Love you Dean, but we need to get up."

"Yes. I don't want to be late for work. Thank you for taking care with me and making it so special. I love you Christian."

I lift her chin and kiss her loving the sound of that.

I walk in and Mucimi and Teller come running. I kiss Dean's lips and bend putting the cast in front of me to balance. She walks into the classroom and they both hug me. Mucimi is scared. He saw the vision through Aquyà. Jesus these kids are going to be fuckin' strong. "I'll get with Jeremy and Dakota and we'll do what we do little man. Protecting you is our job." Teller lets me go and takes Mucimi back to the classroom. Aquyà is at the door watching me. "You need a minute?" He nods.

I throw him the daycare room and follow him in. "The ancestors said you will teach what is needed. Mucimi needs a way to shut off from everyone."

I'm fuckin' shocked. "You've jumped?"

He nods, "My dad jumps with us then comes back when we are ready."

"All of you?" I'm relieved they didn't go alone.

"No, Phoenix, Teller, Mucimi and Justice. Dad said we have to wait until you teach the rest. They don't go yet and Brandon and Stella don't jump." This confuses him.

"Brandon is like Jacob. He is support for the Protectors. Stella is like your mom and grandmother. She will make the world better, but doesn't rely on the past to do that."

I see when he gets it and he nods. "Will you teach Mucimi how to shut the visions off? He's not sleeping right and worries all the time. Phoenix is worried too. He said Mucimi is too little to see so much."

I'm hit with a vision of Phoenix and Aquyà together, but older. They are leaders and will work together. I push it away and focus on Aquyà. "I'm trying to get time to teach him Aquyà. Everything has been coming at us and I'm having trouble making the time for him. He's not sleeping?"

He shakes his head no. "You could teach him at night. Do you need to be with him?"

I shake my head no already working a plan of action in the back of my mind. "I'll work with Mucimi. Try to keep him calm and I'll start tonight. Yeah?"

He jumps to me. "Yeah. Thank you my Warrior Protector."

I hold my laugh and give him a squeeze. "You're welcome Aquyà. Let Phoenix know."

He nods. "I already did."

I laugh as he runs out. Fuckin' kids.

I pull up to Security and suspend up the stairs. Nekanis stays right with me. Uncle Steve holds the door and I'm surprised he's still here. "Needed some time. Somethin's wrong with the kids."

I nod. "I got it. I need to see Prez."

He nods. "Office."

I tell Nekanis to go eat and throw him that I'll be in Prez's office. He goes to the break room and I go to Prez's.

"Listens good."

I turn surprised he's following. "Yeah." I knock and walk in. Uncle Danny is sitting in front of Prez's desk. "I can come back."

"No, I need to talk to you." He looks at Uncle Danny then Uncle Steve. "You're driving me fuckin' crazy. While you're here nothing is getting settled at the MC. We need all of us to get through the next few months. The biggest threat we're facing is against you. The fuckin' fanatics aren't helping, but they aren't anything compared to your shit. All that happened, all the explosives, vehicles and men, cost money. I don't have the people here to follow all that and deal with the threat from the fanatics. You saw what Mucimi gave us. This will take time and planning and I can't afford the people to do that while they're running down leads for you. Go home. Settle your shit with Pres and get everyone working on the leads we have. Dakota is waiting at the hangar." Fuck. He isn't asking.

They look at each other and Uncle Danny stands. "He's right. We have the PD and MC-Baxter's spinning their wheels waiting for direction and we're playing shuttle service here. Let's go VP, we got shit to do."

I watch them walk out and Prez sits hard putting his hands in his hair. "They make me fuckin' crazy." I can see that. He sits up and pulls a file. "Your list first. I had to shut the boards down, but saw you've added sheets."

I nod as he opens the hologram board. "We have another vision. The kids are upset. Mucimi got it from Aquyà. It has Mucimi running scared, Aquyà calling him to keep going and Brandon shot running to help him."

"Fuckin' hell. I need a way to help that kid, he can't be watching all this at fuckin' three." He stands and paces.

"He isn't sleeping. I told Aquyà I can work with him at night. It calmed him and Phoenix."

He nods. "How likely is that to work?"

"He'll spend a lot of time with the ancestors because it helps calm him. He's strong Prez. I can show him how to shield and stop what's coming in until he's with someone or ready to deal with it. Kind of how Jeremy works."

He stops pacing and looks at me. "You can stop them now?"

"Not stop them, but shield until I'm ready to look. I still get hit with some, but it's not the constant movie in front of the now."

He understands and sits. "You're changing fast. This is good. Mucimi has a chance at a normal life?"

I laugh. "There isn't anything normal about any of the kids Prez. He'll make it to happy though and it won't take as long as I did."

He's surprised then smiles. "You made her yours. I'm happy for you Brother. You deserve happy after the fuckin' nightmare you've lived."

I throw him chin not knowing what to say to that.

"Do you have anything else on Brandon?" he asks and I'm glad to be off Dean. I shake my head no. "Let's get to the list."

He's got two old houses that can be used for the readers when they get here. There's a storefront by our PD that can be used for processing and he's got Shilah ready for the influx of people needing jobs. Nothing jumps out at me so he moves to the pipeline. José has spots going on all major networks and Mitch has social media spots all due to start today. A donation has been made for legal aid and food for the protestors. RVs are being delivered along with insulated tents and generators. Jamie has men with equipment to clear the trucks blocking the road so everything can get through and Ben has media already there recording the progress and stories from the protestors. Since jammers are off, everyone is putting up the stories and people are noticing.

I'd say I'm surprised by all he's done and it's not even nine, but he's Prez and this is what he does.

"If there's nothing else, Dakota is waiting for you to show. You need to see if this reader can be helpful and the MC needs direction on what to do with him."

I stand. "I need to see Jeremy and Aubrey first. I'll let you know when I can."

He throws chin and I'm out the door. I get Nekanis in my truck so we can make the trip to the hangar. I call Dean to let her know I'm out of the yard. The whole yard conversation has me laughing when we board the chopper. Uncle Danny is not amused. "He didn't tell us we were waiting for you. I could have gotten breakfast while you took your sweet time getting here."

I sit and Nekanis leans against me. "He didn't tell me until five minutes ago that I was leaving." I hold my smile thinking Prez is making a point.

I connect to Aiyana letting her know all that's happening. She's excited and drops me to go see the Elders and check out the Facebook feeds.

Security is at the hangar and takes me to MC-Baxter. Jesus the whole front corner is black with soot going a good fifty feet high and new plywood is covering the damage.

Walking in I'm stopped and have to show ID. I'm told Jeremy is working with Geek. Something is wrong, but he's not sharing so I hunt him down. Coming down the hall I hear Pres. Fuck someone is in trouble. I see it and move faster.

"Stop! What the fuck?"

Pres actually growls at me. "He should already have this. I'm not explaining myself to an Officer from another fuckin' Club!"

I look at Jeremy. He's shutting down. Fuckin' Brothers. "Maybe you should. He's not a fuckin' geek. He's HS, trained and working to keep you and your whole fuckin' Club safe. Why is he even here?"

Uncle Steve and Danny walk in and sit down. Pres looks like he wants to rip my head off. I don't move and wait for an answer. He looks at them. "Glad you decided to show up. Why does this kid think he deserves answers from me?"

"Saved your life. Deserves answers," Uncle Steve says and Pres looks shocked.

"We have a fuckin' list of injured and lost a Brother and BS. You two take off and don't answer a fuckin' call. Kids that don't take orders when they're given. Our building has a fuckin' hole in it and now fuckin' kids demanding answers showing no respect." His hands go in his hair.

I touch Jeremy's arm. "Go to the KC and wait for me."

"Do you see this?" He looks at me. "He is a member in the MC. He takes his orders directly from me until I see he follows them!"

"No. He's the Brother that got here in time to stop a truck from blowing your fuckin' ass up. This whole building went with everyone in it. He saved your Club and this is the thanks he gets for it? You want to know what he saw?" I throw him the pictures as I'm talking. "Devan took off.

Brenna drank herself to death. Elizabeth commits suicide. Kate falls into depression and never climbs out. The Club doesn't make it. The PD falls apart. Drugs run rampant here, which is a source of comfort for the kids trying to find peace with the loss of so many members. For Jeremy, all that loss loses him Aubrey because there's no Security to have his back. What was going through his head as he was getting them here, against your orders, was he needed to make sure you survived. With you, the vision and drive. With you, we have hope. He is not an MC member that refused to follow orders. He is an MC member with more vision than you'll ever understand and knew what he had to do to make sure you lived."

Pres sits down stunned. I look at Jeremy. "Go to KC and wait for me."

He looks at Pres, but Pres's mind is spinning with all I said and showed him. He throws me chin and walks out.

"I get that we are just the kids to you. You don't know about visions because you don't get them. Your kids do. Your kids have all that Wall did and more. You can keep holding them back and punishing them for what you don't understand, but Wall thought you were the man with the vision needed to make a difference in the world. He was Mohegan. Did you know that?" He shakes his head no and looks like he's going to pass out. "Wall is with our ancestors and gives us the peace and strength we need to keep going. Life is fuckin' hard as a reader. Visions are worse. That's why Wall stayed in his rooms. The visions were too fuckin' hard. We get to see what happens after too. Seeing everyone you love die time and again is bad enough. We don't need to fight you every step of the way just to keep that from happening. What happened to Aubrey before is nothing compared to what happens to her in the new visions. Jeremy can't handle much more Pres. We need him to keep us all safe. Since he was six years old he's proven himself over and over to you. He's an adult now. I think he's earned a little more respect than he's shown. Wall would have given him that. He gave it to you."

I look at Uncle Danny and Uncle Steve and throw them chin then look back at Pres. "I'll be in KC when you want to shoot me. I got people to see and shit to do." I hear Uncle Danny laughing as I'm walking down the hall. I suspend down the stairs stopping people in their tracks, but I just keep going. I'm fuckin' pissed that no one told me all that's been going on.

Nekanis jumps in the SUV and Security takes me to KC. Jeremy is sitting on the couch looking at the wall in front of him. Ricky comes out pissed. "He showed here like that. He shut down Brother. I haven't been able to talk to him because he was chained to Security. I got all the kids working on Diego's new program. I didn't know what else to do with them."

I look and pull what I can. "They walked out?"

"Yeah. Jeremy helped them shield so you had some time to get back on your feet. Since you're here you can talk to them. Pres is pissed."

Fuck. No wonder he's so fuckin' mad. "I think I just made that worse Brother."

"Fuckin' great. Princes taking apps?"

I smile, but see he's serious. Jesus. "Let me try and fix this."

He doesn't think there's a fix here. He walks back to his office and I call Prez. "I need help. Pres had Jeremy working as a geek and I came in on him yelling at Jeremy for not getting something fast enough. I stopped him and told him the vision then what happened after. It wasn't a pretty picture. The kids walked out on him and Jeremy is shut down in the KC. Ricky's asking if you're taking apps and he's completely serious. He wants out—feeling like a

273

babysitter and not a part of the Club. I haven't seen or heard a thing about the reader yet." I take a breath and wait.

"I have Dakota meeting with Jeremy. He'll be there in a couple of minutes. Abel is flying me up, I'm twenty out."

I hear him moving and see him on the stairs. "Thanks, Prez." Now that I've fucked everyone's day up I look for Devan to find out about my reader.

He's in with Diego and I pull him out. The reader is too sick for anyone to get much from him. Devan thinks we need to give him time to recuperate in order to get anything helpful. That works just fine for me. I ask about the kids walking out.

He sits. "This whole thing is a fuckin' mess. We have Ricky, but he can't do shit for anyone. He tried to get to Jeremy and got dismissed right in the middle of Ops. It was bad. Ally walked then all the kids did. Even Victor is here. Pres is wrong Brother. Ricky is President of the Little Brothers. That used to mean something. We used to mean something." He walks back to the meeting room. Jesus. He wants out too.

I stand against the wall and look in on all of them. They all feel like they don't matter here. I see Prez on the chopper and throw him all of them one by one. 'Get them all at the KC. I'm less than ten out.'

I call to all the Protectors and tell them to get all the kids here. Mase and Colt walk through the family door hall and Mase stops short seeing Dakota with Jeremy.

"What the fuck did he do to him now?" he yells and everyone starts coming out of the offices.

Dakota stands and looks at me. I throw Prez is ten out. He nods and focuses on Jeremy. I wave Mase over. "It would be good if you don't incite a riot. Abel is dropping Prez in less than ten."

"He bringing apps?" Mase asks and Colt laughs thinking he'll fill one out.

I tell everyone to find seats and Ricky has Blake and Victor bring a table up from the back. Everyone is moving chairs from the offices and meeting room. Tiny and Bob come in. Then Patches and Tess. When Kate and my mom come in I look at Dakota. "Oh fuck."

He throws Prez just landed. Amanda and Penny come in with Marty and Geek. What the fuck? I start looking for why they're all here and see it's the same as the kids, but from the parents' point of view. This is fuckin' bad. I throw to Prez so he's prepared. Nancy comes in with Judy and Sandy. I'm surprised to see them, they don't have much to do with KC. I look and see why. There's a whole area that I never looked at before. Seeing everyone's concern, I should have.

Dakota stands when the elevator door opens and Prez comes in. 'He is not responding Prez. Perhaps Aubrey can help,' he throws.

I look for her. She's sitting in her room, but disconnected. Prez looks at me and I throw it to him. He puts a tie in his hair and pulls Ricky to the side.

Uncle Danny and Uncle Steve come in with Pres following. He doesn't want to be here and is bitching them out in his head. I look the other way. No one is saying a word.   .

Prez and Ricky walk to the middle of everyone and Uncle Steve pushes a chair out at the first table. "Sit." Pres glares at him, but sits down.

"We seem to have a bigger problem than I thought was happening when I left Princes. If it is not resolved today my answer is yes to you all. We have the resources to cover you and would not turn you away." Pres is glaring at him and stands up pissed.

"Sit and listen," Uncle Danny says and Pres sits.

Prez looks around. "I think what you're looking for will be easy to accomplish if Pres understands the concern. Remember, he is not a reader and does not fully understand what impact or support that implies."

"That's the problem. Our abilities are great when it helps him get what he wants, but he doesn't get that we can't shut them off when he doesn't need us," Colt says.

"Sitting around waiting to be called nurses. We're not even working part time. We only work when they need a reader or help because someone is off. At Princes, everyone has a real job. Billy said he works five days a week. José said you need help too. We have readers here that can help Christian. You understand what we go through," Blake says.

"And you're not afraid of the girls," Elizabeth says and everyone snickers.

Prez holds his hand up. "You're wrong. I don't get visions, so I didn't understand. Christian taught me a hard lesson. It's not a mistake I'll make again, but it was a lesson I had to learn."

Kate steps forward. "You learned it though and fixed it. The problem here is our kids are undervalued, unappreciated and want to move. If they leave, we lose their parents too. I know Tiny and Nancy looked at houses down there. Geek and Marty are considering it if Jeremy leaves. Cloud and CJ won't stay if this isn't fixed. Amanda and Bob won't let the kids go alone. Rich, Tess and Patches want someone that not only understands readers, but sees the kids as the capable men and women they have grown into. Everyone is looking for the same thing here. You're right Little Ben, there is an easy solution, it isn't that it hasn't been talked about, it's that it's been brushed aside for years."

Prez nods and turns to Pres. "Years is a long fuckin' time Pres. Are you ready yet?" Uncle Steve laughs.

Pres stands up. "You'd all leave?"

Judy suspends and moves toward Pres. "I'm Judy. You don't really know much about me. You think I'm just a kid and I have nothing to offer you. I didn't grow up with you, but I have visions and read. I saw you die in the explosion Jeremy stopped. Then I saw you treat him like he did something wrong. I never wanted to work for you, but I don't want you to die. You will. The next one is worse and you die." I step forward and Prez puts his hand up stopping me. "Your family too. The kids move and so do the Officers. You get so mad that you don't let Little Ben help. Then you die. I don't want you to die." Pres sits down, looking a little older.

Brenna stands and looks at Pres. "I don't either Dad, but you don't leave us much of a choice here. We have more readers here than the Princes and the reservation, but you put Protector Ops with them. We can all read you. You did that so it wouldn't get in the way of what you think of as 'real Ops'." Prez's head swings back to Pres. He's pissed. "When you need a reader, you find us, but the rest of the time we're stuck here without much to do. You don't think much of us."

Elizabeth walks to Prez. "Every one of us made HS before we hit seventeen. I'm twenty-six Pres. You think I'm at the Bakery because I like it?" She laughs. "I rank higher than you do and I bake fuckin' cinnamon rolls waiting for you to see that I can do the job. I'm tired of waiting. I know Little Ben wanted me to stay close to our mom, but Jesus, at least at Princes I can work at a job I'd like. You get to." She hugs Prez and moves back to the wall.

Geek walks up. "You, Steve and Tiny are my family. I grew up watching you make the world better for everyone. Everyone, but our kids. Everything they said is true. The first kids out; Little Ben, Brantley, Jessie, Darren, Taylor, Joey and Sheila. They worked, the little ones even worked through Little Ben. I was so proud that they not only learned, but taught us what they were worth. Something got lost when they left Ben. My boys are readers, I don't even know what the hell Half Pint is, but she needs direction and guidance. She's floating through life like Brenna said. That's not a life for them. What's going to happen to my boys? They're better on the computer than Jeremy was at their age, but they want HS. I don't want to see them used like Colt. Harley doesn't even have a chance at HS, but Colt is only called when it's convenient for us. Poor Aaron had to prove himself, then ended up running to the Princes just to have something to do. He sat down here day after day waiting for the call that he was needed. He's *your* son. What happens to *mine*?"

"You know I'd give my life for you," Tiny adds, "I've been telling you about Judy and Sandy for years. You saw Judy. She needs a job doing good like the Princes do. None of the kids have purpose here. Geek is right. With direction and guidance, they can make a difference just like you did. We've always been happy Pres, but they aren't. It's like watching the life being sucked out of them. We were supposed to make it better for our kids and we aren't doing that." Tiny doesn't move until Pres nods. Thank fuck. He sees there's a problem and he may be the reason.

Prez looks around. No one steps forward. "We need a minute or twenty." Everyone is throwing chin. Prez walks toward Ricky's office and throws for me and Dakota to follow. I fall in behind Uncle Danny. I think Uncle Steve is pushing Pres. Ricky is in his chair and Prez is behind him. Dakota stands behind Prez and I stand on his other side. Pres is sitting in front of Ricky with his head in his hands and I think it's symbolic.

"I was in this position not that long ago. You helped me see where I'd gone wrong. Teaching Christian and seeing Christian were two different things. This is your crossroad Pres. What do you want to do here?"

Pres looks up and I'm shocked at the pain in his eyes. "I fucked up their lives. I need to fix it, but I have no fuckin' clue what I need to do here. How do I give them what they need when I don't even know what it is?"

Prez takes a minute to answer him. "You have the people and the knowledge, you're just not using them. Ricky understands the kids better than anyone here and he's still stuck in the KC. Pulling him for meetings and ignoring his advice isn't working for anyone. Half your Club is ready to walk. Your solution is sitting in front of you."

Pres looks from Prez to Ricky. "Will you move to Security and help keep the kids happy?"

"No," Ricky says and Pres sits back. "I'm not going to be used like they are. If you're not serious about real change I'm done. I've spent years watching them be turned away by you. I've tried to tell you, but I'm dismissed as if I'm a Prospect. I've worked like everyone else and deserve more than a token office with a bone thrown to me whenever the mood strikes you. Jeremy is out there completely shut down. I can guarantee Aubrey is hiding somewhere the same way." I nod and Pres sees it. "You can't fake this one. That room is full of readers that see what you're thinking. If you really want change, you need something that shows them you mean it."

"Office connected to yours empty. Was Little Ben's, but he left," Uncle Steve says.

"You know he's right Ben. The girls deserve to be in HS. The boys should be working every day. They're better than what we have. The Protectors should be recognized by the Club. If you don't open Security to all of them, they're walking and so am I. Ricky can run a Club. He's been making money forever. He's HS and has never been given a patch. He can train and understands abilities more than you know because you've never asked." Uncle Danny shocks the shit out of all of us.

279

"You'd walk away? What about PD?" He's thinking *what about Kate*? but he thinks she'd go too.

"You aren't seeing that the problem is you. You don't understand what the kids need, but won't make the one move you need to keep your Club. Everyone else can see it Ben. Who do you think replaces you?"

Pres looks around honestly wondering who that would be. "Ricky?"

"'Bout fuckin' time," Uncle Steve says and I clench my jaw.

"Now that you've got that, what are you going to do to fix your Club and keep your Officers?" Uncle Danny all but rolls his eye.

Pres stands up and I see his mind working through this. He paces behind the chairs and I want to look at my watch, but keep my eyes on him. He's going around and around and I throw to him. 'Put Ricky in the office next to yours and groom him to run the MC. He is your replacement and you've wasted enough time. Listen to him, he's fuckin' smart as hell. Get the kids on the schedule and learn about their abilities so you can use the information to run your Club. And stop holding the girls back.' I just threw the last in, but I hope he listens.

He looks at me and I look at Prez to see if he's pissed. He's watching Pres so I look back at him. "Thank you Christian, I have wasted enough time. Let's go. I have a Club to fix."

Uncle Steve laughs. "'Bout fuckin' time."

Pres stops and looks at him. "My replacement means your replacement."

"Good with that. He can do the fuckin' paperwork."

I crack up and Prez hits me. We follow him out and I watch the relief flow through everyone. He's typical Pres easing everyone's mind apologizing and explaining how he got to where they are now. Kate mouths, 'thank you' to Uncle Danny and he smiles pointing to me. I look away.

Pres tells everyone he's moving Ricky and grooming him to take over—someday—and everyone laughs then we all cheer. I think Tiny is actually quiet, but I yell for both of us. Prez hits my arm and I stop. He laughs shaking his head.

When Pres is done, everyone is around him wanting his ear. He pulls Ricky to his side and I see the kids see it and approve. Prez looks at me. "You done?" I nod. "Let's get the fuck out of here before they start the party."

I throw to Ricky that we're out. He turns and salutes Prez and throws a 'thanks' to me. I smile shaking my head.

"You will not be able to get more than one or two if you bring Mase with you. Jeremy is not available for support Christian."

Prez looks at me. "It's a no from me." He sits at his spot at the table. "If we need to wait until you can do this alone then we wait."

Mucimi yells in my head, "No!" He throws pictures of the woman.

"She will not make it another day Prez." Dakota throws the pictures to Prez.

"I'll go alone."

He considers that and stands up. "One fuckin' thing that's easy today would be good."

I keep my mouth shut and tell Mucimi to stop with the fuckin' pictures. It's not helping. He stops and Prez looks at Dakota. "He goes alone and we're waiting for him every time he jumps back. We stop when it's too much even if we just get the woman out. Mucimi and Aiyana are there with us to support him."

Dakota smiles. "A very sound plan my great Warrior Leader."

Thank fuck! Prez looks at me. "We shoot for three. If I see it's too much we stop. I'm not fighting you or the fuckin' kids on this."

I nod, "We stop when you say."

His hands go in his hair. "I need to get José to reschedule a meet and we'll start. I should have taken Ricky for my fuckin' overflow."

Dakota laughs. "He is not needed here Prez."

Prez stops with his hand on the door. "Maybe you should do the fuckin' paperwork." He walks out and I crack up.

Dean

Sheila comes in the classroom and right over to me. "I brought your Jeep Dean. It's fuckin' sweet. Come see it."

I look at Holly and she nods smiling. "I'm so excited I almost hug her. "This is the best day yet! I can't believe he bought me a car!"

Sheila is laughing behind me. "When they put me on you today I thought it was another shit job. I'm glad it was for this. Let's take this baby for a ride."

I giggle walking out the door. A little blue SUV is sitting right in front with a red bow on the top. "I love it!"

"Look at the back."

I walk to the back and see the prince logo on the right bottom corner. "Is that important?"

She nods. "The grill was changed out too so you're easy to recognize as Princes. If shit's going down and you need to move fast or abruptly, the townspeople will give you room. They know not to fuck with anything with the logo. Our PD won't stop you either—unless you're a danger to you or someone else I mean."

Damn, I love this place. "So, I can drive without a license and no one will stop me?" My heart is going to beat right out of my chest.

She nods smiling. "If you get stopped, you tell them to call Jessie and he'll deal. Chances are they'll let you go without calling anyone. No one wants to call Jessie—ever."

I love their nutty rules or code or whatever today. I walk around looking at every inch of my new, shiny blue car. "Get in the fuckin' thing and let's go already," she says, but she's happy.

I run to the other side and climb in. This is so cool! I have a car! I look at all the indicators. It's even four-wheel drive! Sheila tells me about tracking and how the phone works from the steering wheel. She points to the corner over the windshield. "When you start it up you have a live feed that goes to Security. They don't have time to watch anyone full time, but they will check that it's you driving and log you on the tracking board so alerts aren't thrown."

"What does that mean?"

She smiles. "Don't pick your nose while you're driving and if you have a problem hit your flashers. The alert goes to Security and they'll call into you or get you help while watching your feed."

I nod, this is good. I won't get stopped, I have help if I need it, and I've never seen a woman pick her nose while driving. That's usually a man thing. I start up my brand-new car and back it up.

"I set the good stations for you. Hit the button on the wheel to roll through them or volume." I leave it and just drive. "You don't drive like this is new for you, why don't you have a license?"

I wave my hand at her. "I've been driving since I was fourteen. My dad taught me and let me drive through an old industrial park where we used to live. I was homeschooled and couldn't handle people touching me so driving was a way to escape for me. When I got older, I took my mom everywhere. She was going to take me if I got stopped, but I never got stopped then we were running and I couldn't get it or they'd find us."

She points the way and we're on a backroad with woods all around us. "These roads through here are set in grid format. They all connect in a big square. Your GPS will show you, but if you're good with direction you won't need it up here. It's a good place to drive while you're thinking shit through."

I nod, she's so nice showing me this. I've missed driving and now I have a place to escape to. I turn on the radio and make the outside square. She's got my favorite stations set and I get us back without thinking much about it. When I pull up she's smiling. "You don't need a license around here, but you will if you leave the towns. Princes don't control the other PDs. Your GPS has our borders on it. Stay in them and you're good."

I must look like a Cheshire cat smiling from ear-to-ear. "Thanks Sheila and thanks for bringing me my awesome new car and taking me out. I bet you had other things to do today."

She does the chin thing and gets out. "It's just a regular work day for me so getting you this afternoon was odd, but fun. I'm happy for you and Christian. You both lived similar lives and you fit."

I'm smiling again. We so do. The kids come out and everyone is climbing through my new car.

When Christian pulls up, I turn the radio down and get out. I'm surprised when he slides out of the passenger seat. Nekanis jumps down right after him and stands beside him. I really like the dog. He's like the other dogs standing guard to keep my amazing boyfriend safe. I jump on him wrapping my legs around his waist and he takes a step back laughing. "You like?"

I have never jumped on a guy, but him stepping back and leaning on his truck strikes me as something wrong. He sounds funny too. "Are you okay?"

He squeezes me holding my head to his chest where I can't see his face. "Yeah babe. Just tired. You like the Patriot?"

I smile, he's a good boyfriend. "I love it, but not more than you. What's wrong?"

"He really is just tired. It was a busy day for our Warrior Protector. He saved four lives today. We are very proud of Christian for doing what he was meant to do," Dakota says from behind me.

I look up at Christian. "The readers?"

He nods with a smile. "Yeah, it went well. Prez has them on their way here. Security will pick them up and get them the rest of the way safely."

He's so damn good! "I'm proud of you too. Thank you on behalf of all the readers." I kiss him and he growls making me smile. "I was going to drive you to dinner, but we can order in."

"Not a chance babe. A new car needs to be driven. Sheila says you're a good driver. Let's ride baby."

Oh, my God I love this man. "Yes!" Dakota laughs and I unwrap my legs sliding down.

Security helps get the kids back in while Dakota carries Nash and Chance in. Holly hugs me quickly telling me, "Go have some fun."

I giggle giddy with excitement. Nekanis jumps in the back seat and Christian rolls the window for him then sits. He slides the seat back and pulls his leg in fighting to get it through and over. He doesn't say a word, but gets himself settled. I lean in and kiss him. "Thank you." He smiles and I wonder again how the hell I got so lucky.

"Where are we going Little Pixie?"

"Sheila showed me the woods, it's a good place to drive, but I only saw the ocean a couple of times. Can we go there?"

"Anywhere you want. We need to stay in the yard though. HS is going to be busy tonight."

Yes! "Serenity brought me to the docks one night. It looked amazing."

I pull out and he tells me where to turn. "You didn't go out the whole time you lived here?"

I shake my head no, seeing the water in the distance. "She had enough to deal with without me adding worry to that. After my parents died I stayed in hotel rooms or the house here."

He squeezes my leg. "Sorry baby. I didn't pick up that you were here, then in danger, until she brought Chance. We can explore everything here. Do you like being outside?"

I smile thinking of my drives and hiking. "I do. Even in the winter I drove my mother nuts with taking off to see one thing or another."

He laughs. "I was the same. We should go to the reservation this weekend. Nunánuk is excited to meet you. You can see where I lived for a couple of years."

286

"Yes." This is going to be the best week ever. After living with so much pain and fear, life is looking up. I'm enrolled in school, got a boyfriend, Serenity is happy and I get to go out! "It's so beautiful here. Ohio had some pretty spots, but it's like living in a picture here. Everywhere you turn is worthy of a painting."

"There's a bluff up ahead on the right. Pull in and get your fill baby."

I shake my head smiling. "Did I tell you I love you?"

"You might have mentioned it." He laughs pointing. "I love you too babe."

That is never going to get old. Eliza was wrong, he doesn't just show it, he says it too. "Oh. My. God. This is amazing!" I jump out and run to the edge of the cliff. Water is smashing into the rocks below. All you can see is the water for miles. It's like the movies I've seen. I wonder what it's like out in the middle of all that water. A shiver runs down my back. That would feel so lonely. I don't think I'd like that.

Christian's arm goes around me and he pulls me back a step. "The wind up here can cause you to lose your balance." Just as he finishes a gust of wind has him holding me against him. I wonder if he saw that in a vision and shiver again. He lets me go and I feel his jacket around me then he's pulling me close again. "It's a sight I never get tired of."

I nod burrowing closer. "It's absolutely beautiful. I've been to the Great Lakes and a bunch of smaller ones, but nothing like this. Is it lonely out at sea?"

"The first time my dad took us out on a boat I felt the total disconnect from the land and hated it. I don't go that far out anymore. Something holds me closer to land. Nunánuk said I have roots to the land and need the

287

connection. I like fishing and skiing, but I don't go so far that I can't see my home."

"Are you true Indian?" I know he was adopted and all the kids are considered half Mohegan.

"Yes, we had to be tested and we all have Indian in us, but me and Joey are Mohegan."

With his light brown hair and shining blond streaks, I don't think he looks Indian. His personality and mannerisms are very much in line with what I know of natives. "You don't look like your dad and Mase." He does have those green eyes that I've seen on some of the other Indians here.

"I am an enigma." He laughs. "Before my mom took us we were beaten by my father. Joey tried protecting me and he broke her back. She was in a wheelchair for a long time and I always felt responsible. It was later that my mom let us read the court documents from our blue books—that's what they send from house to house in foster care. Anyway, the blue book said he planned on killing us both because we were Indian. He wasn't our real father and wanted better than 'half breeds'. When my dad had us all tested, we were the two most unlikely Mohegan's in the family."

What a terrible life that must have been. Having visions, not being able to touch anyone for more than ten seconds and feeling responsible for Joey. "I'm glad you found your mom. Are the abilities tied to the Indian?"

He kisses my head and I love the feeling. "I believe so, but Jeremy and Jacob are not full blood Indian and Jeremy is the most powerful of our ability kids. Although the Little Brothers aren't far behind. Some of the kids that aren't Indian like Zeke, Blaze and Blake or Harley and Colt, Devan and Brenna, all have abilities, but they are all connected in some way to the first known reader in the MC who was Mohegan."

How interesting is that? Holy Moses the people in the Club really are a tight knit group. "Did you research all this?"

He laughs. "I don't sleep much. When I started getting the visions more I stayed away from everyone and trained or looked shit up. Mohegan is not known for light skinned, light haired people. They do have a different eye color and those were made Shaman because the tribesmen thought the color was a sign from the ancestors. At one time a book was written about the Norse populating America and our people being a mix of Nord and native. It was later proven wrong through DNA, but is still passed down by uneducated people. Wall, the first known reader in the Club, is now an ancestor. When I was on the reservation with Nunánuk I got many visions of the Club and how they came to work for good. Wall hated stupid. He wouldn't let the Brothers act or talk stupidly. He tried to educate as many as he could with finances and life lessons. His vision was passed down and is still followed today. Part of that vision is that different isn't worth more or less, it's just different." He laughs. "It's the second time today I've mentioned him and I don't think I've ever said his name before."

I turn and look up at him. "I like history and the real-life stories that are shared in families. I love listening to your history and about your ancestors."

"You will love Nunánuk." He kisses me and I hold on. When he puts me down he's smiling. "The little things—like seeing that smile and your eyes shining after I kiss you—hit me hard. I thank the ancestors every time I get to touch you and see that reaction."

"I still can't believe you picked me."

He laughs walking me back to the car. "And here I thought you picked me."

I shake my head as he waits for me to sit and closes my door. I wonder if Mohegan accounts for the weird and oh so sweet code they live by. He takes me to a restaurant in the center of town. We see Brothers from the Club and Christian does the chin thing, but doesn't talk to them. When I ask, he says it's a chin lift showing respect. They are weird men.

Chapter Eleven

One week

Christian

We walk in and Phoenix comes out of the classroom. "Done needs to come back to work."

Since I didn't get pictures I'm wondering what he's talking about. He throws me Security walking behind Dean. Then helping her put supplies away. Then cleaning the tables. What the fuck? I walk in the room and he's behind her and reaches over her for a bin she's trying for. As soon as I see what he's thinking I slam him back against the wall. The bin falls and Dean jumps back glaring at the pussy.

"I told you I don't need your damn help!"

I step back and watch the pussy nod. "I didn't mean nothing by it."

Her hands are on her hips and she's not in the mood for his shit today. "Done didn't come in the room unless he was asked to. He didn't follow me around and he didn't stand on top of me. Isn't your job by the door?"

The pussy doesn't answer, but Dean doesn't care. "I need to ask Jessie apparently. Take your disgusting thoughts and stay at your post or station or whatever you call it, but keep away from me and the kids. Every one of us knows what is on your mind and we don't like it. As a matter of fact, I'm just going to tell Jessie what you're thinking, if the boys don't first." She bends to get the bin.

The pussy is trying to move, but I hold him where he is. "You make trouble and you'll see what's on my mind."

She stands and walks closer to him making me proud. "You think threatening me will make this better. I thought the Club didn't take stupid people. Every room has

291

cameras in it. If they didn't pick it up before they have it now. And just so you know, I've taken down men that are bigger than you. Take your stupid and your threats back out to the door WHERE YOU BELONG!"

I walk closer and the pussy tries moving again. "Babe. You hitting him or am I?"

She waves her hand. "You can, I have a damn class waiting for these supplies. He's trying to get me in bed with him." She gives him a look. "As if." She walks away and I laugh.

When I look back at the pussy I'm not laughing. "You know who I am?" He nods. "Then you know who she is. Every fuckin' day I'm here. You should have clued in before now how this would end." I roll pain through him and hold his scream.

Jessie runs in with Taylor. "Jesus. I got him Brother." Jessie walks toward him and I let him go. He falls to the floor and pisses himself. "Jesusfuckin'Christ. Coder I need Clean-up in here." He cuffs the pussy.

I don't tell him it isn't needed. He needs a body pickup. I find my little spitfire pixie and help her with the lesson she's doing. We have a good time and I get my fix with the kids. Chance stays on my lap the whole time and for some reason this makes Mucimi happy.

When I get back to Security, Prez is waiting. "You could have just hit him."

I shake my head no. "He was coming back for her and he saw Phoenix behind me." I throw him the pussy's thoughts. He winces and throws me chin.

"MC needs you up there to explain shit to Pres. Ricky is pulling his hair out. Abel is ready when you are."

I nod. "I just talked to Jeremy. He didn't say anything about me being needed."

His hand goes through his hair. "Since Pres apologized to him and Aubrey they've been steering clear of him. Aubrey said every time he sees them he's trying to give them things. You know Jeremy. He doesn't need anything so everything he gets he's giving away. Aubrey thinks it's funny because Jeremy gave Pres's leather to some homeless guy in the City."

I turn around laughing. "Christian." I stop with my hand on the door. "Mitch has the brace for you. I'll let her know you'll be at Security."

"Thanks, Prez." We walk out and I suspend down the stairs and get Nekanis in the truck. "Let's go see the crazy assed Brothers Nekanis."

Abel lands at MC-Baxter and tells us he's waiting. I throw him chin. "I'll call to you when I'm ready. Go eat or whatever, it will be a while."

That makes him happy. We go in and I don't have to show ID this time. I see pictures and I'm glad they finally added me. At Pres's office, I turn left and knock on Ricky's door. "Thank fuck Brother. I swear the man forgot English all of a sudden."

"I don't understand why *I'm* here. You, Devan, Elizabeth, Colt, Harley..."

He puts his hand up. "You're the guy that runs it, he wants to know what you do and how it works. Since I don't do visions he wants a better understanding of how you know what the fuck is happening."

I shake my head. "I told him how the visions work."

He nods. "I think now he's willing to hear it. He's trying Brother. Elizabeth and Harley are partnered and running like Sheila and Eliza." I nod already knowing this. They ran Ops, shocking the shit out of Uncle Steve and Pres, two days ago. You'd think he would have asked while I was here.

He nods and I shield. "He's got inner circle waiting and Mitch will be here in about an hour and a half. Amanda will cut your cast off in an hour and Prez has Jeremy showing with her."

I nod and follow him down to the meeting room. He laughs at the Brothers watching me suspend down the stairs. "Hopping up and down doesn't work for me."

"It ain't the Badass way," he says thumbing us in.

Pres's hands go up in the air. "I was just going to send a Prospect to find you."

What? I just got here like five minutes ago. Rich laughs. "The newly enlightened Pres is a little impatient."

Uncle Danny and Geek laugh. "Have a seat Brother this may take a while." Geek pushes a chair out and I raise me over it and sit.

Ricky laughs. "Badass."

Pres watches then thinks Ricky's right. I roll my eyes and wait. When I was here for the Ops he was asking Ricky shit that was pretty obvious. He didn't need the answers he just wanted to make sure Ricky was on the same page. Now he's all about Ricky like he was for Prez.

"Are Danny and Ricky readers?" Fuck, the first fuckin' question he has is this?

"They're not mine to tell Pres. I thought you wanted to know about Protectors?"

Uncle Danny is relieved and Ricky just smiles. Pres throws his hands up. "Someday someone will answer that fuckin' question."

I nod. "That's not today. What do you want to know today?" Everyone laughs, but I keep my eyes on him. He has to understand I can only tell him so much.

"How do you know what everyone is doing? I've watched Ally and she isn't getting OCs or calls from you. Terry calls her, but she's never talked directly to you, unless you're here." He thinks I should be impressed with his stalking of Ally.

I smile and answer him in his head. 'I talk to her every day just like this. You don't need to be a reader for me to talk to you or even control your movements.'

He's surprised, but curious. "Show me."

"On you?" He'll fuckin' shoot me. He nods and I think I'll never have this chance again. Smiling, I lift his arms up and suspend him from the ceiling. Everyone thinks this is funny.

"Okay. I got that one." He's nervous I'm going to drop him so I set him down gently and release his arms. "That was fuckin' weird." I laugh. "So, you talk to everyone in their head every day and that's how you know what's going on?"

"Yeah and we jump every couple of days, usually after training, so we connect and stay on the same page."

He nods with everything running through his head. I decide to shield and wait for his questions. "The kids that aren't Indian jump?"

"Yeah."

"Can anyone jump?"

Fuck, I see where this is going and want to shut that down. I need to be honest since he's seriously trying to work it all out in his head. "If they have a strong guide, yeah."

"You can take us to the wind?"

Fuck. I look around Geek, Rich, Uncle Steve, Bob and Pres is a lot to carry. My dad and Uncle Danny can get themselves there and back. "I need Jeremy or Aubrey after."

"Why?"

"It will drain me to carry everyone. If Mase is here he can help."

Pres looks at my dad. "Can't you help?"

"If you were a kid I could, but you're all grown fuckin' men."

Pres nods. "Geek find Mase and see when Jeremy is due in." He looks at me. "Jeremy can help get us there too right?"

Since Jeremy is trying to avoid him I don't want to throw him under the bus, but I don't want to lie either. "He can, but he's focused on other things right now. Changing his focus puts people at risk."

"Will you explain that?"

"Jeremy runs different than everyone else. He sees everything, but can focus on one thing while everything is going through his head. If he sees a threat or something that needs to be changed, he does it. If it's bigger and he needs to watch other things happening, he throws to me or whoever can make the change without changing an outcome to worse."

"A Protector?"

I shake my head no. "He throws to Ricky, Jessie, Brantley, Taylor, Prez, Dakota, Uncle Danny, VP, Mase, Jacob or my dad." I look at Rich and he nods. "And Rich."

He runs through the list. "They aren't all readers or Protectors."

"No."

"Why are VP, Ricky, Danny, Taylor and Rich on the list?"

I don't look at him, but Uncle Danny throws HS. "They're all HS, and Jeremy trusts them. He wouldn't throw

296

to someone he can't be sure of. The outcome has to stay how he sees it. Changing a vision is risky at the best of times. With shit happening all around us we can't chance mistakes."

This is all shit I've explained already and I have shit to do. 'Your explanation will further the vision my Warrior Protector. Show him the patience he needs to further that. It will be a benefit to all of us.'

"Yeah, thanks Brother." Pres gives me a funny look. "Fuck. Dakota was giving me advice. Sorry Pres. Too much happening all at once."

"Dakota gives you advice about our meeting?"

I push the vision away and raise up standing behind my chair. Nekanis walks beside me while I pace. "I had a vision running, Jeremy not wanting to stop at the Lab, Geek finding Mase pissed about being called in and you asking about stuff I already told you. Dakota was telling me to show you patience because it furthers the vision we live by. I didn't mean to answer him out loud."

"Do you need a minute?"

I look at him. "Yeah, I need to talk to Prez and Dakota."

He nods. I lean against the wall. 'Dakota I need you to get Security to the school. Tell Prez the vision with Brandon is going to happen today.'

'He is here Brother. HS will cover them.'

I see the fight. HS makes it. "Mucimi. You see?"

'Yeah.'

"Throw to Aquyà and Phoenix."

'We see Christian.'

"Get Holly and Dean to the back with the babies and girls. Wait there for Jessie."

'You see?' Aquyà asks.

They have everyone moving now. "Good job Little Brothers. Throw to Dakota or Prez. I'll keep watch."

I stand up and look at Pres. "I'm ready. Jeremy will be here in ten and Mase is here." Fuck! He looks stricken. "Without a threat, I sometimes talk out loud." Jesus I'm fuckin' losing it.

"There's a run on the kids and you're ready?"

"I'll watch, but HS makes it."

He nods, not believing me. I look at the board and throw the school with the kids in the back then Jessie and Taylor riding toward it. Eliza is running in the door. I stop throwing and look at him. "Sheila is already in."

He watches me for a minute then his mind settles. "Can any of the kids here put up a threat like that so we can see it?"

"You only have Jeremy and Aubrey that get visions like that. Elizabeth gets pieces from everyone else like Prez. Judy has no interest in HS and has never offered so no."

"Jeremy and Aubrey."

I shake my head no. "Jeremy can't be tied to a chair to throw visions on a board Pres. If you try to keep his mind on something like that, he can't see the other things happening. Aubrey is linked into Jeremy, they're bound and work together like one mind."

He doesn't understand. I shield him and watch the school. When they're clear I sit.

"Kids safe."

I nod to Uncle Steve. Mase walks in and sits by me.

"You can put the visions on the board for us," Pres says and I laugh.

"Sorry, I'm not sitting in a chair throwing visions for anyone."

He's getting pissed. "Why?"

I throw the original vision and let them see. "If all I do is throw the visions then they happen." The table explodes when Brandon gets hit. "You can't keep thinking that tying our hands to one specific job will keep everyone safe. We aren't just HS with one job to complete. Too many other things are happening for us to stop for that one job."

He nods finally getting it. "You seeing the kids, talking to Dakota, Jeremy and Mase plus answering me plays all at once."

"Yeah and Aiyana is happy with the Vets at the pipeline, Terry wants to know if the threat was linked here or if it's the lunatics, and Colt is asking if he's out for the day because Mase is here."

"Anything else fitting in there?" Geek asks.

"Nekanis needs to go out."

They laugh. Pres watches me. I wait. "So, all the kids have more than what I see as a threat, but can't always say what the threat is and may react and do things to keep us safe that I never know?"

"Thank fuck!" Uncle Danny says and I nod.

"How will I ever know what the fuck is going on with them?"

"Ricky knows and they're all HS and loyal to the Club. Plus, they're the Officers' kids. Why would you ever think they'd do something that isn't keeping you, the Club or other people safe?"

He's stunned by the question. "I never thought about it that way."

"Maybe you need to trust that Wall's vision is just as important to us as it is to you."

I raise up and stand again. "Look Pres, we can keep going around in circles, but I can't give you vision, or make you a reader. Your purpose is to keep the vision alive and ours is to make sure that happens. Just like with Wall, that vision will be passed down. Those words he said to you were true. You gave that to Prez and now Ricky. They will pass it to others and the rest of us will make sure our Officers stay alive to see more and guide us in the right direction. Like VP, Uncle Danny, Geek and Tiny. Their purpose is to keep you alive—that means keeping the vision alive. For the kids, we've been doing it a different way, but the purpose is the same. It's always been the same. You need to trust the younger generation to do their part and do it without you understanding every step we take to accomplish it. You have no clue how to program, but you have no problem letting Geek do that job. You need to have the same faith in us. Jeremy should be your example." I stop pacing and look at him.

"When the fuck did you grow up?"

"The point is we *all* did and you need to see we have your back—remembering the lessons of our fathers and yours." I wait for him to go through all I said and look for a Prospect. When he's at the door I open it and tell him to take Nekanis out, get him water and wait with him until I open the door again.

VP laughs and I shrug. Pres is still reeling from all I said. "I don't mean to rush you, but I don't have much time. If you're serious about jumping, we need to do that now."

He nods. "What do I need to do?"

"Relax. I'm going to put everyone on the table. You'll all take forever if I don't." I lift them and put them all above the table. "Sitting is best." I lower them then sit with them. "Mase stay with Pres. Dad settle everyone so we don't lose them. Keep your hand on the people next to you and don't let go. Spinning and black is normal. Just feel and relax." I close my eyes. "Now." We jump and I feel the push from Dakota. "Thank you, Dakota." We fly over the reservation and they're all quiet. "The rock Mase." We land and sit. "The ancestors guide us in our purpose. They heal, giving strength and peace when we are in need. Giving their wisdom is not an obligation to them. They share that knowledge freely if we are of pure heart and mind. We will never be given abilities if our purpose is destruction."

Pres nods and his breath catches. "Wall and Hawk?"

I nod seeing them across the lake. "Ancestors." I see Nunánuk walk to them. "They guide us in all we do Pres."

"The ancestors are pleased my wise Protector. You have shown their guidance and wisdom has not been wasted on you."

"Thank you Co and Nunánuk for allowing our visit and showing what needs to be seen. As always, appreciation is felt for our fathers and their lessons."

"Are you in need of guidance Christian?"

"Not at the moment, Nunánuk. It is enough to see and feel all who have passed before us. Their guidance and strength will always be welcome and appreciated."

"You need to return Christian before you are too weak. Jeremy waits," Co says and I'm starting to feel it.

"Thank you my wise Shaman." I look at everyone. Pres, Uncle Steve, Uncle Danny and Geek are still staring at Wall. Catching Mase's eye I nod. "We need to jump back." My dad throws me chin. "Now."

The ancestors and Co push and I feel Jeremy pulling. When I open my eyes, I lay down. Jeremy puts his hand on my arm. "Stupid."

"He needed to see. It will do more than me telling him shit over and over."

My dad leans over. "You're right. I'm so fuckin' proud of the man you've become Son."

I smile and close my eyes. They talk around me excited about seeing Wall. I don't hear anything from Pres and look. He's thinking about the vision and making sure it passes to the kids and grands. 'Trust in us to keep those that carry it safe Pres. We are ready to give our lives for the vision.'

"I see that now. You brought me so I could see what you've been telling me is true?"

I turn my head so I can see him. "Yeah. I could have brought just you, but they needed to see too. Nunánuk helped me give you the language so you understood all that was said."

When I can, I sit. "Pres, if you have anything else, Ricky can answer or knows where to find the answers. There is nothing more I can give you, but to say *trust in your people*. They wouldn't be here if they didn't believe in you."

He throws me chin. "Thank you Christian. I won't let you or your ancestors down again."

I push the vision away. "Je, I need to get to Amanda."

He nods. "Locker room."

"Fuckin' great." I look around for my little man. "Mucimi, can you help Mase get me to the locker room?"

I'm lifted and laugh. Pres watches smiling, my dad opens the door. "Come Nekanis."

Amanda cuts the cast off and washes my leg. I can't take much more of her touching me. Jeremy is doing what he can to help, but I'm still feeling the jump.

302

Mitch walks in and I groan. "I can't do more."

She smiles. "I don't have to touch you to do this. If you can sit you can pull the Velcro yourself."

She's so happy I smile at her. Mase and Jeremy help me up. She explains and Jeremy lays the brace out for me. When she moves to check the band, Jeremy stops her. "No. I'll do it." He checks and tightens it. "It's good."

Mitch nods, but isn't smiling anymore. "What do you need?"

"Healing and time. Too much today," Jeremy tells her.

She gives him a look. "If you'd show me how you heal I might be able to help."

He shrugs and I see his concern, but I'm feeling dizzy. "I need to jump. Nekanis come." I feel him beside me and lay back.

I open my eyes on the chopper. "Fuck."

Jeremy is sitting in the chair. I try to sit up to ask what happened, but I can't push enough to sit. 'Relax. Mitch's hand was on your leg. Didn't see it.'

I look for it and see everyone in the locker room then Jake and my dad moving me on a board to the chopper. When I see everyone pissed, I push it away. All the fuckin' shit I've done and her hand on my leg just showed everyone how weak I still am.

'How the fuck do you figure that? It's our job to watch out for you. We didn't do that. You shouldn't have jumped knowing Amanda was cutting off the cast. All the fuckin' Officers and no one thought to keep watch while you were already drained.' Prez is pissed, but I tune him out. He can yell at me in person.

The chopper lands at the Compound and Taylor and Dakota get me in my truck bed then home.

* * *

Dean

"What the hell happened this time?"

"Mitch made him a brace so he can still walk while healing. Amanda cut the cast off then Mitch was talking with her hand on his leg. It wasn't noticed until he was out," Taylor says and Christian closes his eyes.

"How long?" Don't these people watch for stuff like that? My mom and dad were all over stuff like this.

Taylor looks at Jeremy. "Couple minutes. Maybe four, five." I just met him a few days ago, but he's supposed to be the healer. He looks away. "Sorry."

I walk out of the bedroom and go for a ride to the woods. Someone is following me, but I ignore them and drive. He keeps doing everything to help everyone else, but he's got no one making sure he's okay. I turn toward home and hope the nutty Brothers are gone.

When I walk in they're all here. Jessie, Darren, Aaron and Taylor are at the table. "He isn't awake yet?" I ask.

"Prez was pissed so we came down here," Aaron says.

I look at him trying to get this straight. "Why is he pissed?"

"The Officers didn't watch over him when they knew Amanda was cutting the cast." Taylor takes the fight right out of me. They understand and Prez is mad. This is good. I nod and go up to the room.

I hear Prez talking and slow my steps. "You shouldn't have jumped with them."

304

"I had to. Pres is just getting what all this means and he needed to see we have his back. I would have been fine, but Mitch was touching me. After Amanda took the cast off I needed a minute to get it together. I couldn't move her at that point."

"Jeremy isn't a guard for you. Someone should have been watching out."

I like Prez, he's right, someone else should have been watching out for him. I step through the door and they stop.

Prez looks from me to Christian. "I'll talk to you tomorrow. Call to me if you need me."

"Thank you," I tell him as he walks by me. When I turn back Dakota is holding his arm. Christian watches me like he's worried. "Another one of those days."

He smiles. "It was. I got my new brace though. I can bend my knee and even run with Nekanis once I get used to it."

"This is good." I climb on the bed and lay my head on his chest. "If this keeps up I'm quitting the school and watching over you myself."

He laughs and squeezes me tighter. Then I fall asleep.

Chapter Twelve

One week

Christian

I'm taking Dean to all the places she hasn't seen that mean something to me. At the church, we stop in and see the Pastor. "Christian! I haven't seen you lately. You're looking good and rested. Who is this with her hand in yours?"

"Pastor this is Dean, my girl."

Dean smiles and steps back when he moves to take her hand. "I'm sorry, but touch affects me."

He smiles like it's no big deal. "Like Christian and yet you can touch each other?"

I laugh. "Go figure."

Pastor shakes his head. "The Lord and His mysterious ways."

Dean is looking around at the tables.

"Is Gus around?"

Pastor nods. "We put a table in the back corner for him." He doesn't point, but jerks his head toward the right.

"Thanks Pastor. Let me know if you need anything."

"We're doing good right now. Plenty of help and food."

I take Dean over to Gus's new table. "Christian. How are you and how is Taylor?"

I pull a seat out for Dean and sit beside her. "I'm good and Taylor is Taylor. Nothing keeps him down Brother. This is my girl Dean. We're riding the circuit today checking on my friends. How are you doing Gus?"

He smiles. "I got me a job."

I'm surprised and smile. "Good for you Gus. Where are you working?"

"Eleven to four a.m., at the manufacturing plant. I'm loading trucks in shipping."

I laugh. He's proud and should be. "Fuckin' nice Brother. I'm happy for you. If you need anything get it to Jessie or Taylor at group or have Pastor call."

He nods and I see he's done with company so I stand and guide Dean out. "He's a Vet with PTSD. Not the friendliest guy I know, but he tries."

"I saw. That's a lot to deal with, I mean the crap in his head. I was surprised he got a job. I'm happy for him too."

The shit people live with always amazes me. "He's getting help and goes to Jessie's meetings. It's been good for him for a while now. Not everyone is as lucky as Taylor and Gus, but we've been at it for two years and it's getting easier for a lot of them. Next is the homeless neighborhood."

When we get off the bike at the neighborhood Alex and Prince pull up on the side of us. "Brother." He's excited, but trying to hold it in. Prince jumps off and waits on the side of the bike.

"Hi Dean. I'm glad you're here." He moves to hug her and stops. "I won't hug you so you don't get hurt."

Dean smiles at him. "Thanks Alex. I'm glad you remembered. I always feel bad telling people."

He shakes his head no. "A lot of people can't do hugs. They are the best, but hurting people isn't good. We know how to be good Brothers and don't hurt people. Right?" He looks at me and I nod.

"That's right Alex. We promote good and do everything we can to help people." He's so excited he's ready to float away. I smile waiting for him to tell us.

He smiles big. "I have good news for the neighbors Christian!" I tell him in his head to spill. "The dog food company is giving food free. It's the good food too. We get to order for the dogs on the computer and they deliver the food to town three's loading docks. The Mayor said he will deliver to the houses and neighborhoods. That's big news, right Christian?"

I slap his back. "That's the best big news I've heard all day Alex."

He beams. He's so fuckin' cute. "I'm telling the Supers so they know. They need my email too so I can order. Right now, I just have to know how much."

"I'm just showing Dean around and checking in. See if they need anything while you talk to the Super. Tell me in your head like we practiced."

He bobs his head up and down. "I will Christian." He walks away and Dean giggles.

"They're so fuckin' cute. Ally will have to top this one. She does the same things Alex does so everyone is treated the same."

She squeezes my fingers. "That is so nice. I love how everyone is treated the same here." We walk down the first row and I say hi to some of the residents. Dean stops and looks back at the rows of houses. "This is like the MC Compound."

"It is. Uncle Danny made each neighborhood a theme. This is Mass. We also have a Rhode Island, Key West, Eastport, Boston and the new one Seattle. I think he was getting bored."

She laughs. "He's amazing. It's so clean and the people look happy."

I nod. "They are for the most part. This is what they can manage, so we keep them small. The building has food, mailboxes, showers and lockers for them."

She nods taking it all in. "Let's get to the Vet house. Last year Prez moved the teens to the side of the Vets here and in town two."

She nods looking sad. "There shouldn't be such a need, but I'm glad the Princes are helping with it."

I wait to start the bike. "The neighborhoods are being picked up more and more. Providence, two towns right outside of Boston, Connecticut has four that I know of. They're popping up all over the country. Lily put a book out on how to do it, so people are doing it."

"Amazing."

"It is." I get us to the Vets and feel something is off. Taking a minute I look, but I'm not seeing anything yet. Pulling shields, I open so I can get anything coming at me. I stand still while I'm slammed with shit all at once. Jesus. Holding Dean's hand tighter I go through everything, but don't see why I'd have the feeling that something is wrong. I hit my mic. "Guardian to Ops."

"Protector Ops this is Mimer, Guardian," Terry answers.

"Mimer something is off. I'm not seeing it, but I feel it. Can you get my Security to the Prince Vet house?"

"Roger Guardian." He pauses and I know he's talking to Brantley. "HS can be there in fifteen. Coder can be there in five."

"I can wait for HS Mimer. I don't have a threat just a feeling. Nothing is seen." Dean looks up, but doesn't seem fazed by this. Easy.

"Roger Guardian. HS is fifteen out."

309

"Roger." I start walking to the house. "These are homeless Vets. Most have jobs or go to training at the church. They get moved from here into apartments when they're ready. Brothers check in with them at least once a week and update progress on the Prince website for the other Brothers. We do the same for the PTSD Program, but this isn't as closely guarded. The PTSD forms are watched pretty close and Jessie monitors that everyone is doing their part. This is pretty broad and only one or two contacts a week are made." She nods and I love that she's genuinely interested in the programs and how they work.

Inside we talk to the RA. They have a Vet moving out this week. Everyone is in high spirits. Aaron comes in and talks to a Vet he's been watching out for. He has PTSD and is from an MP unit. I tell Dean and she watches them while I talk to another that started working at the market down the road. He's excited about the job.

"You call me when you're ready and I'll come have cake with you." I'm referring to him moving out and he's happy. Every time someone makes it out they get charged up thinking they can make it too. It's fuckin' awesome to see.

"I'll call you Christian. Can I still do the teen mentor if I leave?"

I love hearing this question and we hear it a lot. "We would hope you would. It takes all of us to make it work Bryan. Getting out doesn't mean forgetting those behind you."

He nods happy he can still take a kid fishing. I hold my laugh because some of the best conversations happen fishing. I slap his back and take Dean toward the door. 'We're waiting inside. Take your time Brother.' I throw to Aaron.

We talk with a couple of guys about the new training they signed up for. After a couple of minutes Aaron comes in and I give a wave pulling Dean out. I'm hit again with a feeling that something isn't right.

"Where to Brother?"

I'm weighing the options. "I think Security until I figure this out."

Dean looks up at me. "Can we stop at the Reader house? Just one. We don't have to stay long." She has a hopeful look on her face.

I look across the street and think. I'm not getting anything, but a bad feeling. No one is throwing shit at me. A few minutes with the readers can't hurt. "To the Reader house Brother," I tell Aaron.

He laughs. "Whipped."

I smile. "I fuckin' am." I kiss Dean before she gets on behind me.

Aaron shakes his head. "I would be too you lucky bastard."

Dean giggles and we're off. At the Readers' house, we talk with a few of the residents and Dean makes plans to come with me for a class on shielding Thursday. I can't wait. She's interested in the paperwork and helping at this house. I'm fuckin' stoked to have the help, but with her here I have another reader that can see more than the words we're told. I kiss her and she laughs.

"I'm so excited. I can do this after work or at night and it's not too far from home." She's holding my hand tight so I give it a squeeze. This is going to be so good.

Before I get on the bike I'm looking around. "Get her back to the house Brother."

Neither one asks questions as Aaron takes her back. As soon as I hear the shot I see the pussy aiming for Dean and spin. I'm hit in the back and the wind is knocked out of me.

"Christian!" She turns.

'Get her in the fuckin' house!' I throw to Aaron.

I shoot the pussy aiming at me again. Sonofabitch. I'm leaning on the bike and look for the other pussy. As soon as I see him I know he's covered from here. I turn and throw a shield around Dean. She's fighting Aaron, but he picks her up and carries her up the stairs. Another shot hits me in the arm and one hits the shield. "Motherfucker!" I switch the gun to my other hand and find the pussy shooting at Dean. He's moving closer, using the parked cars as a shield, but I throw him fuckin' pain like he's never had and smile when he screams. A bullet just misses me and I'm looking for the pussy. Aaron is shooting and talking to Ops. I throw him the pussy on the ground and move to the side as a shot is fired my way again. Sonofabitch! I see it and throw to Aaron. The second-floor window across the street explodes and I pull the sonofabitch out. He screams until he hits the ground.

Taylor pulls up with Tag. "Are we clear?"

"I don't know. I can't see me, but I fuckin' hope so."

'Yeah Christian.' Jeremy says. 'Good job.'

"Jeremy says we're clear," I tell him and look around. The warning I've been getting is gone. "They set up right in front of the fuckin' Reader house."

Taylor looks at Tag. "Take two and check out the apartment." Looking at me he says, "Jessie is on his way with Jax."

"I need to check on Dean. Aaron had to pick her up to get her in the house." I walk toward the door.

"Is she okay?" Aaron asks walking toward me. He's worried because he touched her.

"I can't read her. I'm checking now." I walk in and I'm instantly pissed. "Get away from her! Touch affects her."

The two women jump and pull their hands away. "We didn't know. She just passed out and we were trying to help," the big woman says. She's afraid she's going to get thrown out.

I shake my head kneeling by Dean. "She had to be carried back in. She was probably feeling that. You touching her would have put her out."

"I'm sorry. We didn't know."

I lift my Little Pixie. "I'm here babe." Standing I look at the women. "She couldn't tell you. Touch for her is like getting zapped. It scrambles her brain. She'll be okay with some rest." I turn and walk out knowing they have questions, but my girl is fuckin' out. "I need a ride," I tell Aaron.

He talks to Brantley and I sit on the steps holding Dean to my chest. 'Dakota, can you help Dean from there?'

'I will try Brother.'

I watch her, hoping she wakes up. I want to jump, but there is too much happening.

'In the truck. Jump in the truck. I can help from there Christian,' Dakota says.

Fuck. I look at Aaron. "I need to jump in the truck for Dakota to help."

"I'm sorry Brother. I didn't know how else to get her in."

"She'll be okay. Dakota can meet me and help." I hope. Jessie and Jax pull up and talk to Taylor. I see the SUV coming down the road and walk toward it.

"Take my bike to Security. I got the truck," Aaron says opening the driver's door. A Security Brother takes his keys smiling.

313

I get in and Jessie stands at the door. "You need to get to Nick's. Prez's orders."

"I need to jump so Dakota can help her."

"Then jump on the fuckin' way. You got hit in the back and your arm is dripping blood every-fuckin'-where," he growls and I nod. No point pissing him off. He slams the door and I jump.

"We got this baby." I fly above the lake and see Dakota in his tree. "She hasn't woken up Dakota."

He nods holding her hand. "She will be fine, but she needs to learn to shield and command so touch does not incapacitate her. She will never be safe if she is this sensitive and has no way to stop it."

I have no idea how sensitive she is. I've seen the kids touch her. I shake my head. I need to get on the fuckin' ball and teach her more. At this point it doesn't matter how much she can take. I look at her and think he's right. She's tiny and touch has her out and unresponsive. Anything could happen to her like this. I hold her tighter.

When he steps back I look up at him. "She will sleep. I will check on her when I come in later tonight."

"She's okay though right?

He nods, but he's not happy. "She needs the lessons Christian. Touch is worse for her than you. Her body cannot take so much energy with no way to get rid of it."

Fuck. "I'll teach her Dakota. Does she have the ability to shield?"

"Not like you. She can attain a level of shielding that will help her stay safe, but I do not believe she will ever be completely safe from touch if it is sustained contact. You have the ability to feel then command. She can learn to command and shield for the initial shock, but taken by surprise—I fear she will always be in danger."

"Can I shield for her?"

He looks at me surprised. "I do not know my Warrior Protector."

"When you have a minute to ask, can you? If I can shield her I will." I look at her thinking I'll do whatever it takes to keep her safe. My Little Pixie doesn't need to go through this shit for the rest of her life.

"I will ask. I will stop in later Brother."

He flies and I watch him thinking there has to be a way around this and I'll find it. We jump back and Aaron is standing in the open door. He looks at Dean then me. "Dakota couldn't help?" He's pissed at himself for touching her.

"He did. She's going to sleep for a while apparently."

With a nod, he steps back. "Prez is on his way."

"Fuckin' great."

He laughs and opens the door. We walk into the back and Beth takes us to a room. "What happened to her?"

"Dakota saw her already. She's sleeping. She was touched by Aaron then two women at the Reader house."

She nods thinking this is bad if just that touch has her out. I nod and she smiles. "I need to see where the blood is coming from." I hold Dean away from me and take my shirt off. "You do realize her being in the air like this is freakier than I usually see from you."

"I'm not letting her go so do what you have to so I can get her home."

She's still smiling. "You could put her in the bed."

I shake my head no. "She needs to feel me."

She puts gloves on and looks at me. "I'm going to have to touch you." I nod and brace for it. "She feels you hanging in the air like that?"

"Yeah."

Nick comes in with Prez. "That's not something you see every day."

Aaron laughs and walks to the door. "I'll be outside."

"It's a graze, but deep," Beth tells Nick.

"Shit. Okay, get the suture kit ready." He looks at me. "Prez said you took a shot to the back. I need the vest off."

"It's fine."

"Take the fuckin' vest off and let him see," Prez says looking at Dean. "I saw you shield her. Why is she still out?"

"Dakota said her body can't take the energy with no way to release. I could only throw a shield around them. I don't know how to shield her if someone is touching her. I'm not a healer. He'll check on her later." I clench my jaw when I pull the Velcro on the vest. Moving it in front of me, I spin it to see the back. Fuck. I'm fuckin' lucky I had it on.

His eyes snap to mine. "You saw Dakota? You jumped to him?"

"No, we met at the reservation."

Nick stands on the side of me looking at my back. "I need to touch for a minute."

I nod and he pushes on my back making me see stars. "Stop."

His hand moves away. "It will be sore for a couple of days. Since you walked in here carrying her you don't have damage to your spinal cord." He smiles. "No more than

316

the big fuckin' lump and bruise that is." I roll my eyes at him. "Your arm needs stitches."

I shake my head no. "I can't take much more. Dakota isn't here and Jeremy is in Mass. Can't you just cover me?"

"We could try the super glue thing," Beth says.

I smile. "Do you have to touch me?"

Nick laughs. "Very little. I'm willing to try it and this is a time it would matter."

Prez moves closer. "Can't you let her down and get stitched up?"

"No." I'm not putting her on the table. Right now, she feels my arms around her and she'll keep feeling me until I can hold her again.

He doesn't ask any of the questions going through his head. "You need to get her a cut."

"It's due tomorrow."

Beth comes in with super glue and opens the package. She's excited to try this and I can't help, but smile. Women are funny. Nick sits on the stool and looks at the line across my upper arm. "I'm touching." I nod and he opens the cut. "This is fuckin' deep Christian. Stitches would be better."

"No," I breathe out when he moves his hands. "I can't take more on Nick."

Prez throws for me to put her down. "No. He can super glue me or just cover the fuckin' thing. I'm not letting her go."

"Jesus you're stubborn. Just super glue him," Prez says smiling. "I can relate Brother, but she's out and won't know that you put her on the bed."

"I'll know. She needs me. I'm not letting her go."

He shakes his head, but he's still smiling. Nick starts squeezing the super glue on me with tweezer things holding the skin up as he goes. I hold my breath. Fuck, it burns like a bastard.

"Done Brother."

I breathe. He gets me covered and I pull Dean over to me. "Thanks Nick and Beth." I stand and feel the pull on my back.

"I'll check you in the morning. Eight or so."

I nod and walk out. "Almost home baby," I tell her getting back in the SUV.

The kids are waiting on my steps with Done and the dogs standing on the side of them. "They said they can help," Done says hoping I won't be pissed.

I smile. "I'll take it." I carry Dean up the stairs and the kids follow me in. Nekanis runs up the stairs coming back to check where we are. When I put Dean on the bed he jumps up and lays beside her. Since I didn't give him any commands I find this funny. "You're a good Brother Nekanis."

Mucimi climbs on the bed with some help from Brandon. Aquyà, Phoenix, Teller and Justice get up without a problem and sit beside Mucimi. I watch them put their hands on him and think the little Badasses are supporting him. Jacob comes and chants then the boys do. I put my hand on her leg and jump. Hawk is waiting. I tell him all that's happened and how I just want her to wake up, but I get no advice from him.

Jessie, Prez, Brantley and Taylor come to collect the boys. Jax comes in and says the meeting is set for Saturday. I look and see they're having a community meeting.

Prez looks at me. "We need their help. Too many readers could have been hurt today."

318

I nod, surprised he's reading me. When they leave, I hold my girl against my chest while Nekanis lays against her back. My dad calls and I go through the day with him. Everyone is checking in and I throw to all of them that she's sleeping and I'll let them know when she wakes up. I love every one of them, but—fuck—I need a minute to think.

I order dinner and tell the guard to leave it on the counter then jump with Dean and sit on the rock overlooking the lake. Hawk sits beside me and I settle. I think about the last few weeks. We've been everywhere and seen everyone so they can meet her. I smile thinking about Tess. She had Dean talking to her forever. It was cute, the pixie and the fairy, both so happy to meet. I'm so glad the family is letting her do this slow and not showing all at once. My girl isn't good with crowds and they're respecting that. I remember reading everyone and not being able to shut their thoughts down. That's how I ended up on the reservation. I smile remembering Nunánuk words 'your little one.' She is too.

I kiss her head and talk to her about the things we've done. She had never been on a horse. It was fuckin' funny. I ended up putting her in front of me and riding to the water. She loves seeing the ocean. She loves everything. Even taking Mucimi and Chance canoeing was a happy day. I expected her to want to bring them home when we were done, but she wanted to go eat and we brought them to the park. I think she loves them as much as I do. Something is pulling me, so I jump back.

When I hear the chopper, I groan. Fuckin' 'rents. I keep my shields up not even wanting to know. They're too much sometimes. Nekanis jumps up when they come in. "Friends." He lays down putting his head on her back. "Good Brother."

Pres, Uncle Danny, Uncle Steve, my dad and Tiny walk in. Maybe I should have looked. "Why is she still sleeping? Little Ben said Dakota saw her," Pres asks and I see his concern.

"He said her body can't handle the energy without a way to release it. Mucimi and the boys were here too. Dakota will check on her when he gets back." Everything is running through his head and I shield from it.

"Needs a dog," Uncle Steve says.

That's not a bad idea. "Yeah. I was thinking I could shield for her, but I don't know how." They all just look at me.

"Dog," he says again. I nod.

Prez comes running up the stairs. "Jesus."

I look at him and smile. "Yeah. I need to get up and walk."

"Your back must be killing you. Do you need something for pain?"

"No Prez. I didn't take the last pills. It's too much." I raise her up and slide out. It takes me a minute to stand and move the pillows. When I put her down Tiny laughs. I look to see what's funny, but they're all watching me. "Since you're all here I need to change." I get shorts and take them to the bathroom.

"You got hit in the back?" Pres asks.

I lift and turn. "Yeah."

They're all watching me again and I'm glad I'm shielding. Sometimes I feel like I'm on display. It's fuckin' weird. I change and pace the room. They aren't talking, so I stop and look around at them. "What?"

Everyone looks at Pres so I do. "You're going to figure out how to shield her?"

I nod. "I need to do something. She can't go through life like this. Dakota said even if she can command shield from the initial touch he fears she'll always be in danger and her body can't handle the energy. If I can find a way to shield for her I will."

"Dog releases energy."

Uncle Danny looks at him and rolls his eye. "He already agreed to the fuckin' dog."

"Shield like you did today?" Prez asks.

I pace. It feels good to move. "I don't know. I was shielding them from bullets. I never thought about another way. If I could read her I'd know and could do something, but I get nothing from her unless she's excited or scared like today."

"Why was she scared?" Tiny asks like I did something to her. I roll my eyes and pace.

Prez answers for me. "She saw him get shot. Aaron picked her up and we could see her fighting to get away, but he brought her in the house and was covering Christian. Shots were coming from every-fuckin'-where."

Pres puts his arm out stopping me. "Why didn't you see it before it happened?"

"I don't see me."

"The other readers do."

I see where he's going. "They would bring it to Dakota or Prez. They can't tell me if it alters something else."

Everyone looks at Prez. He nods. "He felt something off and called for HS. There was no time or day, just the vision. When I found out he called for a bad feeling I sent Taylor and Tag, but him and Aaron were already clear when they showed."

Pres's hands go in his hair. "You need to be covered by a reader."

"There isn't one available. We've been through this."

They go back and forth and I get a fork and move my food up. Since they aren't fuckin' leaving, I move beer and send one to each then sit on the bed and eat. "Your food is down Nekanis," I tell him. He jumps down and runs down the stairs. When I'm done, I bag the tray back up and send it to the kitchen trash.

"Do you do anything normal?" Pres asks. I look at him wondering what he's asking, but I don't pull the shield.

"To him, it's normal," Prez says.

The bag? I move me back to the floor and pace. Shielding while I can't read her is impossible. Maybe Dakota will have something. They're still going on about the kids. I just realize my dad hasn't said a word. I walk to him and see he's worried. "You haven't said a word."

He nods. "There's not much to say. You're taking a dog and I think that's a smart move. You've already told us why there isn't anyone to partner with you and they aren't really here for anything, but to show support. You were shot and your girl was hurt. You're able to deal with both without us, but I wanted to see that you were okay. The fuckin' crazy Brothers are just comic relief at this point."

I laugh. "Thanks Dad. I'm fine."

He nods. "I see that. I'm proud of you Son. These fuckin' fanatics need to be stopped."

Dakota comes in smiling. "I had hoped I would not miss the obligatory visit from the 'rents."

"Just in time. Thanks Brother." He touches my arm and I look back at my dad. "It wasn't the fanatics. They were aiming for me and Dean. It was to hurt the MC."

I look at Dakota. "I'm good Dakota can you release more from Dean?"

"You need the tissue mended. Super glue is not really a medical treatment. Nadine is sleeping. She does not have energy to release. The boys did well for her."

"Super glue?" Tiny asks and I laugh.

Prez smiles. "He wouldn't let Nick touch him so he could hold Dean up in the air."

I turn back to Dakota while they pick that apart. "Will she wake up tonight?" He shakes his head no. "Will you be here long enough for me to take Nekanis for a run?"

"I will stay until you return Brother. Someone needs to keep the 'rents from covering you in body armor and partnering you with Danny."

I crack up. "I'll be twenty minutes. Call if you need me."

"I will Christian. Go take your dog out and stretch your back."

I grab a shirt and suspend down the stairs. My dad follows me. "I'm just going for a quick run."

"The brace works for you."

"Yeah. I love it. I can't stand without it yet, but it keeps me moving as if my leg is fine while it's on."

"She's incredible." I see a happy Mitch in his head.

I smile. She is. "Nekanis out." We start and my dad paces to me. Nekanis runs ahead and I smile. He loves being out as much as I do. We see Taylor and Delta, but don't stop. He throws chin and keeps running the other way. I'm feeling my leg and back when we walk in so I suspend up the stairs. 'Rents are still here and Dakota is holding my Little Pixie's arm. I bend and breathe deep. When I feel his hand on my shoulder I stand straight.

"I'm good Brother, should I be worried?" I indicate Dean.

"Always, but she will be fine. She needs time for her body to heal. She is getting that now."

I nod. "Thanks for staying."

"I would not miss the chance to see the 'rents in all their glory." He's got a serious look on his face, but I crack up. He's so fuckin' funny. "I will check in on her in the morning Brother."

I throw him chin and look at my girl. "We were here, why did you wait for Dakota to be here? We wouldn't let anything happen to her," Pres asks.

I look around. Prez is gone. I guess I have to answer. "If she woke up he can calm her. His touch is healing. If you touch her now she'll be out longer."

He nods and I pace. I wish they'd go already. Uncle Danny stands. "They don't need us here tonight. Christian and LB have it handled. We can't change or fix anything and Christian can do anything they need. I'm going home." Tiny follows him out throwing me chin.

My dad hugs me quick. "Proud of you Son. Call if you need me."

"I will Dad. Thanks for coming. It feels good."

He smiles and walks out. Pres and VP are watching me. I wait feeling impatient. "No one gave you the vision they saw," he says it in a resigned way. I nod. "I don't like that we almost lost you today," Pres says.

I smile. "I can't say it would make the top of my best day list either. It's been the way we've always worked. It's as it should be Pres. The bigger picture is always the hardest view to see. Our purpose is keeping the vision alive and working to make it better for more. I'm just a small piece of that picture Pres. I have no problem giving my life for that cause, especially if it means someone else that carries that vision makes it. It's as it should be."

He takes that in for a couple of seconds. "You're not pissed at them for not telling you?"

I'm surprised. "I understand what changing the outcome means better than most and know that even for me, it is what it is. I don't get the benefit of visions of me. I trust my Officers and family to do what's right, even if it's hard for them to do that. Even if it means I don't make it. We have no regret in us to look back at Pres. Every one of your Officers would die for you and not think twice about that decision. I don't understand why it's so hard for you to see that we would do the same. We've been doing it for years. I would never be pissed at anyone for keeping alive what I've freely given my life to defend. Like I said, it's as it should be."

Uncle Steve stands up. "He's right. Leave 'em alone. He keeps sayin' same shit over and over. Problem isn't you need it, it's you seein' it. Not his problem. Let's go." He throws me chin. "Good Brother, but stupid fuckin' questions get old even for me."

I laugh watching him pull Pres out. Thank fuck, I think, as I turn back to my girl. I take a quick shower and come in raising her up. It's almost two. I slide in, but can't take the feel of my weight on my back so I suspend. Nekanis sits watching. I lower and call him to her. When he lays with his head on her back I raise us all up and close my eyes memorizing the feel of her against my chest and down my side. Her heart is beating against me. I've never felt anything like that and spent time a couple of nights ago trying to figure out how the feel of her heart calms and focuses me. We are connected through that beat. That's the best I came up with. She's mine and that's how it was meant to be. Her heartbeat is my life force. As it should be.

I jump relaxing on the rock. All is calm in my mind and the spirit world. I look for my Protectors. They're relieved the day didn't go as they saw. I smile, I am too. I hold her closer. I wasn't really honest with Pres; losing her

325

would be my one regret. Her hands on me is a dream I never thought would really happen. Knowing it's the same for her is a comfort only when we're all safe. She freaked waking up without me. I don't ever want to be the one that causes my Little Pixie tears or pain. Dying would hurt her and that hurts me. Knowing I wouldn't change it doesn't help.

Chapter Thirteen

Christian

I move the laptop when I hear the door. Nekanis is up waiting for me to tell him what to do. I smile. 'Friend.' He relaxes against Dean. I move the bag up and bring the jewelry boxes to me. I can't wait for her to see them. If she ever fuckin' wakes up. If I hear the word patience one more time I'm going to lose it. I shut the phone down and shielded just to get some work done. They call here then tell *me* to be patient. I shake my head. Crazy bastards.

Taking the boxes, I look at the ring then charm bracelet. Te Jess has a bracelet like this and I love that she still wears it. It still means something after all these years. I want Dean to have that too. I only put ten charms on it, but it's cute and the jeweler said I can add to it every year.

I put it down and pull her cut out. It's a princess cut with the Protector patch. Turning it, Blackhawk draws my eye. My name will be on her. My heart skips a beat and I smile putting my hand over it. I want that reaction every time I see it.

She moves and I lower the cut and boxes turning toward her just in time to see her eyelids flutter and open. I feel it again and smile moving her hand over my heart. "It's so good to see those beautiful eyes baby."

She smiles. "You're okay."

"Better now that you're awake."

She squeezes me and looks up. "I saw you get shot."

"I was at Security earlier. We wear vests whenever we go out. I picked you up and never changed."

She leans toward me and kisses my lips. "Thank God you didn't. I need the bathroom." I lift her and move her to the door. I love that giggle. "I love the service Christian, but laughing doesn't help."

I set her down and she moves fast closing the door as she goes. I'm sitting here smiling like a pussy. I shake my head and look at Nekanis. "Thanks Brother." He jumps down and walks out. I guess his job is done for now.

She climbs on the bed and my dick is hard. Jesus I need to control this better if I'm going to get through this. "Now that I can think, how long was I out?"

"Almost a full day." I sit up and pull her to me. "It was a slow fuckin' day too."

She laughs and kisses me. "I'm sorry you had a slow day. My parents just let me sleep it off."

I look at her, but decide to save those questions for later. "I have something for you." I lift the cut to me showing her the front. "This is my cut. It's a symbol of my commitment to you." I turn it so she can see the back. "I'm 'all in' Dean. That means we work for everything. Every smile, every touch, every tear. We don't divorce, leave or intentionally hurt each other. I will work for us Dean. With everything I do you're my first thought. That's for yesterday, today and tomorrow. You will always be that for me. I'd be honored if you'd be my old lady and wear my cut letting everyone know you're mine."

She's smiling and nods with tears ready to fall. I kiss her and get the cut on her. "It looks best right there, babe."

She giggles. "I'm an old lady like Holly! I can't wait to tell Serenity." She tries to move, but I hold her still in my lap.

"In a minute babe." I raise the box and watch her face fall. What the fuck? "The old ladies like the paper with the cut. The Brothers that are 'all in' don't give a shit either way, knowing what the cut means, is enough for us. Either way, the ring and cut mean the same thing. Will you marry me Dean?"

She's nervous and not talking. She's also not taking the ring. My heart speeds up. "You don't want to marry me?"

Finally, she looks at me. "We don't need to get married. I understand what the cut means to you. I don't need the paper."

This is *not* working like I thought it would. I just gave her the option and I'm let down that she took it. "Are you sure?"

She nods smiling. "Yeah. If I change my mind we can always get married later."

I'll be changing her mind. "Will you wear my ring?"

"If you want me to yes." I slide it on her finger feeling a little better. She doesn't want to marry me sits heavy on my mind. I wish for the millionth time that I could read her. I put the bracelet down on my bag not sure what to think. "Now I'm calling Serenity. She's going to be so excited." She bounces off me and runs out of the room.

Seeing the cut on her doesn't feel like I thought it would. I jump hearing her laugh.

Dean

He's been quiet all afternoon. I can't believe I'm wearing his cut and talk enough for both of us. When I told Serenity all he said, she wanted to throw a party making me laugh. I could do a party. After running and being scared for so long a party sounds like just the thing to kick off our new life together.

He stops at a restaurant right on the water. "Serenity is throwing us a party."

"Why?"

My eyes snap to his as I sit down. "To start our new life together. I thought you'd be happy?"

His face changes and he puts a smile on. "If it makes you happy, I'm happy babe. Whatever you want." If the smile reached his eyes, I'd believe that more.

"What's wrong Christian?"

He picks the menu up. "Nothing babe. When's the party?"

Maybe something is going on at work. I get excited all over again. "She's getting Jess to help her. They'll let me know. She said old ladies need to help with an old lady party." I almost stomp my feet, but catch myself and look around. Old lady. I love it.

We eat and he relaxes. He wants to go to the reservation again. Since everything makes me happy today I'm all for it. People get seated on the side of us and are arguing. The woman cheated on her husband, but is mad at him. I'll never understand people. I try closing doors, but she's pissed and everything she thinks keeps messing with my head.

"Let's go babe. The ride will relax you." He stands and I look at my plate. We didn't finish, but he's leaving so I can relax.

I hold his hand and stand, but don't look at him. I can't even sit and eat like a normal person. Why he picked me runs through my head. He's not moving. When his hand reaches for me I look up at him. "I'm sorry."

He shakes his head no. "I should have paid for the tables. Next time I'll remember." Bending he kisses me right here at the table. "Let's ride." He throws money down and

330

walks me out like it's no big deal. A shiver runs through me. That's Badass.

When we get home the guard is holding a bag and hands it to Christian. He passes it back to me. "Can you hold that to the house?"

"Yes. I think I can make it." I laugh. He ordered food. He's the best boyfriend. I wonder if he's my old man. I'm waiting to ask until I can see his face. Somehow, I think that will be something I don't want to miss. I've never heard anyone say old man when referring to their men. I don't mind being the first. I giggle.

"I wish I could read where that's coming from." Reaching back, I give him the bag.

"Somehow I think you wouldn't want this one."

He takes my helmet off and kisses me. "I want them all. Every thought every smile, everything and anything that would help me understand you."

I shake my head no holding his hand while we walk in. "You got a whole lifetime to figure me out." I giggle. "I hope you never do. It will keep life interesting."

Pulling the trays out of the bag he smiles. "Yeah. Because the visions, suspending and jumping to the spirit world gets boring."

I laugh and can't stop. Everything bubbles up then out. He lifts me holding on and I wrap my legs around him leaning against his chest until I calm. "This is the best day ever. I love you Christian Blackhawk."

He kisses my head. "Love you too my Little Pixie old lady."

I start giggling again and look up at him. "Are you my old man?"

He smiles. "Christian works."

I loosen my legs and slide down him. "Everyone always says old lady when referring to the women. You said we don't get to leave or divorce, which I love by the way, but I'm not calling you my boyfriend for life. Old man it is."

He rolls his eyes, "Partner, paramour, lover, all of those fit. If you think old man is how you want to label me, whatever." He doesn't smile as he says it.

I sit thinking about five years from now and calling him partner, paramour and lover. I don't think I can even say lover to someone I just met. 'This is my lover Christian.' Yeah, no, that isn't going to work for me. I let out a sigh. I'll try old man, but he doesn't look like that thrills him. I don't know why. I'm excited to be an old lady. Really, I'm excited to be *his* old lady. He's such a good boyfriend. "Thank you for ordering the food. I was hungry."

He does the chin lift thing, but he looks a million miles away. With his work and vision stuff he must have something going on. I finish eating and stand behind him. I kiss his ear. "You're the best. Thanks for the awesomest day. I'm going to take a bath."

"Okay baby. I have some shit to do. I'll be up in a little while." He clears the trays and throws the trash away.

I'm surprised, but with everything going on he needs to work when people need him. Going up the stairs I think about the van that parked by me and Serenity's apartment. They were there one night, then I heard shots and they were gone the next morning. He kept me safe and I didn't even know him then. I get in the tub thinking of my old lady cut. I let out a squeal then laugh.

I open my eyes when I hear the door. "I didn't know you were waiting for me."

I smile. "I wasn't really. I think I dozed in between all those teenage dreams."

He sits and starts washing me. "Teenage dreams?"

I wave my hand and splash him. "Sorry. You know, living with the guy of your dreams, vacations, kids, all that stuff."

"Yeah, I hope the kids are small like you. Short-Blackhawk is a hell of a name if they aren't."

"Short-Blackhawk?" I don't want my kids called Short-Blackhawk. "I thought they'd just be Blackhawk."

He shakes his head no. "My kids won't ever think they're bastards. They'll have both our names so they know they're always wanted by both of us."

I just nod. Since I'm not pregnant this isn't something I need to think about right now. "I already washed up. I'm ready to get out."

He stands and I'm raised up. I smile the whole time. He's never going to be boring. After drying every spot on my body, he smiles up at me. "Done baby."

When I'm lowered, I pull him down. "Love you Christian. Thank you." I walk out and drop my clothes in the basket. Two steps into the room and I'm lifted again. "I can get on the bed Christian."

"I can put you on the bed, but I was thinking of something else babe. Are you too tired?"

I look over at him and see the smirk. I'll play. "Nope."

He flips me so I'm looking down. This is different. Hands slide up my body from my feet as I watch him undress. It's the craziest feeling knowing he isn't actually touching me. My legs get massaged going all the way up. It feels good and I let out a moan. He looks up and smiles. "You're going to like this babe." He picks a box up and throws it in his drawer. What was that? It's from the jeweler and he whipped it in the drawer like it was nothing. I think back, this is where he had the cut and ring. He had something else for me? I want to see. Why didn't he give it to me? "If you're too tired we can do this another day," he says in my ear and a shiver runs down me.

"No! I'm not too tired. I was thinking of something. I'm done." It all comes pouring out of my mouth in a rush.

He laughs from above me and I feel his real hands go from my waist to squeezing my nipples while the others are stroking me faster. I moan pushing my chest into his hands. "You like rough babe?"

The question throws me for a second. "I guess. I like when you bite me."

He slaps my ass, after the initial shock I'm not expecting the second slap and moan with how that feels. My pussy is throbbing with need and I roll my hips. None of the hands are there. "Looks like my lover enjoys the fuck out of rough. Let's go with that first." The hands on my nipples squeeze harder. My body bucks into those hands loving the feel of the hard squeeze then the soft caress right after. "Love to see you chasing it baby." His hands slide up holding mine above my head. "I'm going to make this beautiful body sing for me babe. Just relax and feel me around you, inside you and right here above you." Hands move closer to my throbbing pussy and I buck my hips for them, but they move to my ass. Damn hands! I growl in frustration. "Relax my little lover. I'll make it good for you." I try, but those hands aren't making it easy. "My name on your back means no cover babe. You good with that?" His hands finally slide to my pussy and I can't think.

No cover, pregnant...oh my God. "Don't stop! That feels so good." I cry out trying to will his hands to stay right there. The lower half of me is jerked up and his mouth is on me. Heaven. This is heaven.

I'm ready to come and he moves. "No, please."

"Shhhh baby. I just needed to taste you." The hands are stroking me again and the throb is almost painful. He's kissing my neck and I feel his finger slide to my ass. He's done this before and I moan knowing how good it will feel. "That's it baby relax into me." His finger slides in me and I push my ass back liking the foreign feeling, but trying for something more. The hands start stroking again and I cry out. My skin is sensitive and feels every touch as if it's igniting lighter fluid through my veins. I'm going to die before I come, but it feels so damn good. He slams into me, I'm not expecting it and yell. "So fuckin' tight baby. It feels good without the cover. When you come, push baby, push down and give me everything. It will be good babe."

"Yes!" I cry out wanting to feel good.

He's everywhere. I feel his bite on my shoulder, a slap to my pussy, something catches fire inside me and those damn hands feeling so good everywhere. I scream his name and push.

Christian

Holy fuck. I'm gasping for breath and feel us lower. Holding the air in I raise us up and move the towels with us to the bathroom. Jesus I'm fuckin' spent. She has the sweetest scent dripping off her, but I don't have the energy to do more than breathe it in. I stand her in the shower and move the handheld to clean her up. When I'm done, I dry her, or the towel does, and lay her on the bed while I shower. Without the brace, I'm suspending and feel the energy draining out of me. I put me on the bed and place her against my side with her head on my chest. I jump feeling her heartbeat run through me.

Sitting with Hawk, I tell him how it worked. Everyone hears it, but seeing it and the feeling it threw on me was fuckin' awesome. I Googled it while she was in the tub earlier to make sure I didn't miss anything. I smile and look at him. "I didn't miss anything. An orgasm like that will make her want more. Maybe enough for her to marry me."

335

He just looks at me, but I know he is agreeing or maybe I just want him to.

When my mind and body are settled, I jump back. I need a plan. I get the laptop above me and think. There's no fuckin' way my kids are going through life as Short-Blackhawks and I see that doesn't make her happy so I'm using it. Today it hit me she won't use lover as a label either. She's too innocent to call me her lover. I laugh. We'll use that too. What else can I do?

She got a couple of outfits, but Nancy didn't send much. With Dean saying they were nice, but not acting all girly with the new clothes I got the feeling she'd wear them—but not be happy in them. I look for Serenity and pick through her brain. I see Dean like she is now but dig deeper then stop. Serenity has memories of her in the craziest clothes. She's in neon bright eighties clothes, skater style and I'm surprised to see biker black with zippers and chains. Everything she wears she has a hat and boots or matching shoes for. My Little Pixie is cute with her hats and the big fuckin' smiles I see. She looks free of worry. She gets hats for Christmas and I'm struck again by that carefree emotion she lets show. She's safe and comfortable with them.

I watch her walk away from Serenity and get in a car. She's dressed in that funky skater style with her hat and two different converse sneakers, but she looks sad. It doesn't work with the clothes that make me want to smile. Serenity doesn't stop watching her so I don't. As she drives away I see her tears fall. 'Someday baby girl, when it happens I'm throwing you a party.' She turns watching the car in the distance. I jump out and look at the laptop. Serenity has been buying her clothes from wherever they could afford and Dean wears them without complaint. Why wouldn't she get clothes now? Darren was getting their money to them from the insurance. I look and see him helping her with the paperwork. Maybe it's not in yet. I shake my head. She wouldn't buy clothes with her new school bills and no actual need for the clothes.

I pull the laptop closer and search for what my old lady wants. I back that up smiling. "What my lover wants." I need to keep that one up.

On a site that sells every fuckin' hat in the world, I'm sick of shopping and can't even remember all the shit I ordered. I put it all on a spreadsheet and send it to Nancy. Jesus. She can find her more shit. I ask her to find hats and shoes to match whatever she sends and close it all down. Thinking about the clothes, I know Nancy will nail it. The look is similar to how Sandy dresses except for the biker clothes. I've never seen Sandy like that. I can't wait. She moves and I check time. Jesus, four fuckin' hours of shopping.

She moans and I tighten my arm around her. She's worth it. Her hand slides across my nipple and I suck in a breath taking the shot of adrenaline straight to the balls. She smiles with her sleepy eyes and pushes herself up. "Whatever you did, I want more."

I laugh. "It was all you babe. Extreme release is yours whenever you want it. Just another service in the Short-Blackhawk pleasure chest." She winces then kisses me.

"I'll never complain." She kisses down my chest and licks my nipple with the flat of her tongue.

"Fuck that feels good," I moan out loving the little smile on her lips.

Her hands are all over me. I hold my body still so I can feel every second of it. When her hand wraps around me I move with her. "Jesus babe I don't know how you could make this any better."

She looks at me and I see the uncertainty in her eyes. It passes and she's got steel replacing it. "I do." She's got my dick in her mouth and I'm not moving.

337

"That would do it." I push back moving us so I'm leaning against the headboard and can see her. "Watching my dick slide out of your mouth fuckin' does it for me babe. That's so fuckin' good." She sucks harder and my head spins. Jesus. Her hand moves higher and she scrapes her nail across my nipple. I moan trying to keep control. *She fuckin' does it for me* is an understatement. Her hands on me would be enough to lose my load in them, but her fuckin' mouth is killing me. She strokes down my sack and I explode.

With my heart beating normal again I tighten my arm around my Little Pixie old lady. She got me off and fell back to sleep. I smile thinking I could do this for life. Losing the smile, I wonder again why she won't marry me. I feel like she's sure and 'all in' too. Why doesn't she want my name?

I raise her up and move pillows under her when I slide out. "Out Nekanis." I throw shorts, the walking brace and sneakers on and run. My back feels better and I don't notice anything, but the muscle burn from my leg.

When I see Taylor, I start walking. He had another dream, but is feeling good right now. I OC it to Prez and Jessie. "Brother. You're up earlier than usual."

He smiles. "Yeah. I got an hour before Precious is up. You doing okay?" I nod. "Beth gave Dean Mitch's book. I thought sleep would come easier for you all relaxed and shit."

I laugh. "That explains a lot. Thank Beth for me and no, sleep hit her not me."

He laughs. "You're fucked up Brother. You need to talk?"

"Yeah." He turns and we start walking. "She won't marry me. I gave her the cut and told her the old ladies like the paper with it and she said the cut is enough."

338

He stops and turns toward me. "She gets what the cut means?"

"Yeah, she's making plans for forever, but I can't read her. I've got no fuckin' clue what she's thinking. What if she thinks I'll turn into the fuck-up I was and walks?"

He shakes his head no. "Who the fuck put that shit in your head? No one thinks of you as a fuck-up." He's pissed thinking it's all in my head. I want to tell him that would be an indication of a fuck-up, but he keeps going. "You have fuckin' readers begging for the chance to work with you. Give them the job of reading her for you. Find out why she's okay with just the cut. Maybe she doesn't need any more than that."

That would be a good thing to know. He could be right and I'm stressing over nothing. "Yeah. Thanks Brother." I turn and start walking then stop. "Taylor?" When he looks back he stops and faces me thinking this is important. To me it is. "At the MC, I trained with everyone else. When everyone was sleeping, I trained. I did everything I could to be ready for when I was needed. You were already gone the first time I was at the Club. Every fuckin' time the whores felt bad for me, they called me the lost boy. Shelly ended up the only one I would see. She didn't look at me like that. She was so much older, but I didn't give a fuck as long as I didn't get a pity fuck." He looks down thinking he should have been around. "It wasn't the women that thought of me as a fuck-up, just the lost boy in need of their pity but it was the Brothers Taylor and some of the KC. They didn't understand what I could tell and couldn't. They would see me and think every single fuckin' time they did, that I was a waste, I was a fuck-up. Years of being a fuck-up to them had me moving to the reservation where I wouldn't let anyone down. I'd give Jeremy, Tess and Aubrey what I saw and stayed away. I don't say I was a fuck-up because it's what I think. I know I've changed from that man, but I can't change what other people think. Some still see me as either the lost boy or the fuck-up."

He's right in front of me and hugs me holding on a little longer than is normal. "I'll kill them all. Who the fuck thinks you're a fuck-up after this last month?" He runs his hand down his face. "You have enough shit to deal with. You don't need fuckin' asswipes throwing doubt on you Brother. Tell me and I'll take care of it."

I smile. Like Darren asking who to shoot, the Brothers that believe in me have no doubt at all. "It doesn't matter anymore Brother, but you thinking it's all in my head bothers me. I have purpose and focus now and the ability to fix the shit I see. You matter Taylor. My family sees only me. It feels good and I don't want to go backward with doubt in your head about what's in mine."

"I didn't know Christian. I wish to fuck I stayed and helped when I was needed. Hearing the shit that was going on when I was away fuckin' sucks when I can't do anything about it."

I slap his back. "It is what it is Brother. We've all made it to the men we were meant to be. With everyone running in different directions I'm surprised Mom and Dad aren't gray and drooling in their rockers."

He cracks up. "Yeah, we were a handful." He shakes his head then focuses on me. "I can see where people can alter the way you think about yourself. Never have I thought of you as a fuck-up. I hate the way it rolls out of your mouth so easily. Get it out of your head Christian. If it weren't for you none of us would be here. That's about as far away from a fuck-up as you can get. Stop saying it for me Brother. Knowing how you got those thoughts in your head is worse than wondering. Yeah?"

"I'll work on it. Thanks Taylor."

He turns running the other way thinking he still wants to kill the Brothers. I shake my head and look at Nekanis. "I fuckin' love my family and the Brotherhood."

Chapter Fourteen

Christian

On the way home I connect with Jeremy and Aubrey, telling them my plan. Jeremy fuckin' laughs. Aubrey agrees right away. She's asking Elizabeth and Blaze to help. I know Blaze will tell Harley and Sandy. This is working out well.

My old la—lover is still sleeping. I shower and dress then raise her up and slide in bed lowering her onto me. As I'm doing it I smile. Sometimes it's fuckin' great to be me.

When she opens her eyes, she's smiling. I hope I get to see that every day. The world is perfect for that one moment. "Morning my Little Pixie lover."

Her smile gets bigger. "You're awful chipper today."

"Could be from the phenomenal fuckin' blowjob you gave me or I like to see you smile when you open your eyes. Either way it's a good day."

She laughs. "I feel the same. You're amazing and I like your smile."

"I need to get to work early. Do you need a ride?"

She shakes her head no. "I'm driving my awesome car with the Prince logo. I'm pretty sure I won't get stopped from here to the school."

"You're feeling okay? You were out for fuckin' ever." I watch her closely, but she shrugs it off.

"I'm fine. I've been out for longer, but I don't feel all foggy like I used to. I actually feel a little giddy."

I can't look at her face any longer and moan taking her tit in my mouth. Her hands go right in my hair. I fuckin'

341

love it. "I gotta go little lover." I kiss her pouting lips. "I like the look of those lips."

She smiles. "Bye Christian."

"Work, my Brother." I smile following Nekanis out.

At Security I pull up my sheets and find my people on tracking. I have a reader class and training at the MC today, but we have lunatics running around trying to get a foot in the door up there. Uncle Danny needs to be warned, but I'm not going anywhere near MC-Baxter. Pres is driving me crazy.

I get to the meeting and see Princes has some shit jobs going on and I'm glad to be hopping up to Mass.

Just as I hit my office, Nancy calls excited about the clothes. She didn't think the clothes fit what she heard about Dean and was waiting to meet her. Since we were due up there this weekend she'll have the clothes and hats at the shop for Dean to pick through. "I don't want her picking through clothes. She's been wearing whatever they could afford since everything she owned burned in the house with her parents. Just send everything you get for her. I'm getting rid of anything she has now." She laughs then hangs up. "People really need to learn to say goodbye."

"And not talk to themselves," Terry says sitting down.

"Yeah. What's up?"

He doesn't want to ask. I smile wondering why he came in. "Jacob is here and Billy said he'd help if he's needed. Prez said it was okay. Can I go with you to training?" He talks so fast and it's muffled in the back of his throat I take a second to get what he said. "I swear Christian, I won't get in the way." He thinks I'm going to say no.

"I don't think you'd be a problem Brother, just the opposite, if you know how they're trained you'll be better prepared in Ops for them."

342

He's so relieved I almost laugh. "I got twenty minutes, right?" I nod and he runs out of my office saying he'll meet me at the truck.

I connect with Aiyana and I'm relieved everything is calm there. I've seen nothing today that causes me concern. Checking on Dean I watch her in the classroom. Brandon has her laughing and I'm struck by that carefree look. It's just like the one from Serenity's memory.

Since all is right in my world we make our way to the truck.

Dean

The kids help get everything cleaned up and put away. I still can't believe they're working on a way to clean water. When I walk out to the front with the baby and Nash, Done picks Nash up giving him a hug. "I missed you little buddy. You doing good?"

"We've all missed you Done. I'm so glad you're back. The subs were sub-par."

He laughs. "It's not good to hear that, but it feels good to be missed."

Beth pulls up and we get the kids out to her. Since I'm done for the day, I decide on a ride. I let Done know where I'll be and wait for Security to pull up behind me. I start my first class next week and I'm excited and nervous. My mind jumps to Christian, he was in good spirits this morning, I hope he's still smiling when he gets home. I flip on the radio and start singing with Marc Anthony who croons about needing me then marrying me. I'm smiling the whole time. *I'm already an old lady Marc.* I flip the station and it tells me this is Blake Shelton. That's weird, he's a country singer. He sings about God giving him me. I hit the station again and get an old song about going to the chapel.

What the hell is going on here? I hit another station and Train wants me to marry them. I shut the radio off.

I'm an old lady. Christian doesn't need the paper and I have no one to come for a wedding. I put up my doors and realize I'm humming the Marc Anthony song. Damn I've got it bad. I smile and make my way home.

Christian

"Babe, I'm at the reader class. How far out are you?"

"I'm in front of the house. I'll be right there." She hangs up.

You'd think a simple goodbye would be easy. She's at the door just as I open it. "My damn radio is broke. Every station is love songs!" Her arms are waving around and she's glaring at me like I did it.

Fuck, who could pull that one off? "I'll have someone look at it tomorrow babe. Right now, I have a class. You ready?" I keep the smile off my face and guide her to the back parlor. Our readers are waiting. It's a good class and Dean is updating my sheets as I move from one reader to the next. Shilah comes in and talks with people throwing what he's getting from them. I give it to Dean, but she's reading right from him. I step back and watch smiling. This is working out well.

When Shilah is finished, he stands in front of us. "Shilah this is Dean my lover."

I see the shock on his face then he smiles. I hope to fuck he's blocking her. 'I am Brother.' I relax and he looks at Dean. "Nice to meet you Dean. It's about time Christian found his woman. When are you getting married?"

Her face is beet red and she looks away. I smile and wave my hand at him. "She's wearing my cut. That's enough for her."

Dean just watches as if we're a tennis match. 'She seems happy with that.' He throws to me then nods. "That's all that matters. Glad you're happy Brother."

'Seems?' What the fuck does that mean?

'I get the feeling there's more to her just wanting the cut. There's a sadness in there.' He looks at two readers talking.

'Thanks Brother.' I look at Dean. "Shilah is the man with the jobs. He needs to get these people working and I'm fuckin' starving. I'll have someone pick up your car from here. My radio works and you can get your fill on the way to eat."

She bounces right to happy. "Thank you! The radio thing is driving me nuts. Sheila set my stations to classic rock and new rock. The stupid thing had country singers on it."

I throw chin to Shilah and guide her out smiling the whole way. Dakota and Prez could change music. Jeremy and Aubrey too. Fuck. Mase and Devan could do it. I have too many fuckin' people that could pull that one off. As soon as we get in Bruno Mars is singing about marrying him. I bust out laughing when she hits the station, button. Aerosmith is on and she relaxes. "Maybe it's just the music babe."

Her hands start waving while she talks and I clench my jaw. "There was sixties music, country and some God forsaken ballad that sounded like opera. This is not normal. Something is wrong with the radio. I had good music last time I drove it. I need some discs."

I smile. "I'll get you discs babe."

345

"Because you're the best." She leans into me for a kiss.

I take her to the Italian place by the PD and throw Smithy chin as we walk by. He stands then is on one knee and I'm holding in my laugh. I stop and watch holding Dean against my side.

"Emma I've waited a long time and don't want to waste another minute of my life without you as my wife. I don't have another fifty years to give you, but I'll give you what I have and make it good for you. Will you marry me?"

Everything is quiet as if everyone is waiting for her answer. "Get your fool self up. Of course I'll marry you. No need for a hip replacement before it's time." I crack up. The whole place is clapping and I'm thinking I need to thank someone. I wish I knew who that was. I slap Smithy's back and I kiss Emma's cheek congratulating them. They ask about Dean and I tell them the same thing I told Shilah. Dean is blushing and trying to pull me away.

We take our seats and I ask her, "What babe?"

She leans forward. "You keep telling everyone I'm your lover," she whispers.

I lean forward. "You are," I whisper, then sit back. "I don't like old man, partner or paramour. You don't have a problem being my lover, do you? I thought you were particularly happy last night."

I get another blush and smile. "Well, no, but the way you keep telling everyone is embarrassing. You could call me your old lady."

I clench my jaw and shake my head no. "I don't like old man so I won't call you old lady. No one ever had a problem with it, but I can see where it isn't politically correct and could be offensive. If my Little Pixie lover isn't happy with it, I'm not using it."

The waiter shows before she can answer and we give our order. She's quiet and I let her think. Since she's not stressed by the people sitting closest to us I'm happy to eat and watch emotions play across her face. They know me here and don't sit anyone too close so it's a nice meal. I ask about her day and she smiles telling me about the kids and clean water.

Chapter Fifteen

Two days

Dean

"Really? This is all for me?" I walked in to the bed piled high with bags and he's standing here smiling.

"Yeah babe. Why don't you take Nekanis for a walk and I'll get it put away?" He would too.

"I can help."

He shakes his head no. "I did this. I'll clean it up. Go relax on the beach. I'll be done with this in an hour."

A Prospect walks out of the closet with two big bags and drops them at the door then goes back in the closet. Since this is considered normal only to freaky MC and Prince people, I take the dog for a walk.

I sit and watch Nekanis playing in the surf, after a while Serenity sits by me. "Hey sis. What's up?"

"Freaky shit. There's a mountain of clothes on the bed and Christian says they're all for me." I'm totally disgusted by the thought of more damn clothes that I didn't get to pick.

Her hand takes mine and gives it a quick squeeze. "I'm sorry baby girl. If I knew I would have stopped him."

I nod. I know she would have. I know I should be more appreciative, but I want to cry. It's been so long since I felt like me, the real me. I miss my happy clothes and dressing for how I feel. Now I just throw whatever I have on. There is no me in anything anymore.

I stand up. "My hour was up about twenty minutes ago." She stands and walks with me feeling bad about the clothes. "How is the job?"

She's happy. I smile, it's about time. "I love it. Every day I love it more."

I laugh. "This is good. I'm so happy for you Serenity." At the house, she gives me a quick hug and keeps walking. I take Nekanis in and go right to the bedroom. I stop short in the doorway. There's a hat tree standing in the corner by the closet door. He knew. He knew and fixed it for me. Tears fall and I walk to the closet. I see right away he got me the clothes that I miss so much. Serenity tried, but there's only so much you can get at Walmart and Kmart. Walking in I touch the shirts admiring the colors then the black old band shirts. How did he know? Hats line the shelves above my clothes. He must have bought a whole hat shop. Nekanis brushes my leg and I look down at him. That's when I see the boots. I fall to my knees touching boots and shoes, he even got me sneakers in funky colors with bright laces. I sit and cry. He knew and fixed it.

"What the fuck? I thought you'd be happy. Did I get it wrong?"

I laugh and look up at this amazing man. "You got every single thing right. Thank you Christian."

He lifts me to him and walks out of the closet to the bed. "I'm never understanding women. Why the tears babe?"

"You knew and fixed it." I wipe my face with my sleeve. I'm not ever wearing it again anyway. "I was just thinking there is nothing of me in my clothes. I thought you got me more clothes like the last ones Nancy sent."

"Some of these are from Nancy. She didn't think it sounded like you so I looked in on Serenity and found you in your fun, carefree clothes. It's not quite what I've seen you wear and I liked the smiling you in her memories so I got those. If you want something else just get it. Nancy has some stuff at her shop for you to look at, but there are a million fuckin' stores and I'm sick of picking clothes."

I laugh. He sounds disgusted. Oh, my God! "You picked my clothes? And all the hats?"

He shakes his head no. "I picked a bunch, like four hours' worth, then sent it to Nancy so she could see the style and colors and she did the rest. I told her to get matching shoes and hats for you, she went by what I already got and filled in all the rest. I hate fuckin' shopping babe."

I laugh. "I don't know what I did to deserve you, but I'm so damn happy you're mine. Thank you Christian."

"Why don't you go find some clothes that make you happy and I'll get dinner on the table. I need to pull the food off the grill."

I kiss him and jump up. "Okay!"

He laughs walking out.

Christian

I get everything on the table and stand looking at it. I bring a vase over and decide it looks stupid sitting there empty so I move it back. I get napkins under our silverware and think that looks better, but not great. Trying to find something to put on the table I'm distracted by the flash at the window. I look and smile. Getting a jar, I send it out and collect three fireflies. When I put it on the table I think it's perfect and turn the light lower. She laughs from the doorway and I swing around.

She's in jeans with holes on the legs and a bright blue shirt with paint splashes all over it. Her shoes don't match, but one has blue on it and the other is black with blue laces. I look up at my Little Pixie who looks like a Little Pixie and smile. "Love the hat babe." She's got an old-fashioned man's hat on, but it works with the clothes.

She laughs. "Me too! I love everything you picked. Thank you."

"You look like a Little Pixie." I walk to her taking her hand and put it over my heart that just skipped a beat. "My Little Pixie." I kiss her thinking this is about as good as it gets. She's happy and looking carefree in her clothes. I like the carefree and I fuckin' love the hat.

"I love you Christian. Thank you for everything you do. I like the lightning bugs on the table too."

I bring her over thinking they work with the carefree look she's wearing. "Love you too babe. I thought the table was missing something. They work."

She laughs and we sit to eat. "This is great. I need to thank your mom for teaching you to cook."

"My dad grills, mom cooks in the house. He taught us all outside and mom taught us cooking inside. They were a great team to grow up with. Do you want to go up to the Club for a little while? The Officers show up there a couple times a week. We don't have to stay, but I should show." She nods happy with that and I'm relieved.

After dinner, she lets the fireflies out and puts the jar in the dishwasher smiling. She's so fuckin' cute in her mashed-up style and that hat. I wrap my arms around her and kiss her neck. "I can't wait to see what you're wearing tomorrow."

She giggles making the whole thing complete. I drag her out and up to the Club. As soon as we hit the door I get a feeling and pull shields. The MC, fuck. I connect with Devan and Ricky telling them what I see. Keeping my eye on Dean while she's talking to Eliza and some woman, I tell Darren what's happening. Aquyà is in my head telling me what they saw. I guess he's the speaker for them now.

"I need to get up there," I tell him taking a step toward Dean.

His hand on my arm stops me. I move it away and look at him. "I'll get them home and meet you at the hangar." He starts talking to Ops to set it up.

I nod and make my way to Dean. "Babe, shit's happening at the MC. I need to get up there."

She looks scared then her face relaxes and she smiles. "Stay safe Christian. I'll see you when you get home."

I kiss my girl and move people out of my way so I can make the door without interference. The Brothers are mumbling shit. Maybe I moved them a little fast.

Dakota is doing his flight check when Darren boards the chopper. The readers are scrambling, but Uncle Steve has them focusing and calmer than when they sat down. Devan goes through the Op with them and I see everyone smiling when Ricky walks in.

Darren waves his hand in front of me. I focus on him. "They good?"

"Getting focused for the Op. We have about half an hour. Did you get Pres?"

He shakes his head no. "My dad said they're on a date night. Dad's on his way in."

Jesus. I look for him. Fuck. They're in their room. I throw he's needed in Ops and get the fuck out of his head and their room smiling. "I told him."

He shakes his head. "I don't want to know."

I laugh, "No, you don't." I remember the first time I saw my mom and dad. I can live without that shit in my head.

"Get someone on Pres. He'll be leaving the Compound. Elizabeth and Harley would be helpful." He nods and calls it in.

I look for Jeremy and find him in KC with Aubrey. 'Je we need you.'

He stops throwing at her. 'Yeah. We'll be there.'

'You should have gone for the meeting.'

'I got it,' he says. Lowering to the floor he puts his hand out for Aubrey. 'Time.' I leave him throwing the pictures I got to both of them.

Ops is looking for Pres. He's not out yet. I look hoping he has clothes on at least. He's at the door kissing Kate. 'Leave now or that will be her last fuckin' kiss!' I yell at him. He jumps and turns. "I need to go now," he tells her walking out. Kate is laughing and I hope it stays that way.

I'm dropped at the Compound making me think Dakota must know something. "There is quite a bit of knowledge in me Christian. Some of it even helpful." I laugh jumping out. "Be safe Brother."

I look back at him and see what he does. Fuckin' hell. A Security bike is waiting and I climb on as Pres pulls up. "You ride in between us."

He looks pissed, but nods. We roll to Elizabeth and Harley and Pres looks at me. "VP, Tiny, Danny, Bob, Digs, even fuckin' Geek?" He's thinking the girls won't work if this is his last ride.

"None have what it's going to take to get you to Ops today."

Jeremy pulls up with Aubrey on his bike and throws us chin. "First." I nod and Pres rolls his eyes then asks Geek if VP is tracking him.

Uncle Steve comes over pissed. "Took your fuckin' time. Kids are all that's gettin' you here."

Pres hits his mic off and glares at me. "Mic stays on. If I can do this so can you. The visions aren't fuckin' quitting Pres. Let's get you to Ops."

353

I see him hit his mic and we follow Jeremy. "Elizabeth and Harley keep us clear from behind. We have the front."

"Roger Guardian." I feel their focus shift and thank Elizabeth in her head. She's not happy seeing the lack of confidence in Pres.

"Je."

"Got it. Now Aubrey!" Jeremy yells. A truck flies right over us and I laugh. It lands nose down, but sits just like that. Fuckin' kid is too much.

Pres closes the distance between us and Jeremy. He's getting it. We make Main and see it's like a fuckin' war zone. Who the fuck has this much money to waste on this shit? I push it away and shield Pres from the fuckin' bullets coming from every fuckin' where.

"Elizabeth, whatever it takes to stop from getting hit in the back," I tell her and focus on what's coming.

"Roger Guardian."

"Jeremy turn away from it and take us around."

The stubborn bastard shakes his head once. "No. We got this. Keep him shielded."

"Aiyana, can you help?"

'I am with you Warrior Protector.'

"Shield Pres while I keep the stubborn fuck clear," I growl out. She laughs making me smile. It's just another day. I keep it in my head and brace.

"I am with you also Christian. VP allowed me a headset and I will help where I can." Dakota says and my mind relaxes.

"Thanks Eagle Eye. I need you to push with us as soon as we get a visual on the trucks."

354

"Roger Guardian," Dakota says and I feel him in my head.

"Aiyana."

She cuts me off. 'Co and Kaya are here Guardian. We have this.'

I smile at her try for levity. "Cover Pres, no matter what happens, you get him to Security. The shield will work once we get past Jeremy's fuckin' show down."

Jeremy laughs. Devan tells us the trucks are circling waiting for us to make the middle.

Jeremy turns fast and I hold Pres to my side moving him with us. He hasn't said a word, but I don't have time to look. Devan says the trucks are widening their circle to follow us. I see where Jeremy is going and think he's fuckin' smart. Getting rid of them is better for everyone away from main roads and neighborhoods.

The reservation land up here isn't set up with grid like roads and the roads are a fuckin' mess. I see the first truck then a vision of a line coming from the front and another from the back.

I look at Pres. "Sorry Pres. I'll get you down as soon as we're clear." I move his bike to the tree line and lift him up to a high branch. "Keep him covered Aiyana. Elizabeth, hit the trucks coming from behind. Blow every other and the rest will go. This is a straight shot. Just ride the line and steer clear of shit flying."

I see the bikes swing around and shake my head. How the fuck did they miss seeing the skill here?

"Roger Guardian," she says like it's just a ride.

Jeremy is a good half mile ahead of me and I see the fire roll from Aubrey. She's hitting every other truck. I hit the first and third and spin back toward Elizabeth. The last trucks are shooting. I lift her bike and she shoots the pussies like it's a normal day in the fuckin' crazy MC.

I roll fire down the line shielding them from shit flying and they ride back toward me. "We had it Brother."

I nod. "I need to get Pres to Ops." They follow without bitching me out. I lower Pres and he still doesn't say anything. Jeremy looks at me smiling. I shrug. He can shoot me later. I need to get him to Ops.

"Thank you, Aiyana. I've got Pres. If you can help in any way here, it'd be appreciated."

'Roger my Guardian,' she says and Jeremy cracks up.

"That puts you using procedure better than me today Aiyana. Thank you." I speed up, seeing Mase and Colt in a fuckin' brutal attack. "Elizabeth, town two. Devan, get her to LP1 then Mase. Elizabeth, work fast—no mercy and move. Mase and Colt will need your help."

Pres looks at me while the radio goes off in my head. "I can get to Security. Go help Mase and Colt."

He's fuckin' sick if he thinks we're leaving him here. "I just did." I see he's going to argue. "The job is a select few for us. You're one of those. We do what we can for everyone else, but you are the job today." He throws chin, and thank fuck, isn't going to argue. We hit a real road and fly to Security. Someone's taking shots as we pull in. Pres ducks. "You're covered," I tell him just as Jeremy yells.

"Fuck!"

I look back. "Aubrey cover both of you and get inside. I got Pres." I pull Pres's jacket getting him in the door behind them. Jesus. "Most people work with Security. I'd think you would get how that works," I say moving us to Ops.

"Watch how you talk to me and they weren't aiming at me." He's pissed at me?

I open the Ops door and hold my temper until it closes then swing around facing him. "Watch the fuckin' feed and see how many bullets hit the fuckin' shield we held over you. Jeremy was hit shielding you instead of himself. Lose the attitude that this is a fuckin' game to us and look at what's happening around you. If you don't clear this threat you're not making another birthday. We can fuckin' shield you, but they're catching on. The vision was you dead today in the middle of the fuckin' yard." I throw up the picture on the center board of him on the ground with two trucks burning around him. His helmet is rocking twenty feet away from him. "If you keep the attitude and assumption that no one knows what you're thinking, I won't have much help in keeping you alive for the next one. Open your fuckin' eyes Pres. You can shoot me, but I'm still the guy keeping you alive. It's a risky move on your part seeing as how you DON'T FUCKIN' TRUST ANYONE UNDER FORTY. I need to help Uncle Danny and keep Mase and Colt safe. Watch the fuckin' feed." I walk away and straight to Ally and Devan at our control. Ally high fives me.

I'm pissed. I thought we were past this. Pres walks to Ricky and Ricky shakes his head no. I throw to Jake to look at Jeremy's arm. "It's flesh and on his forearm," I tell him. He hands Pres his headset and walks toward Jeremy and Aubrey. No one has said a word to Pres. I'm glad they're fuckin' pissed too.

Ally hits my leg and I look at the screen. "Fuck!" I jump to Uncle Danny and hold the bike up giving him a push higher. The ground explodes under him.

"Thanks Brother," he laughs as I lower him just past the big fuckin' hole in the ground. Crazy bastard.

I look for Mase and Colt and see Elizabeth and Harley have them clear. Thank fuck something was easy today.

357

Devan handles this way better than I ever could. I don't want to be running Ops. He stops talking and looks at me. "I'll do it. VP hasn't changed anything I've done."

Good to know, but there are fuckin' bullets flying right now. "Later." He throws me chin and gets back on with the Team.

I watch the boards, helping where I can, for three fuckin' hours. This sucks. While the Teams roll in, the other controls are watching the boards. Uncle Steve pulls Pres to ours and tells Ally to put up the feeds so he can see what a fuckin' pain in the ass he is. Pres wants to shoot him, so I move away.

Dakota comes in smiling. "Good job Brother. You are always interesting to travel with."

I laugh. "We may not be invited back."

Since he's still smiling I guess I'm wrong. "Just the opposite our great Warrior Protector. You will be sought for council because of your commitment to the job."

I push my hair back. "Oh Jesus, not by Pres I hope." The fuckin' guy still wants to shoot me.

He laughs. "Ricky and VP see much clearer than Pres. He will not shoot you."

I throw him chin. That's something. "Are we ready?"

He shakes his head no. I see the meeting room and my head falls forward. Fuckin' great. Our Team walks in and I tell Devan and Ally they're done for today. I let Jake know what to watch out for and walk out behind the Protectors.

"This is fuckin' bullshit," Colt says as soon as the door closes.

"I want to move down to Princes. I can run Ops from there," Devan says and it isn't a question.

"Me too," Ally says surprising the fuck out of me.

Elizabeth takes a step forward. "I'm not leaving, but this shit needs to be sorted."

I nod and look in the meeting room. There are already Brothers gathered in there. "Use my office Brother," Ricky says from behind me.

He follows us up and tells the room he's in. Boards and lights come on together and everyone sits or leans against the wall. Since I didn't do shit, I stand letting the Brothers that need the seats sit.

"Devan, I have Jacob running from Princes."

Jeremy stops me. "Need him here."

I think about that. "Okay welcome to Princes Protector Ops."

He smiles, but it's not real. He's pissed at Pres. "I'll be there tomorrow."

I look at Ally. "Jacob isn't a reader. He needs someone that gets it on control. Will you consider staying for a while longer and giving Jacob that support?"

She bobs her head up and down. "If you need me here I'll stay. I work good with VP and Devan, but Jacob is nice and knows I'm smart."

What the fuck? I look at Ricky. "There was doubt and we cleared it up tonight."

Fuckin' Brothers. I nod looking at Colt then Mase. "I would like nothing more than to take you at Princes, but the bigger threat is here. I don't give a fuck what people think about me or you. The job is the same either way. You being at Princes just means I need to arrange your travel back here daily."

They nod, but they're not happy. I move my hair and look at all of them. "Our job isn't to decide who is worthy of

359

protection. Our job is to protect however we can. This is new to everyone. Seeing you moving objects and fighting the way you do is new to everyone. Give them the time to take that in. We *are* making progress. Sometimes it's too fuckin' slow for our way of thinking, but it's still progress. I can't be more proud of you than I am right now. Knowing you all saw what Pres was thinking and you still did the job threw relief on me. Let him think what he wants. He made it here and has to deal with VP—to me, the job was easier."

They laugh. I look at Dakota. "Very good advice Brother. They are meeting."

We file out and Ricky stops me. "Thanks Brother."

"I did nothing for you Ricky, but I'm glad you're happy. The purpose was keeping Pres alive."

He nods. "I got that. I also know that if he's gone I am." He keeps walking. Fuck. Brothers need to get a fuckin' clue before they fuck it all up—and they called *me* the fuck-up. I shake my head and walk into the meeting. Pres throws me a look, but keeps talking. I roll my eyes and lean against the wall waiting for him to finish.

When the Brothers leave, I tell the Protectors to stay. Pres gives me another look. "You can think about shooting me all you want. We both know it isn't happening. You need to hear the changes being made so you can adjust. Devan is moving to Princes tomorrow. Jacob will move up here to keep Jeremy in line." The Officers laugh. "Ally decided to stay and support Jacob. The rest of the Protectors are pissed, but understand the job is protecting you and the Club regardless of what you think about them."

Uncle Danny stands up slamming his seat into the table. Everyone jumps. "Another one! I lose another fuckin' kid because you're too stubborn to see what's right in front of your face. And Ally? They fuckin' fly, throw fire, control people with their minds! Christian saved my fuckin' life today, holding my bike up, WHILE HE WAS IN OPS! What the fuck do you need to see for you to believe they have your fuckin' back? It's a back that I'm losing interest in taking by the way!"

Pres is stunned, but his mind jumps to fight. "You don't know why he's moving."

Uncle Danny suspends himself and stands on the table. The room is stunned and silent watching him. "I know. I know what you think. I know how you talk down to them. I know you always thought of Christian as a fuck-up because you didn't understand. You don't understand now. You've done as much damage to our families as you've done good for the community. The scales are just barely balanced right now, when those scales start tipping the other way, I'm done."

Pres watches him and I see it isn't where he needs to be. "All this time you could read me?"

I walk out. What the fuck ever. My dad puts his hand on my shoulder and I stop. "All along it was Pres thinking you were fuckin' up?" His hand drops.

"It was better when it wasn't said out loud. He's not the only one, but his cut deep." I turn looking at him. "He jumped right to Uncle Danny holding back from him, but still sees me as a fuck-up and now every Officer and Protector knows it because Uncle Danny threw the pictures while saying it."

Dakota sticks his head out. "We need your help Brother." Everyone is yelling in the room behind him. Jesus.

"Because walking back in there is a good idea right now," I mutter making my feet move. Dakota fuckin' laughs.

Uncle Danny is up in the air as if he's sitting in a chair just watching everyone. I shake my head. I guess it's one way to come out. I wouldn't ever have told if I were him. He throws me chin and I look around. Devan is yelling

361

at Pres. Tiny and Colt are throwing points in between Devan's.

"Stop!" I hold them all stopping Devan mid-sentence and look at Pres. "I thought protecting you would be easier now. It was fuckin' easier when you had no clue. Devan is at Princes tomorrow. Jacob is moving up here." I look at Jeremy.

"Tomorrow."

I nod turning back to Pres. "Tomorrow. We don't need anything from you to keep you alive, but some courtesy and a little respect would go a long way. Uncle Danny was right. There is nothing more we can say or do to show you we've got your back. The rest is up to you." He's pissed thinking I can't tell him where Devan lives. "You're wrong Pres. My job is leading the Protectors and keeping the vision alive. I'll do that however I can. Your help would be appreciated, but I don't fuckin' need all this."

"I believe the ancestors will be helpful here Christian. They can explain what we are missing."

My eyes snap to Dakota's. "I'm not carrying his ass anywhere tonight. This isn't a threat to him and I'm fuckin' tired." I throw. 'Giving him peace is not at the top of my fuckin' list.'

He nods. "I understand. Perhaps Mase can help."

I watch Mase nod and Uncle Danny lower himself. "I'm not helping." He walks out. Tiny fights my hold and I let him go and watch him follow Uncle Danny. Ally and Devan follow with Harley and Elizabeth.

Uncle Steve kicks a chair. "Sit, take the tiara off and listen. Gettin' tired of sayin' it too."

"You knew all this time and didn't tell me?" Pres sits glaring at him.

I throw my hands up. "Good fuckin' luck Brothers. I'm out." When I turn, my dad is at the door. "Can I get a lift home Dad?"

My dad drops me at the Compound and I jog home. He is pissed, but never said a word—which made for a long ride. I spent it connecting with Aiyana, Kaya and Co thanking them for their help. I find Devan and Jacob both packing with the help of Prospects. They're both happy with the change.

My girl is sound asleep with Nekanis laying against her. He watches me and jumps down when I walk closer. I raise her and slide in. What a fuckin' day. Her arm goes around me and I jump. Hawk sits beside me and I tell him all that's happened. I follow his line of sight and see a vision of Wall talking to Pres. I push it away. When Pres went all in for Ricky I thought his deeper thoughts changed too. I knew what he really thought about me, but it looked like that was getting better too. I should have looked.

"It was not yours to see then Christian." Nunánuk sits beside us.

Maybe not, but it would have been fuckin' helpful. I think about the visions and reading people. "My focus is changing Nunánuk. I see more of the vision and the need to protect it."

She smiles looking at the lake. "As it should be my grandson."

I let the ancestors wash through me, feeling the peace they leave behind down to my bones. I wasn't lying to Dakota that I was tired. I'm feeling that now. I jump back and sleep.

Chapter Sixteen

One week

Dean

The reader class is happy today. More people have jobs and are settling in the apartments Prez bought. I still can't believe he bought apartments. They are a unique kind of crazy.

Christian's arm goes around me. "We're out babe."

I take his hand and start walking. If he tells one more person I'm his lover I'm going to scream. I think of anything happy I can grab onto. "Mucimi was happy today. He said you got them all. Does that mean the readers are all safe?"

He takes my hat and puts the helmet on me. "No, but the ones in harm's way are. There are probably tens of thousands of readers around the country. We focused on the ones that were destined to die."

Wow. "Are they all coming here?" Prez needs more apartments.

He laughs and puts his hand out for me. "No babe. They'll stay where they are for the most part. We'll keep helping those in need."

That's good. I kiss him because he's such a good guy. He's been quiet for a couple of days, but today he started talking again. "Are we safe now?"

"Let's get to the Club and I'll tell you what's going on."

I smile glad I dressed in my biker clothes today. Holding on, I think about all that's happened since he found me hiding in my closet. To say they move fast is an understatement. I'm an old lady, have a job, I'm going to school and I get to help him here with the readers. Plus, he's been working with me and Mucimi every night so I'm able to focus more and block better. I decide that life is good, as I get off and wait for him to take the helmet off me. He seems to like putting my hats on so I always wait and let him.

He smiles popping it on my head and leans against the bike. Pulling me by the belt, he lets it go when I'm in between his legs. "The lunatics are still out there. They have a direct line to us and it will never be over. Since there aren't as many and they're seeing they can't really hurt us, the fight here isn't so dangerous. There are other fanatical groups that will make a run at us. Their hate isn't focused on killing Princes so much as religious beliefs and changing the way we do things here." He pauses so I nod. "We have a bigger threat that is MC related. When they get their heads out of their asses we can deal with that and hopefully get back to living without Ops every fuckin' day. So, to answer the question, no we'll never be completely safe, but together we keep each other alive. I can't wait to make it back to living for stretches of time without a direct threat."

I smile and kiss him. "Thank you for answering. What is up with people hurting people so they believe the same? And oh my God, the MC needs to get their damn shit together. You work too hard."

He laughs pulling me into the Club. Music is blasting and he pulls me right to the dance floor. He's been teaching me to dance for our party next week. I love dancing with him. He's wicked good and I like his hands on me. After two songs, we get a drink. The men always stop and talk to him so I sit and watch. He's funny and happy to answer their questions or talk about the Vets or homeless which always reminds me of the things he does that I don't see. Tonight, a skanky guy stands by him and he rolls his eyes before looking up at the guy.

"Before you open your mouth she's got my name on her back. You don't know me, but I can guarantee you don't want to know me the way you're going to if you say what's on your mind."

The guy gives him a look. "Being your *lover* doesn't mean she doesn't want anyone else. My name would look good on her too."

My eyebrows hit my hairline and I look at Christian. The guy is a pig, he's already got me undressed and in a dirty bed. I see black and look back up at him. His nose starts bleeding, but he's standing there frozen. I put my hand on Christian's face and turn him toward me. "He isn't worth it. Let's dance Christian."

His face relaxes and the man falls. Christian lifts me and carries me back to the dance floor like nothing happened. That's a little scary, but the man was a pig. I hope he's okay. When I look over a Prospect is pulling him across the floor. Maybe Nick is here.

When a slow song comes on he spins me around and pulls me to him. I laugh and hold on dancing just like we practiced. Dakota and Jess glide by and smile at us. We aren't that good yet, but we're getting there. When the music stops Christian leads me to the outside of the floor and stands me in front of him. We watch Dakota and Jess dance and they're amazing. I always think of Dakota as reserved, but he can dance and it isn't a waltz. I look at the other men and they're dancing just as sexy as Jess and Dakota. When Jessie walks to them I turn around. Them grinding with Jess in the middle is more than I need to see. Christian smiles and pulls me away.

Just before we hit the stairs a woman stops him. "Christian! I haven't seen you lately." She's got a big smile on her face and I want to slap it. She's been with him. He stops and looks at her. She walks the other way and he watches. I don't get any more from her and look up at him. I'm kind of hurt, but it's not like I can pinpoint why.

"I'm not a kid. I grew up in the MC where sex is part of life. What I had to do for relief embarrasses me now that I have you and know what it's supposed to be."

I think about that and can't really argue it. He's a grown man and did live with all this sex around him. This place has a room that they have sex right out in the open and no one says a word about it as if it's normal. That couldn't have been easy when he couldn't touch anyone. It wasn't easy for me and I didn't grow up seeing what he did. I nod and he brings me up the stairs.

He unlocks the door and guides me in. "Before you ask I've been the only one in that bed. I bought it when I moved to the Compound."

That's a relief. I nod not sure what to say. "It's a nice room. Why do you need it if you live on the Compound?"

He watches me, but answers just when I think he won't. "For probably everything going through your head, but also when we're locked down, all the Officers can stay here. It's closer to Security. If we're drinking, we can sleep it off here or if someone needs us we can be here for them." His shoulders relax and it looks like a slump to me. "I'll have your name added to the door." He says it like it's the last thing he wants to do.

"I like it just the way it is."

That gets a smile. "You do? No Short-Blackhawk?"

I shake my head smiling. "I like just your name on the door. It looks cool."

There goes the smile and the shoulders again. "Yeah." He waves his hand. "So, this is our room. I'll get you a key tomorrow, but you only move around the Club with a Blackhawk, the Officers, or the old ladies with you. Don't go anywhere alone."

I nod and he takes my hand walking out. Okay, this was just show and tell? He moves people by the door and we walk right out. He takes my hat and puts the helmet on me. "What's wrong Christian?"

He shrugs. "I'm tired. It's been a busy day for me and I didn't sleep last night."

My poor man doesn't sleep enough and he was at the MC all day yesterday. "Take me home Christian. I think I know a way to relax you." His eyes show me love and he kisses me. I don't think he's telling me everything, but maybe he can't. They've been in Mass for a couple of days now. I can't imagine what they're going through up there, but he comes home and still treats me like a princess. I hold on and smile thinking about him being pissed that he missed the dinner I made for him. Yesterday Beth showed me how to make clam chowder and you'd think it was a five-course meal. He was impressed that I even had those little oyster crackers. He's a funny guy, but appreciates all the little things and always shows me how much he loves me. I climb off and smile when he takes the helmet off and puts my hat back on me.

"I love you," I tell him and turn around going up the stairs. I can help him relax and maybe he'll sleep.

"I need to take Nekanis out." He's standing on the first step.

I grab his hand and pull him up the stairs. "I got him. We'll be back in a little while. Go relax my tired Protector. When we get back I'll help you with that too." I giggle, kissing his cheek, and hop down the steps following Nekanis to the beach.

Christian

This is why you don't fuckin' lie to your old lady. I flop on the bed and lose my clothes pulling on a pair of shorts. When I lower down I jump. She's never marrying me. Now she thinks I need to relax to sleep. I hear them come in and she's trying for quiet. I bet she thinks I'm sleeping. Since she does, I stay and think about the week.

Pres seems like he's jumped on board, again. I haven't bothered looking any deeper because I really don't give a fuck. I throw a rock in the water. I haven't looked because I don't want to see me through his eyes. I need to stop the lying shit or I'll never be worth anything to anyone.

"Very wise my Warrior Protector." I turn seeing Dakota fly over.

I'm happy to sit with him for a while. "You have not asked, but Dean may change her mind if you tell her the paper matters to you."

I shake my head no. "I'm not forcing my name on her Dakota. If she wanted it she'd have taken it." He looks at the water, but doesn't say any more. I feel Dean's heartbeat against my side and stand. "Thanks Brother." I jump back knowing she's asleep.

Working for a couple of hours I get everyone settled for the next Op we'll be running. Hopefully Uncle Danny and Pres are talking before that. My dad and Tiny aren't talking to him either. Since they're not on my Ops, I'm not too worried about them, they'll come around. Ricky and VP have been calling the shots. I was surprised when VP let Ricky run the first meeting. He's right though, if Pres isn't going to show, Ricky should be running it. He's doing a good job too.

I like working with Devan. He gets shit before I have to tell him. Jessie sees it as a plus. Jacob loves being closer to Jeremy and Aubrey and talks to me every day. I can hear how proud of them he is every time he talks about them. He's pissed at Pres too, but likes working with Ally and VP.

I need a way to get the Protectors connected again. They're all doing the job, but it's not fixed. This will only last so long before they all want to move again. I put it in an OC for Prez hoping he can figure something out.

I send the laptop to the dresser and have the charm bracelet come to me. I still think it's cute and know she'd love it with her quirky clothes and style. It fits her more now with the funky clothes. I smile thinking about her in the biker clothes. She's perfect and the fuckin' hat always gets me. She moves and I close the box sending it back.

"Wait." She sits up and reaches for the box. Fuck. "I saw you throw this in the drawer a couple of weeks ago, then forgot all about it. I was going to look at it when you weren't here." She smirks at me, but I don't know what to say. "It's obviously important to you. Can I see it?"

I'm not lying to her again so I need to just give it to her. "It's for you. I think you'll like it and I can add to it. I thought it would mean something to you too."

She nods, but her brows draw down. "Why didn't you give it to me before? If I didn't see it, you would have put it away."

I shrug and open it. "I'm giving it to you now." She's watching me and doesn't look at it right away. I don't know what the fuck to tell her so I wait.

When she looks down she smiles. Thank fuck. "It's beautiful. Thank you."

"The jeweler made the cut on it and put stones and shit on the others." I'm nervous and watch her look at them.

She stops on the cut, the bike and the little laptop. She laughs at the phone, pixie and boot. "You're right it does mean something. I really like the wave, tiara and the D&C. What's the ribbon with the S?"

"Sister or Serenity. He made that one too."

She nods. "Why didn't you give it to me?"

Jesus. I push my hair back. "Getting the charms to add means something to me. Te Jess has one that Uncle Steve adds to all the time. She still wears it and he bought it for her when they first got together."

"You didn't know if it would mean the same thing to me?"

I nod looking from the bracelet to her eyes. "Yeah."

She leans down and kisses me. "I love it and knowing that it's important to you makes it that much more special. Thank you."

She hands it to me and I put it on her. "I guess our anniversary can be the day I gave you my cut."

Her eyes snap to mine. "That's why you didn't give it to me? You weren't sure of our anniversary?"

That is, in a way, so I nod. Then shrug. She laughs. I get up and throw the box away then look around for anything else to do. "I'm sorry, but men are so funny."

I look at her. "Men?"

She waves her hand and the charms make a little chime sound. "You know what I mean."

"No really. Men because you've been around so many and you'd know or men meaning me and my stupid fuckin' gestures?"

She freezes and I realize what I just said. "I'm taking Nekanis for a run."

"Don't leave."

"I'll be back after we run." I walk out, hearing her call me. I'm such a fuckin' idiot. In the mud room, I sit to put sneakers on, but hold my head in my hands. She doesn't want my name, she doesn't want to marry me and I gave her that choice. Now I'm taking it out on her because I didn't want her to take it and she's got no fuckin' clue. I take a minute to breathe then go back up the stairs. Fuck. She's in the middle of the bed crying because I fucked this whole thing up. "I'm sorry baby. I've got shit fuckin' with my head. Walking away isn't an option and you don't deserve it."

She looks up at me. "Is this 'all in'?" She hiccups with her red eyes and tears still falling.

I nod feeling like a dick for doing this to her. "I shouldn't have walked away." I lift her up and sit her on my lap.

"You were coming back?"

What? "Of course, I was just taking Nekanis for a run. Why would you think I wouldn't? I gave you my cut babe."

Her arm moves and the charms hit together again. "I don't know anything biker. What if I say something too stupid and make you leave?"

I smile. "I couldn't walk out the door after our first fight babe. 'All in' means forever. It's not some weird biker meaning it's just English meaning actually forever."

"Oh. I like 'all in' even more now. Why were you so mad?"

I move tissues to her and watch as she cleans her face. Her eyes are swollen and red because I was a dick. I owe her the answers to every question she has. She's watching everything I do so I keep my face blank. "You don't corner the market on saying or thinking stupid shit babe. I've done some pretty stupid things in my life too and Brothers thought of me as the fuck-up of the family. Not my family, but it took me time to realize they didn't understand how much I could read and see. They had no idea how to help me and I had no idea that they wanted to. I'm not proud of it and I don't like talking about it."

Her face scrunches up so cute. "I can't believe the Club would think of you like that. You save everyone all the time."

I love her for giving me that and kiss her little red nose. "Now. Before I could only tell them what was coming. Sometimes they'd be pissed if I didn't tell them things I saw. It's only been the last two years that I've been training and growing into abilities. Since Dakota is here, he explains shit better to them and they understand more now."

"I'm sorry I laughed. I only meant men are different than women. We think different."

"Yeah. As soon as I said it I realized what a stupid fuck I was. I'm going to do and say stupid shit, but I'd never walk babe. Every night I'm here and we'll talk about what a dick I'm being. I never had an old lady or even a girlfriend. This is new for me too."

She giggles and my heart catches. "I'll meet you in our bed. I'm sure my damn mouth will lead to more fights, but I'm new at this too. I like that you didn't leave and love knowing you won't."

I kiss her head thanking the ancestors and Mucimi for bringing her here. "Never baby. I love you Dean. You don't hurt what you love. I'm sorry I hurt you."

Her charms make a noise as she moves and I think I'm going to love hearing that sound. She turns so she's straddling me. "I never got to relax you."

Fuck. "I have a better way to relax. Guarantee we'll both sleep."

"Oh yeah?" I nod loving the challenge in her voice.

"It's called the numbers game. We start with seven then move to sixty-nine."

She giggles. "I don't know seven, but I know what sixty-nine is."

"You're going to love this." I raise her up and lay myself down sitting her down on my face.

"I really like the numbers game," she moans, moving for my mouth.

Chapter Seventeen

Two days

Christian

"If you keep riding my leg I'm fuckin' the shit out of you."

"Yes."

I flip her to her hands and knees and move behind her. My fingers find her wet and I slam in moaning. "Fuckin' perfect." My hand wraps her hair and I wish it was longer, but I get enough to hold her head back and slam in again.

"Oh my God. Yes!"

Her yell spurs me on and I picture my hands running down her from the front. "You like my hands on you my beautiful Little Pixie?"

"Yes!" she yells.

Raising us up I let her hair go and flip her. "I need to taste you baby." I move down, smiling at her grunt of frustration. As soon as my mouth is on her she's moaning with her hands in my hair.

She's bucking into me and I hold her tighter. "Oh, please don't stop."

As if I would even consider it. I suck her all in shaking my head in a no motion. Stroking her inside gets her purring then I get my scream. "Love my name on your lips when mine are on your sweet pussy."

I angle her so her head is lower and slam back in knowing my dick is hitting right where she needs it. "Take it Dean." Seeing her already so close has me moving faster. Raising her higher, she grabs my arms and I like the feel of her nails on me. I get her tit in my mouth and suck hard then bite the underside. Her hand moves pulling my head into her harder. I picture my hand slapping her and she's bucking into me again. "I love your tit in my mouth beautiful." Needing deeper I move her out, but picture my mouth on her tits sucking and biting while I'm slamming into her. Watching her head move from side to side, I move towels over the bed. "Baby you're going to give it all to me." Fuck, it feels like we're sucking the air out of the room. "Push babe. Push and it will feel so fuckin' good." Stroking her inside she screams raking her nails down my arm and I lose it. We drop to a few inches above the bed and I'm fighting to keep us up and move with the strangle hold she has on my dick. Jesus. Feeling the heat run through me I lower us and empty into her with a roar. Falling forward, I land on my elbows and bury my face in her neck. Holy fuck. "Whatever you're doing to me don't ever stop. Don't ever fuckin' stop, baby."

It takes a good fifteen minutes, but I finally feel able to get us cleaned up. My hip is on the wet towel and it feels like shit. My girl doesn't need to wake up feeling dirty after she gave me all of her. I raise us up and get to the tub. It's the only thing I can do without the brace on and feeling so drained. She moans when I lower us down. "Love you my beautiful Little Pixie." I get us clean and dry. She's still out of it, but she stands leaning against me. I lift her moving us back to the bed. Fuck, I move the towels right to the washer. I'm losing it if I can't even remember to clean the mess we made.

Dressing in shorts and putting my shirt on her. I think about talking to Dakota about healing my leg. This fuckin' sucks already. I check my Protectors and see the MC already starting to get antsy. I need to sleep for a couple of hours. It's just hitting four. This will work. I get us comfortable and close my eyes then smile. My girl doesn't think I'm a fuck-up.

376

Nekanis sits in the seat beside me on the chopper. Since I'm not running Ops, Prez keeps me with Princes HS. I don't need the coverage and told him I'll just run with whoever they had, but he shut me down saying MC HS won't get me. What he was thinking was Princes will make sure I come home. I threw him chin liking the way that felt and have had a Princes partner all week. Today my partner is Jessie. He's got shit swirling in his head when he sits.

Dakota lifts off and waits until we're out of Princes air then talks to us in Mohegan. I've noticed he always switches languages until we're over the MC. I should ask, but let it go and listen to him tell Jessie about Destiny getting her breakfast yesterday. I shake my head smiling. The fuckin' kids are unreal. She's two.

Mucimi is throwing me pictures while they talk. The last is Pres hugging me and I push it away. My job is keeping the people that protect him alive today. Nothing Mucimi sent is new to me so I thank him for the heads up and focus on what's being said.

When they're quiet Jessie asks, "What's going on with Pres?"

I shrug. Prez gave him an update last night at the patio. Since I wasn't there, but saw the conversation, I tell him what I've seen. "He's letting Ricky run Ops with VP. He knows Ricky reads him and has been staying away." I don't tell him Pres was so pissed almost everyone in the room was readers, he threw his chair through the window. I'm pretty sure Tiny gave him that since they talk regularly.

"Baxters are looking at taking over PD." He watches for my reaction. I was surprised to see it in his head a couple of days ago, but it works out so I just nod. "You've seen it?"

"I talked to Kevin yesterday." He's surprised, but doesn't ask everything that brings up for him. "It works out. Their concerns are legitimate and they have the people, with the MC in place, nothing much changes."

377

He nods, but he's trying to figure a way to ask for more detail. "Pres is okay with this?"

"I don't know. I've stayed away. Since he's letting Protectors cover him on his Security detail I'm not that close. The first time I showed, after Dakota took him to the reservation, he still wanted to shoot me. Since I like living and he's not under a direct threat I've been keeping the lines up making sure no one gets in or close enough to become that threat."

He's pissed, but not at me. "That's been a fuckin' week. He's been to Never Never Land almost every fuckin' day."

"We need a way to get the Protectors aligned with him again. If you can do anything to help, or you see something I'm not, just tell me. We can't keep running with this disconnect."

"You don't think you're part of that disconnect?"

What? "I'm here every day doing my part to keep threats away from him. It would be fuckin' nice if they focused on where the threat was coming from and not just the Ops. I've brought it up and I'm shut down. The Officers are still pissed and Ricky is following orders. He says there aren't many, but keeping the borders safe is the focus. I'm not a fuckin' miracle worker here. Aside from doing my job what can I do?" Since he's talked to Baxter's and Tiny he knows what I'm saying is true.

He thinks about that. I focus on the Protectors and see Ally is happy today—she's going for a girls' night out. She's so cute deciding what she's going to wear. I jump to Jacob. He's ready for the day. Quickly making my way through them, I stop on Jeremy. He's working at the lab, but I can't get anything going through his head. Aubrey is with Mitch and Carolina. Pulling away from them I see Jessie watching me.

"Vision?"

"No. just checking on everyone. I see through the visions now. They don't hold me like they used to."

He doesn't understand, but I don't explain. I seem to have to explain shit to everyone and it's getting fuckin' old. I've got no problem telling Prez where I'm at, but I've already told them how the visions work for me now.

"There are many things changing in our great Protector, Jessie. He is just realizing the strength in his abilities and adjusting to keep up with them. Visions are no longer the concern they were because he controls them."

"You need to stop calling me the 'great Protector' and shit. It throws negative on people. Especially the Brothers that don't know me."

He jumps to English, thank fuck we're close. "I did not see that my—Christian. I will adjust my language." He starts talking to MC Air and I watch the Compound pass under us.

"Brothers still have a problem with you?" Jessie asks and sounds baffled.

My eyes snap to his. "Yeah. They've got no clue what's going on."

"Jesusfuckin'Christ. My father can fix that." His look is fierce and I'm reminded of just how deadly Jessie can be.

I unclip my belt and stand. "He's not in the fixing mood lately. I could change that, but it would be a misuse of my abilities and I'm supposed to protect him—not control him. I don't give a fuck what he thinks as long as he stays alive." I open the door and jump out. Nekanis walks beside me.

I hear him and Dakota talking, but push it away and clear my thoughts. Aiyana jumps in my head. 'The Army Corp of Engineers is stopping the pipeline!'

379

I smile and stop walking. "That's great Aiyana!"

'It is a start. The company refuses to listen, but the Vets have kept everyone safe. I am here if you need me my Warrior Protector.'

"Keep me updated with the pipeline and thanks Aiyana. Thanks for the help. I'll call if I need you, but it should be an easy day. I've got nothing happening until later." I start walking again.

'As you will Christian.'

Uncle Danny is at the door smiling. "Great news." Jesus.

"I can see you coming out is going to be a pain in my fuckin' ass." We walk by and he gives Nekanis a pet laughing.

"Always keep them guessing." He turns to the chopper. "They know the way." I look and see he's got news, but I don't touch it. He follows me to the meeting room. Just as I thumb in he touches my arm. "Thanks for not asking."

I throw him chin walking in. Mase's face lights up and I laugh. Fuckin' kids. "No, she isn't agreeing, but I'm good with it."

His smile changes to a frown. "I saw you take her to your room."

"I'm glad you're getting better, but that better be as far as you ever go."

He gets pissed. "I don't need your shit in my head, but I thought the kids had it covered and she finally said yes."

I stop and Nekanis stands beside the door. "The kids? They've been fuckin' with her music?" She's still pissed about it, but I'm smiling. They're too fuckin' much.

He nods. "I can't read you, but I thought you were happy last night."

I was for the minute I thought she agreed.

"I can't read him either," Harley says. The Protectors go around the room saying they can't read me.

Dakota comes in and everyone is quiet. He threw for them to give him a minute. Ricky and VP walk in and watch everyone wondering what's happening. "I can read Christian, but only certain areas. As a Prophet, it is not necessary for me to see all his thoughts and plans. With our—Christian, his intent and the ability is my focus. I see his heart and get his reasoning. It is enough for our ancestors, our great Leader, and our cause." Wow. That's kind of cool. I throw him chin.

"So, he reads everyone, but no one reads him?"

Jesus. My head falls forward and I wait. No one says a word. You'd think a week would be enough to cool him down.

Dakota puts his hand on my shoulder. I see the Protectors see it and stand straight shrugging his hand off and throwing for him to explain. "He will not read you Pres. He is open to everyone in the room, but not you. His last thought is of you want..."

"Enough! Jesus. We need a way to fix the fuckin' disconnect here not make it bigger." I turn and throw chin to Pres. He still deserves respect.

He looks me right in the eye, but I don't see his anger. "We have a disconnect? I thought things were running well." That look says he's confused.

What? I look at Ricky and he's smiling. 'He's clueless.' He throws and I want to laugh. Harley, Elizabeth and Colt turn their heads away. Rich, Blaze and Blake actually laugh. I sit.

381

Pres looks at Ricky. "What time are we starting?" He means Ops, but Ricky gets it.

"Sometime around lunch."

"I'm eating early," Uncle Danny says and everyone is laughing. It feels good. Jessie says he's going to lunch with him and I laugh. Fuckin' Brothers and food.

"Got shit to do," VP says and everyone shuts up.

Pres walks forward and looks unsure until Ricky steps back throwing him chin. When he steps up I see something has changed. "I need some time to hear and fix this disconnect. I wanted to let you know how proud I am of your ability and effort to keep the Brotherhood and our communities safe. Without the combined efforts of our new Protectors and Ops planning and execution we all wouldn't be sitting here today. Thank you, Brothers." He throws chin and walks out.

I'm pulling what I can get from Ricky. He watches me smiling. I peg him a finger and he laughs. "If you'd read him, you'd see for yourself."

He's right, but fuck. He still thought I was a fuck-up for putting him in the tree. I push my hair back and think. They go through Ops while I pull from them. Everyone is cautious of the new change, but excited.

Jessie hits my arm. 'You paying attention?' he's yelling in my head.

'I sent it to them earlier. Nothing's changed.'

He nods and looks back at Ricky. When they finish, Ricky and Jessie stay. Jessie has questions and Ricky stayed to explain when I get pissed. I smile seeing it and he pegs me a finger. "Explaining isn't one of your strong suits Brother. That's why Pres always wants to shoot you."

Jessie laughs. "You send the Ops to Ricky?"

I nod. "And Uncle Steve. I tell them who needs to be where and they pair Security or HS and whatever they need to do their part."

He nods. "No wonder my dad hit the fuckin' freaky trail so hard."

Me and Ricky crack up. "I don't plan their Ops, just where the Protectors are. I don't have anything to do with their shit."

Ricky doesn't stop laughing and Jessie is looking at me like I'm nuts. "Brother, in a matter of like two fuckin' months everything in MC world was flipped around. Ricky's running fuckin' Ops and from what I know, half the Club. You're the go to for whether they go on living and Uncle Danny is as fuckin' freaky as Mucimi."

I smile at him. "Your kids are as freaky as Mucimi—they all are. I just tell them where Protectors need to be and Ricky was born for this job. I didn't make or control any of this shit. I'm just trying to keep ahead of it." He shakes his head no. "My job isn't fuckin' controlling shit, it's just keeping the vision alive. That's it. I didn't ask for it, but it's what I'm meant to do. As long as I do the job I don't get all the fuckin' talking about it."

He puts his hands up. "I see that Brother. Relax. I see where your focus is narrowing, but didn't realize how much until right now. Dakota says you need a pure heart to do your part. I see nothing, but good in you Christian. I'm just trying to understand where the disconnect is and how I can help."

I nod blowing the fight out with my breath.

"You need a fuckin' handler Brother." Ricky is thinking Devan being here was good and wonders how to get me to see the changes from their side. Since I'm on their fuckin' side, I push it away.

383

Jessie stands looking at him. "That's my job. I got this Brother. Have Pres watch the feed. It may help him understand." Ricky nods and walks out.

I pull my phone to call Prez and Jessie puts his hand on mine then pulls it away. "I'm just calling Prez. I don't know why everything is such a fuckin' dramatic event here, but he gets all this."

He slaps my back. "Let's get lunch and I'll explain it." I roll my eyes and we follow him out.

Dean

This is my first field trip and I'm excited. We're going to a battleship docked at town four. I've seen it from the bike, but never up close. The kids are excited and Holly had them learning about the ship and some of the men that sailed on it. One became quite the accomplished writer and kept daily logs.

"We're ready," Done says from the door. Holly nods and he takes Chance. I follow with Mucimi and Aquyà. Stella is bouncing around and Brandon takes her hand walking in front of me. Honor is with Holly and Phoenix. Teller and Justice walk in front of me.

I'm thinking they're good at field trips and Justice looks back. "If we want to go on more we need to show we're responsible."

I hold my laugh and nod. "Got it. I'll do my best to be responsible too." No hanging out the windows yelling at cars for me.

He shakes his head no and keeps walking. Holly is laughing and she doesn't even know what I'm thinking. Damn kids.

We pile into a huge SUV and get everyone settled and belted in. Prez gets in with us and I'm surprised. "Christian and Jessie are at the MC. HS is short today so I'm in and Sheila and Aaron are our Team leads."

Wow. I didn't expect him to explain it to me.

He smiles. "For the old ladies, I explain." He nods to Done and we're off, with Prez inside and two teams outside.

We talk about the ship and Prez asks them questions. I have no idea about the guns, but the kids do, so I listen while watching out the window.

What the hell? I look at the billboard again then look at Holly. "Does that say marry him Dean?"

She looks where I'm pointing and laughs. "No, it's for an ambulance chaser."

I look again and shake my head. It's not blue with white writing anymore, it's an office picture with red words on the side. I am losing it. Prez looks back, but doesn't say anything. He must think I'm nuts. First the damn radio, then the discs, now street signs.

Done pulls in so I put up my doors and leave it for later. We spend hours on the ship finding out every single battle it went through. Mucimi is excited, sad, then asks a million questions through everyone else. It's weird and funny. In the gift shop, they look at everything then Justice hands the woman money as a donation from the Little Brothers. Prez laughs and writes her a check. She tries to give the kids a toy, but Stella asks for a book, then the boys want one. They are the strangest kids, but so damn smart and sweet I think the woman would have given them everything.

We take our happy group home and they're talking about everything on the ship. I tell them my parents were going to go on a cruise for their thirtieth anniversary this year and they start talking about the dinner cruise ship. The

MC and Princes run it and the money goes to the schools. How damn cool are these people?

Prez laughs. "You should get Christian to take you on it."

Being trapped on a boat full of people far from land does not sound like a good time. He nods. "I didn't think of that. You need a place where you can go to relax and just have fun." I forgot he is a reader.

I can't help smiling. "He takes me everywhere. I like the reservation. His dad said he can help him build a house there."

He turns back looking out the windshield. "Cloud is a good carpenter; his house is beautiful and he built his grandmother's house too."

I just realize no one else is talking. I look around and they're all looking at their books, even Chance. We're close to the Compound and I see more bikes around us. Something has more Security with us. I watch, but I'm thinking about Nunánuk's house. It's a log cabin that looks like it's right out of a book. We don't need anything that grand. I can't wait until we start building it. We can go there to relax and have fun. The reservation has everything right there. Mucimi throws me pictures of houses and I laugh. Then I stop and look at him. Could he? "Did you change the sign?"

"No." He holds my eyes and I nod. That's a whole lot different than throwing pictures in my head.

At the school Prez wants to talk to the kids so me and Holly go in. They carry their own backpacks so we have nothing, but ours on. "That was a trip. I hope we have more."

She laughs. "You were good, so we'll take you on the next one. It's to the sundry building. The kids are heating it with plastic and filtering the water. Stella is excited for that one."

386

I laugh, she's six.

* * *

Christian

'Mase, a bike is coming at you. Rounding the corner, he's hiding a gun.' I turn with Jessie and fly toward the truck that's trying to outrun us. "Now Mase!"

I move to the side and Jessie takes the driver's side as I slow the truck. Devan is talking to Mase and VP to Colt and Blake. I'm pulling on the truck, but the driver is hitting the gas. I throw pain through him and stop the fuckin' truck. Too much is going through my head. As soon as I stop I pull off my helmet then the ear piece.

"Devan I can't keep Ops in my ear. Shut off my helmet from MC Ops too."

'You're good Brother. Tell me if you need something.' Thank fuck he talks in my head without all the chatter.

Cars are going around us when PD pulls up. Jessie hands the pussy off and looks at me. "You need a minute?"

"No, I get them all without the piece and it's fuckin' distracting. I can tell them what's coming without all the extra chatter." I put my helmet back on.

"Where to Brother?"

I like that he's not asking me to explain shit and tell him, "The backyard."

We hit the truck that was waiting for the pussy that PD just picked up and we're done. "MC-Baxters."

I let everyone know where we're headed and get Jessie's conversation with VP. The other Teams are rolling in. I'm fuckin' beat. Dakota meets us at the door. "Another good day Brothers."

387

I smile because it was. Dakota holds my arm as we're walking to the meeting room. It's weird, but he's throwing energy that I need—so I take the weird with the help. I sit and jump. Brothers are showing, but I stay on the rock until Ricky and VP come in. When I jump back I feel VP and look at him.

"You good?"

"Yeah I'm good."

He laughs. "You are, meant the ears."

Everyone laughs. "I can talk to them without it, all the rest is just a distraction."

"Devan said that. Don't wear 'em on Ops. He shut your helmet down. Tell him if you need it back."

I planned on it, but getting the okay is good too. Elizabeth and Harley walk in and everyone cheers. "Good fuckin' job," VP tells them.

Elizabeth liked that. She throws him chin making me smile. Harley is watching Bob and gets chin giving it back. Nice. It's about time they got theirs. The 'rents will never know what it feels like to train for so long just waiting to be called. They deserve this.

We get the status and Brothers file out. Dakota stops me from standing. "One more Brother." He points to the boards and Prez, Darren and Devan are on it.

I throw them chin and move to the other side of the table so I see them there. Ricky sits on one side of me and Dakota the other. I'm shielding from both of them.

"Dean doing good?" Ricky asks.

"Yeah. She's excited about the party. You bringing your girl?" He tries to block me, but I see it.

"No. She doesn't do crowds, but I'll be there Christian. I wouldn't miss it."

388

"Shield for her. I do it for Dean all the time. We've been in restaurants and the Club no problem."

He sits back. "If I was you that'd be easy. I struggle shielding myself from all their shit."

Dakota sits back and I smile. We should have sat at the end. "I can teach you to shield better. After this we can look at our schedules and add it in. We do not need to be together for that."

"Thanks Brother. Everything is getting louder lately. It's good, but fuckin' hard to make it around the Club now." I hear relief in his voice, but think about his words. He's reading more now.

VP, Jessie, Uncle Danny and Pres come in. I throw chin and look up at my Prince Officers. Pres sits at the head of the table and I'm surprised. He doesn't normally sit.

"You can read him. I've been all through his fucked-up head and see the change, even when it happened," Uncle Danny says.

I nod weighing my words. "No disrespect Uncle Danny, but when you were pissed everyone in the fuckin' room saw me coming from the whore's room shaken. They saw you look at Pres and exactly what he was thinking. It's not a memory I plan to relive. I get what everyone else is thinking. I can get deeper and have. I just don't need to anymore. I got what I needed from him, nothing else is needed for me to do my job. My commitment has not changed. If anything, it's stronger and more focused now than ever before."

He nods and looks up at Prez. "You're blocking all of us?"

I look at him and see Darren's question, but answer Prez. "I am shielding, but I think that's changing. I don't want everyone's thoughts before they're spoken. I'm not shielding you from my thoughts."

"Explain Dakota," Ricky says making me smile.

"This is not so easily explained. Daily I am trying to keep up with the changes. I can tell of the man I see from visions. Christian becomes hard like VP. He does not like explaining now and later only explains to me and our great Leader. He does not see his abilities change, but feels them after we notice. He will be the most powerful of ability Brothers and the ancestors say that is how it should be. His heart is pure and mind is clearer without negative thoughts from others. He will avoid those and continue to do his job. When he says he does not need approval, he truly means it. His focus is the vision and nothing or no one else."

I look at him. What about Dean? He smiles. "Dean is there as well." My whole body relaxes. This is from visions and she's with me.

"He already took what he needed from me?" Pres asks.

I'm not answering this a-fuckin'-gain. "He did. He pulls information from people when he needs it. If he has questions he will look for answers, procedures or memories. He does not need to ask, he just looks and takes what he needs. If you took a class he will find your notes and thoughts on the subject."

Jessie laughs. "I could have used that."

Pres doesn't look happy and I look up at Prez. 'What is this? I've got real shit to do.'

He nods. "I'm asking you to give him a few minutes."

I nod turning to Pres wanting to hurry this along. "You would keep me alive hating the man, but protecting the vision?"

I nod. "Yeah." His hands go through his hair. "Pres, I respect the fuck out of what you've done. I saw the old Club. I saw the shit you dealt with. Even after the Princes

390

split you worked for the vision. I don't hate you. I'm just not a little kid needing approval to accomplish what I'm meant to do. For years, I lived with your thoughts—hoping one day to be needed—but every fuckin' time, seeing what you thought of me." I shake my head. "By the time I was fifteen everyone was on a leaderboard, but me. I was already ahead of them. For me to see that negative and how much I'm worth to you, in your mind, will take away from what I need to do. I mean no disrespect, but I'm not going backward. It isn't necessary and I'm happy being right where I am." I haven't taken my eyes off his so he sees the truth in me.

His jaw clenches and I wait. "So, it's the vision, not me, you're protecting?"

Jesus. I stand up looking at Prez. He's watching Dakota. I'm not going around in circles. I pace, but don't answer. "Yeah." Prez answers for me.

"Why is explaining this so fuckin' hard?" he asks like this is all on me.

I stop and turn. "I have shit going on and I'm here, again, explaining the same shit over and over. You've gotten guidance from every fuckin' person here and Wall. Why the fuck do I have to answer too. I'm just a fuckin' Protector—not a Prophet, a Leader or inner circle. Use what they're giving you and let me do my job." I don't add, that doesn't require fuckin' stupid meetings, but I mean it.

Uncle Steve laughs. "This will be fun." He throws money down and everyone follows. I look at Prez. 'Is there a fuckin' point here Prez?'

His hands go in his hair. "There was Christian, but we're so fuckin' far from it I don't know what the fuck to tell you." He looks at Pres. "Dakota told you about his unwillingness to explain. You're jumping back to pushing his fuckin' buttons. If Dakota says it, it's true. If Christian says it, it's true. Their abilities work off a pure heart. You know that too. Get over him not bowing down. At this rate, it will never fuckin' happen. You had a point walking in, maybe you should get to that."

Pres is pissed. I move above the table to the door. "Nekanis." I don't need more of this fuckin' shit.

"Wait!" Pres yells and I stop and turn. "Apparently, I need to get used to a level of disrespect I don't normally see." No one laughs.

I just look at him. Seriously? For fuckin' years I lived with it. I catch Dakota's eye and he tells me to wait. I lean against the door watching Pres run his hands through his hair.

He looks right at me. "Knowing you are the most powerful Brother throws me. Knowing you hold my life in your hands throws me but knowing it's the vision and not me you're protecting kills me. I know I did that. I didn't understand and hurt you in ways that will never heal. That's not easy to live with." He pauses and I think he's waiting for an answer.

"Nope, it wasn't, but it's not an issue holding me back anymore. I'm good Pres." I turn and he stops me again.

"Jesusfuckin'Christ will you sit for a fuckin' minute and hear him out?" Jessie barks at me.

I pull out the chair by Uncle Danny and sit looking at Pres. If Jessie tells me to sit, I sit. Pres is deciding what to say. "You sat because he's your Officer?"

I nod.

Ricky stands up looking ready to spit nails. "This meeting had a purpose. Christian, Pres gets exactly what *your* purpose is. LB showed him the boards and how it all works. He *has* gotten advisement from all of us and your ancestors. Knowing what your purpose is and how we keep the good moving forward, we're offering you a seat on inner circle here at the MC. We need your skill and insight to keep going. He gets it and we have a vision from the readers that he actually does get it."

I stand up. "No, thanks Brothers. I'm honored, but I'm not even inner circle at Princes."

"What the fuck? You most certainly are. Prez just meets you at different times." Jessie's into barking today.

I move around so I can see the board and Prez is smiling. I smile and shrug. "I didn't know, but thanks anyway Brothers, I'm already inner circle."

Everyone, but Pres and Ricky laugh. "Why?" Pres asks.

"Because of that. I already explain shit too much. You will still get what I have. You still get the protection. You still get the advice. Whether you use it is up to you. I'm doing my job no matter what meeting you drag me into. It's a fuck of a lot easier if I don't spend fuckin' days explaining shit. I'm honored, but not interested in more meetings. You have people here that can answer all your questions. I will tell you, again, you need to get to the source of the attacks. Running Ops for-fuckin'-ever will get old for everyone. You have the information and the warning I gave you. You're too focused on what isn't important. Your life and Aubrey's are still out there. For every day you waste, the Princes are even more under the gun. Fix *that* Pres. *We're* fine."

His hands are in his hair. "The Baxters stepped back. They're jumping into the PD."

I nod. "It works well and it's not where your focus is needed." I look around the table. "This is the fourth fuckin' time I've said it. If you don't get on the fuckin' leads, he dies. I don't know how to get that across to him. Maybe you can. I'm not saying it again. This is why—you ask and don't listen." I look at Ricky. "Was there anything else?"

He sits looking defeated and shakes his head no. "Thanks for running Brother. We'd be fuckin' lost without

393

the Protectors." He throws me chin. I throw it to the table and we walk out.

"Thank fuck that's over. We need to see Jacob in Ops." I thumb in and he's waiting.

"I knew you wouldn't take it. You good Brother?"

I nod. "Yeah, why wouldn't I be?"

"Jeremy said you were pissed."

I wave it away. "Not at anything except wasting fuckin' time in meetings explaining the same shit over and over. I need to talk to you and Devan. Jeremy will keep training Aubrey, but the MC needs to get the fuck over themselves and work the fuckin' leads. Anything you can do to push that will help."

He nods. "I'm in with Geek. I'll talk to him and Tiny. I'm pretty sure Bob and Rich will help. Pres is thrown by all things freaky. I'm glad he finally got it, but even I feel like we're running out of time and I'm not even a freak."

I smile. "You're our freak Brother. Can you get with them today?"

He's watching me and I pull the shields to see what's happening. "I'll go right now."

I'm slammed with visions again and turn away. We walk out and wait in the chopper. I jump and sit with Hawk until I feel them close. When I open my eyes my dad is standing outside the door. "Can I have a minute?"

We get out and he walks away from the chopper toward the back field. "Playing it straight. I am not asking because I want you to take it. The question is will you reconsider inner circle?"

"No. It has nothing to do with anyone, but me, Dad. I don't need more fuckin' meetings. I can see meetings without being there. Nothing changes for me. I'm just not roped into a fuckin' chair while I can be doing something else."

He smiles and nods. "Got it. You were fuckin' amazing today. So fuckin' proud Christian." He hugs me quick and walks away.

I smile climbing in. Jessie's watching me. "Cloud's good?"

"Yeah."

"You threw Pres again. He thought you'd take the seat."

I shrug. "I don't know how to get them to listen. Sitting in meetings isn't doing it."

He nods. "I see it Brother. Hearing he's going to die hit me. He's worried about the seat and everyone was pointing out the warning. I think their inner circle is going to work with Ricky on it."

"Thank fuck. Jacob is talking to Geek and Tiny. He thinks Bob and Rich will jump in too. Any way we can get them to focus is good. Maybe Uncle Danny, now that he's not PD, can get them moving."

Surprise is on his face. "You went to Jacob after the meet?"

I nod seeing he thought I was walking away. "What the fuck do I have to do to show I'm all fuckin' in?"

His hands go up. "Relax Brother. With him brushing the warning off, *I* would have walked. I don't doubt your loyalty or ability, but he does tend to push your buttons. I just thought you'd keep running from the outside."

I see it. "I am. I'm going around him, but at the moment that's where I'm needed. When I need to move closer I will. I don't have a problem with any of it or even Pres. As long as I don't have to keep explaining shit."

395

He laughs. "Thanks Brother. He's a lot even on the good days, but he's my dad. I don't know how the fuck Uncle Danny puts up with him."

I crack up. "That's why he's always at Princes."

He gets serious. "You really didn't know you were inner circle?"

I shake my head no. "I wasn't told. Inner circle meets and I wasn't invited."

He nods. "Prez thought one-on-one with you would work better. You've been meeting him right along."

I almost shrug, but stop myself. "I didn't know. I'm honored and glad I don't have to sit in the extra meeting."

He laughs and we're quiet until we land. "The old ladies are heading up there to do a girls' night out."

What? "When?"

"Tonight. They weren't telling Dean until today. We got everyone covered. You shield everything?" He looks surprised.

Fuck. I should have gotten this. I got Ally, but didn't look at it. "I've got a lot going through me. I've been running through shit like a slideshow. If it isn't a threat I'm moving before I look closer at it." I need to slow shit down.

"Good to know there's no threat." He climbs out and we follow.

I throw him chin and point us to the Compound. Jessie follows me to the gate and makes a turn heading out. I'm not pissed about the escort and smile. Her first night out. I connect with Elizabeth and ask her to shield for Dean while they're out. A crowd won't be fun for her if she's getting everything coming in. 'I'm on it Christian.' I smile. My girl will have fun. Taking Nekanis for a run I'm glad I'm not feeling any pain and remember I need to ask Dakota about healing my leg. My days are long, but today was a good one.

* * *

Dean

I run in the house so excited to see his truck already here. "Christian!"

He looks up smiling. "Yeah babe."

"I'm going out with the old ladies! All of them!"

He laughs. "I heard. Elizabeth will shield for you, so you have fun."

I stop. I didn't even think of that. "Thank you for doing that. I wasn't thinking. You take me everywhere and I never have a problem."

He's still smiling. I move to him and sit on his lap. "You'll have fun. The old ladies are a fuckin' trip when they're out. You'll be singing the whole way home." He laughs.

I hop up. "I need to find clothes!" I almost take a step, but turn back and kiss him. "I love you."

I run hearing him laugh. Since it's old ladies I do the biker chick look. Someone has really good taste and makes my life easy. With a leather skirt, white tank and my cut on, I find my boots and the perfect hat. I am so excited.

"Babe the tights are ripped."

I spin around. "That's how they come."

"Jesus. I'm so fuckin' glad I'm not up there tonight. You look like a little biker pixie." He doesn't look happy.

"Is that bad?"

"If anyone goes near you have Sheila take them out." He's so serious when he says it.

397

I laugh. "Will do. What are you doing tonight?"

"I need to meet Devan up at the Club. Then I'm waiting for you. I'll never get to sleep without you."

Up at the Club? "Devan lives here now. Why up at the Club?"

His eyebrows frown. "Making an appearance and I need to talk to him. It works."

I want to go with him. "Jess said Jessie has a meeting and everyone was going there."

I nod. "I'm meeting Devan after it. It's only an hour and Devan will be done by then."

Will be done. The whores?

"You don't want me at the Club?" He's still frowning. Damn.

I wave my hand. "I want to go with you. Now I'm rethinking girls' night out. Dancing with you sounds like way more fun."

He laughs. "Go have fun with the old ladies. I'll take you dancing tomorrow if I'm not too late."

I smile at him. "Okay."

He walks to me and the look in his eyes has me seriously rethinking girls' night out, until the pounding starts on the door. He smiles. "Sheila's here." He kisses me and she's yelling for me to get my ass in gear.

I laugh and he steps back. "Love you Christian. Save me a dance." I run hearing him laugh. He doesn't dance with anyone, but me. I giggle going down the stairs.

I like the helicopter and practice blocking on the way up. Serenity is so excited, I can't help but laugh. I read her no matter how hard I try to block. She's never been on a helicopter and has the most ridiculous questions.

We're brought to a huge building and everyone is wondering why. This is Security where Christian has been working out of. I'm interested in seeing this so I keep my mouth shut. Ally comes running and stops right in front of me. "You're here!"

Everyone laughs. "I am and I'm so glad you're coming with us."

"I won't hug you, but I want to. I'm supposed to bring you inside. Follow me please." She's so cute.

I giggle. "Lead the way Ally, I hear you're the woman with all the secrets, I'll follow you anywhere to get one."

She laughs. "We don't talk about Ops because someone can get hurt. We have to be good Brothers and keep that close. I can tell you Harley likes a Brother. You have to ask her for the details. He's to die for."

Oh man, Harley is young. This may not be the secret I want to hear. The picture Ally has in her head is a guy in his late twenties. Inside she points down the hall. "Everyone can go down there and grab some food. I have to bring Dean in here."

She puts her thumb on the keypad and the door vibrates. No one is walking down the hall and I'm glad. Why do I need to go somewhere different?

Ally looks back when I don't follow her. "It's just Pres. He wanted to talk to you."

I look at Sheila not sure what to do here. Eliza saves me. "We all go or no one does. She can't be touched and this isn't cool Ally. She's Christian's old lady."

"I am here Eliza. I will keep her safe. Pres had a valid concern," Dakota says from behind everyone.

Eliza moves so she can see him. "Still not cool. Would you want Jess in a locked room with two Brothers?"

399

He nods. "I see your point. I will bring Pres to the cafeteria and we can sit away so they can talk. I will be with them so Nadine can be comfortable."

Eliza looks at Sheila and gets a nod. There's something going on that they aren't saying and I can't read. I'm usually good at reading Eliza, but now I wonder if she lets me read her.

"Let's go get a snack and we'll wait together. *Where we can see you*," Sheila says from my side. I like Badass on her.

I nod and we walk. This place is massive. The cafeteria is as big as a restaurant. They never do anything small around here that's for sure. I'm good with a fruit cup, but put it on the table and walk to where Dakota is sitting with a man I've seen before. He was at Princes.

They stand and I'm nervous. "This is Pres, Nadine. He was away when you met Kate and you were sleeping when he went to check on you and Christian."

"I saw you at Princes. It's nice to meet you. Thank you for checking on us." He smiles and I relax. He's thinking I'm cute all dressed up to go with the women. He can't be bad if he thinks like that.

"I'm happy to see you awake this time. Please sit." I do. "I've fucked up about as bad as a man can where Christian is concerned. I was given some information and hope to fix something that's bothering him."

I can't see what he did wrong and look at Dakota. Do I ask? He tells me 'no' in my head.

"You accepted Christian's cut, but don't want to get married," Pres says and I watch him giving him a nod. "Is there a reason? Are you not sure about staying with him?"

That's what this is about? "That's not it at all. He said he didn't care and other than Serenity I don't have anyone to go to a wedding." I feel the tears and blink them

400

back. "My parents died a few months ago and I never thought about getting married, but they aren't here."

He nods and moves to take my hand, but Dakota stops him. "No Pres."

"Sorry. I see why you demanded to be here." He looks at me. "It matters to Christian. I know I'm not your dad. You don't even know me, but I'd be honored to walk with you to marry Christian."

It matters to Christian? I think about all the crazy songs, proposals and the billboards. "Is he changing my music and making people propose in front of me, like every damn place we go?"

Dakota laughs. "No, but if he thought to do those things himself, I am sure he would have. That was different people. I am sure he does not know all they have done."

"It matters to him and other people found out, so they were messing with me to change my mind?" These people are crazy, but so damn sweet.

"Yes. Like you, we never thought he would find a woman he could touch. Marriage and babies were never part of his plan. Now you're here. I'm not pressuring you one way or another, but just wanted to tell you it matters to him and I'd be honored to stand in for your father." They are amazing.

"I will stand with you as well Nadine. I know Jessie would too."

I laugh. They aren't kidding. "Why wouldn't he tell me it matters?"

Pres looks at Dakota so I do. "He will not force you to take his name. He offered it and felt you did not want it. Men are stupid when it comes to women. The choice is yours to make. I can tell you Pres just wanted you to be aware."

I nod. He wants to marry me. Short-Blackhawk is a stupid name for kids. Everything flies through my head. The room at the Club, his mood swings, introducing me as his lover to every damn one. I start laughing. "I really miss having a mom and dad. I bet they would have gotten it right away." I shake my head glad they're smiling. "Can we get married before the party? I don't want to tell him though."

Pres laughs. "We know someone that just got the paperwork to perform the wedding. We can do that. So, you and Serenity?"

"And his family," I add smiling.

"We will take care of it. All you have to do is show up thirty minutes before the party. Both Pres and I will walk with you."

"I can't wait. You won't tell anyone, right? I want to surprise him."

"I will get the rings with help from Nancy. We won't tell anyone else," Pres says and stands.

I'm so excited! "Thank you for telling me. I'm sure in a year or two I would have gotten it." They laugh and Dakota brings me back to the women. I hope they tell the paperwork guy.

'I will tell him.' Dakota says in my head and I'm ready to spill it to all the old ladies. Luckily, I keep my mouth shut.

* * *

Tess is so happy she has me cracking up. She knows and I didn't say a word. "I don't want everyone to know."

"I can help with that." She has a musical little laugh making me smile. The bar is huge. They tell me it's rowdy, but no one ever comes close to our corner. Amanda's husband is watching over us with a wall of Security boxing us in. There's a whole conversation about him talking.

Joey tells me they're all crazy and takes me out to dance. She's fun and so damn happy like the rest of them. She can move with her crutch and I'm impressed. We talk about my class, but it's too loud to do much talking. We make plans to meet at Dunkin' with Holly. I'm glad she lives with us at the Compound.

When we get back, Serenity is telling them about my hats and how I dance using them. I hit her to shut up, but she doesn't. Of course, they all want to see it. Damn sister. "I grew up with just my family. There wasn't much for me to do as a teen so dancing was it. I'd watch the dances and keep playing them back until I got them then add the hats in. They were my only friends, until I moved here, so I made them my partners." Everyone is quiet for a minute then right back on me.

CJ laughs. "In this place, if you got it, we want to see—then learn it. We need something to keep life interesting."

Kate, Jess and Nancy all agree. These are the old ladies that have been here forever. How do you say no to them? Since there's a wall of Brothers facing away I agree.

Serenity tells me to do the *Dirty Dancing* one. "You have the right hat for it." I laugh and Sheila goes to have the music changed.

Tess hands me a drink. "Courage," she says making me laugh.

My face is burning and I don't know if it's the drink or embarrassment, but I get up and wait for the music to start. Holding my hat up as if it's at partner height I start moving to the beat smiling as if I'm so happy to be here with my partner dancing. I move the hat, jumping back in time to my bedroom and I just dance. When the beat picks up I roll the brim down my arm and wait for it to hit my fingers. It hits my fingertips and I flip it up, spin and catch it plopping it on my head for a second then we dance as if it's my partner again. I roll it down my leg and flip it up snatching it and plopping it on my head at the last beat and they're all clapping and yelling. Amanda lets out a whistle and I look around smiling until I see the wall of Brothers watching me. Oh damn. I put my head down and Bob laughs.

"Cute, Shorty."

My eyes snap to his and I smile. "You do talk. I knew it." He laughs turning around.

Tess tells me to show them how to do it. When she tries to go find hats, Bob stops her. "I need hats Bob. We're just borrowing them." He rolls his eyes and looks at another guy. The guy walks away smiling and I wonder if he's a reader. "No, he just doesn't talk much. They know I won't quit until I have hats so they'll get them. That's why Kate sent me for them." She giggles and I crack up. They certainly know how to move around the Brothers. Nancy talks to Bob and comes back to us. I wonder what that's all about, for like five seconds. The Security guy has hats!

We get all kinds and do a line dance throwing them up and catching them with little quirky moves in between. We're all laughing and move right into the next song. Eliza thinks this is cool and adds moves with Jess—throwing the hats to each other. I sit watching them thinking they are cool as hell old ladies. Ally is right there with them. Beth stays right by her showing, then encouraging her to do more. It's so damn cute.

CJ sits by me. "I'm so glad Christian found you. You're amazing. He's spent his life alone too. It's like you were meant for each other."

Oh my God. She's going to be the best mother-in-law in the world. "Thank you. I wish I could hug you right now."

She smiles. "We were warned about touching you. Bob would probably point his gun at me if you got that close."

I crack up and see a hat fly toward us. I catch it and look over. Sheila is pissed. "I get the fuckin' demented hat." I laugh and throw her mine.

Kate sits smiling. "Mitch is going to be pissed she missed this for a boring benefit."

MC Jess laughs. "I'll tell her all about it."

I look around and notice people are watching behind the wall of Brothers, but they won't let anyone in. Some of the guys want their hats back. A Prospect is let through with a bag and walks right to Nancy. Bob collects hats while Nancy hands them out. I'm sitting here laughing like crazy watching them decide what looks best with whose outfit. They're too funny. When they settle with the perfect hat we all dance again.

I am officially tipsy or maybe drunk. I switch to water and keep dancing with all my new friends. This is the best night! I'm getting married and these women all like me. When I get back to the table Tess hands me another drink. "I can't. I'm trying to do water to keep standing." I giggle. "If I drink too much no one can lift me to get me home."

She gets a serious look on her face. "That's one way to be a responsible drunk." She gets water with me and I laugh more. They're awesome crazy. That's what I'm calling this happy, go with the flow, not normal behavior. Awesome crazy. Oh boy, I really did have too much to drink. I drink more water and stand up. "You fit right in Dean," Tess says following me.

I blink my eyes like crazy. I never had friends and never expected anything like this. I'm so glad Christian found me.

Tess giggles. "We are too. Show me how to do the spin thing."

We dance with our hats.

Christian

I hear the chopper and smile. My Little Pixie is home. I hope she had fun. Elizabeth loves her and said she left her with Tess to watch over her.

'I will need you to get her home Brother. She passed out on the way.' I hear Dakota smiling. They must have had fun.

"I'm on my way. Come Nekanis. Dean is home." We run up toward the gate and make it as Dakota is setting down.

When I open the door Lily, Beth, Jess and Dean are out. I laugh. "Fuckin' awesome time. Watch the feeds Brother, she's perfect," Sheila says slapping my back. They all climb out laughing and talking. It must have been a good time.

When everyone that can walk is out, I climb in and lift my girl. Dakota is moving Jess when Prez and Taylor show.

I get a ride with Taylor and carry my girl to bed. She's so fuckin' cute in the biker gear and hat. The fuckin' hats get me. I smile undressing her. Once she's in bed, I get undressed and move her to my side.

I pull the laptop over and have to look for Geek's password. When I get it, I watch the feeds. As soon as she's standing alone on the floor I slow it down. Then I smile. She's fuckin' adorable. My little biker pixie can dance and she's fuckin' good. The hat cracks me up. She flips it, kicks it and dances like it's part of her. When I see Security taking

406

hats from people I'm laughing. The old ladies are right there with her. Joey, Elizabeth and Sheila surprise me dancing right beside her. I watch the whole thing then send it to Taylor and Sebastian. Everyone else can get the feeds.

I'm watching it again when Taylor pops in OC. 'Don't fuck it up. Love the hats.'

I laugh. I do too. My girl had fun. I shut the light and move the laptop giving her a squeeze. I jump with a smile and tell Hawk about her first girls' night out.

Chapter Eighteen

Christian

Walking into Ops I feel the change. I saw it on the way up, but actually feeling it throws relief. They're working with more than Ops as their purpose. Ricky's in Uncle Steve's circle. They watch me walk toward them. "I'm just letting you know I'm here, but I need a bike up here Ricky. Can you get one for me so I'm not on different bikes every day?"

He's not still upset I didn't take the seat and smiles. "VP covered it Brother. He had all the Protector bikes marked with the colors too. You have a locker with gear here, but he didn't order any pieces for you."

"Sweet. Thanks VP. I'll bring some gear up."

"New Kevlar suits. Mitch sent Protectors first. HS is next," Uncle Steve says making me smile.

"She should have done that the other way around, but that's good too. Are they heavy?"

Ricky shakes his head no. "It's like wearing leather. She's fuckin' unbelievable with design Brother. She got the colors inlaid in black."

Nice. "I'm at KC for training, then back here at three. You set?"

I see they're making headway into the source and again, I'm relieved they're working together. "I had a question about Jeremy. You have Colt with Jeremy and Aubrey. Do we need HS partnering with them? You usually don't have him on our list."

I think about what I can say here. "HS won't be a help with them. Save the team for Digs." I look at Uncle

Steve. "You need to watch Air today. Dakota will be helpful."

He watches me and I see his brain click to high speed. "Up or in Ops."

"Up." I turn and we walk away. Security takes us to KC.

I have Mase, Colt, Jeremy, Aubrey, Blaze and Blake. "Today promises to be as exciting as yesterday." They laugh. "Jeremy shut down the feeds."

"Done."

I look at them. It seems like we've been at this forever, but Jessie was right—it's been a short time. "Our threat isn't just to the MC. Colt, you're on with Jeremy and Aubrey today. I want you working on throwing shields over them while shit is coming your way. Jeremy, throw at him and Aubrey so he's working to cover you under pressure. Aubrey, throw at Jeremy and shield under Colt's so nothing hits any of you until you see he has it." With nods, they suspend above us.

"Blake, I want you working with Blaze on controlling from farther away. She's got the control now, but from Ops she needs to control more. It can be small objects for right now, then we'll move to people." He takes her to the locker room.

I look at Mase. "Jeremy and Aubrey again?" I nod. He looks away. "I don't understand why they have to live like this Christian. They don't do anything to anyone. If it weren't for them needing to eat we'd never see them."

He's right, but wrong. "You're not thinking about how they can benefit other people. Money, controlling others and visions are all people see with them. It's greed and power that's their biggest threat. Today we work to keep that away from them. Yeah?"

He stands. "Yeah Brother. What am I doing?"

409

I take him to the rock wall. "Move fast." He rolls his eyes at me. I push and I'm at the top of the wall looking down. "Fast."

His mouth is open looking up at me. "Fuck Brother."

I push and I'm beside him. "I need you to move quickly from place to place. Look at where you want to be and push like you're suspending, but push hard and just be there."

"Is this how you help us from Ops?"

I shake my head no. "I control from there. This is different. Start practicing and we'll move you on to the bike."

He does and I check the other teams. Nekanis is hiding under a side table by the couch. I don't blame him—this is freaky shit. Jeremy is laughing throwing everything at Colt and Aubrey. Shit is flying fast up there. Since it's working, I look for Blaze. She's in the locker room whipping plastic cups at Blake in the kitchen. He's giving her pointers while deflecting. I go to her. "Try for heavier now."

She smiles. "No problem."

I see her move a plate. Blake yells and we hear it shatter. I smile walking away. Ricky will need plates with the new table.

Walking out, Mase appears on the side of me. "Good fuckin' job Brother. That didn't take long. You think you can move something with you?"

He laughs and is gone. A chair falls and smashes on the floor and I crack up with his yell of frustration. "Fuck!" He's in front of me looking at the chair. I guess Ricky will need chairs too.

"Feel where your body is connected to the object you're moving. Don't just hold the chair. Split second

410

assessment—feel where it is in your hands, against your body, and the space it takes up. Once you get that, push *feeling* it with you."

He moves and another chair falls. "Sonofabitch!" He gets it with the next try and laughs.

I watch Colt throwing and defending for Aubrey. 'He's got it. Aubrey isn't shielding,' Jeremy tells me. Nice.

Mase is moving around with his chair making me laugh when he starts moving it in different positions. I call them all over and Mase lands sitting in the chair. Jeremy laughs then pulls from him how he did it. I shake my head smiling. "Keep practicing. I want you to show each other what you've learned and practice what you don't have yet. Mase, you're with me on the bike. Colt, you're Jeremy and Aubrey's shadow today. You shield them everywhere you go. Blaze, you're at Ops control and Blake, you're running with Mase in about an hour and a half."

I look around the KC. "Blaze and Blake, clean this up, but I don't want you moving from where you are to do it. Control everything you need to get it spotless again without touching or physically moving anything."

Diego walks out of his office. "Is it safe?"

I laugh. "Yeah Brother."

He walks out with his head swinging from side to side then up. "Terry's gonna be pissed he missed this one." He's looking at the broken chairs and plates.

Blaze and Blake laugh while they start cleaning it up. Diego just watches.

"Later Brother. They'll get it clean." I walk into the hall with Mase and Nekanis headed to the house. Jeremy, Aubrey and Colt are going up to the Lab.

Mase goes for his bike. "Brother remember the chair?"

411

He looks around then walks to the side. Pulling a dirt bike out of the shed he's smiling. "Ready."

I laugh, but nod. It's our dad's bike. On the first try he moves to the driveway, but it's slow. We sit on the step watching. He starts moving faster. Dad comes out probably wondering what the hell Mase is doing. "You're not working today?"

"I'm on in half an hour. How the fuck is he moving like that?"

I smile. "Suspending, but fast."

Mase gets cocky and moves to the top of the hedge line, then falls through with the bike. I move to him laughing and pull the bike off him. My dad holds the bike while I pull him out of the bushes. "I need to work on that."

We crack up. "Next time use *your* fuckin' bike," my dad says, but he's smiling.

"I actually ride mine."

I walk away. "I'm at Security. You're on in forty-five Mase." I hit my watch for Security to pick us up.

When the SUV pulls up my dad waves it away, "I'll take you. My chopper is at Security." I nod and we get in his truck.

"I'm glad he has you teaching him. He's happier working every day."

I smile. He is. "Yeah."

"Your mom loves Dean. They had fun last night."

I nod. "Did you see the feed? It was fuckin' cute."

"Love the hats." He laughs. When we're almost at Security he looks at me. "We're looking at a house by you. It's two away from the Compound."

I knew, but don't say it. "Pres is in line Dad."

412

"Why didn't you take the seat?"

Fuck. More explaining. "I don't need the seat to do my job. Everything I said was true. You weren't in the meet, but I didn't lie to them either. I don't need more meetings. I need them to find the source. I'll do my job no matter what, but the meetings don't work for me. I spend half my time in them explaining abilities over and over."

He smiles. "Pres is in line and you didn't take the seat so you don't have to explain." He laughs. "I love my fuckin' kids. Tiny said you weren't taking any shit from Pres. I thought you were done with him."

I'm shocked. "Not even close Dad. His life is my job. The ancestors are clear on what we're meant to do. I couldn't walk if I wanted to. We have so many people counting on us to get this right. I wouldn't walk away from them either."

He pulls in and looks at me. "I spent the night thinking it was over here. I don't want Mase growing up with no direction and under-appreciated."

I smile. "That isn't yet Dad. I'm actually pretty good at this job." He laughs and I put my hand on his arm giving it a squeeze. "He's just getting what he's worth here. That means something today and it will tomorrow too. Don't jump yet if that's your concern. When you walk in you'll see the difference."

He nods. "I'll take your word for it." He gets out and I'm smiling. He trusts me.

We go down to the locker room and I change into the new Kevlar. It's cool as shit with the logos in black and much lighter than I thought it would be. Switching out my pocket shit I get the brace on, but can't use the pockets on that side. I dump my shit into the others and head up to Ops.

Seeing Dakota, I walk to him first and wait until he's done picking Uncle Steve's brain. I don't know how he

413

catches the thoughts running so fast. When he's done, he steps back.

"Do you have some time to heal my leg? I still can't stand on it without the brace." I see it play out in his head. Fuck! "Can you heal it enough for me to stand on it?" This fuckin' sucks. I want to jump, but stay to hear him out.

"I will do what I can. In time, you will be able to stand on it, but you will always have a limp." I see me older walking away from him fuckin' limping.

Jesus. I throw my helmet and walk out. I walk down the hall and sit. Nekanis leans against me and we jump. Nunánuk and Hawk are waiting. "I'm okay Nunánuk. I just need a way around it."

She smiles and sits. "I believe you will find it my grandson. You are a master at finding solutions. This will be no different. Is your leg painful?"

I shake my head no. "Not with the brace. It's fine even working out."

Her eyes smile. "You've already found the way around it."

I shake my head. "I guess I did. Why is everything so hard?"

"Easy doesn't teach you humility, compassion, or pain. Without it you would never know what happiness truly is." She's gone and I think about that.

I think about Dean. She made hats her life when she had no one else in it. She was so happy this morning because she had friends and no one had a problem not touching her. She's never had that. She'd never know without first going through the hard. Now she's the sweetest woman I know.

I guess we all learn the same thing, but in different ways. I got this. I have the way around it. I'll see if Mitch can get something a little easier to fit over my clothes since I can't fit this one under the Kevlar. That will be my way around it.

We jump back and my dad is beside me. "Jeremy stayed with Phoenix and Teller in the operating room."

I smile, he's trying to find a way around it too. "I'm not them though. They don't have a problem with touch. I'd never make it back Dad. That's why they didn't tell me. Jeremy saw it. I'm good. Nunánuk got me straight. I need to ask Mitch about a different brace, this one won't work with the Kevlar, I lose the pockets with it outside."

He shakes his head smiling. "Fuckin' proud."

I laugh feeling it deep, "Got that Dad."

Back in Ops Uncle Steve watches me then smiles throwing chin. Dakota is relieved and Ricky doesn't know what to think. I throw him chin letting him know I'm good.

Ricky calls all but Security control to the meeting room. We go over everyone's position and I smile when Geek comes in upset because he's late. When Ricky's done, he tells Geek and Officers to wait. "You got something?"

Geek smiles at him. "Yeah, but I'm not sure of the tie in. I'll get back on it as soon as we're done today."

I like the way Ricky is thinking. "See if Brantley can cover you on control for Ops. If you need more let me know and I'll find you people."

Geek smiles. "Victor would be good. He's like a dog with a bone. I'll call Brantley and cover Ops. Can Jacob cover for Victor?"

Ricky looks at me. 'Not today Brother. Maybe Billy or Jason?' "Jacob is needed today, but I'll find out if we can get Jason or Billy."

Geek throws him chin walking out. He's already calling Brantley.

415

I look at Ricky. "You need more chairs and plates in KC."

He's surprised then smiles. "I'll get Diego on keeping it stocked."

I get back to Ops and see Ally telling Blaze about going out last night. Jacob is watching the boards. Perfect. "Jacob, Blaze." They turn. Ally turns back to her monitor. She's cute. "Blaze you're on the side of Jacob working through the boards as a distraction to the pussies any way you can. Jacob work around what she can do. If she's got someone looking one way you get the team to hit them from the other side. Make everything she can help with count. If you see something she can do, tell her so she's working right with you. Yeah?"

Blaze smiles big. "Yeah."

Jacob laughs. "Terry is going to be pissed."

Ally spins around smiling. "I'll send it to him."

I laugh walking out. "Devan, I'm moving down to the garage. They have me on a new bike so I need a minute to get used to it."

'It's fuckin' sweet Brother. I have nothing on the boards yet.'

I see the Protector logo and smile. All our bikes are in a line in front of a bay door. I know mine right away. My Prince number is on the back inlaid in black. Fuck, he went all out. "Thanks Uncle Steve." I can see him smiling. Fuckin' Badass all the way.

A Brother hits the door open. "VP had the Garage working all night to get them done. Baxter boys were up there adding shit for you. They got dual boards or something and special lighting."

I nod. It's like the Princes HS bikes. If Jared worked on them they work by thumb print. I try it out and love the

416

purr. The panel is digital and I already love it. I check the lights and see we have an outline of blue low lights and the regular head and tail. I run the outline and get off to see it. Jared is a genius. They're understated, and will be visible at night—but not blaring. Hitting the board, I see the full Ops board. There's no glass on these, just a cutout for the hologram board. I hit the 'P' and it flips me to Princes. Fuckin' nice.

I try it out and know right away he did something to the engine. I fly out to the back field and test it with my gun in each hand then turning and stopping. Mase hits a hill in front of me and we play hide and seek moving the bikes by suspending. I'm happy to see him keep it low to the ground.

I'm listening in at Ops, but see a plane coming toward us from the south. "VP, a plane, I tagged it yellow, coming our way." I turn heading back to Security. Mase follows talking to Jacob. Rolling under the building I tell the Brother to top me off.

"Devan, a plane tagged yellow on the MC board."

'Roger Guardian, I picked you up. Your new bike has a mic. VP said you're talking out loud more and he didn't want anything missed.'

I laugh. "Roger."

Elizabeth and Harley roll in and check out their bikes. I see Pres didn't have a problem getting here today. They ran shuttle earlier, but Devan gave them some down time because they ran so hard yesterday. I'm glad to see them both smiling. "Go change, we got company coming."

Harley smiles, but Elizabeth isn't happy. "We need a locker room."

What? "You don't have lockers?" I'm looking for Uncle Danny.

Elizabeth's hand goes on her hip. "No. We have plastic drawers in a fuckin' closet."

417

"I'll fix it."

She nods and follows Harley. Jesus.

I pull my phone. "Uncle Danny, the girls are changing in a closet and have plastic drawers as lockers. Can you get them a locker room?"

"What the fuck are you talking about?"

I see him coming down the stairs. "I'm at my bike. I'll see you in a couple." He's pissed and I'm glad.

He doesn't show and I look for him. I don't really have time to wait around. Blake shows and runs up to change. I connect with everyone and see no problems. I hear the chopper go up and know I have to go.

"Protector Ops. I'm rolling out. Everyone will be ready on schedule. I need to talk to LP1 about lockers. Can you remind me after Ops?"

'Roger Guardian.'

Aaron comes running down the stairs. "Sorry Brother, my dad's going off about crazy shit that he thought I needed."

"Girls don't have a locker room here. They change in a closet."

He stops. "That *is* fuckin' off." He throws his leg and I'm rolling. "Nice skins."

I smile and speed up. I love the black on black. We run through town until we hit the backyard. All old ladies are supposed to be on the Compound already, but Amanda and Penny are still in the backyard. "Green truck moving through the backyard." I see it playing out before we turn and move me to in front of Amanda's shop.

"Fuck Brother," Aaron says and I tune him out pointing my gun at the driver. His hands go up and the truck stops. "Pickup Lightfoot."

418

I don't move knowing he's going for a gun in a couple of seconds. Aaron gets closer and the pussy's hand goes down. I shoot.

"Clean-up Lightfoot." He changes the order. VP is giving him shit about keeping up with me and I laugh. "He just went from my side to the other side of the fuckin' street! No one can keep up with that shit!" Aaron's looking at me as if I did something wrong.

"Do you see where he's stopped?" I holster my gun and ride. "Old ladies were supposed to be on the Compound a half an hour ago, MC Ops. There was a reason for that. Show B3 the feed. I had ten seconds to spare there." No one is answering me.

"Princes Ops. Check MC tracking and call them on the fuckin' phone if you have to, but move people where they belong. There's a know playing out here." I can't tell them how it will play out, but maybe they'll look for the way someone knew Amanda was at the shop.

'Roger Guardian. Coder is on it.'

Thank fuck. We ride up Main to Power Plant Road and I stop. "Stay alert Mase." I watch them running and see Aaron is antsy. "I'm watching them. Here." I hit the board on and flip it from Princes to MC.

"Why don't I have that?"

I roll my eyes. "I'll ask VP to get you one."

Security is picking up Amanda and a very scared Penny. "Throw HS to Digs."

Devan is right with me. 'Roger Guardian. Eagle Eye says connect.'

"Roger." Reaching Dakota, I see he's already airborne. 'Pull your shields Brother. I believe that perch you are on is not a good stopping point.'

Fuck. I throw to Aaron and get the fuck away from the coast. Jesus. As soon as we're down the hill all hell breaks loose.

Jacob has Blaze working to get Mase and Blake clear. I run toward Elizabeth and get slammed with a second plane coming from the water. I throw it to Devan and we keep moving. MC Ops is scrambling. Prez is watching and throwing orders to Dakota and Brantley.

Jacob and Devan are sticking with the plan and running as if they're alone in Ops. I see Jeremy on the move and throw to Aaron, 'Bikes coming from the south.' "Be ready Elizabeth."

'Roger Guardian. I see it.'

I stop the cars and switch the lights to red—blowing through the intersection. "Shield now Elizabeth!" We come from behind the bikes and take the two in back. Elizabeth and Harley are coming at them shooting.

'Christian!' Jeremy yells.

"You got this Jeremy. Aubrey, you throw just like you did with Colt. You keep Jeremy clear, Little Bit. Colt, shield and throw everything you have. I'm two out."

'Roger Guardian,' Colt says sounding calm.

I push a car back and fly around the corner heading to the reservation. 'Jeremy turn at the next crossroad. We'll come from behind them.'

'Yeah.' He's calmer than a few seconds ago. That's something.

There's something up with the feeds. *Rolling blackout* pops in my head. "VP, rolling blackout?"

'Yeah. HS is rollin' slow.'

"Get my helmet on. Elizabeth help where you can." They're the only team clear right now. I see it and yell,

"Jeremy don't stop! Go over! Colt shield and spin around heading the other way. I got them." Aubrey screams and I push them up. "Aaron get to Colt!"

He's shooting as I hit the woods. The bike is light making the trail easy. "Slow down Brother and we'll clear them from this side."

'Aubrey.' Jeremy is pissed.

"Kept you clear and helped lift you. She's clear Je. Let's make sure they aren't back tomorrow." I see Dakota shoot the plane over the water. One down.

'Yeah.'

Jeremy spins right in front of me and hauls ass going back. I could sit here and just watch him throw his anger out there, but he's a healer. This isn't his fight. "Mase move toward me Brother. We have two that will try to run."

"Roger."

I see the fire rolling and have to blink. It's not a vision. "Not in the woods! Wait until you're clear!"

"Sorry," Aubrey says and I hold my laugh in. Holy shit, she's pissed.

Aaron is hitting the pussies from the side and I see a pickup explode. "Now Aubrey!" She rolls her fire and I push it. Pussies are under the fuckin' truck and I send it right to them. Colt is waiting and rides on the side of Jeremy shooting in a straight line as they ride. "Good job Colt. Get them wherever they were going."

"Roger Guardian. We're at Security in four," he tells me. I'm surprised. Jeremy has been avoiding Security. Mase and Blake have the two that were running. Aaron rides up to me and stops. I look back. Fuck. This is a lot of money being thrown our way. I hope to fuck the MC gets it soon.

When I turn back Aaron asks, "Aubrey clear now?"

I nod. "For now."

"Fuck."

"We're clear. Get the Protectors with HS to help clear this." I see PD rolling out to help so they shouldn't be out for too long.

"Roger Guardian. Prez said that was an impressive hour and good fuckin' job." I can hear his smile. He's not used to getting that and I'm glad he's down in Prince Ops.

"Thanks for keeping us running Devan. VP says it's all about the control."

He laughs then starts talking to the other teams. I turn and ride to Security at a nice sixty. The reservation roads aren't the best in places, but it's a good ride. I'm starting to think that any ride where I'm not being shot at is a good ride.

Walking into Ops everyone cheers. I look around and Ricky laughs. "For you shit head." I smile. This is nice. Nekanis stays by me. I'm surprised. He usually waits by the door.

Jeremy is at Air control and I see why. "Dakota."

'We are moving over barren land Brother.'

I watch the boards behind him and see the plane explode. It's like a movie seeing it up there like that. I just shake my head.

Jeremy spins around. "Thanks." He stands and I give him a quick hug.

"Nekanis Kuwômôyush."

He says it back smiling. Aubrey moves over to us. "Mitch and Jeremy worked on a cuff for Dean. It's to help with energy. Something with ions and neutralizing. Look in his head for all that. Anyway. It won't help for long, but Mitch said it will help for initial contact."

My throat closes. He was working on this for Dean when all this shit was going on?

'Yeah.' He throws me directions and how it works and I'm lost.

I put my hand up. "I don't need to know all that. It's a few seconds?"

"A minute, two tops." I hug him again and he laughs. Aubrey pulls him toward the door giving me a finger wave. I watch her pull Jacob down and kiss his cheek then walk out with Jeremy.

I look at the cuff and laugh. He found a way around it. Fuckin' Brothers.

The meeting room is empty so I sit and jump. Nekanis is running with Hawk and I'm happy to relax and watch them. It was a good day all around.

"You are at peace my grandson." She sits beside me.

I smile. "I am Nunánuk. It was another good day. I'm learning to enjoy all the little victories."

She laughs. "It was difficult to walk with you through such hard times, but you have learned your lessons well, grandson. Today was a big victory Christian, for our family and our tribe. It is okay for you to feel pride in a job well done."

I look across the lake feeling everything run through me. When I turn back she's gone. I smile calling Nekanis.

When I open my eyes Aaron and Dakota are here. "Nunánuk and the ancestors are very proud today," Dakota says smiling.

I nod. "Yeah."

Aaron is watching us wanting to know what we're talking about, but I'm leaving it alone. "How long are they going to be?" he asks.

"Twenty minutes," I tell him then smile seeing he's going for food. "Bring something for your dad." He throws me chin and Dakota laughs.

While no one is here I throw to him. 'They have a good two weeks before this shit starts up again.'

'It would be wise to keep that close.'

Fuck. 'I see them working, but they're not taking the warnings. How do I make them understand?'

He gives me a sad smile and I see they still have some work ahead of them to mend the Club. "Sometimes it is enough to lead the horse to the water. Sometimes it is better to drop it in the middle of the lake and hope it swims out. Today you dropped them in a lake. Bob and Digs are not happy Brantley had to call from Princes to keep their women safe. Bob ran Clean-up. Your father is not happy no one is running Air Ops and Jeremy stepped into control. VP and Ricky can only run so many stations and so many teams. This is a very big organization without the benefit of Security stepping into HS Ops."

"Why didn't they pull Geek and Victor back?"

"Jake and Jerry would have worked, but they were pulled by Baxters to the PD." That's not an answer, but I know he won't say more.

"Where was Pres? He's here." I see him in his office.

He looks out the window. "Making amends."

Shit. He's not mending the Club. "I didn't know. I was hit with so many visions at once I couldn't follow Ops."

He nods. "You kept people alive Christian. That is what you are meant to do. The MC will get through this and

424

you will be a big part of that. For now, we must let it happen as it will."

As far as plans go this one sucks, but with Dakota saying it, I guess it's our plan. Brothers show in a steady stream and they're not very happy. They're wondering what happened today.

Bob comes in pissed and leans against the wall. "Thanks, Christian."

I throw him chin.

Ricky, Uncle Steve, Uncle Danny and my dad come in and none of them are happy. Uncle Steve stands at the head of the table. "Lead and control was pulled to PD right before Ops. Left us no Air and no Clean-up. Princes ran two HS teams. Christian cleared biggest threats and sent Protectors to clear with us. MC dropped it and we'll fix it. No casualties, two injuries. Brothers with Doc. One fell off his bike other took a hit to his foot." Everyone looks at Uncle Danny. I clench my jaw.

He moves back and Ricky moves forward. "Again, the Protectors, Princes and Dakota helped clear the biggest threats. Cloud ran Air from the air. HS had its problems with lost feeds and dropped orders, but we had no casualties. Not an easy day, but two hours of hard shows us where Baxters will be missed. I'm glad our lesson was today and we made it through. That wouldn't have happened without the dedication and skill you showed us here today. Thanks for having our backs. Ops will run better for the next one. That isn't a hope or dream, it's a guarantee. There will be changes made and we will have the people and support you need to do your jobs starting tomorrow. Together we made it through today and together we came out stronger because of it. Thank you Brothers for another job well done."

I smile. Nunánuk just said that to me, not in so many words, but she doesn't talk much. Dakota laughs while the Brothers are thanking Ricky.

"Protectors stay with the Officers." Ricky stops Harley and Elizabeth from leaving. Everyone sits, but Bob, Digs and my dad. "Today would have been as bad as losing the Officers. Thank you for your part in keeping Jeremy, Aubrey, Mase and Amanda with us." He looks around the table. "We need help. Losing Jake and a control so close to Ops with Rich on HS hurt. It can't be repeated. Who is ready for HS now?"

Everyone is surprised. Elizabeth is ready to float away she's so happy. "Brenna, Carla and that kid Mendez."

Uncle Danny looks down. Pres will fuckin' flip. "Get with Rich and bring them in to run training for assessment." She nods and he dismisses them telling them they did a good job today.

I'm still watching Uncle Danny waiting for him to say what's going through his mind.

My dad steps forward. "If there's no Air control, I'll do it. We have pilots that can't run without a lead. Today we were fuckin' lucky Dakota isn't one of those pilots."

Ricky nods. "The job is yours. We can't assume Jamie will be here when we need Air Control. You're right, we were fuckin' lucky it was you and Dakota up there."

My dad is relieved.

"I'll run lead too," Uncle Danny says and I look at a smiling Dakota.

"I'll take it. The Brothers may be safer." Ricky has us all laughing. "Bob and Digs, I know you're both pissed. We lost Jake and Jerry literally ten minutes before Ops was set. If I had known the old ladies weren't covered, I would have moved them. It won't happen again." He looks right at them and I'm proud of him.

They both throw him chin. "Pull me to control next time Ricky. We have HS and Security that could have covered today. Pull me when you need me," Digs tells him.

426

"I will Brother. I'm not going to lie to you. I was just trying to keep ahead of the teams. LB ran lead for us and Brantley was running Ops control from Princes. I knew we'd be short, but not that short. VP gave me direction, but it was so fuckin' fast and you don't get all the words. I'm in Ops until I get what the fuck he says without having to stop and translate. I won't let you down again."

Digs is happy with that.

"Are there any questions?"

"Where's Pres?" Tiny asks.

Ricky steps back and VP moves to his side. "His office. Didn't answer then Bob showed, then Jeremy." Everyone has questions, but no one asks. "That's it? We're done." He walks out followed by Bob, Tiny, my dad and Digs.

Ricky plops down in the chair. "Holy fuck that was so bad."

"The Brothers left happy. The Officers are stepping up instead of bitching. It wasn't a perfect day, but it changed how the Brothers see you and threw relief where it was needed." He looks at me as if I'm nuts and I smile. "It did."

"When the fuck did you become Dr. Phil? You better watch it or they'll be dragging your ass to more meetings where you get to explain all that shit."

Dakota cracks up and I'm out of the room so fast I yell, "Later," as the door is closing.

Uncle Danny, Tiny and my dad are in the hall and I slow down shooting for a normal pace.

"Mitch will have a new brace for you tomorrow and she's making a wider leg on the pants so it will fit under."

"Thanks Dad. I'll see you at the party." I throw them chin and tell Nekanis we'll wait in the chopper.

I start connecting with the team. 'You did it Blaze. I'm so fuckin' proud of you.'

She laughs. 'It wasn't as hard as I thought it would be. Thanks, Christian, for teaching us.'

I go through all of them and end with a happy Mucimi. He's so fuckin' cute throwing me pictures of Jeremy and Jacob dancing with Aubrey. "We did it little man. Thanks for the heads up." He giggles and I laugh.

Chapter Nineteen

Dean

I'm going to die. It will be deliriously happy and well satisfied, but I'll be dead just the same. "Do not stop!" I moan at him when I feel his hand shift.

He laughs like I'm kidding. "Never babe."

The hat falls and he stops. Dammit! Once it's back on my head his mouth and hands are back in place and I roll my hips grinding against his mouth. "Please, you're killing me here."

"Oh, baby we need to make our anniversary a day to remember."

I feel him inside and think I'll never forget it. My whole body has fire running through it when he does that. He moves fast flipping me around and sliding in way too damn slow. "Christian! Harder."

"Mmm. My demanding Little Pixie."

My arms fly out to the side like I put them there. Holy crap that's hot. He's everywhere and slamming into me. I don't even care how. I feel him inside again and whimper.

"Push my beautiful Little Pixie," he says against my ear.

Oh, my God! I scream and push.

Christian

I grab onto her and fall on the bed cradling her in my arms. She's fuckin' killing me. Falling back, I hold her on

429

top of me and laugh while trying to breathe. At least we were over the bed. Shaking my head I calm down and get more air into my body. Jesus, I'll never forget our anniversary. Holding her I feel her heartbeat against me and take it all in. Every place she's touching me, every movement of her breath, it's all mine. My sweet Little Pixie. After fuckin' forever I feel like I can move again.

Lifting us I stand and feel my leg. Shit. I hold her tighter and walk feeling every step. As soon as we're clean and dry, I get the brace on and bring my girl back to bed. There's shit everywhere. I send the toys to the bathroom to clean them and move the sheets off the bed. Watching clean sheets cover the mattress I'm smiling. We never made dancing last night, but hit the adult store in town three. Boxes and wrappers are all over the floor and nightstand. Since she doesn't like anything but me in her ass I send the plug, beads and vibrator to the trash. I have no need for the furry cuffs, but she wanted them so I put them in the drawer with the rest that come back clean and dry. It strikes me again that it's good to be me.

I move the hat back to the tree remembering the look right when she came. My dick swells and I shake my head moving Dean back to the bed. Once she's covered I get dressed and get Nekanis his walk. It's just past six when we head back and I feel Prez. 'Coming up the beach,' I throw.

'Coffee's ready.'

I smile and keep walking. He walks out when I hit the top step. "Here."

I take the coffee and sit. "They have some time before the next wave hits."

He nods. "We'll be hit first." He got it from the boys.

"Not the way you're thinking. The religious nuts are gathering, but HS can handle it. We have no major threat to us for a while. We're watched, but with Security running

430

they aren't getting close enough to get at anyone. We just need to keep ahead of them and shut down their plans."

He laughs. "Oh, that's all."

I smile thinking about it. "Yeah."

"The reservation?"

I look in on Aiyana and Co. "Peaceful at the moment. The pipelines are going to push for legislation to block the protestors. There's already a suit against the federal government for right of way access. With the contaminated water and oil leaks finally publicized people are noticing and fighting against it. Baxters help with that. Ben and Mitch threw in." I look to see if he's interested. He is. "More communities will be hit with contaminated water which will be bad for them, but good for the cause. Some are in areas that oil is a main source of income, so it will be a hell of a fight, but one that's known nationally. There's another issue that's brought to light with all this publicity on water and oil. Natural gas is running pipelines down south. Pretty much the same scenario as the oil."

"Fuckin' people. Oil kills the water and gas kills the air. When the fuck will everyone wake up and see we only have this planet to live on. Whole countries are switching to natural resources. We need fuckin' help in Washington."

I put my hand up to stop him. "Baxters didn't move for the reasons everyone thinks. They're all in with the MC, but have some plans for change. We'll see the beginning soon. It's just what we're hoping for. This is why Aiyana and Mucimi calmed. It's in the distance, but will happen."

He's looking, but I know he can't see it. I'm glad when he doesn't ask. "Your readers are learning fast. I saw Mase moving like you and Elizabeth is as fuckin' Badass as it gets."

I smile because she is. "Mase has some work ahead of him. He's got the ability, but he still needs to work on reading. They're all still growing. In time, they'll be unstoppable. Between technology and abilities, I think the vision of the Clubs helping more communities is safe."

He spends some time thinking about all I said. I'm happy to watch the dogs play in the yard while he does.

"The readers?"

I've thought about this and don't see where anyone can be hurt. "We'll get more, but I don't think they're here to help right now. I see some as working for the cause to keep all readers safe, but no one stands out as helpful to the Club yet. The kids will bring more."

He rolls it in his head again. "Helpful to the Club yet? The kids?"

"Yeah. The kids are growing too. Aquyà is keeping Mucimi on a tight leash. I don't say it because it's bad. Right now, Mucimi needs to learn to follow a chain of command even when it's Aquyà and Phoenix. These are lessons he needs to become who he's meant to be. With everyone growing in ability, the last thing we need is another Jeremy running wild. Aquyà is making sure that doesn't happen." He wants to ask about them, but I can't give him anything else. I let him see it and wait.

"Jeremy made a cuff. Can it help so you can get the surgery?"

I look at the water. "No Prez. It's for Dean. She'll be able to handle initial contact for at least a minute." I breathe deep. "I don't come out of the surgery. That's why they didn't say. Mitch is bringing me a new brace and having new pants made so the brace fits under them."

His hands are in his hair, but I keep my eyes on the water. "Sorry Brother. If there's a way, she'll find it."

I nod. "I'm okay with it. Dakota says I won't always have pain without the brace, but I'll limp. I just haven't told Dean yet."

432

"You think she'll care?"

His tone has my eyes meeting his. "I can't read her and it drives me fuckin' nuts. What if she gets sick of me and all this fuckin' needy shit?"

He laughs and I'm pissed. "Since Dakota told us what you needed and gave you the tools, you are the most un-needy Brother we have." He laughs. "Just between us. Jessie, always feels inferior because he has no abilities and doesn't feel as smart as the rest. Taylor, thinks his PTSD makes him weak. Dakota, feels he's making everyone work harder dealing with his visions and no touch shit. Darren, thinks he's missing shit all the fuckin' time." He waves his hand. "*Darren*." He shakes his head thinking Darren's crazy then he thinks we all are. "Everyone in inner circle carries a bag Brother. Once we figured out what you needed, yours fuckin' emptied. I know Pres hurt you, but I'm not seeing that. It's not your load to carry anymore, now it's his. That leaves you with a brace Brother. Not fuckin' bad for what you went through." He's so passionate I smile.

"Yeah. She won't care."

"No, she won't. Do you have anything else for me?"

I shake my head no feeling better now that I dropped this all here. I guess that's why he's the Leader and we're all working to keep him alive. He's a good Leader for us.

"Go tell your girl so she can laugh at you for worrying Brother. I need to get Lily up."

I smile putting the cup on the table. "She's up. Thanks, Prez."

"Shit." He goes through the slider fast.

"Nekanis. Let's go see Dean."

He comes right to me and I wonder why until I feel Uncles Steve and Danny. Jesus. A day without them wouldn't hurt me.

433

I walk in the side door and shake my head. "I would have put the coffee on if I knew you were coming."

Uncle Danny laughs and I roll my eyes. Before he opens his mouth, I push to check on Dean. She's still out. I come down the stairs and make another coffee.

Uncle Danny kicks a chair out for me. "How do you do that?"

I shrug. "I push."

He waits for more, but I'm done with meeting time today. Uncle Steve laughs. "Got her dog."

I look and see a pretty husky by Nekanis. How the fuck did I miss that? "Thanks, she's for touch and protection like Nekanis?"

"More Hawk or Max. Fierce Protector. Nekanis don't need that, but protects her too."

Ricky's words play through my head and I translate. He's like Hawk and Tess's Max when we first got them. They were fierce protectors. Nekanis doesn't need that with me, but he'll protect Dean too. I nod. "Thank you. With the cuff, it should be easier, but she'll need everything I can give her."

Uncle Danny's surprised. "It works?"

I smile. "She touched a cashier last night handing money over. She took the hit reading, but the contact didn't hurt her and Nekanis is a help. With all the fuckin' ability you'd think healer would show, but I'm still waiting."

They laugh. "Leaves somethin' for the rest of 'em."

"Yeah."

"She still can't block?" Uncle Danny is looking at me as if I'm not doing my part. "She's getting better, but a crowd is too much still. She'll get it, but never be freaky kid level."

434

He nods and Uncle Steve stands. "Need to see my boy. Got shit to do."

I smile pushing my seat in. "Might want to give him some time. He's busy."

Uncle Danny doesn't move. I see everything going through his head and just throw him answers to what I can. "He's in line. That's why my dad took lead. He was ready to move and is still pissed, but working to make it better. Baxters isn't my story to tell, but you may want to keep Kaleb in your sights. He's got some reader ability that works for good. Tiny comes around soon and so will Digs and Bob after a while. They never had to work with leadership struggles so this is new for them. They will learn from it and appreciate it more when it settles. I'm not talking about fuckin' surgery again. I'm getting a new brace and I'm good with it. Not explaining shit means to you too. I'm not repeating shit either."

"Fuckin' little Badasses. If you wouldn't hang me from a roof, I'd shoot your foot."

I laugh watching them leave. I hear her bracelet and spin toward the stairs then drop my head. I need to stop saying shit out loud. "How much did you hear?"

"I'm never going to be freaky level? Are you going to get sick of shielding me?" Her tears fall gutting me.

I move and lift her up cradling her against my chest. I like her right here, but could live without tears. "No baby. I'll always do everything I can to make that easier for you."

I sit and she looks up at me. I hate the fuckin' tears and wipe them away. "Why me? I'll need help for the rest of my life. That's a long time to put up with my damn baggage." Her eyes fill again and I kiss them.

"You know my schedule. *Whenever the fuck I'm needed* is too much for some women to handle. I'm about as freaky as it gets with abilities. Talking to people in my head is normal for me. I found out yesterday that I'll be in a brace forever or limp my way through life. I have dead ancestors that I visit regularly and a live family that's as fuckin' freaky and crazy as they come. If I get too much energy I'm helpless and need a dog and at least one from the freaky farm to help me move again. I think you're getting the short end of the stick here babe. I count myself lucky that you're willing to wear my cut."

"Your leg never healed?" Fuck.

Everything I said and it's the leg she's worried about. I want to just jump, but she needs to know what this will mean. We may not be having an anniversary after all. "I can't have the surgery. Jeremy got a vision that I don't recover and saw it through Dakota. I can't have someone's hands on me that long, so it's either the robotic brace, or I limp. Limping isn't Badass so I really only have one choice. The brace." I hold my breath.

"I'm so glad you know all these people and can get the brace. You don't limp in the brace and I like your Badass." She smiles.

My breath comes out in a whoosh. "You don't care that I need it?"

I get the look. Shit. "Seriously? You're like a damn super hero in real life. Iron Man has a whole suit. Captain America has his shield and you have a robotic brace. I can live with a brace as long as it brings you home every night." Her arms are flying and her bracelet is making sweet chime sounds as she talks.

I crack up and hug her to me. "Fuckin' love you babe."

She giggles and life is perfect.

436

Dean

I can't believe he doesn't know. I might be able to surprise him yet.

"What do you want to name your dog?" he asks while we're cleaning the kitchen.

Really, it's cleaning itself. I only put my plate in the sink. I smile thinking women around the world would be so jealous of my self-cleaning kitchen. I kiss his lips for making me the luckiest woman on the planet and look at the dog. "I don't think she likes me. She hasn't come near me yet." Of course, the dog walks to me because I said it. I put my hand out tentatively.

"She's trained babe. She won't ever hurt you."

She puts her head under my hand and lifts it up. I laugh. "I never had a dog. The others don't really come near me and Nekanis is more human than dog." I pet her head then bend down and pet her body. When she leans into me I fall on my ass and laugh. "Pretty girl with the bright blue eyes. What's your name?" She sits right on my lap. "You're almost bigger than me." I look up at a smiling Christian. "She's sweet." I feel all through her silky fur and she moves so I get her belly. "Nekanis is my brother. How about my sister?"

"Ituksq, my sister. She'll protect you by keeping people away and she helps with energy. Between the cuff, Ituksq keeping people away and her healing, you should be safe in the towns."

This is the best day and I'm not even married yet! "I should take her for a walk. Do you think she can play Frisbee like Delta and Nekanis?"

He nods watching me love on my new dog. I already love her. "Let's take them to the reservation. We can see all she knows. Uncle Steve is crazy with the training."

This day just keeps getting better. "I need to get a hat and boots. Come Ituksq." She jumps up and is waiting like she's at attention. "How cool is that?"

He laughs and we run up the stairs. I get the perfect hat and cowboy boots and meet him back in the kitchen.

He hands me some tiny bones that he gives to Nekanis. "When she does good you give her a treat so she knows. You don't give them for everything, but when she listens and it's the first time you command something, she should get a treat. Later you give them a couple times a day, but it's just showing she's doing good and deserves the attention. Just like we do with Nekanis. Yeah?"

I put all, but one in my pocket. "Yeah. I got it." I look at those pretty blue eyes. "Out Ituksq." She walks to the door with Nekanis and I smile. I love it. I hand her a bone and pull one for Nekanis. "Good job four-legged family."

I open the door and see Frisbees float to the truck. Shaking my head I think, it's never going to be boring that's for sure. He opens the back door and they jump in. I feel like we're on our first family outing and giggle. On the way, we talk about the house his dad will help build. I have no idea what houses need, but I want a gym for him and room for my hats. He thinks I'm funny, but says he'll make sure the hats have room.

I hope the people blocking him have an easier time while we're away. They were worried because he sees everything. Once we get to the Rhode Island reservation I'm too excited to worry.

We play Frisbee and my dog is awesome! She can do everything that Nekanis can. Like they're twins. Sister is a good name. After we play he brings us to the water and we lay on a rock looking up at the sky. The dogs lay down together and I can't help, but smile.

"You like your new dog."

I giggle. "I love my new dog. It feels like a family."

He smiles and moves my hat off his chest so he can see me. "We are."

I guess we are. The best damn day yet.

Christian

"Old lady party. Get out!" Sheila yells as if that scares me.

I laugh and sit at the table.

"I need a pen! Dean where do you keep the fuckin' pens here!"

I'm out the door and across the street before Dean answers her. Fuckin' women. It's a fuckin' party. I smile. It's her old lady party. She deserves to have them make it special.

Nekanis catches up to me and we walk the beach. We have some time. It's been another good day. Nothing is coming in that's a threat and everyone is relaxed. It dawns on me that everyone has been quiet today. I'm glad they are. I needed the time with Dean to just relax.

She likes the Rhode Island reservation, but my dad will help me build a house in Connecticut. I can't wait to start. She's easy with everything we went over, making me smile. She's pretty easy with most things now that I understand her better. I still wish I could read her.

Coming back up the beach I see the next chopper land. One more and they should all be here. A vision of Aiyana and Co hits me and I smile. Them showing support for her means everything to me.

'Brother, Dean needs you right the fuck now!' Mase is yelling. Jesus.

"Where?"

'Side door Activity Center hurry up!'

Fuck. I push and step through the door a second later. "What happened? Is she okay? Did someone touch her?" They're laughing and I'm fuckin' pissed.

"Relax Brother. Come have a drink. She's on her way and wanted you to be here," Jessie says and I relax.

I find Mase. 'Don't ever fuckin' do that again.'

He comes up behind me and I turn. "Sorry Christian. Dad told me to get you here fast."

I see it and lean back. What the fuck? "She's marrying me?"

"You're like the fuckin' Grinch of surprises," Jessie says throwing his hands up.

"She's marrying me? Today?" No way.

I feel her and turn. She's in a white dress with neon colors down one side. There's sparkly shit in her hair and her beautiful blue eyes are shining at me. I push, moving to her, then hold on getting her up in a classroom without an audience.

"Christian!"

Fuck that might have been too fast for her. I put her down and hold her face. "You're marrying me?"

She's shaking. "What the hell just happened?" she yells.

"You want to marry me? Today?" Why won't she fuckin' answer?

Her hands start moving and I hold them. "I did, but I don't even know where we are. You think you can take freaky down a couple of damn notches so I can get married?" She's still yelling and I kiss her.

She pushes me away. "I lived with no damn music, billboards telling me to marry you and people proposing every damn place you've brought me. Today I'm supposed to get married and make that dream come true for myself and we're God knows where instead of actually GETTING MARRIED!"

I suspend us back down stairs and she screams. Everyone is laughing, but I can't take my eyes off my soon to be wife. "We were just upstairs."

"Oh. Thanks for making that quick. You think we could...oh, I don't know...GET MARRIED NOW?"

I laugh. "Anything you want babe."

I look for Pres, but he's not up here. "Are we fuckin' done in Never Never Land? I got a party to get to," Jessie says making me laugh. He stands in front of us and my family gathers around.

I look back then at him. He's marrying us? Oh my fuckin' God this is priceless. "All yours Brother."

"That was fuckin' cool by the way," he says smiling. Everyone laughs.

We listen and repeat his words and I'm surprised he didn't swear once. As soon as he says I can kiss her I do until she laughs. "They can't pull us apart you know."

"Yeah."

"Jesusfuckin'Christ. Mr. and Mrs. Blackhawk! Everyone welcome your new Princess into the Club. I need a fuckin' drink." He throws the paper and walks away making me laugh. I don't let my sparkling Little Pixie go as everyone welcomes her. I'm glad it's just Serenity, the Officers and my family.

Pres steps up and Dean takes his hand for a second. I'm shocked and look at him. "Thank you for walking with me. It mattered and made this the best day yet."

"You made this happen?" Everything he did for this hits me. I close my eyes for a second letting it sink in. He helped get the paperwork for the license pushed through and Jessie's license to marry us a couple of weeks ago. He walked with her in place of her dad. Even has the cabin and Security set up for us so we have a place to go tonight. That's what he was doing yesterday. Fuckin' Pres.

"No. I told her it meant something to you and she decided it meant something to her too." Typical Pres.

"You're right. This means something to me." I hug him shocking the hell out of him.

"Brotherhood means never alone. I'm so fuckin' glad you're not alone anymore Brother," he says so only I hear him and walks away. I feel that hit me deep. He fixed the disconnect.

I can't help but smile. "Love the fuckin' Brotherhood."

~~Until the next one faithful readers~~

Happy Reading!

Keep going for a sneak peek at MC: Ricky, Book 10 of the MC Series.

MC: Ricky

Coming Soon

"Just go. You'll miss Christian's party. Of all the days, he's the Brother that deserves everyone there."

I'm shocked. "Of all the days? You knew?"

His hands go through his hair, but I'm not smiling today. He turns his head looking out the window. "I knew she would try again. Judy and Dakota have been shielding for me. For like a fuckin' year. He showed one night and stopped her, then started shielding. I didn't want anyone to know. With all the shit happening then the shit with Pres, it was too fuckin' much to deal with. Trying to keep people focused was hard enough without my shit mixed in the middle of it all." He takes a breath and his head falls forward. "Once Pres moved me up I couldn't say. It was a weakness and would have been used to keep me in the KC."

"What the fuck are you talking about? You had a girl that was ready to kill herself. You think the Brothers would turn their back on you?"

He looks right at me. "Yeah, I do. You think they'd move me with something like this hanging over me? The same Brothers that are pissed because they had no fuckin' clue about the kids, the Protectors, the ones that laughed at Christian—for fuckin' years. Yeah they would."

"Ricky, not one fuckin person that matters would turn away from you."

His hands wave in front of him. "No, they wouldn't, but pity would have played out here. That's what happened. Dakota saw it and warned me. Judy offered to help and I took it. I couldn't walk away from her. She was broke and I couldn't be her reason. With that, I would have been seen as weak. Pity is a funny emotion. Dakota says it would have held them back from adding more to my plate."

Fuck. Dakota wouldn't say it if it didn't matter. "You didn't love her?"

He looks away and I know. "I did at one time. I can't say I was all in with her, but I did love her. I saw her giving up and sent her to therapy. I took her everywhere thinking the same happiness I was feeling would wake her up. Nothing made her smile for more than a couple of hours. No matter what we were doing she'd always fall back to that quiet, morose personality until that's all there was. She gave up. I knew more than a year ago that it would never work for us, but couldn't walk away. She was always nervous, but with just us? She was happy and full of life. Little by little she was gone and it was more like an obligation."

He's not talking to me anymore. He's just getting it out. I get two glasses and a bottle and pour. Jack can't hurt—especially tonight. I put my hand on his back and the glass in his hand.

He looks down at it. "What the fuck did I think would happen Elizabeth? I had to psyche myself out just to go home. Put on a happy face." He laughs, but it's not happy and I feel that pain for him. "I always thought that before walking in the door."

I refill his glass and pull him to the couch with the bottle and my glass.

He tips his glass for me. "Judy is shielding for me. You should go to the party. Christian deserves everyone showing for him. I hope his girl is happy. I've never met her. He shields for her too because she doesn't like crowds either. I hope to fuck she's not depressed like Beckah."

I smile. "She's not. She's like Tess, a slip of a woman, but so full of life and fuckin' cute. He calls her his

445

Little Pixie and it fits. She's not able to shield or be touched, but she's fun, funny and loves him. They were made for each other—she's showy and happy where he's quiet and unassuming. She wears hats with everything. It's adorable." I smile thinking about Dean and her hats. I love that woman and I hardly know her.

He smiles. "He deserves it."

I saw how the Brothers treated him for years and have to agree. Uncle Danny throwing Pres's thoughts at him showed all the Protectors why Christian went to the reservation. With me, my father would kill anyone that touched me, so being a teenager was fuckin hard. For him, some actually laughed, but the elders that saw him leaving the whores rooms thought he was a waste—to his family, the Club and the Brotherhood. It was fuckin sad. I kissed him one day trying to help, but he couldn't take it. How the hell do you live not touching people? He found his girl though. I smile. He got the girl and deserves every bit of it.

"I'm glad it's just shielding for her. I thought it was more like Beckah."

"No. Not at all. What started you with her?"

We drink and he talks. His body relaxes and I'm happy to see it. I thought we'd need a ride from the morgue, but he pulled it together and made it back fine. Well as fine as you can be when your girl jumps off a fuckin bridge. I'm so glad it wasn't the bluff at the Club.

At one we're laughing hysterically and he finds another bottle.

Ricky

Pounding is going to make my fuckin' head explode. I cover my eyes and make it to the door. "Dad. God, don't fuckin yell today. I can't take it."

He's quiet and my head knows that's wrong. I move a finger and look at him still shielding my eyes. He's looking at the living room so I turn and freeze. Elizabeth is holding her head with a throw blanket barely covering her naked body.

"He's going to kill you," my dad says and I barely hear him.

"He's going to kill me," I agree.

About the Author

L. Ann started with the Baxters and is working on her fourth series, The Protectors. While her books feature ex-SEALs and Badass Bikers, L. Ann is writing about the strong women that these men need in their life to help right the world's wrongs and keep their small part of the world safe. The women are extraordinary, strong and determined to make a difference.

The men fight for right in every book. Yes, they kill people. Yes, they shoot at the bad guys' feet to cause them pain. Yes, they throw tampons at each other regularly.

That being said, they do these things while stopping human trafficking, bringing their Club into legitimate businesses, fighting gangs to keep drugs away from their town and kids, keep women sheltered safely while trying to stop domestic abuse. These are men that don't leave a Brother behind. They don't treat women as possessions and they don't cheat. Respect takes on an honorable meaning. Women and kids are cherished. Everyone is looked out for and everyone is equal.

L. Ann has made an amazing Club, tackled the taboo subjects and made it easy to imagine living in a world where your protection comes from the freaky kids, SEALs and Bikers.

With readers writing about rereading the series over and over, she feels like she's told her characters' stories in a way that would make them proud.

Every book will make you laugh, every book will make you angry for the wrong that happens in the world. Every book will make you cry for the pain that a character feels. Every book gives you hope that we may just get it right yet.

Author contact links:

Connect via email: mailto:l_ann_marie@aol.com

Connect with me on Facebook:

https://www.facebook.com/author.l.annmarie/

and

https://www.facebook.com/lann.marie.3

Check out my website: http://www.lannmarie.com

Twitter: https://twitter.com/LAnnMarie1

Other books by L. Ann Marie

The Protectors
Christian Book 1
.★.═══════.★.═══════.★.═══════.★.
Princes of Prophecy
Prophet Book 1: http://a.co/d4kvNN1
Reader: Book 2: http://a.co/2fnBniC
Leader Book 3: http://a.co/j0YrU6y
Enforcer Book 4: http://a.co/jcysz8m
Coder Book 5: http://a.co/gMArhyO
Sniper Book 6: http://a.co/ghUPQDS
.★.═══════.★.═══════.★.═══════.★.
The MC
Knight: http://a.co/drLpl5V
LaPonte: http://a.co/b3tYTaP
LaPonte-Karr: http://a.co/9q2xch5
Pres: http://a.co/aWErBHQ
Blackhawk: http://a.co/a765z4b
Tailley: http://a.co/h6KD5An
Callahan: http://a.co/eIzq1My
Brighton: http://a.co/dJ900LL
Moniz: http://a.co/i8q8ZM3
Behind the Scenes: http://a.co/eEpfH4F
.★.═══════.★.═══════.★.═══════.★.
The Baxters
She Found Us: http://a.co/1LuiEaa
Our Wife: http://a.co/4iqSmcI
Our Angel: http://a.co/dVMurUd
Jake: http://a.co/iZe1w5I
Rayne: http://a.co/7yE00JD
.★.═══════.★.═══════.★.═══════.★.
Stand Alone
Spying Eyes: http://a.co/ic4qbvT
.★.═══════.★.═══════.★.═══════.★.

Made in the USA
Lexington, KY
14 March 2017